Experiments

At

3 Billion

A.M.

Alexander Zelenyj

'Experiments at 3 Billion A.M.'
Alexander Zelenyj

Copyright 2009 by the Author. No part of this publication may be reproduced by any means, electronic or mechanical, without prior permission from the Author.

Published in 2009 by Eibonvale Press
www.eibonvalepress.co.uk

Cover art and interior/exterior design by David Rix
www.eibonvale.co.uk

Printed by Lightning Source
www.lightningsource.com

Author Photograph: Point Pelee, Ontario, by Rachel Blok

ISBN
978-0-9555268-4-8

Paperback Edition

www.eibonvalepress.co.uk

Publication History

The following short stories originally appeared, often in greatly different form, in a variety of publications:

The Potato Thief Beneath Indifferent Stars – published in anthology, Unparalleled Journeys II, Journey Books, 2007

Blue Love Maria – published in Whispers of Wickedness, 2004, and reprinted in Upfront Magazine, Issue 79, 2005

The Stealing Sky – published in Jupiter Magazine, Issue 11, 2006

Teenage Pirates and the Ghosting of Texas – published in Death Bus, Winter Issue, 2006

The Loneliness of Strangefire Dancers – published in Noneuclidean Café, Issue 2, 2006

The Prison Hulk – published in Revelation Magazine, Volume 3, Issue 4, 2006; and in anthology, Revelation: Volume III, Fourth Horseman Press, 2006

Night Symphonies – published in Revelation Magazine, Volume 4, Issue 1, 2007

The Burning Sadness of Crash-Landed Sleepers – published in Amazing Journeys Magazine, Issue 10, 2005

Tara of the Wine Cats – published in The Cerebral Catalyst, July Issue, 2005

I Humbly Accept this War Stick – published in The Lightning Journal, Volume 2, Issue 1, 2005

Lost in the Penguin Tunnel – published in Crossroads Magic, Summer Issue, 2005

Dreams of the Rocket-Boy – published in The Cerebral Catalyst, June Issue, 2005, under the title *Dreams of the Mantis-Boy*

Love, Death, and Monsters at the Drive-In – published in Revelation Magazine, Volume 3, Issue 3, 2006; and in anthology, Revelation: Volume III, Fourth Horseman Press, under the title *Love and Death at the Drive-In*

The Silly Significance of Running with Soda Fire – published in Revelation Magazine, Volume 2, Issue 2, 2005; and in anthology, Revelation: Volume II, Fourth Horseman Press, 2005

Waiting for the New Reign of the Fire Ants – published in Revelation Magazine, Volume 2, Issue 3, 2005; and extended version of story published in anthology, Revelation: Volume II, Fourth Horseman Press, 2005

Pining for the Lost Love of the Moon Creatures – published in Worlds of Wonder, 2005

Captain of a Ship of Flowers – published in Revelation Magazine, Volume 4, Issue 2, 2009

The Grey Tammy and the Living – published in Underground Voices, December Issue, 2008; reprinted in Euphony Journal, Spring Issue, 2009.

Poppy, the Girl of my Dreams, and the Alien Invasion I Can Detect Like Radar through my Braces – published in Front & Centre Magazine, Issue 2, 1999; reprinted in Revelation Magazine, Volume 4, Issue 3, 2009

Alexander Zelenyj's fiction has appeared in a wide variety of publications, including FreeFall, Front & Centre, The Windsor Review, Revelation, Simulacrum, inscape, Underground Voices, and the Rose & Thorn. He is the author of the short novel, Black Sunshine, published by Fourth Horseman Press. He lives in Windsor, Ontario, Canada, prefers basements, and watches the skies expectantly.

For more author information, visit: www.alexanderzelenyj.com

Acknowledgements:

This book would not exist were it not for the inspiration, support and patience of a variety of wonderful human beings: thank you to my mother for buying me the many paperbacks which called to me from the grocery store magazine racks of my childhood; and thank you also to Imran Qasim, Matt Spadafora, Lindsay McNiff and Kevin Durda, Rachel Eagen, Claudio and Catherine Mary Sossi, and the Dr.'s of Disc, Liam, Mara, and Sean O'Donnell, for helping to perpetuate my nocturnal habits. A special thank you to all the editors who found places in their respective publications for certain of the stories contained herein, most notably David Rix, Brian A. Dixon, and Adam Chamberlain…And of course my infinite thanks to Rachel Blok, to whom this collection is dedicated.

And an eternal thank you to my lifelong pals Ray and Robert, for introducing me to the great mystery to begin with…

For Rachel Blok - darling, alchemist, editor extraordinaire, and the loveliest creature I've ever known - these bottomless rooms of escape.

"And evolving from the sea
Would not be too much time for me
To walk beside you in the sun"

Contents

15	Foreward, by David Rix
23	The Potato Thief Beneath Indifferent Stars
45	Blue Love Maria
53	Black Flies Inside
75	Footsteps to Blacken the Drifts
87	The Stealing Sky
107	The Mighty Ones Listen to the Night
123	Let the Firefly Men Remind You
145	Just Right Under Moonlight
157	Teenage Pirates and the Ghosting of Texas
171	The Loneliness of Strangefire Dancers
189	Onwards! To Memphis!

Contents

The Prison Hulk	**211**
Gladiators in the Sepulchre of Abominations	**229**
Night Symphonies	**251**
The Burning Sadness of Crash-Landed Sleepers	**257**
Tara of the Wine Cats	**269**
In the City where Dreams Wander the Sidewalks	**279**
I Humbly Accept this War Stick	**293**
Lost in the Penguin Tunnel	**305**
The Lilac Perfumes Between the Stars	**315**
Dreams of the Rocket-Boy	**335**
Love, Death, and Monsters at the Drive-In	**341**
Letters from the Laboratory	**353**

Contents

393   The Snow Robins Fly Between Heaven and Hell

419   The Silly Significance of Running with Soda Fire

433   Waiting for the New Reign of the Fire Ants

451   Pining for the Lost Love of the Moon Creatures

461   The Empty Hands of Alvin Calvin Rourke

483   Salty Magic Balloon Trips for the Moon to Judge

491   The Runners Among the Stars

509   Captain of a Ship of Flowers

523   Pigeons or Ashes, and the Final Gift of Jimmy Colley

Contents

The Animals have Seized the Diamond Sea Kingdom   **545**

The Grey Tammy and the Living   **557**

Christina the Bloomed   **571**

I am the Stink Candle   **595**

Grandmother Mars and the Relentless Call to Arms   **613**

Where the War Bird Leads   **633**

Another Light Called 1-47   **641**

Poppy, the Girl of my Dreams, and the Alien Invasion I can Detect Like Radar through my Braces   **651**

Foreword

By David Rix

3 Billion A.M.?

Have you never heard the clock strike that? On those nights when the moon is indeed for lovers and when a blackness that is nothing to do with the night coils around you? You surprise me. Have you really never ghosted your own streets, wherever they are, at 3 Billion A.M.?

Just before I received an email from the other side of the world in Canada, my own life experienced an event that sent it spinning into a sharp down-turn. Without going into details, on a cerebral level it proved an interesting study of how a life can go to pieces in spite of all rational approaches and common sense. In spite of everything you know. At that time, I was doing my own ghosting – of the Thanet Way, in my case. I would take my bike out at 3 Billion A.M. and ride on the local dual carriageway, testing speed on the long downwards slopes and negating the effects of comfort eating on the long upwards ones. Singing names and nonsense in my head and feeling the moonlight. At 3 Billion A.M., the dual carriageway – the main traffic route from London to Thanet – was as good as deserted, save for the occasional night-riding truck, which would sweep past and send me spinning in the slipstream as though I was a kite. At 3 Billion A.M., the silence and quiet and the sense of freedom from eyes is breathtaking.

I think most of us have ridden some sort of road at 3 Billion A.M. – and if you haven't, I might have to kill you.

It was in this state of self-pity and melancholy that the email arrived. A submission – a large one – from Canadian writer Alexander Zelenyj, whom I had never heard of. The email was just one of many and I felt no great reaction to it. In those days, I was rather dully going through the motions of Eibonvale Press, too caught up in dreams in which murder and tenderness were mixed in almost equal measures – and wishing I had not opened for submissions just then, as the gloomy slew of slightly perverted and badly imagined horrors that was trickling into my inbox was not helping things. But what I found when I opened up this attachment and started reading so precisely matched and sang to my mood that I was stunned. Here was something lyrical yet very fresh and clear – melancholy yet oddly positive in that. So much so that it was a hard submission to read. I kept putting it down, working on other things, then forcing myself to press on with it – almost reluctant to touch it, simply because it stirred something that, quite frankly, hurt. It still does, even now as I work on the long job of preparing and illustrating it. It is a human weakness, I think, to be afraid of the big, serious emotions, even when they are genuine. Like an adrenalin-rush activity, it is only something you want to dive into and taste when your life is actually safe and warm.

I accepted the book before I had even finished reading it.

These are diverse stories, ranging over many 'genres' and taking you to some surprisingly different literary worlds. Hints of science fiction, of classic horror, of singing lyrical fantasy, of black magic, of realism, of paranormal. But that old familiar 3 Billion A.M. unites them all and makes them a universe. And, according to modern physics, why not? M-Theory? Where drifting branes collide and spawn an infinite array of universes? The cutting edge of science tells us that, literally, not only anything, but everything is possible – or maybe inevitable – somewhere. In an infinite universe, there is indeed a place where the monkeys have bashed out the complete works of Shakespeare – where you were never born. Where this book was never written. But, if we follow that through to its conclusion, where does that leave fiction? Where does that leave the imagined worlds? After all, in an infinite universe, even the imagined worlds must be real . . . somewhere.

Does that mean that every book, even the most imaginative, is real . . . somewhere? That somewhere the monsters of Lovecraft do indeed rise? That the brash psychedelia of Harlan Ellison does indeed exist – and the gentle, haunting worlds of Ray Bradbury, so similar to our own and yet so different and touchingly strange, can be felt? Somewhere where the dark carnival rides and the Crowd frowns down? Where books are burned and where the Halloween Tree blossoms?

To each writer, a universe.

Some very familiar, yet inevitably different.

But anyway, the dimension of 3 Billion A.M. is not so far away. This universe is very – painfully – familiar. Only one membrane away perhaps. Or maybe even right here beside you. At the end of the day, if you don't know when 3 Billion A.M. is, I can't tell you and perhaps this book can't either. But, for good or ill, those unfamiliar with this hour to at least some degree seem few and far between and to those that know, this book will come with that touch of the familiar that goes way beyond the bleak streets and wild roads of its stages. Hey – it's a large collection. One that can remain by your side for a long time as a companion for those quiet rainy afternoons or nights – even nights when the clock strikes 3 Billion A.M., when the moon is indeed for lovers and is thus filled with pain – as a companion that can be dipped into and tasted for a long time to come. When that happens – when you are stuck walking at 3 Billion A.M. as most of us are – I think it is worth remembering that multitude of universes and the power of emotions. That the absence of emotion or hiding from emotion is more horrible than any feelings of despair.

Emotions are there to sing about.

Experiments At 3 Billion A.M.

"If an experiment works, something has gone wrong."

- Finagle's First Law

"To search for truth is often a lonely business, a darker path."

- attributed to Nikola Tesla, Serbian-American inventor, physicist, mechanical and electrical engineer (1856 – 1943)

The Potato Thief Beneath Indifferent Stars

He found her nibbling at raw potatoes in his field at dusk.

The purpling sky colouring her gently: the thin agile fingers, daintily holding the dusty vegetable. Her slight frame amid the dirt clods and grass spikes, thin and fragile and child-like. The small circular eyes like obsidian marbles above the slight suggestion of lip-puckering mouth. Her skin the colour of green apples out of season, wan and ethereal in the settling gloom.

She was beautiful, he realized, even as his hand with the spade instinctually leapt out and swatted her down into the dirt. One swipe with the rusty tip and over she fell, dropping her potato-treasure in the dust beside her. Her small body was limp and unmoving in the early evening, like a strange fossil record dug up in his vegetable garden bordering the field, harkening backwards to a past unimagined.

He stared down at the thing, stirring a moment later at the soft knocking sound on the air: the metal tip of his spade where his trembling hand caused it time and again to brush the dirt beneath his boots. He dropped the tool and knelt close to her, anxiety overwhelming his actions and making them seem prolonged and too-slow.

A smell of vegetation drifted to him, potent on the still, humid air.

He gathered her up a moment later, and hobbled towards his backyard patio door. He glanced quickly in all directions as he went, to make certain no distant neighbour stood with hands shielding their eyes from the day's final sun-glare, wondering at his strange cargo. Certain that he was alone, as he was always, he slipped through the patio door, bringing the perfume of vegetation with him into his sleepy house.

He'd seen as he'd laid her on the sofa: the slight protuberance above her bare buttocks, the small suggestion of a tail.

The blanket he'd covered her with rose and fell evenly and he breathed deeply with relief. He hadn't struck her too hard, only stunned the live fossil he'd discovered rooting about in his dirt patch potato garden. The dust still coated her fingers, he saw, as he leaned close to where her hand lay across the blanket. He marvelled at their long shape and the nimbleness and dexterity they suggested. He stared, awed at her colour, which was like summer almost in bloom: the last night of Spring manifest and curled silently on his threadbare basement couch.

He knew distinctly and instinctually that it was a female, although he'd seen no physical indication of gender while examining her earlier. Female and young, only a child. This he'd glimpsed in the silent startle of her eyes when he'd discovered her. Their bright astonishment as the foolish old man had swung his primitive stick towards her in his own shameful terror of her strange beauty.

He looked at her sleeping and was struck anew: truly, she was a beautiful creature. And in that instant he named her, for her skin, and he wished her a silent wish: sleep well, Spring Apple. Whatever you are.

And he climbed the rickety narrow staircase, each slat of wood shrieking like a pained animal. Framed in the doorway, he clicked the light off and left the green girl in darkness. Closing the door silently so as not to disturb her slumber, carefully pulling the heavy meat freezer across the kitchen linoleum and leaning its great weight snugly against the door. He felt shameful in the act, as though he needn't behave in so wary a way – as though he needn't have anything to fear from something as delicate and fragile-looking as the sleeping creature. And yet he made certain to stack both a microwave and toaster oven on top of the freezer, and he retired to wakefulness on his living room chair with his rifle pulled down from the wall and resting across his lap.

And when he secured his meagre few minutes of sleep it was only when sunlight returned, savage and like fire, seeping through the tightly-drawn curtains and reddening his face where he rested, poorly vigilant, in his chair. He managed to dream during the brief spell, only a fragment, but when he woke from it he woke with a start and with the image still stirring in his tired, unfocused eyes.

The lush deep verdant stretches of a jungle. Trackless in its depths, and himself lost in the endless green.

He sucked in air perfumed with the scent of just this dream place. Vegetation air. Emerald air. And he rose with a creaking in his knees and, awed and hungry for the taste he was breathing in, whispered towards the blockaded door which led into the basement.

His ear against the wood of the door told him and eventually he believed. From within, from below in the basement:

Birds.

Their music stirred him deeply. He'd always adored songbirds, since he was a very young boy. The surrounding county had reawakened his old love when he'd retired here several years before and listened once more to the A.M. symphonies held in the trees. From the rooftop of the old derelict barn he kept to store his truck and all the many relics from his past which could find no place in his house, and from the roofs and rain troughs and scattered telephone wires of the small Leamington downtown strip which he visited weekly. Often, invisible flying singers perched in their morning positions and soothing him like they once had.

He clenched his eyes together tightly, tried restoring logic to his reeling mind. There could be no such music below his home, in the basement in the earth where cool air remained even during the most stifling of summer days. But his ear remained pressed to the door wood and he eventually could deny it no longer. From below, the symphony continued unabated.

The strangest birdsong he'd ever admired.

Like something electric. Like pure energy sizzling through a thousand robins or blue jays and merging with the music each species had stored in special genetic code inside of them. Altered by the unknown energy source, made more beautiful by it. Made more foreign through its presence surging there within each note. An alien soundtrack from below, and yet he recognized it clearly, like a song from his youth remembered bitter-sweetly. And he was wiping at his eyes where salty trails wound their way downwards and across his dusty cheeks.

Breath pent up, heart a hammering cacophony in his chest, he turned the dulled bronze doorknob. Slowly, he pulled, and pulled more, moving the freezer one inch and two and then two more, until the dark crack between door and doorframe grew large enough for him to step through, and deep enough for him to fear. He stood there, looking downwards into the inkiness, and he was assailed by the sound, now grown louder, more real and indisputable.

His knees buckled again. His heart played a louder thrashing beneath his skin.

Something flitted past him, startling him into a contorted face and urging a small cry from his throat. The flitting thing circled about him, a crimson sizzle whirring through the air at a velocity too fleet for his bulging eyes to follow. Then another whizzing thing zipping past his ear, and he cried out again. He searched for it but could barely follow its quick erratic flight through the kitchen air, its nervous path hugging closely to the adjacent living room ceiling. Only a flash of colour like its sister sizzle, only this one a bright spot of purple too fast for the eye to contain.

From below, there was more singing, familiar but unknown, an old song through alien singers. He paused a moment, gathering himself, and he descended the squealing uncertain steps.

She'd grown a coat sometime during the night.

He stared at her, awed into silence again. Her beauty was overwhelming this morning. He marvelled at her new colour, thinking distantly that perhaps he'd misnamed her, too quick in his romancing of the strangest discovery he'd ever stumbled on. Deeper, her colour, the lush emerald hue of living things. Verdant, and he peered with incredulity at her amazing new coat of fur. Tiny hairs covering her everywhere, soft-looking and lush, a true summer fruit dozing in the A.M. birdsong.

 Around the small couch upon which she reclined he saw with disbelieving eyes the tangled foliage creeping upwards along the wall. The spreading of these leafy tendrils several inches along the ceiling, too, and massing on the bare concrete floor in bunches and tangles. He jerked his hand to his head as the colour-spot flashed close to his cheek: another red sizzling through the air. He looked about the small room and saw.

 There were a dozen or more of the strangest birds he'd ever seen, flashing like beacons from their perches in the creeping vines, among the tangles draping over the couch arms and cushions. Several more were making colourful arcs through the air. He peered closer at one he discovered resting from flight near to him, stepping gingerly from foot to foot along its little sward of green vine.

 It was blue and bright, with unfolding wings like a butterfly's, fragile-looking and silky. He wondered how those tender wings could carry the creature through the air, with its round and heavy shape, almost a perfect globe, the rotund body. But before his eyes, with an electric singing which signalled its intention, the creature became a motion blur of blue and zipped through the air, lost in the basement reaches. It was soon replaced by another, this ball of bird lemon yellow and just as anxious in its foot-to-foot dancings.

 When he looked to her again he found her awake on his couch with her fingers in her mouth. She was licking potato dust from her hands, with a frightened glare in her dark eyes. He examined her now, noting how she still savoured this garden residue. Like a child suckling its thumb for comfort. Like a hungry child asking silently for food.

 He motioned with his hands upraised in an ineffectual gesture of peace. She still eyed him silently and without moving from her tense position on the sofa. He hurried uneasily upstairs and fetched a pail which he took several minutes to fill with potatoes from the garden. When he returned only several minutes later, she was cowering on the couch still, although now with a newly-risen canopy of greenery offering her cozy shelter. He presented the pail to her tentatively, the same slow way in which she eventually accepted his offering. Reaching forward hesitantly, tempted by the uneven landscape of vegetables, eventually snatching one with fingers as dexterous as he'd imagined them to be. She ate with aplomb, munching heartily on one potato after another. Her mouth and fingertips were dusted with field dirt like an earthy powder or make-up. Her eyes watched him watching her through the entire repast.

He stood and stared from his vantage several feet from her until she'd finished off the entire pail and was sucking her fingertips again. He dared to smile at her black eyes, and to try for words in that surreal moment.

"Hello."

His voice sounded strange in his throat, and its odd presence in the room made him realize that he hadn't spoken at all since discovering the creature in his garden. He winced as she recoiled a little at the noise, eyes suddenly larger, rounder in her emerald features. Again, he raised his hands on the air uselessly, trying to convey his peaceful intentions even while she shrank deeper into the old folds of the sofa and her own leafy embrace.

He ventured, in a much smaller voice, "I won't hurt you. I never hurt anything. See?" He looked to his hands and offered a weak smile, feeling foolish and amazed, sleepy and dreamy. Again, he dared to offer her his voice. "I can see that I named you too quickly. You're more Summer than Spring. I see that now." He chuckled. She cocked her head towards the sound, her round eyes relaxing into a curious expression.

He realized the dull ache in his knees then, and gingerly made his way to the ratty love seat beside the couch. He made sure to watch his own shuffling steps so that the green girl would understand his motion to be harmless. He groaned himself into the old cushions, feeling springs prod him through the worn cushion material. Sighing, he looked to her and was amazed all over again.

Had she become greener during his several-second trip across the room? Was her complexion that much more like the deep lushness of jungle foliage? He smiled at the transformation, if that was indeed what it was, and was pleased to see her cock her head towards him once more. Mouth open to say some soothing thing or another, he paused as a flame landed on his knee. He started a little, focused his eyes on the round bird-like flyer stretching its butterfly wings towards the ceiling. It chirped its electric chirp and it made him smile. He looked to the girl, feeling the boy hidden inside of his ancient skeleton settle into his skin and take over the smile he smiled. A wide smile, and open.

"It seems you've brought friends with you, haven't you?" The flame bird darted its small head up at his words, hopping gingerly from one foot to another as it examined him. It lingered, making its little noises like energy-chirpings and watching him with curiosity. He turned to the girl and, pointing slowly to the pail on the floor, said, "I'm glad somebody likes my potatoes besides me. It feels good, you know? To share my garden with someone again. It's always better than eating alone."

He recalled his wife, dead now for several years, and their children off in the cities to the east and to the south who worked their city-jobs and had no time for home-grown vegetable feasts. He remembered the look of his darling kneeling in garden dirt, with daffodils stirring in the air around her. He recalled Mr. Toyota, his faithful dog of unknown lineage, which he'd buried himself in the garden after discovering its inert body lying sideways among the daffodils, heart failure among his flowers. His own heart had almost burst among them that day, too, slamming the shovel tip into the soft earth and feeling somehow cruel in so doing, deepening the hole to fit one wonderful animal among the crumbly, moist dirt and earthworms burrowing their tunnels.

A soft, small sound stirred him from his reverie. A tiny rumble, a gurgle, and he looked to the green girl's belly and smiled at her. She looked to her stomach, too, placing a hand over its small rounded curvature. "That's one too many potatoes, I'd guess." And he chuckled. He actually was able to laugh a little in her presence, an act he realized in that instant he hadn't enjoyed since Maria died years ago. Laughter, and the sight of the strange creature with her large stunned eyes examining her noisy stomach made him shake with it. It was delicious, and he thanked her with the tears in his eyes and with words, too. "Thank you, thank you so much, Spring. Spring Into Summer. I didn't even know how much I needed that medicine."

The green girl continued to watch his now serene features closely, and he thought he saw her posture relax, too. Eventually, she pulled the pail from the floor and cradled it in her lap, savouring the lingering aroma of earth and potatoes. He felt ashamed when he noticed the slight swell on her otherwise smooth head, where he'd knocked her a good bump and sent her to sleep. He winced too when he remembered the rifle he'd pulled from the wall and left leaning at the base of the staircase, in case the beautiful thing he'd found hid something un-guessable and dangerous. He watched her hugging her pail and saw her docile nature. He saw it in her mysterious yet kind eyes while she watched him back, just as openly, just as wondrously.

His dreams had been serene and when he woke he discovered himself in a jungle.

Fronds were thick and waved into his eyes. The whirring of invisible insects surrounded him. Something grazed his arm and he looked and saw a flying silver stick hover close to him and then drift off into the greenery, its transparent gossamer wings nearly invisible on the air.

He stood from his chair, now covered in creeping vines and small flowering buds, wiping the vines from around his wrists and where they'd bunched about his thighs. Something stirred in the bushes at his feet and he glimpsed a large six-legged shrimp scampering along the floor, which was no longer bare concrete but peeked through the greenery as a rich-looking layer of earth. He stumbled speechless through the foliage, bumping his knee softly on the sofa, now cocooned in leaves and chutes and an abundance of small silky-petaled flowers, the species unfamiliar to him. He wondered at the thick clump of these flowers on the spot directly before the buried sofa, their pointed scarlet and green striped petals reminding him of Christmas. Then he realized, the potato pail, and his absent green girl.

He looked about for her but saw only much smaller movements: the gentle bobbing of some strange emerald insect as long as his hand among the fronds; a squadron of silver sticks drifting past in the distance; another of the shrimp runners padding along between his feet; a bizarre rodent-like creature with silver-specked furry body and fleet feet which carried it silently beneath the green layers of the sofa. And a thousand invisible shufflings and tickings and whisperings in the jungle around him.

He turned and was startled to knock his crown against a newly-risen tree, thin and black-barked. He stared in wonder at its branches and their cargo of miniature oval-shaped buds, like purple- and red-spotted alien fruit. It took him several minutes but he eventually found the staircase and ascended it, slowly, because its new floor of grass was slippery with dew.

The upstairs was similarly jungle-conquered, too. Butterfly-birds circled in his kitchen and nested in his cupboards. From the living room came the cacophony of monkeys or some things which recalled to his ears the frenzied cries of simians. He nearly became tangled in the long caterpillar-like thing like a feather boa which barred his path to the back door.

He found her, of course, among his potatoes, munching quietly, a mellow sheen over her eyes. The small earthquaking inside her belly sounded in the cricket stillness, too, comforting him somehow in his awe.

He squatted down beside her, cracking his knee joints and aching his lower back. His whisper was laboured. "You're an amazing little girl, aren't you? I feel as though you've brought me through the old rabbit hole."

Her throat gurgled in response, and her delicate fingers plucked another potato from the earth. He watched her nibble it and saw her tiny teeth sparkle in the early evening moonlight. He turned his eyes to the heavens and watched the stars slowly emerge, one by one, then hundred by hundred. Soon, the star field was everywhere, and he realized that he didn't keep his vigil alone. He felt her eyes following his, and turned to her.

Her small black eyes reflected a constellation whose

name he'd forgotten but whose youthful romance lingered in his heart still.

"Which way?" he whispered to her, and though she made no response, he was happy to note that she no longer shrank from his too-loud old man's voice, the hoarseness of his attempted whispers. "Do they call to you? Which one is yours, or do you call the underground here your home? You certainly do seem to enjoy playing in the dirt."

The green girl gobbled her potato, and breathed in the dust it left floating on the air.

The old man returned his eyes to the sky. He once knew the names of many constellations, had recited them like poetry for his darling, Maria, in the days of their courtship. He remembered telling her once, not long after they'd been married, that he saw a secret design among the stars which reminded him of her. He'd pointed and made his declaration to the night sky: Maria. There you are. Between the archer and the bear. Being brave and strong and beautiful for the world to see, if they only happen to look up.

He recalled the feel of feathers on his cheek after he'd recited these words: her lips, cool and soft, making his meagre poetry worthwhile. He hadn't thought of it in quite some time, because he could no longer enjoy evening skies like he once used to. He felt the old ache throb inside his chest, and he winced at its familiar pain. But he murmured the words then, upwards to the stars. "I miss you, my darling."

When he turned to look at the green girl, he found her eyes watching the shimmering black overhead along with him, a potato forgotten between her fingers. Her black eyes reflected that shimmering sadly, and he believed he understood at least some part of the mystery they held.

He found her star-watching on most nights.

Clambering through the density of his jungle-home, he passed the strange creatures occupying his grassy steps and dirt-covered linoleum. He passed the sing-song trickling of water from somewhere in his basement, a secret water source he'd searched for on several occasions but had yet to stumble upon. Always climbing through his vine-draped patio doorway, fearful of the presence of some horrified distant neighbour waiting astonished for him in his overgrown yard.

But the old man rarely had visitors on his humble plot of land, and his children, all grown and busy inside of their own lives, called only infrequently. Only the green girl, with her black eyes fixed all over the sky. Her posture disappointed with slumped back and sagging shoulders. With dust around her mouth and a rumble in her belly, her coat of emerald bright and lush in the darkness, she was a healthy and thriving beacon drawing his admiration each time he gazed on her, but no acknowledgement or signal from the sky.

He'd taken to sitting with her outdoors every night, even during the chilly final weeks of August. He'd laughed and shown her that she needn't fear the arrival of fireflies in the county, catching one in his hand and cupping it there gently for her to peek through his fingers and admire. Eventually, she plucked them gently from the air, too, and held their burning bodies close to her eyes, cocking her head side to side as if bewitched by their light.

One night while watching her examining a night crawler poking itself from a hole in the lawn, he had murmured, mostly only to himself, "What kind of powers do you own, that you can grow so much in my little home on a diet of potatoes and dirt alone?"

In answer, the green girl had rocked backwards and forwards in a funny little dancing motion where she sat near to him in his lawn chair. Her eyes were closed tightly – as if in mirth or joy, he wasn't certain. But a beautiful moment it was, and one which he thanked her for heartily. "Thank you, child. I haven't known magic like this in too many years." And then he added, almost as an afterthought, "We must grow you some more vegetables, and soon. Or you'll lose your bright colour."

And he cried softly, while she watched his tears with inscrutable eyes.

*   *   *

He found her watching the grass one quiet morning before the crickets had awoken for their playing, staring fixedly downwards at the spot upon which her small green feet were planted.

He realized with a little incredulity that it was the site where he'd buried Mr. Toyota three years before. "Yes," he murmured softly. "It's a special spot, isn't it, my dear?"

The green girl only continued to watch the grass, and feel its warmth with her curling furry toes.

The next morning he discovered a bouquet of flowers growing on the spot. Yellow, like daffodils and sunlight, only brighter and much more beautiful for his eyes to look upon.

Leaning on his walking stick, the old man ventured about his property in search of some sign of the green girl's arrival, finding nothing.

No craft like a star-plucked steel leaf nestled among corn rows, immobile and depleted of some un-guessable fuel. No wreckage or debris looking alien among the wheat, and no other wondrous summer apples wandering the fields and bushes with wide black eyes desperately searching the county horizon.

There were only tractors making deep ruts in the earth, and ordinary gatherings of crows on wooden fences. There was the hum of invisible insect life in the grass and trees, and the crackling sound of summer afternoon heat baking the corn and wheat rows.

And he returned to his little plot of land, remade in its new splendour, and it was like returning to another time and place entirely. His knees brushed exotic and vivid petals and fronds, and a million unnameable smells filled his senses. He drank them in gladly, and his thirst was satiated, and no coat of dust bothered his tongue and the back reaches of his mouth any longer.

He found her in the dirt, examining beetles black as her eyes, allowing plump bumblebees to land on her soft-furred fingers, and cocking her head at a pair of orange cats watching her surreptitiously from among the wild grass.

He noticed that her tail had grown. No longer nub-like, it now made a little curlicue where it lay modestly curving her buttocks, and the delightful sight of it made him adore her all the more. He descended his weight into his lawn chair, creaking its rickety frame or maybe his own, and watched her bury her feet in the soil in delight. He was tired from his walk, and felt the tremor still stirring inside of his ancient knees.

He squinted into the bloody late-afternoon sun, a frown worrying his wizened features, and he murmured, "What shall we do with you, my dear? Whatever shall we do?"

They lingered in the yard, and when the first stars emerged against the deep purple backdrop of dusk, he saw her stare forlornly into the sky.

He watched her in her melancholy vigil, and ached for her, understanding all too well. He murmured, with a sad glimmer in his eyes, "I know, my dear. It's a terrible ache, isn't it? To be so alone, and no one visits you? It makes even the stars less beautiful."

His jungle house in the sleeping county grew, and no farmer or other retiree could guess the beauty he grew there. Or the nature of the first wondrous seed, the small frail child with the bottomless eyes and the coat of green, like a celebration of summer's best qualities.

He wondered if others wondered, distant farmers shielding their eyes from the trickery of sunlight making oasis mirages in the heat-shimmering distance: is that a new tree in the old man's yard over there in the hazy distance? I don't recall that row of bushes bordering his house on the east side; where did it come from? And that strange new sapling, only a trick of the light surely, but its leaves look so dark and strangely-shaped from this distance. Did it spring up overnight?

He continued to wonder himself, and his worry for the girl grew every day. Who could tell what might happen if the wrong person noticed the miracle in the county. Visitors would travel from far and wide to witness the spectacle of this unknown geography, and for a glimpse of its amazing maker.

He braved the unknown one night himself, while his throat was parched but his legs too tired to walk him indoors to refill his empty glass from the flowers-obscured kitchen tap. Reaching over his head, he plucked the round black fruit from the overhanging branch of the new tree. He brought its furry skin to his lips and slipped his dentures deep into its surprisingly soft body. Its delicious moisture refreshed him, its taste vaguely reminiscent of pumpkin only much sweeter, yet with the refreshing tang of orange and some indefinable other ingredient which brought to mind visions of palm fronds and other greenery. And he didn't crave water for the entire rest of the evening.

He'd caught her watching him silently, though, from among the tall spikiness of a strange new cluster of purple flowers with petals like cartoon lips. Tilting her head one side to another. Looking tranquil in her roost. Looking somehow pleased.

He found her as dawn burned the jagged field horizon line.

Her small body was torn and rent, curled up among the daffodils and weeds. Her colour vanished, green to pale off-yellow, nearly white. The awful transformation had transpired sometime during the earliest A.M. hours while he'd slept soundly in the indoors jungle. Her small eyes clenched tightly in her final moments, frozen in her departing terror.

He judged the teeth and claw marks to be those of a dog. A roaming animal from one of the outlying farms, perhaps, happening on the strangest creature it had ever encountered in any of its nocturnal travels. Startled perhaps, in its discovery, striking instinctively at this unknown thing resting where only field mice and grasshoppers were known to roam.

He remembered the haunting feel of the shovel connecting with her small green skull on the evening when he'd first discovered her rooting about in his garden. The deeply regretful feeling of examining her child's body with shaking fingers, stomach churning at the sight of the darkening welt atop her head.

A numbness settled into him, touching his bones and thoughts as he stood staring. Only his heart burned, with an ache he recalled from years ago, when his wife had went to sleep and never awoken again, ruining the peaceful picture of evening skies for him forever; making grass-watching and potato-gardening easier tasks than admiring shimmering constellations of his own invention.

The salty taste of tears, where they rivered down into the corners of his mouth, stirred him.

He gathered her wordlessly in his arms, as he'd done once before, and carried her to the garden. She was cold against his skin, shivering him in the still cool morning air. Her lifeless touch made him recall the morning several days ago when he'd awoken in the lawn chair to find her asleep across his lap, the warmth of her sleepy form making him tranquil and drowsy while the sun rose and illuminated the awakening day around them. Spring, Summer, Life. This was his green girl. She'd never known winter because wherever she'd come from there existed no such season of icy death. This he knew, like he knew a few things about evening skies.

He dug her a hole, beside the grave of Mr. Toyota, and placed her there with tears ruining his vision. He wept for a long time afterwards, his tears keeping his cheeks clean of the dirt powdering his hands and nose. When his legs grew too weak from his digging work, he knelt down before the grave with a popping of springs in his knees, and wept there for a long while, too.

He looked to the new day's sky of sun and distant, wispy clouds, and felt the lingering chill of the night goose pimple his skin. It was the end of August, and he knew now that summer was truly ended.

The old man began calling his children on the telephone, not so much as to become annoying, he hoped, only so much so that they remembered that he was alive and well. His weekend rings became tradition and he made certain to speak with cheer even if he was feeling a little bit glum.

He spent time in his backyard, watching the ordinary birds in his old tree, and listening to the violining of crickets as dusk settled over the fields each evening. And he star-watched with great dedication, too, spending time with each shimmering speck he could find before his old eyes became too tired and he was nodding off into sleep.

The jungle had crept out of his home as stealthily and mysteriously as it had arrived. The morning he'd discovered her among the daffodils even, he'd noticed the limp look of the strange cluster of silvery flowers beside his patio door; the drooping vines looking forlorn and lifeless everywhere; the withered fronds and pale grass, and the silence among the bushes where hidden things had stirred and rustled only days before.

Where the grass had gone to, he did not know. Where the rich soil layering his linoleum and carpets had seeped, he couldn't begin to guess without convincing himself that senility had arrived with his many years to claim him once and for all.

But he frequently visited the spot in his neatly-manicured lawn, beside the grave of his old trusted dog, where he'd once dug another, similar hole, and filled it with a dying beauty. He stood before this spot on the remaining afternoons of lingering summery haze, and even on occasion during chill September evenings when the breeze shook him, making him nervous and rattling the dentures against his gums. And he admired with wondrous eyes, not unlike the wide-open gaze of a child, the strange and amazing tree growing from that very place in the lawn. Very foreign its supple green trunk like a large plant-stem, furred like a tennis ball only much softer to the touch. Unmistakably alien the way its thin, curvaceous branches grew ripe cargoes of round, similarly-furred and delicious fruit among their rich emerald and obsidian leaves. Flowers bloomed there, too, along the trunk and branches, and particularly at the tree's base, where they flourished, clustering wildly and in vibrant profusion. Their crimson and violet hues were radiant, their delicate silvery markings shone in sunlight and moon glow alike.

He took his time standing upon this spot, savouring

the sight of the strange flowers stirring in the breeze, and the fruits bobbing in their places, too, like lush, living ornaments celebrating a season past. And a bittersweet ache pained his chest during such moments, and made it very difficult not to cry.

But in the evenings he found himself less unhappy than he once was. Maybe this was because he could name several more constellations each night that passed, as if the simple act of watching their twinkling light held enough power to part the collected time of years, and make recollection easier to bear.

And when his children asked, on occasion, why his happy tone, or what the secret of county living might be that he sounded so hopeful during their telephone talks, he startled them first with laughter, robust and hearty – And then also with his words, spoken with zestful wistfulness, if such a thing could possibly exist in the universe.

"There are bushes and there are trees everywhere," he tells them. "Everywhere. And they never wilt and die, not really. Winter arrives and ravages the land, surely, but Spring always returns. And those bushes and trees, well, their cargoes sing. They sing songs of beauty that are hard to imagine for city people like you and you and you. And there are flowers that grow out here, and they move to those songs, too. And if we're lucky enough, and we listen very closely, we hear their secret rhythms and we dance with them, too. And I have one very, very special tree, my darlings. It grows in my yard near to my potato garden, and it is a strange and beautiful tree. It's quite an alien and amazing specimen, and the fruit it bears – oh, the fruit it bears! – There's no other tree quite like it in this world, and of that I'm very certain!"

His children invariably chuckled good-naturedly at his words, and made promises to visit him in his amazing county country.

And he always made certain to add one other wonder of the land to his prodigious list. "The stars, my darlings," he told his children. "The stars here are better than anywhere else. Here, they shine and twinkle and tremble, and you can see every constellation that ever formed. One is even able, on occasion, to discover new ones, and old ones emerged again after many long years hidden."

Then he added, "Although, it must be said, that it's always a prettier sight to watch them with someone else beside you. Someone who sees the big sad romance in a picture like that."

And they heard the wistfulness in his dreamy words, and they promised once more to come and visit, and sometimes they found time in their busy city lives to do just that. And when they did, their father gathered them on the grass beneath evening skies, and together they marvelled at the good perfume of the flowers and trees and county air.

"You're right, dad," they invariably agreed. "It's so peaceful out here. And quiet. And beautiful."

The old man nodded at their words, and said, "Oh, there's beauty, my darlings. Beauty and mystery deeper than anything."

And they smiled at his dreamy, romantic words.

And he pointed into the night sky, there and there and there, and he showed them.

Blue

Love

Maria

My boyfriend wrote on a school wall tonight. He wrote: there is a jackal living inside me.

He thinks he's pretty fuckin' cool for writing that there. Pretty rough and tough and ruff and tumble. And he thinks he's the rebel of the world when he tells me he's going to take me out of hell, just going to grab me by the hand and take me away to a good place, like Chicago or a small shanty in the county, overlooking a small river.

Rebel. I want to tell him: You're no Luke Skywalker. You are definitly no mister

Han Solo. I wish he'd just spontaneously combust or some shit like that.

A jackal, he says.
Idiot.
He doesn't even know. And he's known me so long. He doesn't even imagine what lives inside me.

Dear Ralphy, hey Ralphy: I eat your face and your life and your redundant weak little thoughts.

Blue love,
Maria

When Ralph Lamb was found by the small gang of boys, beneath the spruce tree in the tangle of woods abutting his parents' house, the community of Woodslee was stunned. At first, only a select few knew the grisly details of his death: he had been found with no face. It had been removed with some great force of violence. His hands were missing as well, and his feet, too.

And all of his remains, as well as a small area of grass around his body and the lower portion of the spruce beneath which he was found: painted blue. Blue spray paint, thickly layered over his remains, hardened and congealed like a second layer of sad skin.

The letter from Ralph's childhood friend and girlfriend of one year, Maria Reed, was discovered creased and hidden beneath his pillow the day he was found in the woods.

Authorities were quick to visit the Reeds' home, only several houses west of the Lambs' residence, but she was not there.

She had disappeared.

Her parents, indeed, had spoken with the police the day prior, frantic in their worry: their fifteen-year-old daughter had not returned home the night before.

She had said nothing of significance to them that last day they had seen her, said very little at all in fact. But then she was always like this, silent, looking at her feet crossing the ground away from them, always away from them.

One thing, with tears choking off Mrs. Reed's words, and she'd thought very little of it at the time, because it was an old picture: Maria had wandered by her in the upstairs hallway that last afternoon, crying. Her mother had turned after her, considered asking her about it, but decided vicious rebukes were something she couldn't handle that overcast day. And she'd turned and went downstairs, to television voices and less painful breaking news than further proof that she knew nothing whatsoever about the strange human living quietly upstairs.

Maria had disappeared, and her last afternoon at home, she had been crying softly.

The neighbourhood turned into its annual orange and black and brown, and Halloween arrived; and some kids were reprimanded, swaggering teenagers sent home for their tastelessness, all covered in blue paint, their faces hidden beneath hoods, gaping blackness for faces, their hands tied away beneath too-long shirt sleeves. Black jokes were passed in school lunch rooms when a ninth grader opened his brown paper bag lunch to reveal a Sonic Blue Kool-Aid juice box, and it did little to alleviate the fear hanging on the air. Teachers grew red and livid at these discoveries, and detention rooms the community over were filled to brimming with brash, embarrassed girls and boys.

And the younger children, they absorbed strange tales in their own ways, too.

Blue Love Maria, they'd say softly, eyes all over the ground: *she made me do it.*

And pumpkins everywhere were painted blue in the night, and on Halloween night, the jack-o'-lantern faces grinned sadly in the darkness, their light wavering with each cold breath of autumn wind.

Maria Reed was never found. But everyone who knew her said she had always been quiet, and fuming in her silence. And crying. She had cried often, and no one knew why; huddled over her desk in the rear corner of her classrooms, sprinkling her school work with sad showers, wandering alone at the distant edge of the football field during her spares, scanning the iron skies with wet cheeks. When asked about her tears, the anger came forward to help her. And it was sad to see, that perpetual fury, like something dark wishing for sunlight. That's what people said about it, and what they still say.

Legend twists and changes over time, it is the nature of

its life.

Now, in Woodslee, when a girl breaks up with a boy, or vice versa, or when a child leaves home secretly beneath the dark blanket of night time, it is common for their parents and friends and lovers to find their names signed in bright blue ink or marker, and to find the spot marked with a heart of the same sad colour. And this tells a lot, it explains a lot of things.

And this strange influence is seen and heard throughout the small town in other ways, too, and the raised hands and voices of the wild-eyed adults often lower themselves and soften at the words, a little, a little…

Blue Love Maria, the frightened children sing softly, sadly: *she made me do it.*

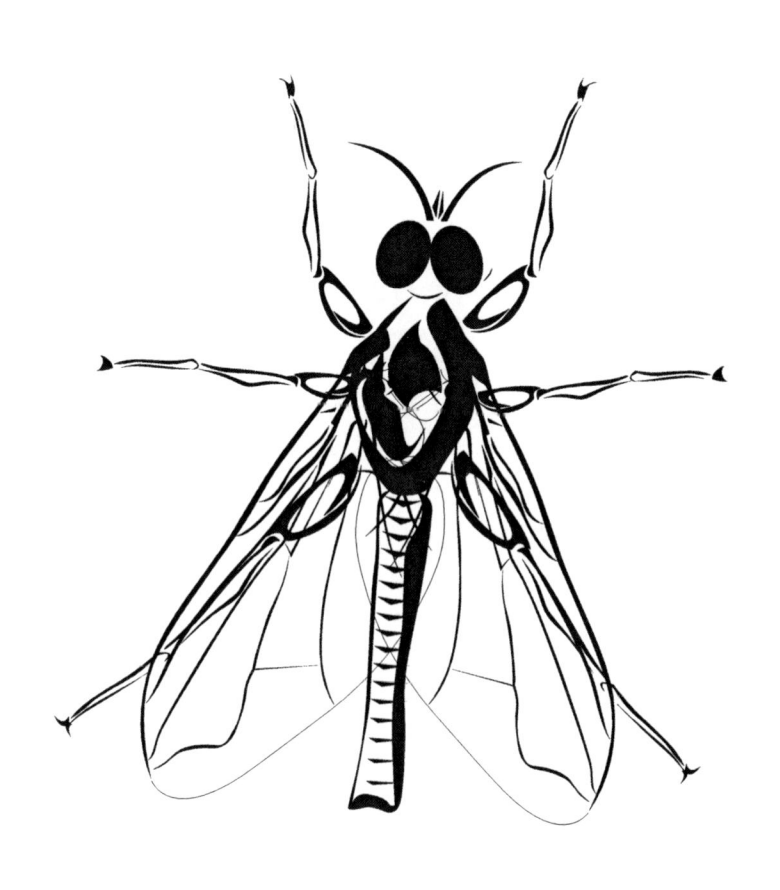

Black Flies Inside

A small dark fluttering across the naked breast.

The movement not inside the computer screen with the girl and the two men climbing all over her, but outside and in the room with him. Startled at the sudden clarity of the realization, he recoiled from the desk, swatting downwards in the same motion with his open palm. Peering close, he saw through squinted eyes the demolished creature.

Grimacing, he reached for a Kleenex to wipe away the wet-ashen remains. The tiny black flies always came in the wee A.M. hours, it seemed. Startling him with their silent arrivals, their mute mad fluttering of wings. Frenetic, their movements, as if they welcomed his attention, and the instinctive death he gave them time after time.

Gingerly, he dabbed at the moist mess of legs and wings and body illuminated by the computer screen's electric light, swallowing it into the wad of tissue between his fingers. He could feel the broken form through the paper, but only barely. He turned and dropped it into the plastic garbage pail beside the desk, a sudden knot churning inside his belly.

He stared after the small bundle in the trash, half expecting to spy a sudden silent motion within. Madly frantic. Stealing his attention again and urging his death-dealing once more.

A moment passed, and he returned his eyes to the girl inside the screen. Still, she screamed as the men grappled her. One inside her mouth, the other between her thighs. The bed quaking with their efforts. Only now the scene had lost its potency, it seemed.

Only tangles of pink flesh and moaning voices disembodied from his former riveted attention. He stared for a long while, following the moving pictures doing their mechanical pumping groaning things.

He felt only tired, though, and found himself rubbing at his eyes. He clicked the scene away, its climax unfinished. He knew how it ended, he rationalized. They all closed the same way. He shut the computer down and stretched, popping things in his bad back. He turned the light out a moment later, feeling unfulfilled as he lay in the darkness.

Cocking an ear to one side, he listened carefully. And when he discerned no sound he listened harder still. Almost as though he yearned to hear a soft, barely audible noise in the bedroom with him. A confirmation of some half-formed idea that had been haunting his thoughts just beyond the conscious realm.

Gossamer-thin wings whispering. Like a message for him to decode in the dark.

But nothing stirred from the shadows and, eventually, he slept.

He'd taken to lengthy showers after being with her in their secret motel pit-stop.

Thirty minutes getting drunk with her and thirty more minutes coercing her out of her pants and shirt the way she liked to be so teasingly convinced. Another half an hour of sex and his final thirty minutes for washing her residue from his skin. Their two hours up once again at their short-stay motel rendezvous en route home from the job they shared. She to her home of husband and two little daughters, he to his apartment and wincing at the ringing cacophony of the telephone because as always it would be Sally. Oblivious and sweet and cheerfully wanting his company as if he hadn't just trod her into the dirt inside of his secret life.

He closed his eyes beneath the insistence of the shower water. He felt its scalding embrace, sensed the steam tendrils curling around him. He welcomed their presence, felt relieved in their heat. He imagined the filth of his ways washing free from his pores along with the accumulated grime of his long day behind him. Another morning and afternoon of working the tediousness of the office, and another early evening of having Barbara after exchanging hungry looks with her throughout the day.

He strained his ears and imagined that he could hear her in the next room, knowing of course that he couldn't. The shower water hissed from the faucet and burned his skin lobster-red. It roared behind the wall inside the motel's ancient network of pipes. It slapped down hard upon the chipped porcelain of the bathtub where the rivulets ran off his body.

But he knew the face she wore on the opposite side of the door. Different from her panting howling mask which he often helped her put on. Through the things he did to her, making her look so urgent, so ecstatic and fulfilled. Her current face looked taxed, with tired circles beneath her eyes and a weary, hurt look glaring inside of them. This was especially true during his showers, while her strained eyes asked him silently: How do I make you feel so dirty that you have to spend some of our limited motel-time together scrubbing me away?

He let the water rain onto him and from him into the tub with a pounding clamor. And still he felt his stay there in the steam needed to be longer. And still he wished for a larger soap bar or better body wash than the small travel-size bottle the bathroom came equipped with. And he only shut the roaring down and reached for a starch-smelly white towel when her voice from the next room came through urgently.

Telling him that they had to leave their secret place right at that instant. Because the motel owner had rang them to remind them that their two hours were up. Because her family was waiting and the day had went away and been replaced with night time.

I can't help myself, he thought at her, silently as always.

Smiling weakly as though the great weight of his fatigue came from a long work day behind him. As if reliably making secret rendezvous and struggling to somehow satiate himself didn't figure into the labour. The draping of long legs over his shoulders and the thrusting motion of his hips. Always the thrusting-dance to buckle his knees in the post-coital aftermath while he shivered under shower waters and hated the guilt eroding anything good that might remain inside of him.

She stood in the door, her smile nearly too bright for him to look on directly. She was only stopping by to deliver him a small gift of dinner. En route home from her job she'd thought of him and his penchant for fish and chips following a day of office drudgery. Her flashing smile and kind eyes while her hands held out the plastic bag with its two Styrofoam containers, the aroma of French fries and deep-fried haddock strips rising delicious between them.

"Thank you," he said, putting his eyes on the bag, seeking but failing to conceal the dejection from his voice, hearing it blatantly like an incriminating indication of his thoughts.

How he didn't deserve her. Sally the Good. The kind one with thoughts always of him and him alone. Taking the bag from her hands, he accepted her little kiss with a perfunctory puckering of his own lips and a strained look on his face. He watched her descend the staircase with the promise called softly over her shoulder as she went: "I'll be by later. I've got some errands to run, but I'll see you tonight."

He closed the door to his apartment and stood with his back against the thick wood. His breathing came shallowly and he felt far away. Setting the plastic bag on the coffee table, he retrieved the remote control and turned the television back on. Slowly, the screen returned to life and the girl and man were there once more. She on top, his face smiling ghoulishly below. The static screen scene with its fuzzy horizon lines, un-paused as he clicked the 'play' button on the remote and their lewd moment continued.

He finished off the Styrofoam tray of fish strips and three quarters of the fries in the other carton by the end of the film. He was aroused and marvelled a little at the fact. His desire to touch himself in the bathroom like he always did after such rabid devotion to a skin movie, even after having only just seen her. After eating the food she'd thoughtfully brought for him and seeing the open look of her sweet face. Her unaware smile as she promised him another visitation later on that night, and the memory of the knowing twinkle in her stare which promised much more than this.

A minute afterwards and he was pretending himself into the place of the man in the movie he'd just watched. The film woman rode him earnestly and cried just as vehemently throughout the riding as she had in her movie. He, lifting his hips high and bringing her to a cacophony of climax ended their imaginary scene together.

He wiped himself with tissue paper and flushed the sodden remnants down the toilet. He stared after the wad of paper spiralling downwards into the depths of the bowl and imagined it sailing on into the sewers beneath the city. Maybe into a river somewhere far away. Maybe the ocean at the end of the journey. Some little imprint of himself set sail into the greater world. A product of his excitement at the idea of a movie woman he would never see or know but whose look of sweet pained ecstasy made him lose control and spout like a geyser into toilet water.

Ashamed, he considered seeing Sally that night, felt drained at the thought. Spent, and in need of sleep to distance himself from his guilt. So that he might awaken and feel the old yearning returned, so that when she was there with him they might both be a little satisfied.

He paused with his hand on the light switch. He turned to the water-flecked mirror over the sink, leaned his face close to the smoothness of its surface. He looked deeply into the grey eyes watching him there, and shuddered. Who was this man? What did he want? Why did he want it? He smelled the tang of his own sweat and thought that he would have to take a shower before Sally arrived. He would stand in the shower and the steam would curl over him and make him new. Freeing. Cleansing, and he could wear almost genuine smiles on her behalf for the rest of their shared night.

But he felt nauseous. His insides churned and his eyes hurt. He felt moist and milky with sweat and very sticky in his unlaundered house clothes. He decided to try for sleep but cringed at the thought of his unclean bed sheets and how much filthier they'd make him feel. He perceived the suggestion of acid at the back of his throat. A ghost-sensation, tickling. And of a sudden his mouth was wide open, aching his jaws, and he was avidly examining the deepest reaches of his mouth and throat in the mirror. Half-expecting to be somehow horrified. Somehow sickened by what he found there.

But only pink gums and twitching tongue muscle. Healthy teeth and occasional dentist trip-veteran teeth adorned with silver fillings or crowns more immaculate than the subtly discoloured enamel surrounding them. A morsel of French fry or haddock bit nestled between molars. The familiar weird shape of his epiglottis hanging oddly like some moist stalactite at the back of his throat.

Closing his mouth, Marcus stared at the man in the mirror and tried to understand him.

There was no motion to draw his attention. He turned his eyes in their sockets and found it as if he'd known of its presence there with him the entire while. Maybe the faint sizzle of its wingtips where they brushed the edge of the bare light bulb. Perhaps a frying leg or flaming antennae sputtering into ash. One of the flies. His haunters, and this specimen languishing brazenly along the old tarnished steel framework at the base of the bulb fixture. Close to the light and heat. He thought distantly that the thing must be blinded at this proximity, baking so near to what must seem like a sun to its miniscule and fragile body.

He leaned forward in close examination of it: The delicate design. Wings like tiny sculpted flower petals. Pretty but so un-pretty.

Then the black flower was in flight, a madly erratic orbit circling about his face. Startled – and angered at his reflexive reaction as he jerked his face away from the sudden motion – he clamped his palms together mightily, catching the creature crushingly. He held his hands together a moment, tightly. Relishing the idea of the thing's demise in his fingers, but not quite feeling its slight form within his grasp. Slowly, he rubbed his hands up and down, imagining the smear of dusty ashes on his skin. A moment passed like this, and he watched himself in the mirror. Thinking how odd he looked: Ashen-faced, with severe eyes and hands clasped together as if in fervent prayer before his bathroom sink.

He parted his palms.

Miraculously, a tiny black flower flew from his hands.

As if he was a magician, and this his cheap or amazing

parlour trick.

Awed, cowed, he quickly left the bathroom. Clicking off its sun and closing the door behind him.

In the throes of his deception once again, he didn't care.

He forgot Sally, himself, the world. Only the woman existed, whose name he'd temporarily forgotten, too, while he grappled with her ferociously in the motel room bed. The grunting from her as he began the old dance, and from him, too. The eventual racket of the headboard slamming time and again into the wall to the rhythm of their motion. Their cries merging with those from the room adjacent to theirs, the sound of two teenage lovers desperate and energized. Neither duo caring in the least that their unions were being heard by another.

When she was finished, he was still thrusting. "My legs hurt," she told him softly, so that he might stop or lessen the enthusiasm of his efforts. Eventually he did, and collapsed beside her. Barbara was a generous partner, though, and soon took him into her mouth while he closed his eyes to the drab ceiling overhead. He let the cries through the bedroom wall tease him along with her tongue and teeth and lips. He groaned low, then louder, enjoying the rawness of the sound, so unabashed in their shared atmosphere of imminent release. Thank you, Barbara. And he called the words out so that she'd hear. "Thank you, Barbara."

Through his ecstatic comfort, through his near-peace: Her low voice, husky and tinged with alarm. The soft-moist sensation below ended prematurely, and he craned his neck downwards in time to see her fingers dabbing at the small tuft of dark hair between his legs. He stared, focusing, discerned the fluttering flower sprouting there among the curly hairs. He cursed, sitting up hurriedly and picking the creature from his loins. Barbara watched a little aghast as he crushed the fly between his trembling fingers, teeth clenched, eyes livid. She saw the aftermath of dust smearing their tips, ash-like, and exhaled audibly.

Marcus, suddenly furious, only shook his head. Only

shaking it harder, more determinedly with each of her attempts at placating him. "It's okay, Marcus. It just startled me a bit, that's all. It's kind of funny, in a way. That it chose there to land."

But he was standing and pulling on his clothes by the wan light from the bedside table lamp. His face turned from hers, watching the work of his fingers buttoning buttons and fastening his watch about his wrist. He felt disgusted – churning stomach again, sweaty and unclean. Contaminated with dark little things. Dark and huge things. And the guilt. How it consumed his thoughts, how it tore him from his place of escape and fixated his attention on absent Sally, wholesome and pretty and with gentle eyes and smiles for him alone. Pristine and pure wherever she was that very moment, whatever it was she was doing.

"Come back to bed. We have forty minutes left here." Imploringly. Her voice wishing to satisfy him. The thin curl of her smiling hopeful lips prepared to finish his trip to ecstasy.

Marcus looked to her briefly, naked and unashamed on the bed. He envied her that, her sense of freedom, as if this sordid room and them in it several days a week were her due, and no less. He hated her for it, too, and felt his jealousy like a tangible thing inside him. A small fire growing bolder the longer he remained in the room with her.

And the thought arrived unexpectedly. It shook him visibly with its sudden revelation, giving Barbara cause to scrutinize him closer from her bed-vantage. The thought rested heavily in his head. A weight rooting him to his spot of carpet in the centre of the small shabby motel room.

They come from me.

The idea dazzled him with its clarity. An epiphany which awed him. A truth he couldn't deny despite its far-fetched implications. Despite its impossibility. Because he knew. He simply knew. Truth.

The filth flies. They came from inside him. From some deep place within him, where all awful things were born for him to bring into light. Deception. His secret life undetected beneath the radar of those who thought that they knew him well enough. His co-workers, acquaintances. Sally. Oblivious and living in the lit world above, while he traveled silent and rodent-like through a nocturnal underworld of his own sculpting.

To Barbara's eager eyes and hopeful expression he only murmured, "I have to shower." And he left her alone in the bed, fuming in silence. And he took his time beneath the steaming torrent, eyes closed and soaping his body ferociously all over. And when her voice through the thin door urged him to hurry because the call to their room had been made minutes before and it was getting very late and she had to go home or else risk arousing suspicion, he only lingered there still.

Rubbing the water into his flesh and washing away what he could along with the frothy lather of suds covering him like a liquid layer of skin. And when he finally left the bathroom to discover Barbara gone and the cleaning woman staring at him bewildered with her hands filled with dusters and vacuum tubes, he felt relief surge through him. He was alone in the world in that moment. Apologizing to the woman, he left the room in a swirl of steam which misted behind in his wake.

She surprised him regularly with her kind words and good intentions.

"I was thinking that up north might be a good place for us. Just for a few weeks. Just you and me. Alone time. Besides, you work too hard. It's summer, after all."

He watched her wearing her unabashedly open expression sitting beside him on the couch, nearly flinching. Such a wonderful girl. Such a dangerous way to be.

And that face she wore helped him make his decision. Right then, like a solemn vow between them.

I swear, Sally – I'm going to be good to you. From now on, you have my promise on that. He'd already made a breakthrough in denying Barbara that afternoon's sojourn to their motel room tryst. Denying the throbbing yearning thing which had knotted inside of him, too. Two washroom breaks and once at lunch – daydreaming her into his embrace and hoping earnestly that no other employee would enter the small room. Because then he would have had to stop his embarrassing activity, despite the protective walls of the stall. Despite his invisibility to others' eyes prying into his secret doings. Because he needed to at least be alone with his daydreams and the events which they just barely contained within their fictitious fabric. At least that, if not Barbara as a reality to hold and touch and fill with himself as he liked.

But of course he only thought these thoughts, leaving them unspoken in his mouth. It was always less difficult to leave the shameful things hidden in their old place.

So he only said, "Up north. That's where the biggest horse flies are. Their bites hurt like hornets' stingers. Bother horses and drive the people insane. The North Bay area's really bad for it."

She frowned, said, "Well, we don't have to. Sounds kind of nasty."

He shook his head. "No, no. Let's go there. The air's clean there. Up there everyone says it's good to just breathe."

She watched him quizzically a moment, lingering her eyes on the strange distant look in his own. Then, smiling, she nodded, and settled into the warmth of him, like an old familiar space good for resting her tired self.

Only their first few minutes of touching each other were ever very difficult for him.

Once through this opening period of kisses and initial disrobing, he always slipped effortlessly into the savage skin of forgetful lust. All thoughts disappeared and he was wholly untroubled as he felt her wetness where she lay back in her bed with her legs open for him to play. Her small pantings grew louder the longer his hands lingered in her warm soft spaces. Her voice small, slight, even when he had her moaning and clutching at his neck for support while he fondled her, as if he was her anchor to the world while she slipped away into some realm of rapture.

Even when she told him with her voice hoarse and laboured and frantic that she loved him. Even then, his selfish vision remained determined and he saw his goal of satisfying himself through to its end. "I love you, too, Sally," he answered her in his low voice while he slipped inside her and began his thrusting-dance. Transforming his lover of six years from quiet panter into howling screamer with the movements of their dance together.

He was either brave or cruel that night as he turned her around and positioned himself behind her with the words whispered hoarsely into her ear: "I love you so *much*, Sally."

Then, inside her again in this new position. Rocking together, they became a new animal. A linked gestalt with one mind, one purpose. He could hear it in her cries as he felt in his own body: Neither of them ever wanted the moment to end.

Then: Through eyelids half-clenched together, he caught sight of it: Movement. Dark little movement where there should have been none.

Eyes wide, he stared down at Sally in the moonlight before him. There, resting on one small buttock, its black colour distinct and alien against the pallor of her skin: A tiny black fly. Unbeknownst to her. Fluttering its wings madly. As if seeking to draw his attention. A black butterfly miniature, but hopelessly less beautiful. Vile somehow, in the way it ruined the look of his lover. In the way it re-painted their moment together, reminding him of his own abominable ways.

He discreetly edged his hand from where it held firmly against her buttock, stirring the fly from her and into the air. He watched it flutter away into darkness. Hating it. Wanting to hasten after it and destroy it wherever it circled in the shadows. To turn it into wet powder as he'd destroyed so many others of its kind those last few months.

He only realized when her voice came to him, worrying him from his distraction. He'd stopped their thrusting-dance and, feeling his limpness inside her, knew he couldn't go on.

"I'm sorry, Sally," he whispered hoarsely, and extricated himself from her. He refused to answer her questions of what was wrong, only lingered his thoughts on the sound of his vague words of apology to her. A weak sound in the changed bedroom. Incomplete, and without conviction.

I'm sorry, Sally.

As if it was in any way enough to say to her. As though her goodness didn't haunt him like his awful ways towards her.

A soft cry of alarm from her beside him on the bed. He turned and saw her in the moon glow silvery through the window. "What is it?" he asked, awed by her quiet beauty. "Nothing," she murmured, sounding sullen and a little uneasy, her hands ruffling through her thick auburn curls. "Just a mosquito in here, or something."

He watched her and saw the sad look on her face in the silvery light. She looked pristine. Unsullied and perfect.

Yet he felt a feather-light touch on his shoulder a moment later, too. Wing-tips, maybe, or tiny reaching legs preparing for a nocturnal landing upon him. And he shivered terribly, deeply, and decided that he couldn't turn on the bedroom light just then. Despite the melancholy picture of her beautiful in moonlight before him. Despite the protracted sense of their ruined moment growing more and more severe and weighted with each passing second. Because he was very frightened of what they might find there in the room with them. Something which had been there all along while they'd danced their bedroom dance as though nothing existed which might bring them back to the vile realness of the world.

His final thought as he drifted that night: The young woman cashier from the movie rental store. He'd met her only recently, while she'd rang through his rentals with a shy glimmer in her eyes. He'd nudged their conversation along towards their similar tastes in movies and such even while simultaneously hating the avenues he seemed always to choose in his life. But she made it difficult for him: Her smiling lips, smiling eyes. The slight lift of her short-sleeved uniform shirt where her small-ish breasts jutted. Hidden treasure beneath the blue and silver design of cotton: Fruit delicious and refreshing for him to suckle and drink. 'Maria', her gold-coloured name tag told him, and he referred to it openly and began calling her by her name only minutes into their conversation.

His asking and receiving of her telephone number on the back of his receipt, as if she might be part of some limited time in-store deal with any given weekend movie rental. An added bonus to drive him once again towards familiar warm places and the old aftermath shame. Because some things never changed. Because of some people living their lives unchanged.

He'd met with her twice already. Morning meetings lasting close to forever. Weekend mornings before her shift began, while her mother was still at work and they could be alone with only the cats and the humming of the refrigerator in the unkempt townhouse's tiny kitchen, because oddly she preferred the cool and hard of linoleum to her soft warm bed. Amazing encounters which stretched and he thought might never end, until they did. And then his former sorrow and shame as he headed homewards, fearful of the telephone ringing like an alarm exposing him for the ignoble man he was. And then her voice sweet and like a pretty song melody. A familiar song he knew intimately, and yet she'd only ever perceived some small part of him during their years together.

He fell away into sleep with visions of grape clusters and their sweet taste on his lips.

A choking sound in the early morning semi-gloom.

She stirred, instantly uneasy at the sound because her Marcus had always been such a quiet sleeper. The gurgling quality of the noise made her worry distantly for him.

With only feeble lunar illumination by which to see, she found herself vaguely frightened. She fumbled half-blindly for the light, feeling a greater anxiety beginning its descent over her. Eventually she clicked on the bedside lamp and turned to squint down at him beside her. She would have screamed but just then her own breath was stoppered in her throat.

His open mouth was full of ashes, fluttering moistly in the dark warmth between his teeth and tongue and lips.

Something flitted across her vision.

She jerked reflexively, swatting. She focused, and saw:

The air about her, black with fluttering forms.

Tiny black flies. Drifting through the air. Careening off one another, and fluttering jerkily in different directions. Dotting the off-white walls like some grotesque living wallpaper. Writhing in their masses across the ceiling like one enormous and amorphous creature. A swell of black curving along the ornamental bed frame. A range of tiny stirring antennae and wings on the bedspread and blankets.

Silent.

Their movements frantic but with no sound. Hushed, like an awful secret whispered inaudibly, more suspected than discovered.

The idea grew in her slowly: That she was inside a room of burnt things. With ashes drifting through the still morning air like some deathly unmoving scene of post-apocalypse. She thought of volcanoes and the remnants of those things they swallowed in their lava rivers. She watched her lover and wept, shuddering at the black contagion spilling from his mouth.

Her crying woke him. Squinting into the light at first, then trying to swallow and choking on the attempt. He jerked upright, coughing, gagging, clutching at her instinctually. Spittle like long liquid stalactites stretching from his quivering lips to the crumpled sheets about him. Inserting his fingers into his mouth, attempting to pull the mass of moving black from among his tongue and teeth. From the deeper recesses towards the back of his throat, where the flies clung tenaciously among the moist folds, lining the roof of his mouth. Thick, their presence, and densely compacted as they stole his oxygen. He, like one dying plant in a garden of black flowers.

The dirt flies filth flies.

He cried as he worked his fingers frantically inside his mouth. He wept harder when she tried to help him, cupping her hands pitifully and uselessly before him as if waiting for something holy or wise to exit his mouth and fall down to her.

He had nothing to give her, and only gurgled up acidy vomit and limp, shredded wings while tears made long trails down his face.

* * *

The quiet sounds of early morning drifted through the open window: Birdsong from trees and electric insect noise in the grass. The thin white curtains moved faintly in the breeze, two ghostly virgin parentheses curving the frame of window and the deep purple wee hour sky it held.

Silence in the room, between them. He near to the window, the touch of cool air goose-pimpling his bare arms. She on the opposite end of the bed, perched precariously on its edge as though prepared for flight. He wore his pensive look and she her face of great gravity. It had been a long and strange night they'd shared. His thoughts jumbled and made him numb, and only their names surfaced as he pondered how best to speak to Sally beside him.

Barbara. Maria. The others throughout the last six years.

The millions of nameless black butterflies like ashes in the air.

He shook his head, swatting at the tiny black leaf feather-touching his ear. It fluttered before him, until he crushed it into powder inside his fist.

He'd succeeded in cleaning the physical aspects of the room to some degree, if not its soiled aura and his own tainted feelings. Throwing the window wide, urging the swarms of black flowers into the night in exchange for mosquito squadrons and occasional moths like pale flying lilies. Crushing them beneath the suffocating death of the blanket he'd torn from the bed and rubbed frantically along the walls. Shivering with revulsion at the relenting texture of living things through the fabric and along his fingertips as he smeared the black hosts in its folds. When the murder-act was done, rinsing his mouth with near-scalding water from the bathroom tap and then two mouthfuls of Listerine. Spitting and spitting into the sink until his mouth was dry and tingling with lingering mouthwash energy which did little to quell his roiling stomach and the nausea continually making the world unsteady and his steps in it unreliable. Vomiting over and over again until only yellowish liquid came up, and then he was dry-heaving and gagging miserably beneath her confused, horrified scrutiny.

They hadn't spoken a word. Her intermittent periods of crying quietly and drifting into shocked silence. His hateful yet curious appraisal of the lingering flies in the difficult-to-reach upper corners of the room like some snippet of bizarre wildlife documentary. He'd made no move to comfort her. It seemed a miraculous feat which far exceeded his injured abilities. She shrank from his presence besides, and he wondered if she'd ever allow him to touch her again.

An unexpected flash of bright startled him, like a surprise or miniature explosion in the doomed mood permeating the bedroom. A wish on the air: A butterfly hovering past his shoulder, circling and hanging in the air close at hand. An early morning riser, the first of its family to explore the dawning day. Its wings were large and blue. Yellow spots marked them, reflecting the morning light like a pretty signal or warning.

Sally looked to it, too, admiring its silky-soft appearance, marvelling at its vivid juxtaposition against the dirtied room, her troubled thoughts. Its wings lush and wet-looking, setting off its resplendent yellow-blue hue. A winged globeflower, a flying blossom filled with fire. Like sunshine held in the anxious air, straining to help change its hopeless, sullied atmosphere.

She followed the creature's nervous progress as it explored the boundaries of the bedroom. Brushing against the bureau and tapping with ginger wing-taps against the un-illuminated lamp shade. Drifting across the ruined walls like some surveyor of blackened, war-ravaged terrain. Eventually she saw it return to its fluttering orbit near to Marcus, and risked a glance to his eyes fixed blankly on the creature. With these expressionless eyes like a shark's he reached out with both hands and easily captured the butterfly in the prison of his cupped palms. Quick, easy, efficient, as though he were accustomed to snaring flyers much more fleet than this. Hands like hunters and fingers like prison bars. Within their extinguishing grasp, fluttering fire.

She watched him apprehensively. She cringed at the dead look in his eyes. A lost look, of frost and ice. She saw the small dark moving thing flutter along his upper cheekbone, a black beacon signalling some awful truth she didn't wish to ascertain or ponder.

He turned to her with his new eyes, holding out his hands as if in some gesture of supplication. She fixed her eyes on them, her nape hairs prickling at the sight of the two black flowers fluttering madly among the hairs along his forearm, and another like an obsidian stone landed on his finger near his knuckles.

She stared at his proffered hands, reaching her own hand forward tentatively. The bed creaked with her subtle movement, a too-loud sound in the silence. And yet she didn't take it from his fingers. Something in her lover's eyes, maybe, held her hand. Something behind their deadness. Their lost expression. A depth of sadness she'd never seen there before. Like looking into the mystery of death, two funereal orbs chilling her like the early A.M. air could never. He beheld her wordlessly yet, she realized, with wildly speaking eyes. As if he wished to pour himself out to her but held back for a reason she couldn't begin to guess. A mystery text opened, a person nearly revealed.

They sat like this, on opposite ends of the bed, facing each other in the brightening morning light. The walls about them smudged soot-like where his hands had rubbed with the blanket held tightly, smearing their strange living wallpaper grotesquely. Occasional dark forms stirring in the air, along the ceiling and walls, like surviving warriors of a massacre. Survivors in the killing fields. Time languished, paused. Eternity came over the scene and seized ownership of it completely. Staring at one another: Marcus hoping to glimpse understanding in her. Hoping and wishing that his secret thoughts could be made apparent so that he wouldn't have to use the pain of words to explain himself. After this darkest of nights, he could conjure no words at all.

He thought the thought at her as hard as he was able: *Sally. I'll be clean for you from now on. For you I'll be clean.* She watched him evenly, looking for something in the grey cloudiness of his solemn stare. He watched her very closely, too, wondering at the new thing dwelling in her eyes, as well. Some hint of knowledge, or scrap of suspicion.

They sat this way forever. With morning light purpling the sky outside the window. Stirring the robins from their nests and into a new day. Making them fidget in their places, as though if the moment arrived when clocks un-paused and time continued once again they would be committed to move along in its steady heady tread, too. While bees buzzed and hornets droned. While birds sang and butterflies glided tremulously on the charged yet quiet air. He with a handful of trapped fluttering fire held out to her, she with her new face of fear.

Looking into each other's eyes as if for the first time.

Footsteps to Blacken the Drifts

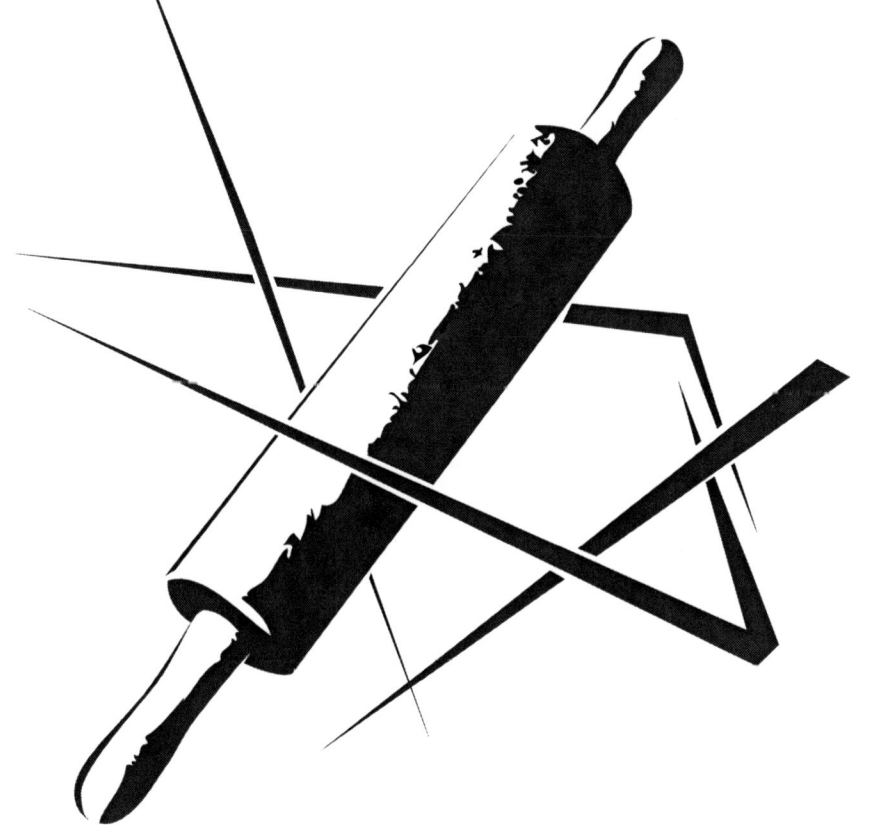

Her house of husband and children were sleeping tightly. It was only her at the window comparing the grey look of her cigarette smoke to the snowfall outside. Only her and the tiny tickings of the Christmas mice in the walls. And the A.M. look of the street turning whiter by the minute, as if the sky's gift to the wee morning world was a pristine makeover. As if she could slip outside now while everyone in the world was sleeping and fall down on the ground, fluttering her parts into snow angels and be cleansed by the act.

From the corner of her eye she saw the grey flash of movement. She turned in time to see by the wan outdoors light a Christmas mouse darting along the base of the wall and scurry behind the sofa. It had been quick, but she'd seen. She named them after the holidays because they only ever came around this time. She joked with her husband and children and said that they liked the smell of her holiday baking and enjoyed the crumbs they all left under the table, in front of the television.

They practiced gift-giving the European way because Peter was from Prague. This was okay with their children because they were as anxious as any children and Christmas Day morning was so far away. So, like every year, the colourful remains of Christmas Eve wrappings and trappings covered the carpet around the base of the cheap plastic imitation pine and there was a collection of assorted dishes cluttering the living room table and making the picture complete in its holiday untidiness.

She pictured them now and practiced her usual count-off: Peter on his stomach with his rear in the air, his pillow bearing the brunt of his snores until she came in, if she came in at all that night. Then, he'd stir, rub at his eyes as if he was wondering who it could be slipping in silently beside him in bed, and try to spoon her while she stared at the wall waiting for him to flop back onto his stomach and bother his pillow rather than her ear.

Down the hall on the opposite side slept Christina. In sleep she was much like when awake and looked like a princess. Golden hair and a pale face like snow. She was jealous of her daughter because she could never look that beautiful again. Her time of beauty had passed already and why shouldn't she wince at it in others?

Her last check in her list was Little Peter. Like his father he breathed loudly when sleeping as when awake. His hair was chestnut brown and always messy no matter her efforts to set it right, and there was always something in his hands that made her nervous: scissors or kitchen knives or Christina's hamster which he all too often handled as if it were a tennis ball. It had become her secret name for the animal, Tennis Ball, and she predicted its death in the hands of her awkward son one day soon. He was always last on her list because she knew him the least and never felt the desire to understand him more. He was last on her list because his bedroom was furthest down the hallway, adjacent to the empty room they never entered anymore. She hated the chill wafting from beneath its door and tickling her feet like some anxious ghost-memory and avoided it and the entire portion of hallway.

There was a slow rustling behind her. She turned slowly and saw: a Christmas mouse exploring a torn shred of wrapping paper. She saw its little whiskers trace the pattern of reindeers and sleigh all over, sniffing for some good treat. The crumbs are closer to me, she wanted to communicate, around the table where we all shared chocolate cake and a batch of my half moon powder cookies and smiled at each other.

She looked outside again. The snow was like magic. It looked surreal, like something stolen from a movie scene. There was much of it coming down and there was no sound and somehow its silent descent made it the most perfect thing she could recall having ever seen. Goodbye car, she thought as she glanced to the white hulk of their old Chevette. Goodbye garbage day, and she liked the look of the lawn corner, where a smooth snowy mountain range resided suddenly where before stinky black plastic bags had hid their family's trash.

She drew a last puff from her cigarette and turned from the window. Her soft slippered step on the carpet startled the exploring Christmas mouse into a fit of motion. It zipped somewhere out of sight. She liked the idea of its tiny eyes watching her progress through the unlit room from some secret nook or crevice. She liked the idea of feeling safe and was glad at least someone in the room felt this way.

The kitchen light was off and she left it like that. She only cracked the refrigerator door and by the frosty glow of its bare bulb searched silently through the utensils drawer. She stroked the knife handles, rubbed the rolling pin up and down slowly. She grasped it gingerly and hefted it out. It was heavy in her fist but only for a moment. The longer she held it the easier it handled. She could envision using it the way he deserved. She had it in her, the strength to walk the staircase to the bedroom floor and go to him in their bed and bludgeon his life from him. While their children slept close by. While the world slept outside their house and the snow turned everything white and pure and like a new place. She could paint their bed red because who would guess it, when the snow fell so silently? Because when the snow fell in silent sheets, as she knew well enough, the whole world often slept as if dead, oblivious to gigantic happenings. And then in the morning, a new world with all its buried events of the secret A.M. hidden from view beneath the virgin white and who would think to ask questions about night occurrences? Yes: she could break him wide open with one or two or a hundred blows to his head and face and watch him spill into the bed they didn't really share at all anymore. She could do this thing she envisioned intermittently every day. Because look at him in his peaceful-looking sleep while she paced their A.M. home listening to snow fall and her heart hammer and hurt.

She replaced the rolling pin in the drawer and eased it closed. She went to the refrigerator and retrieved the carton of milk. The door whispered shut and she drank milk in the darkness. There was enough left for someone's morning bowl of cereal but she only poured it into a dirty saucer and placed it on the floor for the Christmas mice to find. They'd find it, they found everything with their good sniffers.

She ventured to the base of the stairs and considered going to bed. A moment later she was back at the living room window. This time she had tears in her eyes which ruined the picture of outside. It was blurred, and she felt that way, too. She lowered her head until her forehead grazed the window glass. It was pleasantly cold on her skin. It gave her a charge and she stayed this way for a moment. With her face this close to the glass her breath fogged its surface. When she opened her eyes the tears and the fog made an indistinct white wash of the world outside and she liked the look of it. She wouldn't mind living in a world like that if only she could stop crying.

Every day she cried sometime. But Christmas time was worst of all. It reminded her of everything that was wrong and how it was all her fault. It reminded her of secret footprints in the snow in the dead hours of night or morning, it depended on what you preferred calling it. She'd always liked morning: it made it sound like a time when bad things didn't live. You could do things in the morning that would be one way, but if you did them at night they'd be altogether different kinds of things. She liked the morning and made sure to wander the house whenever she could during the A.M. hours. Even though it reminded her of snow footprints unfilled by winter skies. Because it didn't always snow like it did sometimes, on mornings when a walk through the streets would turn your coat and hair white and your heart, too. Even if your heart was black and you did wrong things like leave trails in the snow for people to follow when they wondered what the early morning had that you wanted.

She cried and cried. She wrapped her arms around herself because the cold from the glass seemed to have transferred through the rest of her, too. But she didn't move. She couldn't and she wouldn't move because she should be cold. She deserved to be cold all over like she was wading in calf-deep drifts, down winter sidewalks and across December lawns.

She cried and the world outside became whiter and bigger and it consumed her swirling thoughts until she no longer felt cold at all.

*   *   *

It was always easier once she'd arrived. Then her world made perfect sense. The walk twisted her one way and then the other and her eyes played with tears and then hard resilience. When walking she was either unhappy or dead inside, willing herself to wait just a few more blocks over to the west, only one more yard to cross and then.

She was happy when he was inside her. First his fingers, one two three. His tongue followed and moved inside her for a very long time. She thought of a snake coiling and uncoiling itself frantically inside her. She cried little moans and was eager to let herself loose. When he was on top of her and throwing her legs over his shoulders and filling her up and making her forget the world outside of her and him, then she let herself loose. Then she was happy. Then she was frozen like an ice stalactite and her secret warmth was him and only him.

It was the things he did. It was the things he told her as he threw her around his bed. It was calling her things she wouldn't dare ask someone to name her but he, he'd known somehow. It was calling her these things with his fingers knotting in her hair and holding her face down between his thighs. It was him using his hands to grip her throat and squeeze her until she became scared and then they were smashing the headboard into the wall and sending things toppling on the night table beside the bed. Then they were on the floor and it hurt and she knew he'd keep at it until he was done. There was nothing she could do but being helpless in his hands was okay with her because what else did she want? What else could she possibly want from the world?

They'd been a too-brief couple of winter. Her hush-hush whispering out of the house, taking pains to ease the backyard screen door closed slowly and quietly. Quieter than a mouse as she'd crunch away from their house, wincing at her progress through the hard crust of snow. Every night was secret walks like this because she was able to make them. Her tracks could have been anybody's. Each step closer to him she would grow less inhibited, crunch a little less carefully through the neighbour's front yard and around the side and into his backyard. The key beneath the ice-encrusted rubber mat outside the door and letting herself in and wandering the house. Never knowing just where he was, from around which corner he might bound and grapple her to the ground and drag her into his bed and rid them of their clothes and make her cry good tears.

It was from the bathroom that he'd bounded their final night together. She'd gasped because it was part of the game. He'd cuffed her across her chin and wrapped his arms around her middle while she cried in fear and expectation. Throwing her into his bed he lifted her skirt and felt her. She was soaking wet and he played there with his hands. She was screaming things, calling him things and agreeing with the things he called her. Her eyes were unfocused and staring at the white streams of snow flakes outside. The window was beside the bed. She liked watching the world out there knowing she was lost in the one they shared in his bed. She looked and saw nothing and only felt the man inside her. She looked and saw nothing but then a shadow blotted out the beautiful picture of snow and she looked and it was Peter.

She watched him watching them in the bed. She could only continue screaming because what else could she do? She felt so good. She felt so good she could survive anything. Nothing could stop what was happening then. Then her final high screams and his closing grunts and curses and a final slap across her chest for good measure until the next secret night. She looked to the window with new eyes and knew that she'd seen a phantom. The glass was frosty and the snowfall hadn't abated. On the contrary, stepping outside several minutes later, she found her hair and coat becoming covered quicker than before. It was torrential and she walked home slowly, relishing the touch of the air and the cleaning skies all over her.

You did this, were his only words to her that wee dark morning.

She with her coat dripping melted winter onto the kitchen linoleum, he with the red rolling pin in his fist. Louisa small and frail in the centre of her blood pooling everywhere across the tiles. Her fragile skull split and misshapen and leaking red like a spigot. When someone is ten months old they don't know what violence is. She thought this as she stared at their dead daughter. When someone is ten months old they haven't even had a chance to be human.

She was human, she knew. In that instant all of her humanity came home to her and left her reeling. There was smeared brown all over her palms where she fell down and whined on the floor while he stood over in silence. She felt the weight of the wooden pin in his hand. It owned its own aura like something alive. She wished for it to bear down on her in her moment of weakness and crack her skull and make her thoughts quiet.

Her husband left the rolling pin on the counter and walked from the kitchen. He left her with their daughter and the room to clean up. She sobbed and sobbed and lost consciousness. When she woke up, Louisa was gone from her side but her blood remained. Her husband drank coffee at his usual place at the table. She fetched rags and wiped away the red from the floor and cabinets.

They didn't talk at all that morning or day or night. They stopped talking very much after that night and that night had been many years ago. They only wore smiles and spoke words when Little Peter or Christina was bouncing around them, willing their father and mother to act like parents. They stopped touching each other, even for show when old friends were making holiday pit-stops. It hurt her, their new winter life together, but what made it worse was the certainty of her knowledge that it hurt him, too.

Look what she'd done. Look at what she'd done to the world and the things in it.

The Christmas mice began their visits that winter. She remembered meeting them soon after, she crying on the kitchen floor and two wandering grey specks nosing about beneath the table. They'd eyeballed her and she'd stared back and by the time the sun flared through the window the three had established something between them. They wouldn't hurt her, and she would let them wander wherever they liked.

She watched them now, a different pair than that of years before or maybe the same wiser animals. The one from beneath the sofa, it was he and another, darting about the perimeter of the living room coffee table in the semi-light thrown from the winter window. Go on, she willed them silently. Go wherever you want to go.

A sound somewhere in the house turned her head. But it was only a house sound, some floor boards settling deeper into the earth, or a piece of insulation loosening in the walls of the unfinished basement below. There was no need for alarm. Everything was silent now. Everyone was asleep in the world. Except her and her Christmas mice.

She pictured them now and tried her hardest once again. This time she failed.

Peter was belly-flopping of course, a lean beached whale, but he was lovely. Handsome in only his striped pyjama bottoms, his greying hair a mess but his dozing features peaceful and gentle and pretty. His snores would be a comfort tonight as always if she chose to lie down beside him. His words upon waking his usual: a brief kiss on her cheek and a good morning that reminded her of all her faults. He'd given her everything in their life together and she deserved none of it.

And Christina with sleep in her eyes and long hair a silky sheet down her back, her first words always an account of the dreams she remembered dreaming. She doted on her mother like her mother couldn't help but dote on her. And Little Peter, so like his father with his square chin and delicate hands, what a funny mismatching. With his booming hellos and goodbyes upon leaving for and arriving home from school.

She couldn't paint the picture differently. She couldn't change the colour of her feelings for them like she tried every night. Most especially nights of gentle snowfall like secret promises in the endless A.M. She couldn't find in her family a reason to allow her humanity to wander into the drifts and twirling flakes. But her heart longed for such a journey now. It felt strange inside her and she pictured it black and stark against the streets and lawns and sky outside. It burned and charred inside her like an abundance of wood in a fireplace, but how to put this fire out when it never really simmered lower, not for one endless night?

She turned her head again at a noise: was it a sleeper turning in a bed upstairs, reaching for a glass of water and knocking a clock radio or desk lamp? Or was it only one or two Christmas mice searching for something good to eat?

She strained her eyes and found them again. They'd moved to the opposite side of the room, found a morsel of cake or crumb of chocolate chip. They frolicked about the spot at their discovery. They looked excited, eager. They looked happy.

She stood from her place at the base of the staircase and walked gingerly into the kitchen. She stared through the window into the night. She heard her old names drifting like ghosts on the wind. The names she deserved. The names she won for herself for her secret winter walks. His voice carried them and together they rode the night and reached her ears muffled through the wooden door and glass pane.

She remembered that there was once blood on these tiles.

There was a whisper as she slipped her nightgown from around her shoulders. It crumpled silently on the floor. She was bundled beneath, sweater and turtleneck and an old pair of jeans she could still manage to squeeze into if she held her breath while pulling them on. She pulled her coat from its peg beside the door and stared into the whiteness. She turned her head and listened for a sound in the house.

The Christmas mice were silent. They'd found their treasure and dined and now they slept, gorged and peaceful.

Everyone in the house slept.

She turned to the pane, listened. The world was sleeping everywhere.

She listened hard, very very hard, for an old voice on the wind.

She listened and waited, and the picture outdoors was pristine. It was beautiful. It erased what had once been there and gave it a new landscape. And the tiny sound she heard might have been the tapping of snowflakes across the glass before her or something old inside her that had never gone to sleep.

The Stealing Sky

It only ever took. It gave nothing in return. Not to me, or anyone. And in the icy heart of winter it merged with the distant horizon line until both were invisible and the death of you if you were foolish enough to wander into their stretches.

Your hobby is a passion too fanatical, but I never heard their words. Larry's tone was invariably vindictive, full with disdain: what was his younger brother doing with his wretched existence now? And he answered for himself always with the rolling of his eyes and the shaking of his head in something like resignation and triumphant defeat: his little brother will never learn, just like he'd always said, he'll keep harming himself by trekking away from sensibility and into far-away places in pursuit of nothing.

Maria, God bless her, had tried harder, but futilely as well. It's a difficult task to steer your husband from the one place that brings him peace. I still cry for her, alone in warm places with no one beside her at nights but the old menagerie of cats, Persians, long-hairs of all kinds, and one or two strays with no clear origins. I cry for her but the water becomes crystal beads on my cheeks in this air. It hardens me, too, this air. It's what I've always craved, and I realized it two years into a marriage that had been doomed to fall apart from its beginning. To be surrounded by emptiness. To be alone in the world. I've always felt alone in the world.

I've followed the pies in the sky my entire life, and they've led me here, with the ice dunes and the wolves, where every day feels like midnight because the afternoons are too cold to hint at daytime of any kind.

Wilderness all around: I love this wilderness.

It's where packs of grey-white fur pad across the glacial sheets in search of holes in the snow. I've watched and admired them often from afar, training my high-powered binoculars onto the stealthily-moving dark specks in the distant white: dark shapes moving with snouts low to the ground, circling a spot in the snow, and then their fangs appear, and their breath visible on the ice air.

I used to feel like the snow hare: oblivious to dangers like people told me I was, nosing about in a world too large and crowded for easy exploration. Surrounded on all sides by hungry things whose rabid appetites were attracted to me in my perpetually weak state, with foolish, fearful eyes like a maimed creature falling further and further behind the progress of its herd. And then my throat opened forcefully, unexpectedly all over my place in that old world, red ruining my days over and over.

Until I had to tell her: Maria: I can't go on. This doesn't feel right any longer. Knowing secretly that it never really had, never having the courage to tell her this honestly. Because truth is harder to tell than bear.

She'd be happy for me now, I hope. If she could see me now: I'm a wolf here, in this beautiful wilderness.

I watch my brothers and sisters often, roaming the pristine plains and rolling hills in search of the snow hare camouflaged amid the white. I walk with them often, but bring my rifle, because no one can ever be trusted fully, not even one's siblings. But I only allot them some of my time. The rest of my days and nights – and they're all really nights here – are given to the sky. Between meals taken from the tightly packed tins of reserves – the potent-smelling tuna and sardines, the moist and sickly-looking but hardy beef and chicken spreads and the stores of bread for spreading them on – between these carefully apportioned lunches and dinners, I watch.

I watch the skies for them and I'm invariably rewarded,

given time. There have been weeks, entire months that drag themselves by with no sightings. No visitations, except from the wolves, the quick leaping-by of snow hares, and the long creature I twice glimpsed peering through cracks in the lake west of my outpost; the Arctic sea snake, I call her, knowing that no such animal could possibly exist, yet never doubting my senses when I perceive her there amid the floating blocks of dark ice: sleek and pretty and long, maybe ten feet of her stretching upwards in the million-degrees-below air. My frosty queen, and I wonder if Maria ever considers me here, so far removed from the old world, but content enough with another woman to gaze on every so often.

But I forget everything when I steal a glance at them. Them. My friends, I hope, my salvation, I believe, wheeling through the cold sky above. I follow their intricate designs crawling and darting among the iron-coloured clouds through my binoculars, my telescope. My naked eyes cry tears of exposure to the cold and weep with overwhelming passion too, as I strip myself of the protective goggles I wear as defense against the elements and discard them on the snow at my feet so that I can examine the mantle of the sky unhindered.

I wave my arms at the sky, frantically, desperately, joyfully. I never felt true rapture until I began following the signs in earnest, the tidbits of news in the obscure papers and magazines that are often relegated to the rear of newsstands and the waste baskets of reasonable-minded people with whom I once shared a world. Until the few like-minded convention-goers offered their time and advice and support as I meticulously set about preparing for my great expedition into the icy heart of a Canada I'd only ever chanced to visit once before. Until the many clues I'd discovered elsewhere confirmed what I knew I'd seen on that sole trip to the far North: the miles-away sight of the hanging lights, like giant lanterns suspended some incalculable distance over the jagged profile of mountains, scorching the winter air and striking up some burning thing inside me, too. Like a promise, of some secret and greater truth, and of the betterment of my life if only I could make certain beyond doubtful thoughts of strange Northern Lights-like phenomena and illusory tricks of cloud cover mirage. If only I could fathom the sight of them and their hidden meaning.

I had money. I've always had it and will always have it. My father saw to it, and a free trip through years of schooling and traveling abroad at no real expense to me, it all allowed me to think through the scheme of things around me. I found my heart, which raced in pursuit of darting blips and pies in the clouds to the exclusion of other, more commonplace life goals. I still feel a small pang of guilt at my misleading ways. But I do sometimes think of you, Maria, wherever you are back in the old places.

I blow kisses on the freezing night air, through the window of my bedroom while I wait for sleep which comes only rarely these days. The silver telescope at my elbow flashes under the powerful moon glow, but then the sky begins to snow and darkness descends. I blow kisses and I think of you, Maria, but I must confess – my kisses are for the stars winking through the clouds.

They came to me last night, the most intimate touch I've ever received.

The radio had been accurate: the storm hit that evening, late, and raged and blustered and howled and scraped ice at the windows into the wee A.M. hours. Logic would dictate looking skywards to be a futile gesture under such unpropitious conditions. I abandoned logic years ago, along with math texts and chemistry fictions. Through my battered silver stick I put my eye out into the sky of the gale. I waited. I stole a glance every so often to the digital display on the bedside table: the hours ticked by, midnight, 2:00 A.M., and then in the dead hour of 3:00 in the lonely morning, I saw.

In weird soundtrack accompaniment, the constant tickings of snow and ice on the glass of the window pane gave music to the dancing spots upstairs. I sat riveted on my chair at the window, my eye unblinking to the lens. I watched carefully to be certain, though I knew as the seconds clocked by that I was. I'd been certain for years.

They were hiding behind the bulk of the storm front, moving in a frenetic vertical rhythm with the downwards-falling onslaught of snow debris. Two at first, as always, then, as was also their custom, the others appeared. From the two central spots they grew like arms in opposite directions. They were blurred by the flying snow momentarily, but soon seemed to be growing in size, distance decreasing as what I believe to be my destiny came towards me. They shimmered and shook, Christmas light bulbs of the same luminous hue, a deep kind of blue, the deepest colour of any sky. They shook the storm around them, a new tempest among the wrecking winter wind. They were a cross of lights in the sky, an "x" forged against the backdrop of sky and snow.

    I'd seen this flying "x" before. It had never come so close, though. I stepped from the eye of the telescope because I no longer needed its reach. I shielded my eyes against the brightness of the storm, this new storm coming for me. I peeled the blankets and thick comforter from the bed and took them, along with a flashlight and the rifle, into the closet with me. I huddled down among the boots and boxes and smell of old leather. I quietly slipped the goggles over my eyes in case the immense brightness swept me from my place in the bottom of the closet darkness. I pulled the small carton of ammunition from the top of the box beside me and opened its lid, and the thick metal smell of shells was a tiny perfume of assurance. There was no telling what might happen, and if I emptied the rifle I wanted to be certain there was some hope left to me. I did these things – futile precautionary measures all – because, as always, when the moment of judgement was imminent, I felt fear. I hate being like all people in this way. Better to be a wolf burrowed courageously in the depths of a murky hollow beneath the ice. They know no gods. Or maybe it's always only my instincts rushing to the forefront in protection of me, and I'm more perfect than I realize.

    It must have been nearly an hour since the lights had left me alone again when I realized that I wasn't alone at all. They were with me, tangibly near at hand. I knew this. My bedroom contained myself and them. The rifle in my hands was suddenly very silly, a toy I gripped for no reason, a futile gesture at best during a moment when I needed so much more to help me. I shut my eyes tightly and the tears came, I can't remember their brand, whether joyful or of terror. The air of the closet was cold, colder than hours ago, and the trails that wound down my cheeks took long as they fell. I think they froze there but I didn't touch to be certain because I couldn't move at all while in the relentless grip of my fear. Because the small sound of cracking ice crystals might prove the loudest sound and my undoing.

    I had followed them for years, through the magazines and journals and books and conventions and websites and through the quiet messages whispered to me every night since the fifteenth year of my life. I had followed them through a floundering marriage which ultimately they gave me reason to abandon altogether. They allowed me to forget the world I once lived in and gave to me a wilderness of ice and snow and wolves and the mountains and pine forests in which they live and hunt and thrive. They gave me peace from my tired thoughts and they gave to me a promise of something I haven't yet been able to define but which I'm certain I must have.

    And when I woke and the air was the colour of morning my fear was nearly gone again. And I peeked from my haven of shoe boxes and clothes, clutching my rifle against me, shivering against the icy breeze. I crawled from the space and found the window open, shutters rattling against the wall. I closed it and the same chill breath touched my legs and I went through my small cabin to find all the windows and both doors thrown wide to the winter outside. My feet in nothing but thick woollen socks crunched on a fine powdering of snow as I moved through the rooms, peering into closets and cupboards and cabinets, beneath couches and beds and the desk in my study. This was part of the natural sequence of events following a night of lights, this checking of nooks and crevices. They say abductees exhibit this kind of behaviour, but not everything the books and magazines tell is accurate. I did these things without any real trepidation, but took the rifle with me besides because this had become my habit.

    I moved through the kitchen, peering into cupboards as I went. I stopped, remembering the pantry. I hadn't ventured there at all. I opened the door and was met with impenetrable blackness. I reached and fumbled blindly for the light bulb switch. Its wire tip brushed my fingertips, eluding my grasp. I felt suddenly tense, alert again, as if the mere presence of darkness was all it took to breathe fear into me once again. At last my fingers were gripping the cord and I pulled it and the bulb flickered, its fixture being loose and in need of replacement. It was shadows all haphazard all across the cramped walls of the pantry, the myriad corners and sharp edges of the boxes stacked there and the cutlery hung there on nails casting crazy designs everywhere. Their monstrous shapes, inflated by the madly flickering bulb, made me wince against my will, and crush the rifle between my fingers where I gripped it nervously. Then, for no reason I understood, I whispered: "Who goes there?" I whispered it and nearly smiled at my boldness despite my sudden sense of dread and the rising hair at the base of my neck. I steadied the wire in my hand and the flickering of the bulb subsided. A warm semi-gloom pervaded the small room, orange sixty-watt light, and I stepped fully into the space. I thought then about where I was, sequestered in a small room inside a small shack in the frozen heart of nowhere at all in Canada. I thought of wolves and hares and beards, like mine, grown long and tangled with months of unkemptness and often glimmering with ice crystals while I wander the wastes. And I was nearly smiling once again at the familiar and strange comfort with which those thoughts filled me, though my grip on the rifle remained resolute and white-knuckled.

There was nothing in the room. Nothing was amiss, no jar of peanut butter disturbed or tin of salty fish missing. Even the spiders haunted their same corners, large spaces made cozy with the intricacy of their sticky designs. I made to leave the room but before I did turned to the spider who lived above the tuna. As was our custom, I asked him, "How do you live with no flies for your belly? And where do you come from?" And as was his custom, the spider remained silent and motionless in his web, waiting, waiting for a winter fly to fly into his prison. Maybe he's frozen, and his arachnid friend across the room as well, fossils of a different time and place, summer etched in icy rigidity in my pantry corners.

I closed the door shut behind me, quietly so as not to disturb the sleepers inside, and went into the living room again. Everything was as it always was. A late night and wee A.M. light show, and the morning after. Like any deep northern Canadian wasteland dawn. But no. This time had been different than the others.

95

The proximity of the lights, the presence, the multiple presences in the bedroom, it required something more to be discovered. I went through the cabin again, re-checking the regular dark places. There was nothing. I glanced around myself as I stood in the middle of the living room quarters, helpless. I turned the heat on full and listened to the laboured groaning of the heating system as it re-awakened to fuller life. It was freezing and I donned my coat and with the rifle I ventured outside to smoke a cigarette because I dislike smoking indoors. A vestige of you, Maria, with your good manners and better house-keeping qualities. It was just as cold inside besides.

    The wind was down a bit and it would have been a good morning to light up and puff away while wandering the white dune seas. I dropped the lighter in the snow as I saw it: a fragment of the old world, a jigsaw piece from yesteryear, and her face was pristine in the faded photograph. Her shoulder-length dark curls only set off the ghostly pallor of her cheeks, so round and youthful. The entire picture, its composition with Maria looking downwards into the camera lens, a little sheepishly, but a little mischievously as well; the old quality of it, its faded colour, the backdrop of summer spruces behind her a lighter green here than they were at the time the image was captured. Those trees were once lush, I thought, and it's as if they're dying before my eyes now. And a tremor moved through me.

    The photograph was resting on the frozen ground, as if an invisible hand had dropped it gently in place there on the snow and departed. The photograph's home was thousands and thousands of miles away. Here there were only the wolves and myself. I looked around in astonishment, there were no footprints anywhere in any direction. I took a faltering step forward. I made out the familiar creased upper corner, where the picture had been marred from one too many peelings from our old photo album, our first of several over the years. I reached down hesitantly but didn't retrieve it from the ground. I looked up at the sky. The sky was iron. It promised a vaster storm front than I'd lived through during the night. It sent a shudder through me simply because it was so vast, so colossal. It was the biggest and most awesome thing I have ever seen in my life. I opened my mouth to say something, maybe to utter a word of thanks, but the wind picked up then and made my teeth quake in my gums and I clenched my teeth tightly as I reached for the photograph.

I clutched it to me as I hurried back across the front yard of my cabin. I held the rifle tightly too because it felt as if I wasn't alone. Maybe there was an eye out in the mountains towering broken and sharp in the north, watching my little steps. Maybe it was a telescopic gaze from the belly of a monstrous cloud soaring overhead which followed my scurrying progress.

Once inside, I held her dearly, and I felt longing, and I kissed Maria all over her beautiful round cheeks. What does it mean, having you here with me now, Maria, so unexpected, so unfathomable, perhaps even welcome in some remote part of me. I kissed her repeatedly and put her away beneath my pillow only when the storm renewed its fury and made everything very dark. I paced through the murky rooms, forgetting time. Then I returned to my bedroom and reached beneath my pillow and took her in my hand and stole into the closet, my rifle in my other fist, and I closed the door and dreamed of sleeping.

They leave me things. Gifts, I hope; warnings, I grow sick in even entertaining the notion.

I want to speak their language and offer my thanks for these things, but what common language can we possibly share. That of numbers, because the ancient rules of mathematics are carven in stone, in ice like that which surrounds me everywhere? But what if mathematics is lies, as I've always suspected, all through my years of academic toil? What if we only don't see the superior language, a mother tongue only known to stronger animals?

Maybe the wolves speak it. In which case perhaps I'm saved, because we're all brothers here, sisters and brothers of this wilderness. But then, you can't trust anyone, as I long ago learned, or anything. And what is school for at all if it neglects the important lessons in favour of fictional math and other questionable sciences.

They leave me things sometime in the dead hours of night and I claim them from the snow in the early mornings. Gifts.

Warnings. A story whose ultimate design my small mind is too weak to grasp, because maybe I am only human, and the wolf only a very distant cousin, if there's any blood between us at all.

My supplies ran out two weeks ago and I awoke to discover a snow hare resting before my door. Meat for my bones, and its skin had already been stripped. It frightened me, the raw red look of it, the way something had peeled away all of the animal's winter clothing to reveal the frail creature within. Its eyes were missing, scooped out cleanly, and I couldn't help but wonder where they might be, and if there might be a collection of soft white pelts laid out somewhere in the mountains, among the pines.

I knew they would save me, though admittedly I did doubt them sometimes. Again, the weakness of the spirit they call human. But then I'd become so tired, almost lifeless in my lethargy, and the journey from my closet where I'd brought my hoard of food to the radio room upstairs was unthinkable. The trip up the staircase was unfathomable. The idea of contacting another human voice through the microphone and headset was somehow repellent to me. I'd begun feeling like a sequel to some past version of myself. Where before I'd been strong, and a self-reliant and curious wanderer of these wastelands, now I sought shelter and warmth behind cabin walls. Where in months past my roving eye would watch eagerly for signs of movement on the rolling white dune seas and in the night sky, lately I scanned my world with trepidation; as if fearing something watching me from the surroundings of this wild country, or from the spaces between the stars. Or maybe it was the stars themselves that I feared, because hadn't they begun to assume a strange life of their own shimmering above me every night like a million living things? Like an endless sky field of eyes? Theirs was certainly the wilder country, and my telescoping eye scanned their night sky home apprehensively.

Three days or so afterwards I peered through the frosty window over the kitchen sink and discovered several more hares of varying sizes spread about in a rough circle at the rear door. I crept forth with my rifle leading the way, my eyes gummy and wincing because I'd become accustomed to the darkness of the closet. Even the goggles did little to drain the world of its powerful whiteness.

Only the hares stood out, a handful of blood red carcasses, the snow around them untouched and perfect. Roses in the virgin white. I gathered the animals in a burlap sack and was preparing to return indoors, half-expecting to discover a tawny long-hair cat there waiting for me, or a Persian, royal in its carriage and reclining in the centre of my sofa; or the ghostly touch of a feline the colour of smoke whispering in behind me, trailing between my legs as I kicked snow clumps from my boots. But then I remembered that these animals are from another place and that they couldn't survive here. I swept the perimeter quickly and discerned something a few yards beyond the rear door of my shack. I stole forth cautiously, suddenly very fearful again. What was happening, where had my peace gone to, my solace at my seclusion among these lost mountain paths that only deer know and roam. It was reprehensible, I thought, this change in me, this terror in the midst of my haven.

I stared at it for a full minute before reaching a quivering hand to the icy earth and retrieving the pie. It was tightly bound in cellophane but I could smell it easily. Blueberries, in the middle of this wasteland on the far edge of the world. I pressed it to my cheeks to be certain, waited a moment for the numbness to subside in place of the tingling I knew would come: it was warm. I peeled a tiny strip from one edge of the tin in which it sat and watched amazed as steam curled from it like breath onto the freezing air. Blueberries in the middle of dead winter and my favourite of all her recipes, a fresh pie dropped down from the sky before the door of my shack. I could almost hear Larry, the Larry of old, who became my friend on rare and special occasions only, such as when blueberry pie slices made him dizzy with giddiness and good cheer, and transformed his little brother into someone worth addressing at all. Pie days were good days for everyone, and I might have smiled if my face wasn't frozen and numb with cold, because weren't all my days pie days of a sort?

I rushed inside, closing the door hurriedly, rattling the jamb and sending clumps of snow falling everywhere. I cried as I ate her blueberry pie and I wondered why, I wondered why and how it had come to pass that these pieces of my past were ghosting me in my retreat. Midway through my delicious meal I remembered the lights. They hadn't visited me for weeks, and I knew it wouldn't be long before the walls began to tremble and the windows were thrown wide to the wind outside, sucking the curtains through their maws and blowing pieces of storm into my ramshackle home.

I crept into the closet and fastened the thick steel ring of the padlock through the wooden shutters. I locked myself there in the blackness and listened for the falling of snow inside my cabin, my home, my retreat, my headquarters for secluding myself and following the dancing of the lights in the northern sky. I have money and the radio is only upstairs in the communications room. But the trip is long, and I haven't the stamina. I'm full with fear, and the only sense I can ever make of anything these days is the certainty that I must remain here and wait. I have cans of ham and turkey spread stacked neatly about my ears, a loaf of bread as hard as a piece of the tundra beside me, yet more inexplicably accrued rations recently left in the snow outside these walls for me to collect in trembling hands. I have these items stacked around me like some crooked metallic terrain, and a rifle between my legs, aimed towards the centre of the door. And Maria is inside my shirt pocket, her bright face turned towards my chest, so that I can feel her warm breath. This is her new home, always pressed tight to me and warming me with her perpetual presence. She reminds me that I'm alive, when the waiting becomes too painful.

The gifts have been of all kinds, always delivered secretly by the invisible hands while I listen to spiders spin their webs in the closet darkness.

I've become more anxious each morning, almost giddy with excitement when I steal forth from my hole and search cautiously the area around my shack. The hares have remained the most common, although the slaughtered bear cub was a startling surprise; all of his fur gone and it was so foreign-looking to me, that creature in such a naked red state, that it took me a moment to realize what it was. It was the claws that had revealed it to me, black and long and deadly even for a youngster. Several days later I was expecting to find more animals, some red hares or maybe the mother of the bear cub, but I realized that I couldn't predict them. Their motives were beyond my feeble understanding: it was my high school yearbook that I discovered on the snow outside of the kitchen window, from my graduating year, with every old and familiar nick and groove in its decades-old cover. It was a gift that frightened me tremendously, opening that book of nostalgia to discover nothing but blank pages between its covers, all the faded photographs and text and scribbled messages inexplicably erased. I considered leaving it behind in the snow, but something implored me to bring it inside, maybe the inappropriate and disrespectful nature of not accepting a gift bestowed on you. So I brought it with me and left it on the kitchen table while I devoured red meat, only to stop my meal midway through because of the nervous feeling the book gave me. Since then, it's been locked away in a closet all its own, and I pity the spiders who might have to share their darkness with it.

The moose was the largest gift, and I had to follow the trail of stiff mountain hawks stretching from my front door into the pine thicket across the plain in order to find him. I became nervous as I walked, scanning the horizon in all directions for signs of loping grey forms, the wolves would surely be drawn by the scent of so much death. The trail I followed would be a delicacy to them, it was not easy to catch a hawk in your fangs, and I was certain that their noses would have been excited by this scent of treasure had they been leagues away, which they never were. They were always close, my brothers and sisters.

When at last I stumbled through the knots of thickly growing pines and into the glade, I was suddenly colder than I'd ever been before. I forgot about wolves as my knees quivered and the rifle shook in my hands. It was a gargantuan specimen, larger than any I'd encountered before. His antlers had once made him mighty, but now they were twisted obscenely, reaching outwards from his head as if a mighty force had gripped them and brutally stretched their intricate design of bone up towards the sky. They were the sole part of the moose connected to the upper branches of the enormous pine tree from which it hung, fastened impossibly in place by a thick wad of ice which encased the tortured antlers completely. The beast, like the others, had been stripped of its skin, and hung suspended like a deep red obscenity among the grove of pines.

I stood and stared and trembled for I don't know how long, and at the sharp crack of frozen pine branches parting somewhere behind me, I wheeled as quickly as my numb legs would permit. I held the rifle out towards the lone wolf peering at me from among the branches. Neither of us moved. At last I understood that the animal wasn't watching me at all but was, in fact, peering past me and upwards at the desecrated moose in the tree. The wolf stared at the sight with alert green eyes for a moment, and then turned to me briefly, and then padded off among the branches, leaving no sign of its having visited there at all.

I left, too, following my own winding tracks through the snow, and as I walked, hurriedly, as fast as I was able and with many backwards glances and glances all around me on all other sides, too, I remembered my brother's eyes. And the fear I'd glimpsed in them kept me on course, urged me to remain tight on the trail that led to the relative safety of my shack and a dark closet space.

Above me, the sky stirred with clouds everywhere. And they were oppressive, heavy-looking where they hung churning, as if weighted down too long and prepared finally to burst.

With my miles-long binocular stare I saw: out on the frozen wee A.M. plain of pristine white, between the dark wall of distant pine forest and my perch in the unlit window of my shack, the air stirred. A mirage that confused my eyes and I blinked hard many times but the picture never once disappeared.

A cross burning in the snow. Milling figures or were they wispy columns of gaseous vapour or glowing plumes of fire making the ground about them roiling and angry and the colour of blood. Malevolent: a dictionary opened of its own volition in my mind and selecting and pairing the word to the scene burning before me. I was silly with the rifle in my hands. I was foolish hiding behind thin walls. I was the size of an insect when things as vast as the sky burned the world crimson and set me trembling and weeping from my child's vantage.

Could anything glow warmly like that in this sub-zero wasteland? What kind of secret power did the sky hold? Could it rain down giant torches and keep them blazing amid sheeting snowfall and incredible winds? Was I tumbling from my place on the window sill because my wincing eyes had shown me a suggestion of movement on the snow plain? Was my hurried flight through the darkened shack as headlong as it was because the mirage conveyed determination in its movement, singular purpose as a march was begun across the wastes and towards my intruding cabin in its icy heart?

Was it God that I prayed to as I shut myself into my bedroom closet refuge or did I wonder whether something greater stalked across the plain towards me just then? Were my brothers and sisters the wolves cowering inside their snow holes tonight because their instincts were undeniable in their will to look away from strange fires at all costs?

I felt her in my pocket, her warm-looking face pressed into my quaking chest. Thank you, Maria, for remaining with me during difficult times like these. During endless waits for salvation or truth or some kind of answer to my miniscule life's purpose. I clenched my eyes closed and the warmth rivering down my cheeks were my old tears as I recalled the fading green of photograph trees. But then these trails grew cold as ice on my skin and I only thought of the immense inevitability of some things. Until the air grew too harsh and I felt as if I was entombed in some winter prison of ice. And then I became numb all over and thought nothing at all, and I only felt the weight of the darkness around me like some tangible hold on my existence.

Suddenly the floor beneath me shook and a thud to my temple was a falling shoe box, heavy with old papers, putting stars in my eyes for several minutes. The cosmic swirls and eddies writhed and burst before me while I waited. I gripped the rifle tightly, trained towards the centre of the closet doorway. I didn't breathe. I waited. Among the stars filling my eyes I saw a cross approaching. It turned and turned slowly as the walls around me shook and as boxes tumbled around my ears. It became an "x" that moved towards me. I thought then that I had maybe been rash in trading my old life for this peaceful wilderness of roaming wolf packs and their baying lunar songs. And I had never known the kind of fear that then breathed into me.

I was alone.

I realized: there was me, and the wolves and the moon and the endless blinding whiteness of dune seas stretching to infinity. I had followed the dancing discs of the sky to this place, investigated their fallings. I thought fleetingly of the places I had come from, of the life I had lived before this which meant nothing right now. I'd always craved the deep peace of solitude and now that I felt it so utterly where was my fulfillment? I thought of what it meant to be truly alone in my skin and the thought now filled my chest with ice and made breathing difficult. Then a silhouette of burning figures glimpsed through the grill of the closet door like some strange assemblage of giant fireflies, before tears blurred them all together into a single burning-red and hatefully phosphorescent thing. They were returned and with me again. I wasn't alone, but I felt more alone then than I ever had before in all my life. Then, blinding whiteness and falling things. Then, great fear and I slept.

I dreamed:

And somewhere in my dream I turned towards the north, where a trail of the blackest smoke wound its way into the sky. And I began to walk northwards.

And I walk now, whenever I dream, towards that thin plume of smoke rising like a rent right through the pristine white of the always storming sky.

I looked in the snow again this morning and found a jar half-buried. Its lid was frozen closed and I had to scrape away a layer of ice in order to see inside. I heard them first, buzzing and tapping against the glass walls. Two dozen or more large black flies, their multi-faceted emerald eyes alive with frantic energy as they careened off of one another and the invisible walls of their prison. Food for my spiders.

And I nodded my head beneath early morning winter skies and I went inside, bringing my unthawing spiders their breakfast, waiting for mine to arrive or not arrive. Waiting for the next gift. Waiting for my future, as I've always waited. It's a logic outside my comprehension, outside mathematics and other easy formulae. I don't understand but I obey. It's not my place to question, I am only a man fearful of things greater than him in his ant's life. Gifts of sustenance from above, clues to a puzzle I can't seem to piece together and understand? Perhaps, and maybe one day when I'm stronger and wiser of mind I'll be certain of these things and no longer feel threatened by impending cloud fronts brewing like hell in the distance. Maybe when that day arrives I'll accept their offerings wholly as gifts and celebrate the new emptiness in me, where once there lived persistent doubt and fear; as if maybe something like peace was being stolen from me each day and night that passed rather than that elusive thing being nurtured and helped to survive. Now I'm finished with questioning, and only wait out the cold.

Everyone in their place. Every man, woman, husband and wife, every one of us displaced from his fellow brothers and reborn amid new families and with new dreams.

Every thing in its perfect place. Every dancing, whirling crystal of snow frozen in its place, in its perfect descent down to Earth.

Maybe I'll be braver tomorrow, and I'll venture to the lake north of my shack, and I can walk out onto its frozen floor. And maybe I'll catch a glimpse of the frosty lady who haunts its cracks and deep fissures, my Arctic sea snake come forth from deep blue places to acknowledge my existence in the world. And with my rifle under my arm, I can look upwards and give thanks to the bellies of clouds dark with storm.

The Mighty Ones

Listen to the Night

He was mighty in the centre of the black road, and we would have destroyed ourselves if it hadn't been for the calm blinking of his obsidian eyes in the headlight glare.

I spun the wheel crazily and we swerved to the right, tearing through gravelly shoulder and rolling quickly down the ditch's incline. It was over in a flash and in the silence of the suddenly dead engine and settling dust particles I saw him in flashback: his wide neck thickly corded with muscle, and the handsome grace of his mane as he stared down death in calm dignity, and won. His powerful legs widespread and rooted surely in the tarmac of the road as he waited for his destiny in high beam spotlight. Those eyes like black bulbs in his face, wet and blinking, and me frantically turning my hands over one another as I spun the car into darkness.

We sat rigid in our seats, listening to the gravel cloud descending in its million tickings all over the car. The sudden stillness and silence following the chaos of our near-collision and off-road crash was pervasive. My hands shook visibly where they still white-knuckled the wheel reflexively. Slowly, I let myself calm, exhaling heavily and un-clutching my trembling fingers. I heard Sarah breathing evenly beside me so I knew that she was uninjured, too, and I turned my head towards her a moment later. I saw the wild look of her big eyes in the darkness and knew that she hated me all over again.

An afternoon of energetic make-up sex in two different short stay motel rooms off the 401 and one other time in the car, when we'd pulled off the road and eased through the wall of sun-bleached, flaky corn stalks not twenty feet from the highway, hidden from sight of the vehicles shooting past at high velocities. The whistling of the stalks along the car windows came back to me, the soothing quality of their music as I watched Sarah slipping out of her denim shorts beside me. A knife through hot bread, I remember thinking then as I looked forward to having her again, recalling the hollowness in me even at that thought. One of three frantic pit-stops throughout our day-long journey home after an unsuccessful weekend attempt at vacationing and mending the frayed connections between us.

    Now we sat in tense silence once again, the dropping of falling dirt having subsided mostly to occasional tiny tappings along the roof and hood of the car. I was tired of this swinging existence, always back and forth between extremes of misery and renewed infatuation with one another. Living mostly in the grey area of fragile forgiveness where our words of regret and pledges of continued adoration grew each day to a greater weight of uncertain faith in each other. It could be anything, the subtlety of a gesture misunderstood completely: her sidelong glance in a convenience store at a man receiving his change for the chocolate bars in his hand, just an ordinary man living his life and happened to have collided with the two of us in our cross-country travels in search of peace, and then all the suspicions and anger risen up again in tidal waves. It might be the reminder of my own petulance as Sarah gave a barely perceptible nod towards the attractive woman pumping gas into her car off the highway who she'd caught me watching from the corner of my eye, or the insolent yet somehow casual way she might light up a cigarette after a particularly heated exchange between us; because cancer clouds – as she well knows – make me worried for her and distraught for my future because what if they take her away someday, and what a foolish end to deliver yourself. Then all this stupid language of arguing bullshit futilely with no end in sight will be over and where will that leave me but alone?

    It returned to me suddenly, the impressive picture of him standing there stalwartly, a gargantuan onyx statue owning the road with no hint of fear in his eyes like oil. I said, with too much irritability infusing my words, "At least I missed the horse."

    And suddenly he was there, an immense shadow looming its darkness into the car with us, swallowing the feeble moon glow which had allowed us to see the futility in our eyes. As though called upon by some unknown secret alchemy hidden among the ordinary sound and timbre of my words. He'd come over to the car. He'd drifted over and now sniffed at the driver's side window, fogging up the glass with his wide flared nostrils. His unexpected appearance made me jerk away from the window instinctively, the immense presence of him enveloping us in his shadow. I sensed Sarah jump beside me, too, a cry half-caught in her throat and the creaking of the leather car seat beneath her where she moved reflexively in her place. Beyond my unease at the animal's presence so close to me, the wild look in its eyes and the way it lingered at the glass watching us cowering inside, I was yet struck by its beauty. Its curiosity or bravery in exploring the strange metal creature which had nearly struck it down in the road. Look at him, I wanted to tell Sarah, order her to cease her sullen ignoring of me and take in closely the magnificent sight of him separated from us by only window glass. To just look at the power living in those sleek legs, and the rippling back, so strong and muscular. But I said nothing, because of course she wouldn't care to hear it. I'd managed to save an animal's life and most likely ours as well but small or great feats weren't good enough during moments like those: I'd thrown us into physical disarray and that must have reminded her too much of the way we lived together generally, the world's most confused couple of fools.

  The horse's eyes were black bulbs shining relentlessly into the car, intense yet mournful. Why are you sad, friend, I wondered, feeling suddenly a peculiar kinship with the animal, but didn't ask the words for fear of Sarah finding something in them, some subtlety in their wording or nuance of my speech that might make her hate and renounce me more. So I only watched anxiously as the massive creature investigated the glass a moment longer and then turned about and sipped at the settling water of the shallow ditch. A moment later his thirst had been slaked and he was trotting up the grassy incline of the ditch, and then he disappeared over its rim and soft moonlight was returned and barely illuminating the interior of the car.

  The quick metallic flicking beside me, once, twice and again and then the sputtering orange glow along the nooks and edges of the dashboard as she lit a cigarette and made me unhappy. The stale acrid smell of Rothmans, her favourite brand of cancerous smoke, wafted to me and I shook my head just barely: why do you have to hate me for everything? I just saved a beautiful thing from being broken in the road and here you are punishing me again. But I of course held my tongue, and listened to the loaded silence of her smoking anxiously beside me, her nerves still jangling after our near-collision of minutes before.

She smoked the entire cigarette and we sat in the spiteful silence for several minutes afterwards, breathing acrid air.

The soft neighing brought us both to and we craned our heads to peer through the rear window. We were both a little amazed at the sight of her. I don't know how I knew that she was a girl, but she assuredly was, sleek and small in stature, a child, a racecar-fast colt as white as a snowscape and hovering timidly at the summit of the ditch behind us. She pawed at the grass and snorted nervously and I wanted to tell her to go ahead and pass, we weren't there to stop her or anyone from going on their way.

Then, bravery seized her and I was proven correct about her speed: like a flash she was down and midway up the opposite bank of the ditch, her hooves never stirring the narrow line of dark water at its bottom. Then she, too, was disappeared over the crest of the rise with no sign of her passing left behind, not even the tall grass stirring.

I was going to be brave, too. I looked to Sarah beside me and found her eyes already on my own. They were resentful as always, those eyes, but no longer livid, and maybe a small bit regretful of the bad air hanging motionless inside the car with us. Something else glinted there, too, a suggestion of eagerness, or maybe only a kind of fixed fear. I watched her and nodded for no reason I could understand. But it worked, if it had been a plan on my part at all, because a second passed and then Sarah said, "She was gorgeous. Both of them," with the added stipulation of, "But the first scared the hell out of me just coming up to the car like that, and watching us." A bite in her tone, as if the mysterious ways of animals were my fault, too.

I nodded again, a little relieved that we were speaking a little again, and pleased that she agreed with me: that speedy little girl was a girl for sure, the near-miracle of our agreement on the subject serving as proof enough, and I remembered her white coat and wanted to see her again. "I know what you mean. I mean, what are the odds, right? Two horses like that, just wandering out here. Maybe a farmer somewhere has a broken gate."

The rustling of the tall grass alarmed us for a moment. We turned about in our seats again, both of us simultaneously clicking our doors locked in instinctive apprehension. He was a big raccoon, plump in the belly and rotund all the way around. He too paused briefly in his descent down the grassy slope of the ditch, eyeing us suspiciously through his thief's mask. His whiskers bristled in the moonlight, each hair straight and long and both clusters on either side of his face rigid like plentiful clumps of cactus needles. He watched us watching him a moment, and then cautiously padded downwards, making a ruckus of it through the grass and especially where he splashed recklessly through the shallow water.

We followed his casual meandering progress as he waddled his way upwards, a dark hump parting the tall grass around him. Then he was gone, too, joining the others.

Sarah and I sat in silence, a little uneasy and wholly spellbound. I didn't notice the awful air anymore. I was waiting. We both were, and when the pair of cats, both black as midnight, slinked past us through the grass, stopping only a moment to shine their ghostly emerald eyes at us huddled into our seats, only then did we dare to exhale, because we couldn't hold our breath anxiously any longer.

I wanted to suggest it to her, very urgently because I felt the overwhelming need myself. But I'd known Sarah for years, and so I waited. I'd seen her first when she was a nervy, mouthy teenager with a vendetta against the world, and I'd followed her through the years into honeymoon trips to quiet islands where the air was as deceptively calm as she'd become over the years, seemingly peaceful but with a kind of electrical current running through her every breath. Like thunderheads waiting hidden behind her grey-cloudy eyes. I'd watched her eyes change from the way they once watched me and become filled with a kind of distant regret, as if she could only look at her old mistaken perceptions from a ways away, or else she just wouldn't be able to cope with the things she saw. And through the years I'd learned when it was safe to lead her into untried conversations and unknown places where she might usually feel threatened. Because sometimes this kind of courageous exploration was exactly what she needed, and me, too.

I knew her well enough to catch the expectation in her face. It was in the pensive way she surveyed the moonlit ditch in which we were nestled, and I waited for her to offer the signal. Which she did, and it only took a matter of another five minutes of sitting silently in the car and watching awed as several other silent creatures moved stealthily past us: an immense beaver, a furtive skunk slinking forward with nose grazing the grass, another pair of cats, these tawny but with the same mysterious eyes of green fire as their sisters who'd passed earlier, and a plodding cow, the old bell around her neck sounding dully in the night; we waited and allowed these animals their peaceful passage and sat in awed silence the entire while, until she let out her breath in a sigh I knew meant it was time for us to move, too.

I followed her rapt stare and picked them out right away: on the electric blue air, illuminated like apparitions in the moonlight, the four butterflies danced. They were large, huge, like model replicas of some antique machines of flight, their wax paper wings thin as gossamer where the moon's rays shone through them, yet indisputably powerful as they beat effortlessly on the air, keeping their dance alive.

Sometimes words weren't good between Sarah and I, and we'd loved and hated each other for enough years to understand this by now. Wordlessly, we got out of the car and stood in the tall grass, stretching our dull-aching legs and back muscles and staring off after those delicate air dancers.

They fluttered like veils on the air over the crest of the ditch, and then they were gone and we followed.

*   *   *

The fields would have been spectacular with the moonlight's art alone. A powerful gibbous moon had emerged from behind the evening's iron-clouded sky and set every blade of grass and stalk of corn and clod of dirt aflame in silvery light.

But then we weren't travelling alone, either: our companions were the night's ingredient which took our breath away and gave us good reason to walk in a kind of silence something like reverence.

They were beautiful.

All of them.

The mighty stallion appeared to lead, he was at the vanguard of the widely dispersed column, his sleek sides shining in the distance. The raccoon was there, too, but we couldn't be certain which was our thief of earlier because there were several of his race lumbering along on either side of us now. And now we travelled with a thousand cats it appeared, a thousand agile and taut forms slinking along in every direction, picking their way gingerly but deftly through the large clods of farmer's field dirt. Always a few feet ahead of us, the butterflies fluttered along silently, a ghostly beacon guiding us along, and I caught Sarah eyeing them wondrously every few minutes.

I glanced to my side and found a tiny kitten poking its way through the grass, its over-sized paws comical and clumsy in relation to its frail body. He was adorable, and I touched Sarah lightly on her elbow to show her. She'd been looking all around us, and the look of rapture on her face when she turned to me made me happy, and happier still when it became something a little different, and more specific with regards to me. She was comfortable, at ease, and there was no venom in either of our eyes as we walked, and I even kissed her on her cheek because I wanted to and I knew she wouldn't mind.

Like children we strolled through the fields. Awe in our eyes and magic all around. We believed in its power because its evidence surrounded us.

She leaned across my path and ruffled the fur on top of the kitten's head into severe little spikes. I almost tried for levity and told her that she'd made him into a cute little punk rocker but stopped myself: there shouldn't be words, I realized. Not then, during that strange walk through the fields. I caught her slight frown and grew worried immediately: what was the matter? Had something happened that had made us foolish enemies again? But I followed her eyes and no, it was only the curious sight of our spiky kitten rambling along with a fat caterpillar riding the crest of his back, between his bony shoulder blades. Strange, that the cat wouldn't have felt the insect there and done something to rid himself of his strange cargo. Beautiful, that they rode through the night together.

But then Sarah touched me in return, a light brushing of my elbow with her fingers in a feather-light way, and I followed her wide-eyed stare. A raccoon, one of several in our immediate vicinity, trudged along with his snout pointed determinedly towards the east in the direction we walked. Magically, a ring of fireflies circled his neck like a burning necklace, glowing their warm luminescence into his whiskers and making them look like fizzing sparklers. Sarah and I looked at one another in wonder. Over our heads shadowed shapes soared like miniature missiles in the darkness, whose low hootings told us that our air escort was a troop of owls.

How could this trek through night fields exist, I wanted to ask aloud but didn't for fear of intruding on the eerie splendour of the scene. The two of us, and the animals, all united in the sole purpose of walking to the east, moving through the dead A.M. hours in the heart of a county made mostly of whispering grass and corn and endless farmers' fields. I wondered how our single purpose of walking towards the east remained so determined and unquestionable. How a man and a woman always on the verge of war could put their enmity aside and walk peacefully among such strange company, when all throughout the day and last few weeks their time had been made up of screaming at one another and then relying on the heat of sex to give them temporary respite from their perpetual fury and discontent. I wondered how this one single moment could be so amazing, and whether it could last forever the way I wished it would.

I looked to our butterflies shimmering ahead of us and hoped that it could, and knew that it couldn't. Beside me, Sarah felt the same. I could tell by the way she held my hand, gingerly but tightly somehow, too, the quick furtive way she'd snatched it up from my side, as if she had to act quickly if she was to preserve the moment at all.

    We'd been walking for nearly forty minutes and our numbers had swelled. I exaggerated purposely and told myself that there were thousands of us, millions even, a few million animals walking with mysterious purpose to a destination soon to be revealed and at which we were all eager to arrive. We moved with horses in our ranks, beautiful and sleek, and also with clumsier cows and bulls, some of their neck-bells clunking stupidly and softly on the air. Raccoons expanded our numbers greatly, there were so many of the thieves with their grey fur shining silver under the moon. Insects flew with us, too, and hopped and scuttled, grasshoppers like pepper sprinkled on the drowsy summer air currents and the sound of beetles scuttling secretly and unseen like dry wind-swept leaves in the dirt at our feet. The dense clouds here and there over our heads were mosquitoes hungry for blood, though they sought none and remained well-organized in their flight squadrons. Fireflies like Christmas bulbs shone among us all, little holiday-like signals all to themselves, each and every burning light of them. There were dogs of all kinds, collies and terriers and mutts with untraceable lineages; and an army of cats, their feline elegance and reserve making them the greatest mystery the night held, besides of course our en masse convening and movement through its darkness.

    I felt a new vitality inside of me. My breath came easier. The night air tasted delicious and new. My eyes roamed the landscape and marvelled at the beauty all around. We were strong as we walked, and because I wanted us to be stronger I leaned in close to Sarah and into her ear I whispered: "Sometimes you hate me for no reason."

    I was close to her face, my lips were brushing her cheek, and so I saw how the words affected her: she winced, not quite startled, because she'd been entertaining these turbulent windy thoughts too, but maybe a little furrow of disappointment marked her expression.

Because now? Of all times, this glorious now is when you have to remind us of the regrettable way we are towards each other?

I watched her and she nodded a moment later. Almost imperceptibly, but I saw. She peeked over at me and mouthed the words: you too.

Me too. Yes, she was right. Sadly, we were both very right about each other in this.

We'd spent hours of that day and night highway-driving in bitter silence, an uneasy quiet loaded with the possibility of renewed war breaking out between us. We'd paid small amounts of money for the use of small, shabby sparsely-furnished motel rooms for the express purpose of having sex with each other in attempts to bring us back to some level of normality and stability. Attempts mostly brief and exciting, passionate with anger and regret and transient forgiveness. And, ultimately, they'd been futile: because it could have been a distant look, a certain kind of touch on the skin, any unfortunate reminder of past mistakes, and eventually the skies between us would fill with callous words and their bitter rebukes and then the stale stink of cigarette smoke and then silence and then the whole redundant, tiring process was begun anew. Never the end, only the centre of the endless cycle of becoming more and more tired and unhappy with one another and everything else, too.

I regretted many of my words to Sarah, and knew that many of the reasons she held me accountable for her sadness were valid. And she, of course, knew that she was culpable, too. So I said it, and again I made it a whisper in her ear because intimacy usually solved the problem, however tenuously. I said: "We're fools all the time. But somehow," and I gestured around us, and that's all I said and it's all I had to say. I left it at that, and she left it with a solemn nodding of her head in agreement.

I noticed the giant moth, white as snow, resting among the tangles of her hair at the side of her head, antennae stirring and feeling the air. It looked beautiful there. It looked just right where it was. I said nothing.

She touched my arm as we walked, then let her fingers fall away, an insect's touch in the night. I returned the touch, and we walked side by side listening to the sounds of life murmuring around us. A flat clunking of a cow's neck-bell in the distance, and the drowsy singing of a bluebird from above, wailing a song of love to a companion fluttering in some other air space. The hum of dragonflies like tiny hovering motors, the bass heartbeat sound of an owl hooting forebodingly.

In the distance: light and sound.

Many minutes' walk from where Sarah and I marched, the sky lighter. The bellies of the clouds there were lit with a gentler blue, electric and unreal, and it appeared as though we were headed for that very site. I wondered at that light, and the hulking mass of distant woods I spied making the horizon jagged and threatening, and again at the strange sound of the night surrounding us as we walked. An incredible noise: a distant murmur, a humming in the darkness as of some very powerful thing. An energy source setting the horizon shimmering subtly and tickling the hairs on my arms, at the nape of my neck. A deep hum and thrum, like some great energy collected in one place and set to be released. The giant sound of the night humming like all the power in the world.

But then I stopped thinking these thoughts. It was enough that we shared something like a goal, of trekking towards the blue-lit horizon. I was watching the butterflies dancing on the air and imagined I could hear the tiny flutter of their silk wings. I was content. We walked on.

Every step across the field equated with a rise in pitch of the humming. Like an electrical current sizzling the air and stirring some long-dormant thing inside of me into wakefulness: some sense of wildness, allowing me to walk on despite the untamed, frightening grandeur of the strange scene of which I was a part. Merging me seamlessly inside of its impossible fabric. Perfect, with Sarah beside me unchecked in her strides, too. Some good and vital thing awakened which allowed me to be pulled inexorably closer to the source of the secret power. I felt Sarah's fingers clasp mine tighter, instinctively, and I clutched hers tightly in return. We were together in our long walk, united, a part of this tribe journeying eastwards.

As we neared the copse of trees, my eyes discerned that the formation of walkers had narrowed, three abreast, pairs further beyond these, and finally single specimens of creatures moving into the black belly of the forest. Disappearing within its embrace, while overhead the thicket's jagged outline crackled with promise, an illuminating aura stirring the leaves anxiously like some secret promise in the A.M. The strange night sound was a chorus in my head, humming comfortably, deeply. A loud yet indefinable tumult reverberating in my bones, in my thoughts. The roar of celebration, a chorus like freedom in the night. Maybe animals howled and bayed and screeched inside of that din. A gestalt animal roar coalesced into one song in the night.

We were soon walking along more even ground, with no other animals on either side of us as we approached a narrow path leading into the trees. Sarah's voice was urgent in my ear, "Don't let go of me. We'll stay side-by-side." I squeezed her hand in answer, and it was enough, and we walked on together.

Among the trees I caught sight of miniature flares, and smiled, relieved somehow.

"Those fireflies over there are better," I told her suddenly, nodding ahead beyond the wall of spruces towering over us at the forest's edge. And without thinking, a little apprehensively yet determined still, I reached into her back pocket and dropped the half-empty cigarette pack into the dirt. No more burnings and stinking cancer in the air. And no more words in the night, either. I was finished with them for that night. Our small noises were a blasphemy in the midst of such beautiful cacophony and light.

Around us, leaves trembled and the night roared.

She said nothing as we stepped into the woods and towards our destination beyond them, only stared ahead. The peace in her eyes remained, and I turned back towards the path we were all following and let my eyes soften, too.

Let the Firefly Men Remind You

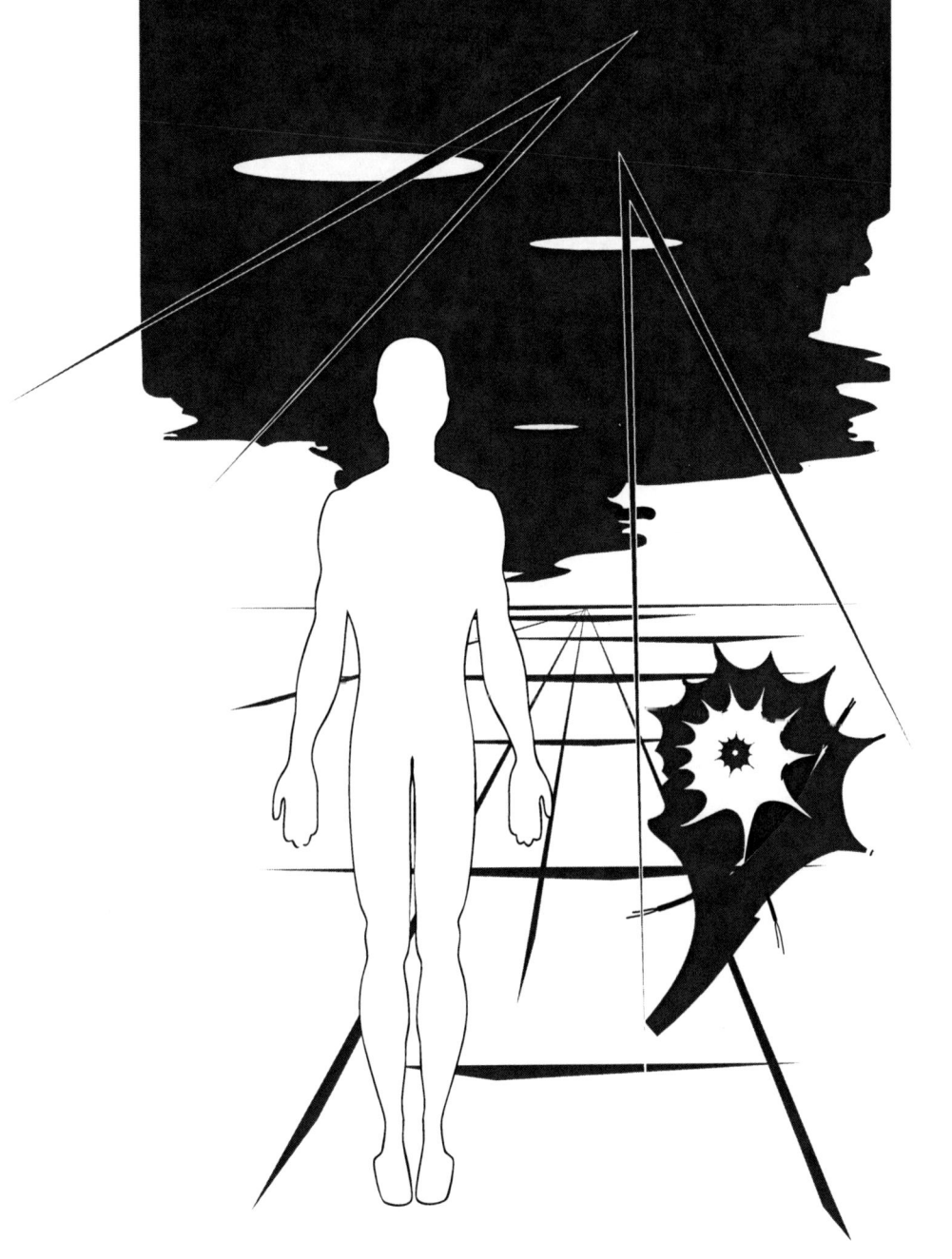

Nothing lasts.

Endless summers fade away, too, with all their strange and wondrous ingredients. And only their ghosts linger. And even though we all knew the truth in those words, that summer still felt eternal, like the most magical and painful summers of your life tend to fool you.

Like hippies so crazed from the acid frying our sizzling minds that we could never claim the truth about the things we'd seen to anyone but ourselves. But we knew it because the mornings following such hauntings found us all pale and cold, and we didn't talk as freely throughout that strange summer as in other, less significant years past. So that was us, day in and out, afternoons drifting by the river behind Natalie's farm house in Comber County while her parents were away in distant Windsor; and the nights were bonfires and pointing out fairy spirits amid the clusters of sparks shooting into the air. In twos, we'd sneak off and kiss our partner behind the first thin wall of trees bordering the deep dark bush where we feared demons roamed with the deer and rabbits. But we were young and crazy with fire between our legs, and the bark of trees scratched at our backs where our shirts were lifted up and over our heads while we were kissed hard into the trunks, disturbing spiders and caterpillars in their crawling nocturnal quests.

Gary was my man most of that summer and we were lost

in each other's touches and whispers when the big fire happened. He was thin and wore his hair long, and his beard, too, all twisted and pubic-looking and so sexy with river water drenching it like some wet animal. We were good together and the funniest thing about us was the knowledge we shared that we'd never last past that summer. I pictured him moving away somewhere else, which he eventually did, to Toronto I think it was, and I knew it then and know it now, that he didn't take my number with him when he went. Just like I erased his name and number from their place penciled into the headboard of my bed back in Belle River.

Maybe it was the sole thing that kept all of us so happy those hot months: our awareness of the transience of all things leading into tomorrow. We never once entertained the idea that we could possibly repeat the grandeur and mystery of those days, and so we weren't too upset knowing we'd never even give ourselves the chance to try. We lived in the very instant of each moment and never considered the existence of time outside of that safe neutral bubble.

Natalie was the same as me, my twin sister it had always seemed in the way she thought exactly as I did, who loved her man's presence beside her every night while the fire crackled and spit wheeling sparks like fireflies around us. But it was only the presence of him she cherished, never any warmth beyond the simple physical tangibility of him being there that summer. We were content enough having another hot body to hold us and to clutch to us when we felt like sharing something good of ourselves.

My man's name was Gary and he spoke like a preacher. Gary Texo, who swore to me that he was a real child of God. The real McCoy, in his own words, with his own carefully wrought-out set of beliefs which allowed him to indulge in any excess he chose while still flaunting the silver cross on its silver chain around his neck. *If you love God, He won't reject you because of your lifestyle, He's bigger than that.* I liked his eyes. They were always looking inwards at himself, as if he were dreaming about himself, and I suppose I really only thought that he was rather self-absorbed and pretty, but I never cared. He knew how to nip at my neck like a vampire and make the skin all along my shoulders ripple into goose flesh. He knew how to remove my bra quickly, he never fumbled with the clasps like so many novices I've known. When he kissed me, he was absorbed totally in the moment, and at least during times like those I knew for certain that he was mine.

    Natalie was a wondrous child, silently wise about the things she saw around her, and so I think she knew it, too, felt it in her petite bones: everything that summer was fleeting, despite the daily slow-poking way we went about the things we did. As if we had all the time in the world left to us. The days tasted too good. The night air was too perfect, a constant temperature of neither too chilly nor too muggy. The mosquitoes were out, of course, but never in droves, and our long-sleeve shirts were adequate enough armour to thwart their needle-noses.

    We were always commenting on geography, it was all around us, a kind of wild, sprawling magnificence. We'd all visited Natalie's farm house before when her parents were away in Windsor, where they went often on business as well as socially to visit their many friends. But it was different then. The tree line rippled better against settling dusk every early evening. The fireflies among the thick twisted trees were more celebratory in their bobbings and flutterings than in previous Julys and Augusts. They'd always been pretty but never quite magical like they were then. And the sound of the river was calmer, the best and most soothing music that stretch of corn country had ever produced. What a soundtrack. What a time. And the sounds of insects moving through the stalks and brittle husks never carried so sweetly on the air.

    But then there were other things at work those days, too. Oddities, peculiarities among the everyday laze and summery haze which ruined our good cheer and brought us down from our drunken spinning reveries. Incidents and happenings we only ever seemed brave enough to acknowledge once the wine had been poured and the acid delivered onto our tongues. The bizarreness of things which always brought us down to lucidity, and that instilled an unsettling ingredient into the days and nights. Which propelled them quicker from their dusks to the following dawns, and just like that another grand yet haunted day was behind us.

*   *   *

I'd found the burning animal at the edge of the woods. I'd been drawn to the flicker of flames from my backyard vantage, and trudged across the field to investigate. Still twitching about in its final death-agonies, croaking horribly. Disfigured from the heat, smoke sizzling from its black, lumpy body, its remnants of fur twisted and scorched. Several patches of the thing's misshapen body still smouldering angrily by the time I'd reached it, little plumes of fire crackling grotesquely in the bright light. I never did discover exactly what species of animal it had been. A small dog, maybe, or a raccoon. Foxes were plentiful in those woods, perhaps one had wandered into the hands of – what exactly? According to Natalie, there weren't very many children in the area, the next farm being located several miles to the east. We'd buried it, Natalie and I, at her request and without mention of it to our friends. They had their own stories to shudder along to without benefit of ours.

One of the summer couples, Maria and Franklin, returning from a trip to the forest with a strange artefact to silence us all and bring our barbecue merriment to a standstill. Unfurling the dirty woollen blanket they'd used for lying down together among the trees, we gasped and didn't say very much at the sight of the cargo it contained. It smouldered, too, the mass of snakes burnt and congealed into a single web-like organism. Black and awful, suffocating us with the stink of its broiled flesh. Scales peeling off and pocking the blanket all over, the stiff calcified tongues black and pitiful on the noon hour air. Maria and Franklin with stunned eyes all over the grass, as if too frightened to show us their faces, or maybe only embarrassed that they'd felt the overwhelming need to share the horror of their discovery with us so that we might offer them some sliver of comfort.

These odd fires and their ashen remains, and the evening occasions of pointing out strange sky-fires to one another, too. The flashes in the air over the treetops, and the pulsing from deep inside the heart of the thicket in the distance, which most of us witnessed at some point during those weeks and attributed half-heartedly to fire bugs or teenagers' bonfires. Like some visual code flickering to us where we reclined in lawn chairs or lolled on grass-stained blankets. Eerie messages we never could decipher, and only wondered over, awed and anxious, and were occasionally curious or brave or high enough to venture towards with our summer partners in tow.

 Strange, strange summer.

Terrifying, but we relished its beauties, too.

 Once, while I was staring into the fire with cough syrup in my belly and Gary's kisses on my neck making me simultaneously drowsy and excited, I noticed Natalie watching me. Her own man, Ted Hansen, was smelling her hair and running his hands across her chest overtop her tank-top. I smiled, thinking it funny that we were talking without words, as we often did, while our boyfriends were oblivious and lost in us. I'll never forget what she said to me then, without words, and it was the most perfect and most defining thing about the whole situation that she could possibly have imparted.

 She smiled, and put her fingers to her mouth and kissed their tips and then blew me the kiss, on the air and sailing invisibly towards me. I motioned like I caught it, and I held it a second, her kiss hot in my hand, and rubbed it into my chest. A secret communication of our own when we needed it most. A reassurance in the mystery of the night. Then we turned to our men and lost ourselves in good places where moanings and less powerful kisses lived.

 Neat-O pranced before us and we laughed, such frantically elegant behaviour for a hog.

 She was enormous, her round belly nearly scraping the straw-littered floor of the barn and spotted all over with dark circles on her white-pink skin. *You look like an inverted night sky,* Natalie said, and I watched her as she knelt in the hay and scratched the pig under her bristly chin. I wondered at her words about the inverted night sky. Always like her to say things that didn't quite make sense when you looked at them carefully, but which sounded pretty and felt endearingly genuine in their intention to define the moment.

 I nodded and bent down and tugged on one of Neat-O's

drooping ears. I held it aloft on the air, liking the warm look of sunlight burning through the thin cartilage. *You're beautiful, Neat-O,* I told her and let her ear flop back down, and I could have sworn that she smiled up at me with her pig mouth and tiny eyes. *You named her perfect,* I told Natalie, and we were watching Neat-O retreat towards her section of stable, side-stepping expertly the piles of manure in the hay. *The neatest creature in the world,* she laughed, and we joked about poor Neat-O's stressful family life, living daily in a perpetual pig sty with her many filthy brothers and sisters.

    We had the radio in with us, resting among farm tools on a narrow shelf set into the wall. The batteries were running out of juice, Black Sabbath droned a little slower than on most days. Natalie bobbed her head in time with the tune and brought my attention to the lyric. *It's a symptom of the universe,* she sang along in pretty accompaniment to Ozzy. *A love that never dies.* Then she said how it sounded dreadful, the way he made the words sound, as if something as ephemeral as love might be capable of doing harm.

    I laughed and said something about the amounts of acid the band probably dropped while recording the album, but I thought about it a long while afterwards. One of many subtle little hauntings making the days nervous beneath their perpetual laze and haze. I thought of my Gary and Natalie's Ted and how neither of us really cared if we woke up alone the following morning. We hung some wild flowers from a hook set over Neat-O's stall, I think Natalie said they were gardenias, and they smelled vibrant in the gloom of the barn. They lit the air up, and we were sure the world's tidiest beast would enjoy their perfume among all the shit and slop.

    We went inside to grab a couple of iced teas and I asked Natalie as we walked whether she was happy. She said: *Yes, I'm happy.* The days were lazy and the nights drowsy and what more could we ask for. I wanted to ask her if she wanted it to last forever, but the thought had arrived in my head so unexpectedly that it worried me slightly and I only nodded and started talking about how the setting sun turned the fields bloody and savage-looking. Like a horizon-long fire. Like a Frank Frazetta painting. She'd graduated from art school the year before and loved the look of powerfully feminine and masculine things so she knew what I meant, and squeezed my hand to show it. She only said one word about it, too: *Primordial.* And once again, it was just her way to be completely right in the way she described the world before her.

Rounding the corner of her parent's house, Natalie tugged on my shirt sleeve, halting me in my tracks. I followed her wide-eyed look and shuddered at the sight: the plump raccoon barring our way, teeth bared ferociously where it stood before the ruin of another of its tribe: a brother, maybe, or sister or lover. A charred obscenity frying the warm air and drawing clouds of agitated flies. The stink of burnt meat on the breeze was potent, violent even, watering our eyes and gagging us while we gulped ineffectually for clean air. Backing away fearfully, we gave the animal the courtesy of solitude with its deceased companion. *Did you notice?* Natalie whispered urgently in my ear once we were a safe distance away, as though we were sharing secrets. *The flies? None of them were crawling on the dead raccoon. Only buzzing around in the air. They wouldn't touch the thing.* We were doubling back in the direction we'd come from, and turned at the noise behind us: there it was, the mourning raccoon, lumbering frantically away from the site of its stricken friend. We watched it lope hurriedly through the field and towards the distant woods, scrabbling over dirt clods and rocks as if it was in some sudden great hurry to be away from the scene.

We stood a while in the warm shade of the house, amid the drone of drifting hornets and bumblebees wandering from flower to flower. It was the unsettling aftermath of a sighting, the jarring post-fire awe and humbled silence. In that moment, Natalie and I were reminded all over again of their presence, the great mysteries of the summer, having been offered another glimpse of the season's strange and immeasurable depth. But after a moment of quiet between us, it was Natalie who saved us with her usual odd observations like unexpected offerings of wisdom. Pointing towards the rows of corn husks burning in the afternoon glare near to us, she murmured, *Corn. Sombre. Comber.* I followed her gaze, and saw it immediately, the morose posture of the heat-ravaged stalks leaning towards the soil, a glum, static sea of greenery shot through with sun-paled yellow kernels like failed attempts at brightness. I shook my head in wonder, wondering why it was that her words made me feel better, but soon giving up on any kind of scrutiny. It's best to take some gifts as they come to you, without question and with gratitude. I worried at the somewhat unhappy gleam in her pensive eyes, and squeezed her hand and reminded her how much we loved this county of dirt and sun and corn rows, and won a smile from her that warmed me more pleasantly than August sunlight could ever.

Eventually we remembered our big thirst and continued on our way, passing out of the comforting house-shade and making certain to avoid the dead animal. The sun put tears in our eyes, and we winced the entire time. I thought as we walked about the beginnings of pictures like the one in front of us, all sun fire and bloody land. The beginnings of big things. But the thought weighed too much and I set my sights on the relief of iced tea moving down my parched throat, and I found that it made me content enough.

They looked good shirtless, both our men, and we leaned back against the hay bales to watch them while we smoked.

Ted Hansen lobbed a warbling spiral toss of the football skywards, his back glistening with sweat or sun tan oil, we couldn't tell which. Gary Texo, my man in dusty jeans and bare feet, pounding across the grass with arms outstretched, running, running, wincing into the glare of late afternoon sunlight. He nearly tripped over the rake hidden in the tall grass but made the catch successfully. We listened to them whoop and cheer like they'd won an important game, but were too tired to applaud their efforts ourselves, and only exchanged weary looks while smiles tugged at the corners of our mouths.

We sat awhile, listening to the dry scratching noises of mice tunnelling in the hay beneath us, at our backs. The air was a little cooler, early evening air, and our cigarettes tasted good then, just right in anticipation of the big supper the men were barbecuing for us. The potent smell of hot dogs drifted to us and we joked about how poor Neat-O must feel smelling that meaty breeze, poor frightened nervous hog.

It was an uncanny ability of Natalie's to name my thoughts before I ever even realized that I was thinking them. I'd convinced myself that I was feeling fine, looking forward to a big supper and getting stoned and hopefully laid afterwards. But then her words were there between us and I woke up from my stupor.

Do you feel scared right now?

I watched her watching me and was nodding my head before I realized with any certainty what I felt. It struck me then: all day I'd been uneasy, tripping over things in and around the house, farm tools, clods of dirt, my own feet, jumping at hog squealings and cursing at the crows squawking down at me from the barn roof and making me edgier. I'd nearly gotten tangled up in the garter snake that crossed my path in the morning outside of the barn, a long specimen zipping madly across the gravel, a frantic blur of movement at my feet, difficult to follow against the earth the colour of its skin. A constant pounding pulse of anxiousness in my temples all day, threatening me with imminent headache pain and nausea. Peering outdoors with eyes squinted in anticipation of some new smouldering vision, another animal roasting in the grass, or a torch of flame dropping like a stone from the air as a burning crow fell from the clouds.

I watched our men cavorting in the grass like they were superstar athletes or children, their jubilant cries small with distance, and I hoped they were careful where they walked. Because there were snakes aplenty in Comber County grasses, hidden like taut leathery ropes among the emerald stretches and wild flower colonies. In the grass where things sometimes burned like strange sacrificial fires, ruining the good smell of gardenias on the air.

Her voice was a whisper. A chill on the air. *Me too. I'm scared, too.*

It was all she said, and we dragged on our cigarettes and listened to the travels of mice around us. A slight breeze picked up, carrying the smell of manure from the stables and mixing it with the scent of cooking meat. I was watching the sky when she told me what I was thinking about that picture, and maybe the bigger picture of everything else, too.

But the sky's gorgeous today.

And she was done speaking, and I only kept looking upwards, admiring the purity of the blue, unmarred by clouds, except in the far west, where the hint of a distant storm brewed. We finished our cigarettes and sat a while longer in our admiration. Even when the v of crows flew into view and coincidentally crossed the path of another which had just taken flight from the barn roof, and for a brief instant they'd formed a cross in the air, scratching out the blue and making us frown.

It began as just another night of fairy dances in the fire and electric cricket song in the tall grass.

We in our regular positions doing our usual things, the tribe convened once more about its fire and revelling in bliss: there was Lawrence like a hippy with his tympani drum on the grass between his legs, its battered skin thin and warped in its centre from weeks of his pounding palms, his eyes glazed with drink and marijuana and staring at shooting bonfire flecks; ignoring Julie beside him, it's where she always was although he only ever paid her very little attention, except for when he noticed her ample breasts through his fog of being stoned; Julie from Belle River, with her quiet way and fragile voice, too timid to remind Lawrence what he was missing most of the time: her nice smile and nice legs and nice way of overlooking his rude blindness, too meek to do anything other than wait for him to notice her at all. Beside them, Madeleine huddled into her woollen blanket, keeping the mosquitoes and her man Tony at bay because she was tired of their stings during the night, his especially; always chiding her for eating too much and smoking too little, barbecue goes straight to your thighs, Maddy, didn't you notice, here, have a toke, you'll love it. Stupid words, she thought, because who didn't crave leftovers like crazy while they were high. She was from Windsor, we'd met at school two years before and become close friends seemingly overnight, amazed at our similar tastes in movies and music and cruel men. And Tony himself, tall and lanky and scruffy with a week's stubble, staring at her and wanting her despite the barbecue in her thighs, too sluggish from marijuana to try sidling first closer to her and then beneath the blanket with her, too thoughtless besides to offer an ineffectual apology for his usual brusque ways. Across from them,

Maria and Franklin were a single animal illuminated by bonfire glow as they pawed and licked each other unabashedly. They'd met for the first time that very week and had mutually decided to live their summer like the lyrics from a rock and roll song, carefree and with abandon. Her long blonde hair spilled over him and he wore his hair the same length, and because it was almost the same colour we often joked about it while watching them: where does one begin and the other end, and in the end we'd only chuckle and return, inspired, to kissing each other.

I watched them all with lazy eyes, old friends some, others only acquaintances who I knew I'd never see again after our holiday was finished, yet all fitting the moment just right: everyone in their place, and the crickets in the grass around us sounded so electric and amazing, too. I sighed luxuriously: Gary's hand resting on my thigh and edging higher, slipping underneath my summer dress, and the bonfire reflected in his narrowed eyes like miniature smouldering suns, the way I liked his eyes best, volcanic and self-indulgent.

We were on fire, too, and so it took a moment for us both to tune into the startled cries of our friends around us. Our mouths were open and our tongues searching for each other, our cough syrup breath hot and ready. There we paused briefly, lips to lips, tongue on tongue, and I suppose this was the first instant I realized that bigger things lived around us; outside of the splendour of losing ourselves in each other and in a sleepy time so slow that minutes seemed to stop entirely.

It was Lawrence, I think, who murmured it through a cloud of pot smoke: *Those aren't fairies, guys.*

We followed the direction of his huge white eyes and saw the line of figures approaching from the edge of the forest. I stared and stared, trying ineffectually to determine exactly how it was that they were illuminated, where was their light source which lit them in green fire like horrific storybook illustrations? I looked for lanterns or flashlights around us to help illuminate the scene but saw none, only the hazy forms provided light as they seemed to shimmer toward us like wavering projector images.

Lawrence spoke again, a volley of speech infused with mounting panic: *Those aren't fairies, guys, holy God, man.*

They weren't fairies, and it was poor unravelling Lawrence who started our sudden and instinctive retreat towards the farm house. Our bottles we left behind on rocks and lawn chairs and overturned milk crates. Some of us left sandals and jackets, too, in our mad flight through the suddenly moonless night. There was no sound except for our laboured huffing and clumsy steps and the occasional hushed curse from one of us. We never discussed or debated our retreat. We only felt a most pervasive nameless dread at the sight of those green lights like fiery men walking from the forest. I couldn't rid myself of it no matter how I tried, refuting my own inadequate attempts at logic as I fled: they weren't will-o'-the-wisps or some other gaseous phenomenon because gases don't move with purpose, and the sight of another sliver of wondrous county geography would only make us sigh in wonder and admiration rather than hurl us scrambling over each other as we ran for our lives. Because something in each of us awoke at that moment, assuring us of danger. A threat to our peace, our lives. Compelling us to flight like no ordinary summer ingredient could possibly move us.

So we scurried like mice in the night, until we were gathered panting in the darkness of Natalie's kitchen. Jostling for a glimpse through the window and into the changed night outside. I think it was Maria who whispered with hot whiskey-breath at my ear: *Oh dear god.* And I reached behind me and took her hand in mine and squeezed her tightly. Because I was watching the burning figures gathering in the yard, too. Their march hadn't ceased. They hadn't winked out of existence simply because we'd turned our eyes from them during our brief dash into the house. They weren't figments of mescaline-tripping or cough syrup cloudiness. They were setting the night alight. Burning silently like enormous torches or mysterious beacons. They were closer and moving resolutely towards us still.

How are they moving, for Christ's sake? It's not fucking normal. I think it was Gary again, poor quivering Gary with his silver cross of Christ hanging among his chest hair, and all his well-pondered beliefs shaken and reeling.

None of us answered him, only let the breath whistle out between our clenched teeth as we stared helplessly. I didn't know Maria as well as our other friends did but gripped her hand as tightly as I could. Because we were there in the kitchen darkness together. Sharing its depth and tension and numbing expectation. Watching in silence a scene which we could never possibly understand. I trembled at the realization of the sentience we were witnessing in the distinctly purposeful progress of the flaming men, walking or gliding towards us where we stood shaking in the blackness. Hovering like some strange species of giant phosphorescent insect awakened from their secret nests in the forest.

Maybe I shouldn't have said it but I was terrified, too, and things just happen that way during times of confusion like those. And so the words slipped out, in a whisper that everyone heard and which made us tremble even more in our shorts and shirt sleeves.

I said: *They look like giant fireflies.*

And they did, with their bobbing gait on the air and the way that they shone, eerie but beautiful too, like a ragged line of lanterns looking strong in the way they pushed back the darkness around them. And therein lay our real terror: because we couldn't look away from those bodies of light, so gorgeous in their burnings, even in the face of the dread they put inside us. Vivid yet indefinable in hue. Frosty yet fiery. Savage and beautiful. Intoxicatingly violent. Mesmerizing and blinding, a collective of dark burning things spell-weaving us to rapt attention. Another summer ingredient blasphemed.

Oh Jesus Christ, look. What are they doing? It was Madeleine beside me, her hand covering her face, eyes wide moons peering through her fingers. I'd never seen her frightened before and shuddered at her new face: she looked like a ghost beside me, pale and insubstantial, a spooked moth that threatened to flutter away at any moment.

We watched riveted: the firefly men had formed a wobbly circle outside of the yard housing the pigs. We could make out the animals' rotund bodies through the crooked fence slats, and then their high shrieks and squeals sounded as they scrambled away from those burning lights. *They better not hurt the pigs,* swore Madeleine, which I'd later think was a sweet thing for her to have said, to have cared for Natalie's animals while we shook and cried ourselves. And I thought of the world's best-groomed pig and I feared for her deeply, wishing she was there with us in the shadows of the house.

Then I realized. And I whispered her name: *Natalie. Where are you, Natalie?*

No answer from the kitchen darkness.

Oh God. It was Gary again and I saw him in the faint moonlight as he gripped his glistening chain tightly in his fingers, tears like silver paint trails down his cheeks. *Oh God oh God,* and we had to tell him with raised voices to calm himself and be quiet, we were just as helpless as those pigs if those lights got into the house.

But we felt it, too, a desperate terror for our friends: poor Natalie, and her man that summer, both snuck off into the woods to have one another among the spiders and fireflies as they'd done a dozen times already those few weeks, as we'd all done some time or another with our August partners. There was no question in our minds that they'd met up with the burning men among the trees. It was something we knew with certainty. And I still feel a pang of shame at the memory, but in that instant I suddenly found myself wishing I could trade one for the other: my Gary, a fleeting and miniscule sliver of my summer, for our Natalie, so much like me in how she looked at the world and understood song lyrics and stroked pigs under their chins to make them grunt and burble in pleasure. A wrongful malice towards him swept through me, and the vision of me hurling him through the kitchen doorway like some man-sized, perfectly-lobbed football or other meaningless banality flew into my thoughts unbidden, trembling me in my rage.

I began to cry around this time and I felt my friends' hands touch me gently in different places. Instinctive caresses in the darkness, because they were there with me, too, in our shared moment of staring into the unfathomable; the burning unknown lighting our summer night terribly and memorably, like no handfuls of sparklers or fireworks had ever done. Waiting for meaning or the touch of fire, or maybe these things were one and the same on a summer night when county forests unveiled their bright yet inexplicably darkly-lit secret cargoes.

Someone else's voice began crying from behind me somewhere, too, disembodied and ethereal. A ghost-moth fluttering in the night. Julie, I think it was, and it was Tony whispering for her to be quiet, soothingly at first because he was terrified, too, but then very heatedly because her sobbing wouldn't stop and it was a very unnerving presence there in the dark. Beside me, Maria was swearing softly, a terrified kind of litany in conjunction with the sound of Julie's sobbing underlying all of her words: *Oh God, oh no, oh God, oh no,* and she was squeezing my hand so severely that soon all I could feel through the numbness was the stabbing of tiny needles in my finger joints.

What was going to happen to us: the pervasive worry which engulfed my mind and certainly consumed the others as well. And then through blurry eyes I saw: among the strange figures that glowed so luminously, in the centre of their circle in the dusty yard with the hogs shrieking madly in chorus, two motionless forms. I think some of us exclaimed in horror and grief, maybe I did myself though I can't be certain.

They were our friends, that pair of unmoving bodies: Natalie and her summer man, Ted Hansen from Comber. They were naked, I could make out the large birth mark on her calf which she felt so self-conscious of, and his lanky limbs looked less wiry, less taut with muscle than I remembered them. They were bathed in the strange luminescence smouldering from around them, and looked small and fragile and helpless in the openness of the yard. Trapped and in the clutches of we didn't understand what, their place secured forever in the midst of the ring of glowing, weirdly-lit figures. Like hapless pawns in a ritual beyond our fathoming. Like meat pieces in the heart of a fire. Like a doomed scene from a Frazetta painting.

And I thought helplessly again of our conversation of the day before: primordial, this picture, too, or maybe an illustration of some un-guessable next step in all our lives.

Then:

One after another in quick succession, as fast as a family of fleas leaping from one region of human skin to another, the figures like malevolent lanterns jumped away into the night air, shooting like silent rockets at light speed up towards the stars. Like that, a flash of hyper-movement, and they were gone, trailing wispy comet tails in their wake. And they'd taken our friends with them. An aftermath glow remained briefly and we watched terrified and hatefully as it faded, until normal moon glow peeked through the cloud cover and coloured the lonely, molested yard forlornly.

We stayed in the kitchen the entire night, staring out into the blackness with wide eyes and hammering hearts. We huddled close, and knelt on the cool tiles and whispered half-hearted encouragements to one another while we wept: *Ssh. Don't worry. We're safe. It'll be light soon. Don't think about it.* It might have been when we cared most about each other, our time together crying in the dark.

When the sun burned bloody over the trees we were there still, until mid-morning when we were all too tired to let fear keep us from collapsing over one another and finding sleep wherever we could, some of us on the living room couches and the rest of us remaining on the cold linoleum tiles. A commune of confused, frightened children dreaming fitfully.

Nothing lasts.

Yet the first thing I recalled when I woke up to the nervous subdued chatter of my friends, and the thing I would recall for the rest of my years, was Natalie's ghost-voice telling me how she felt about it all, summer and its bitter-sweetness.

The days were lazy and the nights drowsy. What else could we ask for?

Yes, she'd been happy.

But the forests held walking lights like men on fire, and the skies said the same thing over and over again when they sucked those figures up and swallowed them and made them into stars winking overhead: it wasn't that simple. The picture of the world wasn't nearly so simple. Savage and bloody, like a painting, like a sunset dipping the fields in the colour of carnage, yes. But simple: no. Not simple. Very difficult. Profoundly intricate and impenetrable, a design bottomless with potential.

We lacked courage and so we escaped from the farm and spoke with one another only infrequently in the years to come, making certain to choose our subjects carefully. We were essentially no more because this was the simplest solution. Eyes mirroring each other's memory of a standstill moment of chaos rending our lazy peace apart: these weren't places any of us wished to look again. Natalie's parents' fruitless initiation of a missing person's search left us more hollow and terrified still, and the only answer we could possibly offer them or the methodical inquiries of the police: *We don't know. We don't know where our friends are now.* And the meticulous sweeps of the surrounding woods and fields by uniformed officers and volunteer farmers' families yielding nothing but spooked local wildlife and occasional inexplicable remains of mutilated animals. Raccoons and dogs, crows and cows, charred and ruined and scattered like blackened obscenities in the countryside. Raising only more speculation, and instilling an aura of even darker mystery over the horrible event.

    I stood in the dust that final afternoon watching the line of their cars filing away down the winding drive that led to the road a half mile to the east. They looked sad, a terrified funeral procession traveling at high speed to distance themselves from the memory of their recent woe and terror. Before I got into my own car, though, I said goodbye to Neat-O, who had remained fortuitously unscathed during the bedlam of the night. I found her rooting about in the hay for some stray food nuggets and I rubbed her under the chin, and when she swung her head sideways in approval I liked the pricking of her bristles on my palm. It's a sloppy world, I wanted to tell her, but only sniffed the withering gardenias and felt suddenly sad because I knew I didn't have time to pick her fresh flowers.

    I had to leave quickly because time felt suddenly against me, an enemy threatening my every moment, and yet even in my hurry I was the last of us to drive from the farm. There was no sign of my friends in the distance, no speeding specks at all, and I felt alone in the world, and the irony, I guess, was that I'd never known so fiercely that I wasn't alone. I scanned the hulking forest which loomed like a threat on the western horizon as I turned from the winding driveway and onto the road. Pebbles ticked loudly along the underside of my car as I sped along, trailing dust clouds. I continued glancing uneasily into the rear view mirror, catching the forest's reflection and wondering what else I might at any moment see there. I felt unreal, divorced from my body somehow, but knew that I'd be crying soon once again. For Natalie, and her man, and for all of us.

It was early in the day and I was glad that the remnants of night sky were no longer visible. No faint star-shimmers or pale hanging ghost-moon like a hint of the larger universe reeling behind the summer-blue atmosphere. I slipped on my sunglasses because of the glare but removed them a moment later because I wanted to feel water welling in my eyes, an illusion of my grief when I otherwise only felt a hollowness filled with fear. The sunlight was welcome: I couldn't bear the thought of seeing all the stars above me and wondering which of the million twinkling dots might hold our friends. An inverted sky, and once again her words were perfect if a little enigmatic. But I drove fast besides, over a hundred even on the narrow winding back roads, because Belle River was a ways away and I was running on empty with no gas station in sight. And the next night of my life was fast approaching. And I wasn't sure what it might hold for me.

I slipped a tape into the cassette player and listened anxiously to the strained whirring of the machine's internal guts as it readied it for play. The tape hadn't been marked, a blank, filled with what songs I didn't yet know. But I knew I'd listen to it all the way through and soak it all up, because I wanted nothing more right then than to make the most of my drive through the fiery-hot day.

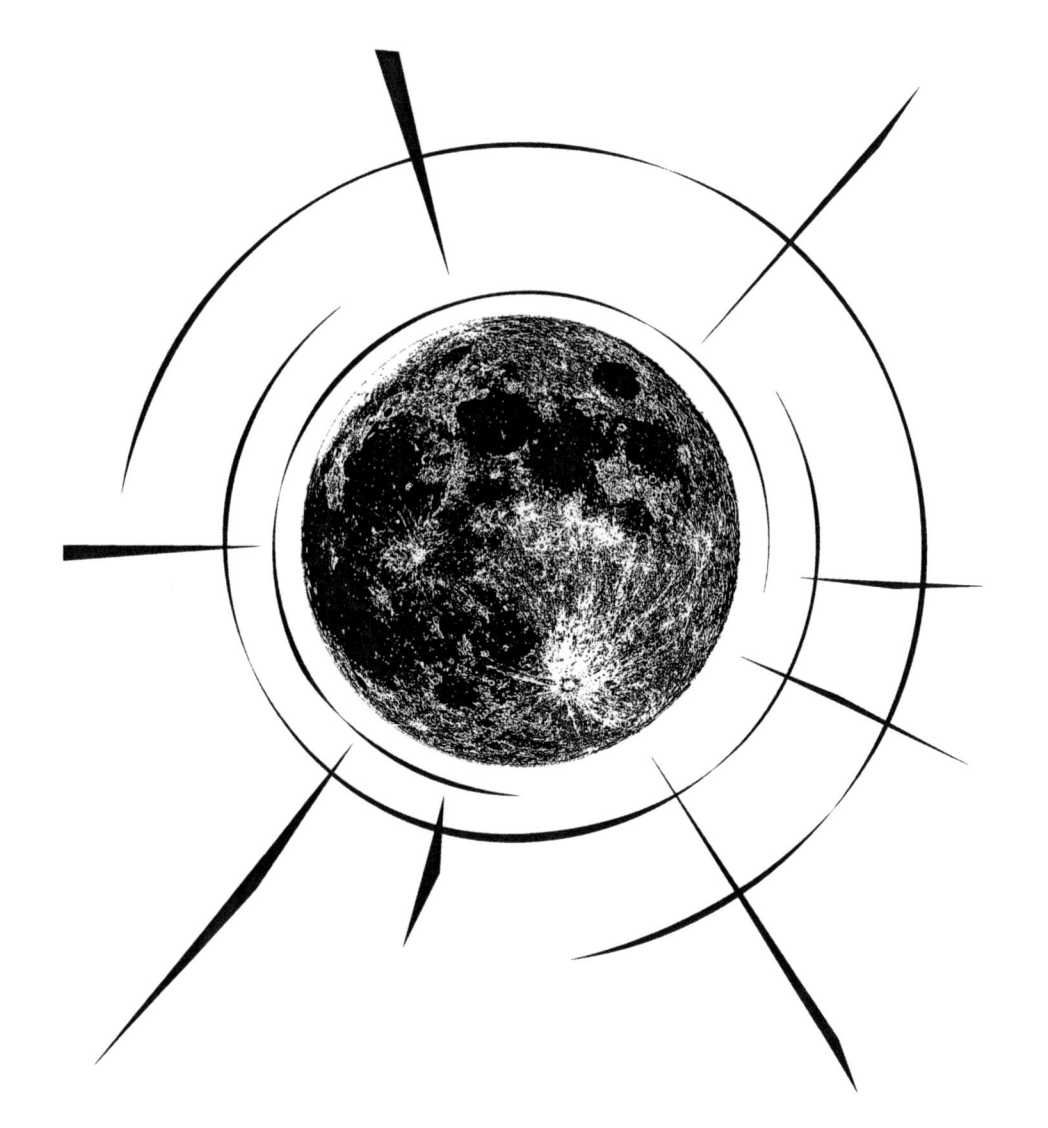

Just Right

Under Moonlight

We only ever made love desperately, as if our town might be going up in end-of-the-world flames later on that humid night. I guess we were perfect couples in all that sticky air, me and the girls who were like moths, flimsy and destined to turn into powder.

All the nights were humid then. Mosquitoes flew like sandstorm specks around our heads in the dark. She used to say how they were like mini-motors in her ears. All the girls said things like that, but not as nicely as her, not as softly. I liked that. I like that still.

It makes my head weigh a thousand tons, thinking of that now. Of miniature motors and air so heavy with pent-up moisture and insect traffic it makes you realize how small you are in the big scheme of everythings. The sight and smell of road kill carcasses red and dusty in the gravel shoulder of the roads leading in and out of town, always with their frenzied atmosphere of buzzing black flies circling in the humidity; sometimes wandering dogs cut down on their way across the roads to the wild freedom of the bush, just as often plump raccoons with their bellies burst open and their guts streaking the tarmac. Summer things, and the stink of them on the muggy air so defining.

But fuck it. All of it. Things aren't so awful now, not really. It's been twenty years and I only really get haunted like this when the air tastes like I'm deep in the middle of July. When the crabapples bloom like blood beads in the trees and bushes. When the seashore stink of late-staying June bugs rides the balmy air, throwing me twenty years backwards. When I'm young again, and it feels as if there might be a little strength returning into my arms.

I think of this past month's batch of girls, consider them each in turn. And it makes me feel foolish, in a way, as if I haven't grown into my adult's skin at all, and what am I doing living the way I did so many years ago? There are still girls to chase, and catch if

I'm lucky, and to forget as soon as I'm able in favour of other girls that set the blood rushing to my temples and fill my brief daydreams with their smiles and legs and other good parts. They're usually older these days but not always, and still very pretty riding beside me with their hair whipping in the wind gusting through the open window.

What a thing, time machines. Dragging you wailing to stretches of lawn where good things lived fleetingly, under roofs of rustling green, and then were gone completely. Dragging you anywhere they will, and there you are, helpless and weak and unwise with only the old words on your stupid lips.

Just tonight, after a date with a good-looking girl named Claire, I caught a song in my radio like a moth in my hand: flimsy and ghost-like, an oldie crooning sadly and taking me backwards; and I mouthed the words out loud, ancient sentences under cover of the old green canopy: *The Boro Brothers. The Boro Brothers came and they went and they took all the girls with them as they drove away.*

Girls were always ghosts in the good old songs we listened to then. They were always in our radios then, being sung about in poems written for them and about them, and the voices crooning in our cars were sad with longing. And there was always a kind of canyon-echo on those vocals, vast and deep and never-ending but resounding in the deepest parts of us all; which was perfect, because doesn't that seem very right when you consider ghosts and how they might sound calling back to you in the night?

I had a lot of those girls, at least half a dozen of the regular ten girls we went around with those days, but none was crazier than Sally. She's my ghost, for sure. And I say this with guilt huge and like a range of mountains lined up rough and jagged and painful inside me, but I can't help it anymore: *I'm tired of all this, Sally. I want you to go away. I want you to stay somewhere where I'm not and I'll come find you if I can when I can if you still want me in another twenty or forty years when I'm left to wander without purpose if that's my fate.*

I don't banish her without good reason: she had the

summer's perfect body. And that's all she had. I never learned one single other fact about that girl, the best one that endless July. Small tits and ass and legs that turned shiny with sweat after ten minutes tangled up in my car. God, I loved her, being inside her in my cramped hot box on wheels, and the leather seats were like thunder while we pummelled them in the night. I didn't need to know anything else because life was perfect on nights like those.

And she listened to records. I learned that about her, too, and I suppose it was the only bit of origin I needed to hear her whisper to me, drowsy with beer and tiny sips of Zambucca like black milk down our throats. Maybe it's why she was better than the others. Maybe that was her spotlight, that picture I saw in my head of her ever since she whispered those words to me just before our first time together under the green canopy: lying on her back in her bed, big headphones strapped snugly over her tawny head, eyes closed, listening to ghosts singing her things.

That's me in the night time, she said soft as silk, *covered in music and floating away on clouds made of good sound.*

Then the Boro Brothers, and the end of summer made from perfect legs and lips and tits and hands rubbing me all over like I was something able to bestow good luck. Pretty funny, in the saddest sort of way, because I must have been the worst kind of luck on Earth, when I think about it. Because what did I really ever give her? There was nothing good about me probably, except for when I made Sally cry out in the dark as if she felt good about everything. And maybe I've been wrong all this time, and that wasn't very much to have given her at all.

That's another thing I knew about her, and I'm never able to figure out how I knew it: Sally was sad. In her eyes and frowns and shoulders when she drifted towards my car after climbing the chain link fence separating the town houses where she lived from the forest where I always waited for her, smug behind the familiar wheel of my sexy hot box. She never told me a thing about it, but then we never told each other anything. We were all about quiet and smiles loaded with promises of groping in the dark, and then the real thing made of getting wet all over and feeling amazing.

Those were good times, good times. But I wish she hadn't

been sad. Especially that July, when winter arrived suddenly in a truck with a dash of flames on the hood and a comical construction company logo, too, and stole everything, even her blue and sexy pouts and frowns.

It's sad to think it, but maybe I knew her more than I thought back then.

Three awful siblings riding with a truckful of sexy and pretty, and it was the darkest night of all.

Police caught up with them a few miles west of town, traveling the dusty back roads under moonlight. They were still carrying the girls in the rear of the stolen construction company truck, mixed in with the dirt-clods and rusty tools. They were already dead, the girls, covered with a dirty sheet of tarpaulin. The chase didn't last very long, the reports said. Some barbwire strung across the dirt and four blown tires and a million bullets thundering in the middle of the late night. And the Boro Brothers dead, a bad legend ended at last. And I hoped they were pierced with a million red holes or at least one per brother in each of their evil skulls, and their shittiness leaking from their veins slow and hard into the shadows all night long.

They came from places like that, I figure. Shadows breed bad things, or so my mother always used to preach as warning for my late nights with my friends. The Boro Brothers, local boys with hollow black spaces yawning malevolently inside each of them. Helping them to land a lifetime in prison for acts unspeakable in our town, atrocities grown into legend among all the teenagers, whispered like warnings or dares and making the rounds of the high schools and pool halls. Only the girl's name survived in the months and years that followed, no one seemed to remember her face or anything else about her. *Poor Jenny LaSalle*, like a hushed warning among the kids, *poor, poor Jenny LaSalle. They found her tied to a beam in the old Peever house, in the basement, duct tape across her mouth, a bullet in her head. Just some kids who were exploring that old shack one June afternoon, and they said she was naked as a newborn baby, and pale as a ghost. I think she was really pretty, too, I think.* My older *brother says so.*

The police staking out that old shack without result, until the big-city investigators were called in because our town wouldn't quit until it could sleep again. A few weeks later and it was Renee Appleyard shriveled and cold and tangled in the cattails at the edge of Little River. A man had snagged her with his fishing line and pulled her to shore, noticed the dark wound circling her neck where her throat had been slit from ear to ear. The town slept even less and the investigators did their best to assuage our fears, vowing to find the person or persons responsible for the nightmare.

A few weeks later and they found Sarah Francois tied and gagged in the cabin in the ravine, catatonic but alive. Another vigil into the wee hours paying off, when the three boys tramped in from the bush, drunk as skunks and just as filthy, I bet: the Boros, surprised at the commotion of uniforms and guns and handcuffs. Caught at last, after plaguing the town's dreams for too many weeks.

Ugly origins for three sick and awful boys. Locked away with no key in sight, good riddance and good restful nights returned at last to our small shaking town.

And then, less than a decade later, the Boros back like ghosts to haunt us all over again. Coming home after a months-long dig with secretly imported tools; a dig that showed them free sky flying over their heads a season and a half later.

Just passing through, the Boro Brothers, famous men with handsome killing-eyes and rugged-squared faces. Three hearts sculpted from stone, a three-towered mountain range chancing to cut insolently through pleasant summer time.

I've always wondered what those boys had said. What they could possibly have sung to cajole four girls of pure sexiness in summer clothes to ride foolishly in a truck taking them to awful places. Did their voices have echo tossing their timbre far into the night? Did the ghosts in their song speak to the pounding in four girls' chests, because those lovely packages of long legs and tight bodies and tossing hair wanted something like romance in the air they breathed that night? Did they have beer with them, and gorgeous-handsome smiles that shone in the night like some secret promises?

I think they must have. Because those kinds of ingredients

work, just like magic. That's what Sally told me, when she asked me to sing along with the songs on the radio, nestling her head into my chest with her eyes closed, looking sleepy as a cat and as at ease as I'd ever seen her. And I did, because I knew a good thing when I had it: I crooned along with those ghost-voices and felt Sally's hands rub my chest under my jacket and then under my shirt. And her little moans got louder and longer the more I sang along, as if the words falling from my mouth were mine and belonged to no one else, except her. As if I was making her special by giving them to her. I made sure to feed her beer, too, lots of beer and then some trusty Zambucca, magic potions, those good drinks, and then she was mine all over again. Easy as pie, that was the joke I always heard in my head while I watched her pulling her sweater over her head or reaching for my zipper. And I'd watch her with huge smiles on my face every time while she lay back like a gift for me to do with as I pleased.

Sally, I know I didn't give you what you wanted that endless July, and I wasn't sorry about that at all. Your legs were perfect and glistening in my car backseat, and you were everything. I spend these muggy days like all the others, hoping fruitlessly that this was enough for you. Knowing, of course, that it wasn't.

And Natalie and Natasha, too, twin sisters of dark complexion and full lips, and what was her name, the girl with swimming pool eyes and tiny bouncing steps, Darla; all of them were amazing but maybe it was only you Sally that tasted like summer in my mouth and smelled like July between your legs. Maybe it was you who was perfect to smoke cigarettes with as the sweat was drying slowly along our bare bodies, who breathed in little pants beside me in strange sweet cadence to Bobby Darin and Del Shannon and all the other bodiless voices drifting like perfect Halloween in my car.

I hope you liked my hot box car and the motel room it provided for our love that summer. Because maybe you made that July endless. Maybe it was you who did that.

I gave you nothing but amazing feeling in your tits and between your legs and maybe you danced away one July night to the sound of something better for you.

But I hope when you used to close your eyes in your bedroom to soundtracks of ghost-singing, I hope you at least dreamed a little bit. And I hope I was there with you in those places, giving you some kind of good reason to meet me most every night that summer.

    And it's time once again and I drive the old streets every night now and the fishiness of the sea from the papery wings of the June bugs rides the air, in concert with whizzing mosquito clusters and moths like pale flowers tapping at the streetlights; and the children do what they do, dashing through sprinkler-rains and hurling tennis balls like some kind of furry meteors into dizzy purple heights of settling dusk. And everything is as it always was, pretty much, except the air is no longer special in its smells and its touch along the wrinkles and lines of my sweaty face. The girls I meet and who ride with me these days are good company, and good-looking, too, but so much less beautiful. And all I can say is probably weak, and it comes out of my mouth the only way it can any more, in song.

    And so hey ghostly girls of old, I dub you the sad sisters of Boro now, and I sing this sad song with its blue title for you and no one else.

    And hey Darla with bounce in your heels and a weekend riding me senseless in your bedroom while your parents were away in the city, foolishly trusting you to keep the house boy-free: the Big Brothers took you away on a wave of summer heat wave air, and I'm sorry to see you go.

    And hey there ghosts of Natalie and Natasha: now you're flying with the Boros on night air currents and I wish I could have your warm skin back in my hands in your living room in perfect July twenty thousand balmy years ago, a dreamy double-teaming for any man with blood for boiling shooting through his veins.

    But really, this song's for you, Sally, and no one else, and I hope that if you can hear me wherever you are, you'll pick up that old miles-deep radio-echo from the old days. So hey Sally, here it is and listen up please: the Boro Brothers took you away in a cloud of county road dust. Hey Sally, don't be sad, wherever you're flying, because I want to know about your frowns and slumped shoulders and sad way of walking through summer forests towards cars parked like beached sharks in the gravel, and maybe one day I'll be able to ask and maybe you can tell me. Or maybe dreams are only just dead things along the shoulders of old roads now.

And one other thing, Sally: it was you and me and no one else who rode nights away in my hot-boxy car under the leaves. For some reason, maybe you can figure it out some day since I can't, it was no one else in that car that I'm still driving through a sweating summer twenty years later. No one else under the old green roof that moved whenever occasional breezes blew. Even today, and tonight, twenty years from the day you ghosted away from me forever: you're still the only rider who's ever given me your kisses inside this car. You're the only one I made sigh and moan and cry against these old seats. And I've never sung to another girl in this tight little space, I've never done that either, and I don't think that I ever will.

And that's my sad shitty song to you, Sally. But the words are sincere, and they're all I can give you.

For now, I have the old records, black vinyl circles spinning their scratchy bodies in my room, and I wear my woofers snug over my ears, and my eyes I keep closed, and I listen and I hear you, Sally, and it's like magic, and you're the best-looking ghost flying anywhere.

July nights are like this often, me and the records and the old voices like echoes which never belonged to bodies, and I sometimes find myself acting it out well into August evenings, too, desperately and like ritual that might save my life if I practice its magic hard enough. I sing along with the old songs, and I try my hardest to match their longing, the sincere way they're singing from the past as if they still want the same thing and that thing will never change. And I feel bad. I feel bad, Sally. I hope the sound-clouds have flown you to green places, and I hope they hold you up high for me to see if I'm able and strong enough of arm to climb a chain link fence or a tree or some other July ingredient one day coming. And your legs, I hope they'll be shining with summer sweat, looking good, looking just right under moonlight.

Teenage Pirates and the Ghosting of Texas

Ghosting a road of midnight children's ghosts: he was at it again.

Fucking bitch, he thought with fire glow in his eyes, and he pushed down on the gas with his sneakered foot. Tires roared along the dirt road, and a million small rocks clinked along the underside of his car as he gathered speed and hurtled through the night.

His fire eyes followed the wavering glow of his headlights over the rough road. He barely noticed as the left beam flickered tremulously, then disappeared altogether, making the speeding universe a little darker about him. The engine chugged like a guitar, a hypnotic roar hammering at his temples.

He shook his head and a high nervous laugh escaped his lips. Fucking asshole, he mouthed, and then muttered aloud into the din of motor and grinding tires and rain of rocks and dust about him, "Fucking little asshole." He glanced into his rear view mirror, saw the wall of dust following behind, said, "I'm leaving you behind, fucker." And he shook his head and laughed again, louder now in melody with the crescendo of noise assailing him in the small space. And he shouted, and his voice cracked. "I'm leaving you behind me, you little fucker asshole."

And he stamped his foot down harder on the gas, but the pedal was at the floor already and he held it there tightly still as the steering wheel shook violently in his hands. The dashboard quaked, too, and so did he, but his tremors grew from his fury. His knuckles were white in their mad grip on the wheel. The muffled-removed jostling of old tools clunked from inside the trunk but the sound only barely registered on his reeling senses.

The soft green glow from the instrument panel and radio

band coloured his hard features. It shone like a pair of electrical phantoms in his fixed eyes, which burned into the unfolding road alongside the remaining headlight. Yet he saw nothing of the path illuminated before him. He perceived only snatches of the darkness outside of the glow, like some bleak mirror to his thoughts.

He drove onwards, past the battered old metal sign which read 'Bridge Out', and he did not see the sign. He did not notice the gross lurching of the car as it ran over the plump raccoon in the middle of the road, did not notice its frozen red eyes caught in the spotlight of his beam, staring madly at coming death.

The wheel shook terribly, felt as if it might tear itself free from its foundation and remain trembling in his hands, as useless a tool for steering through the night as promises made insincerely by the woman he loved.

And he began to laugh again a moment later, and he said loudly and with a note of hysteria into the roar: "I even fucked you right here, so many times. So many hard, good times."

And his words choked themselves off into silence, and he wept low and long, his sobs crushed by the scream of the engine, of the road, of the myriad speeding thoughts careening one from another in his desolate, unhappy mind.

The field of dead lay silhouetted against a backdrop of ugly bush trees, cast into relief by a low-hanging, sullen sliver of moon. He thought of ghosts as he watched the silent scene all coloured in wan light, no sound but the tiny ticking and clickings of his car's engine cooling on the air. And the faint stirrings from behind him in the dirt.

This is beautiful, he thought dreamily, distantly, and he thought how good it would be to live the rest of his life at least like this, as if he were in a dream. I could wander there easy, he thought, easy as pie to wander in places like these.

From behind him, a strangled gurgling, and a scratching sound in the dust.

His eyes remained trained on the black outline of

headstones, the mass of black trees standing like erect sentinels behind. Movies, he thought. He'd seen movies with pictures like these. Horror films with resurrected dead, aimlessly wandering among dark trees; maniacal un-alive people who were friends with the shadows living behind their vapid eyes, covered by their safe darkness, waiting for lusty girls and boys with only warm thoughts on their minds to wander into their clutches. He shook his head, feeling the ache sharply. He lifted the bottle to his lips, swallowed the remainder of syrupy purple cough medicine, cast the plastic bottle through the open drivers' side window. It swished in the tall grass alongside the road, lost amid the grasshoppers and field mice.

    He surveyed the yard before him. He peered beyond the low concrete wall, through the hanging, rusted yellow chain and metal poles set into the earth; this old partition raised as a means of blocking the narrow bridge from access to vehicles. A faint trickling came to his ears, but only when he strained to locate it among his noisy thoughts. He knew it was there. He'd cast stones into the shallow murky stream before. This was a place he'd visited in the past, many times like this when his fury simply wouldn't ebb and the best cure he could think of was to submerge himself in the deep kind of solitude found among corn fields and tombstones.

    The dead end of Texas Road, where ghosts of teenagers decades dead wandered still. Where the distant growl of motors rode the wee morning air like thunder in storm front walls.

    He licked his lips, relishing the syrupy sweetness sticky around his mouth. It made the world easier to drive through, colouring the single headlight beam of his car a pleasant magenta through the filter of his drowsy eyes. And he thought of buried things: his Boxer dog, Montgomery, interred when he was thirteen years old, a trusted friend and confidante wasted to skeletal frame with cancer; his father, wandered off into Florida sunshine and the shade of orange trees, with never a string of words set down on note paper or postcard and sent for him in the mail; his twelfth grade English teacher, stricken with tightness in the whole of the left side of her grey old body, and weeks later asleep with no rise or fall of her narrow chest, discovered sadly in the chair she had occupied for twenty-one years, beneath green chalk boards covered in select points relevant to Aldous Huxley's views on society.

And now this. Now her, too. Just another kind of disappointment when he couldn't stomach any more letdowns. Fuck it. Fuck life. And he murmured, slurred, "Fuck life already. Fucking fuck it." He had no more saltiness left in him. His eyes were dry, red-rimmed, weary. He considered lying back and settling into the comfortable old leather of his seat and closing his eyes. Sleep would come, now that his vision was screened purple. Now that he was here among the stone rows and creek trickle.

Behind him, the strangled groaning again, and sniffling, and then a raucous yipping which persisted for several seconds, seemingly infinite in its life span. He closed his eyes against the unwelcome clamour, brushed the tips of his fingers against the key chain dangling from the ignition. A skull and crossbones, silver and old and mounted with glue on a small placard of brown leather. He'd bought it at a small downtown head shop, bought it from a lanky Indian man who smelled of curry and tobacco and some kind of incense which conjured to mind distant sandy places. And she had been with him. She was always at his elbow in these recollections of the past, clutching his fingers tightly in her own.

And he thought: crossbones: I'm a bloody pirate. In my ship. In my battered old boat. And the seas are rough tonight, and they want us to go down to the bottom. To the very bottom where all the salt gathers.

His mind drifted further away, on rolling sea water courses, through uncharted waterways. There was a threat of underwater dragon in his delirious half-dreams which kept him from slipping into completely deep slumber. It was a leviathan of monumental size. It swam unerringly through the deep marine currents, swallowing manta rays and schools of fish whole, right towards his place in his boat.

She was the greatest ship that ever sailed, his boat.

Out on the rolling green, among the foamy spray, calamity was swimming for her.

* * *

When he awoke, he was staring through his driver's side window at the gaping mouth of the dog, bright drops of red spotting its snout and thin pink canine lips. It was close to his face, leaning upwards urgently through the rolled-down window, a frantic stare in its obsidian eyes. Its breath was warm and rank. It made his head swim. It mixed with the purple taste lining his mouth and sinuses and startled him. He leaned sluggishly away from the animal, shaking himself.

And he thought: I wish I had more purple to drink down.

And this thought was followed closely by another, his initial remembrance when the cold nose and sniffling of the dog had roused him from his fitful sleeping. He thought of dead teenagers, broken and crushed and rent apart in their decimated racing cars, stupid heroes of dusty roads at midnight. He remembered the legend passed around high school halls and grade school yards and lush summer backyards of friends when the afternoons had grown long and games of army tag and hot box tiresome.

Kids used to race there all the time.
Where?
Texas Road.

Texas Road. The name was legend, and harboured spirits in its syllables.

Some kids died there. Two cars crashed there late one night, man. And they all died. It happened right over this little bridge near the end of the road. Huge accident. All dead.

Holy shit, whispered.

And their ghosts still drive there. Ghosting the road. On Texas Road, in the county, with nothing around but corn fields and some old farm houses.

Holy shit.

And the need to visit haunted country was born, in every boy's heart, and the girls who doted on the boys knew they would fly there with them, too; their hearts loud thunder in their throats in the darkness and dust among rows of wheat and the silent farm houses and derelict barns, while the dull clunking of bells hanging around sleepy cows' necks shivered them where they trespassed in the deep night.

And in his car, the anxious whining of the bloody dog grew and became a yipping stabbing into his ears, and then full-fledged barking intruded into the small space of the vehicle, ruining the pillowy hush of the night. He closed his eyes at the renewed pain throbbing in his temples, reached to his side, opened the door. A moment passed. The dog, sensing it had urged some sort of response from him, began a nervous growling deep in its throat, its red nose hanging low and dusting the ground. He gingerly lifted his leg from the car, tested its strength, pulled the rest of himself out a moment later.

The late night air was cold on his cheeks. He glanced at his watch, thought: she bought me this watch. And now it's ruined. Everything to do with her is ruined. She destroyed every memory we share. She broke everything I have. And he removed it, struggling a moment with the frayed leather band, tossed it away into the wild grass near him. The time had not registered on his befuddled senses. He was angry again, and what matter did it make to him whether it was midnight or a thousand hours past, just some other lonely cold hour somewhere in the realm of four million A.M..

He turned about, focused his spinning vision on the growling animal before him. It puzzled him, how the dog seemed to move within a miniature whirlwind, the cloud of pale dust it had raised with its scurryings drifting about it and hovering on the air. He thought: Monty was better than you, dog. He was the best four-legger that lived. I know that because she liked him, too. She loved him as much as I did. That's how I know, you stupid loud dusty dog.

He followed the dog. It scampered ahead of him, backwards from the direction he had driven. His steps crunched into small rocks and dirt, and he distantly thought of his shoes, of how they were becoming more and more coated with dust as he walked. A pale man in the road, he thought, a corpse in the night, but was too tired to tell the dog the words.

He walked after the animal. He walked until he bumped his knee against its head. He stopped moving. He felt its panting hot on his thigh, its snout nudging him nervously. He stood still, listening to the crunch of the road under its paws as it scratched fearfully in the white powder dust. He looked down, saw its wide black eyes watching him pleadingly. It turned its head away, and back to him, and away. He followed the repeated swinging of its head carefully.

There you are. I almost forgot you exist.

She was lying broken in the centre of the white road, her legs twisted and ruined behind her. Blood was congealed and caked thickly across her hands and arms and face. Her grey-brown hair hung into her eyes, and a high cackling came from her trembling mouth. She sounded like a farm animal to his ears in her mewlings and cryings.

He said: "Montgomery is better than you. Best four-legger ever."

The broken woman whined in the dust. Her face was wet with tears, making long trails down her white-powdered face.

He saw her perfectly. She was awash in purple. He was angry still. At the world. At the dust in it. At the way it fogged pictures up in front of his eyes. He said: "We came here before. Did you know that? Me and her. We came here before."

His eyes grew more distant, and the whining from below him didn't reach his ears. He was listening to the echo of his own words in his reeling head. He knew he was speaking of old, good hauntings. Terrible hauntings, really. But still he spoke. "A couple times. Halloween times, mostly. Because that's when you ghost the road. In October time, when the kids all carve faces into fruit. That's when you ghost the road." He smiled at how the word 'road' had fallen from his lips: cool and easy. Hey girl: let's ghost Texas tonight. Texas *Road*. Baddest boy on Earth.

The farm woman at his feet laid an arched hand quiveringly onto his sneaker. He did not notice her, just as he hadn't noticed her at the side of the road on her routine A.M. walk an hour or had it been many hours past. He went on: "It never happened like legend makes you want it to. We'd always used to try. So many tries, but never anything. It only always turned into sex in the back seat." His eyes were open now, watching with fascination his breath escaping his mouth and drifting before his face on the cold Autumn air. He watched it sail away into the night, upwards as if drawn by the silver sliver moon hanging with the stars overhead, and he said: "But once. Once: I laid my hand on the horn. Two times." He laughed. The dying woman clutching desperately at his feet whimpered and coughed dusty red phlegm. He watched a stream of spittle dangle there, a grotesque crimson stalactite connecting her lips to the dirt road. He laughed again. He said, with a fanning of his limp arms in the area about them: "And it happened. Just right here. Two times with my horn. Like every time before. And we waited. I was sitting, hoping but knowing nothing was coming. She was holding on tight to my arm. And then her nails dug into my skin, deep, and it probably hurt, but I didn't feel her then. Because there it was: two horns going off somewhere, pretty far away, but close, too. Answering us."

He looked down at the prostrate woman. A curious look came into his stare then. He said, "They answered me. And we were scared. But I did it again. Two – two more times. And we waited. And a few seconds later, there it came again: two car horns going off in the night somewhere." He kneeled downwards, his nose close to the woman. Her breath was panting and hot and stinking on his face, and he thought of the dog again, which he sensed whining and moving quickly about his feet.

And he said, softly into her face: "We believed in that stuff. That stuff was true. Those kids always together, ghosting this place where they crashed their cars for the last time. And now… Now I hate her. I fucking hate her." Hate. The word did something inside of him when spoken in relation to her. Things did not used to be this way, and what had happened to the world? It could so easily lurch from its regular lazy rhythm of day-to-day ennui to chaos and disarray, and where was the fairness in that? He could bear his thoughts and memories no more. His voice quivered and cracked as new tears found their way back into his throat and nose and eyes. His well of terrible feelings seemed endless then.

And he stood, quickly, sure of himself, purple inebriation no longer slowing his muscles, his movements sure and strong and not very sluggish at all. And he strode off towards his car, waiting for him in the centre of the road, its wide open door like an invitation to a small realm of security.

He climbed in. Slammed the door closed. Locked it and felt safe.

And he reached beneath the wheel, touched his fingers to the dangling keys, and thought: I'm safe, in this ship. This is what I have left, this ship. I'm the pirate king of crossbones and high seas and sailing down roads at night. He turned the ignition, felt the rumble of the motor turn over like the simmer of anger familiar in his belly, chest. And he felt a little bit free. He gunned the engine, rejoiced in the roar. Like waves. Like the feeling of legend coursing through his boiling veins.

He reversed, until he was facing the way he had come.

One quivering beam of light broke the darkness and lit his way, spotlighting the crippled, dying woman in the road before him.

He thought: I'm not lost as long as I'm safe in my ship. I hate her. I hate her.

He watched the frantic dog barking at the light and the noise, and he thought: I'm not alone.

His fingers brushed the crossbones beneath the wheel once again. And the soft tinkle of keys touching sounded in the car. The sound soothed him, along with the gunning of the engine, and he sat back in the creaking leather seat, another sound which pillowed his aching head. And he cast his thoughts back to old whisperings that promised legend to be true.

They still ghost the road. The Texas Boys. They still answer when you call.

And he fought welling tears.

And he pressed his hand upon the horn.

And he listened, past the dying echo of his call out into darkness.

Past the echoless whining of the bloody woman and dog.

He strained ears and body and listened intently, listened hard to the hushed night.

And he hoped.

And he waited, the single headlight beam from his car riding the night like a ghost.

He waited, and would wait, until an answer came to him from some shred of darkness.

The Loneliness

# of Strangefire Dancers

From his bus seat vantage he watched the townhouses drift past. With window grime and scratches juxtaposed against their familiar facades. The way he'd been seeing them for years. From their periphery, no longer from within the comfort of their familiar curbs and catwalks, the narrow driveways where he and his old gang of friends once convened, and in the wild grass field behind the townhouses, where residents hurled junk over their backyard fences while the river trickled invisibly in the near distance.

Terrance saw her face as he was passing her house front and his breathing became pent-up. His usual routine of pulse-pounding and difficult air intake. The inevitable physical reaction his body had perfected over the years. He saw her the way she once looked: hair down and making her wild-looking the way she wasn't at all. Bare feet tucked into grass-stained summer sneakers. Pale skin and supple wrists entwined with hair ties like decorative bracelets because she never wore them the way they were intended. Her eyes large and excited no matter her mood because her single real desire for easy adventure kept them that way. Maintained their untamed look, misleading all the boys who caught that stare and were caught up in it, too, thinking they'd found their ideal match in tomboy charm and supple calves. Samantha the rough and tumble, Samantha the soft. Like a summer-full of dusty boys doing dusty boy-things, couched in the language of a poem.

Then her house was gone and gravity was urging him into the window as the bus lurched around the sharp bend in the road. The exertion of its engine hammering a cacophony throughout the nearly empty bus, rattling the seats and shaking the few other riders visibly. He felt the sunlight on his skin, a burning touch he relished for the easy sensation it filled him with. Sleepy-buoyant, despite his anxious pulse and backwards-looking thoughts.

Her face stayed with him a while, though, long after the townhouse neighbourhood was behind him and the traffic grew as he sped en route to another place of nostalgia. Like a place of ghosts ready to devour him.

Bitter-sweet was the taste in his mouth as he drew within range of the mall doors.

His reflection walked towards him in the dark glass, looking frightened. Frail, as if he hadn't grown up very much since the days of his youth, which maybe he hadn't. His fingers gripped the smooth aerodynamic handle and pulled and a door opened. Terrance stepped through and the cool breath of air conditioned air touched him and relieved the light film of summer sweat glazing his skin. Always a relief to enter his old haven on a bright day after a cross-city trip on a summer bus. He ceased questioning his reasons for choosing that particular day to revisit the old halls and familiar store aisles: the tugging urge couldn't have been ignored. It had pulled at him since the sleepless wee hours, from deep places, drawing him there, determining his purpose with each mile covered by the clattering-roaring bus which had brought him to another place and time.

The food court pleasantly un-busy. Sparse customer traffic perusing overhead menus while cashiers waited indifferently with blank faces. Occasional teenage loiterers beside the pay phones and among the cheerful red metal bubblegum machines and electric-chattering arcade games. Talking and laughing loudly, as if they owned this space. And they did, small groups of oblivious inheritors, as he wandered past them with the cold space growing steadily inside of him, vying for control of his emotions with the warmness this place always put there, too.

"Call her and say it's Bobby," a teenage boy's voice told its friends, and he heard the smile the words slipped through. How appropriate, the words. How perfect the big laughter they urged from the boy's friends gathered among the coin machines, nothing else to occupy themselves with on a mid-July afternoon but time-wasting where they could.

He left the boys behind him. The air cooled his moist brow and he felt adventurous. Like the days he remembered more and more often of late. When he'd been young and luckily bored and he'd had his cronies to perform funny words for, too. Maybe it had been those coin machine kids that had sparked his adventure-mood, he thought absently, knowing that of course it was them and also much, much more.

He took the old short cut. The Treasure Trail, where jewels glimmered unattainably from behind their glass display prisons. In places where children's fingers never strayed. Terrance felt the jeweller's eyes lift from the counter-straightening she'd been busying herself with and touch him as he passed. He cringed at the burning in his cheeks, as if things hadn't changed very much for him. As if any adult might see through him, his body only a transparent casing displaying the little boy misplaced still among the adult geography of diamond rings and necklaces and their small, neat cardboard-labelled prices.

He felt the imminence of the cashier's greeting, maybe a polite ready-made offering of her services in answering questions he might have about the merchandise on display. About the nature of the jewels she guarded, their prices and carats. But he knew something of trails leading to true treasure, and knew also that this cashier couldn't help him find the winding path again, and the elusive thing at its end. And so he hurried past, before she could speak words to him that might hold him in place a brief moment, but long enough to feel the weight of heavy memories.

He knew where to find her because some things remained constant in the chaotic shiftings of everything else.

Her posture still not the best, a slight slouch in her shoulders which always made her look a little sad. Exhausted, listless, and looking forward to peace somewhere else, except her posture would remain and so he always wondered if she'd ever find true comfort.

But she looked good among her animals, at least this if not happiness in her eyes. Her back was to him as she straightened manuals in their wire sections of the rotating display case, she outlined starkly against the background of caged puppies and kittens yipping and mewling a muffled din through the thick glass display window. He admired the somehow cheerful pattern of her uniform, simple with its red collar shirt and beige dress pants. White sneakers looking as if newly purchased because this was the way her job required them to look, pristine like her words of old. He admired the simplicity of her straight blonde hair and wondered what her words were like these days. He wondered how she talked and what her conversations were about, and with whom she shared her thoughts.

A moment later he baffled her with their old joke, spoken close to her ear and making her spin about in her place before the manuals display: "I'm looking for a cute baby tarantula for my mother's birthday." Feeling foolish even as he spoke the words, hearing what might have been some kind of juvenile or tawdry quality with which the passage of time had infused them. Samantha turned and he was instantly familiar with her eyes: their large look of eager surprise hadn't left her stare. A flicker of something else in her gaze for a moment when recognition replaced the confusion marking a small furrow in her brow. Something like unease or trepidation, as time parted briefly, offering a glimpse of something that she'd been unprepared to meet in the folds of its tricky fabric on this everyday work day in the middle of another simple week. But then her old gentle look. A saving look, and he became relieved in that moment and gave her his warmest smile. It relaxed her and she was crushing his midsection in the tightest of hugs a moment later.

"So good to see you, Terrance, my god," and she was beaming and absently toying with stray wisps of her hair where it hadn't been snagged properly to one side with her barette. He did a quick check, tapped her wrist in confirmation and smiled again. She looked and realized, said, "My jewellery hasn't changed much, has it?" Leaving the black hair tie around her thin wrist bone, stark and distinct against her pale skin like cream.

They talked among the chattering soundtrack of puppy

and kitten noises, and the squawking of exotically-plumed parrots. She introduced him to the store's newest arrival, a parakeet the staff had agreed to call Mr. Ruckus for his insistent peels of laughter-like screeches. "I'm sorry," she added. "But we're actually out of tarantulas. Some kid bought our only one last week, strangely enough. The cutest we've got is this old guy," and she tapped a gentle melody on a glass aquarium wall, doing nothing in the way of disturbing the meditations of the wrinkled green iguana lamp-bathing within.

    Terrance stared at her a moment until the silence between them became strange, then paid her his first compliment. "You look great with all the animals around. It's a good version of the wild you've got yourself stuck in here."

    She only smiled at that, as if it made good sense to her.

    He remembered visiting a special place with her once and pointed down the hall. The same cashier eyed them both, flashing a quick small smile. Just another mall couple milling the corridors with window-shopping eyes. He thought distantly that this woman likely saw him differently now. In a better light. In a way which made sense to her, and he hated his feeling of secret triumph in the realization, as though he was actually as content as others might guess he was now that he walked the mall un-alone.

    Samantha followed his gesture and smiled. "We stood there and pretended we'd be married one day." He watched her face closely, knowing she'd missed the hurtful quality in her words, in her too-cheerful tone. Devoid of the potency of the nostalgic terrain which they were recalling together. A sudden surge within him, a tide of red causing his breathing to become shallow and his jaw to work, grinding his molars together in agitation. He fought his fury down and marvelled at his success: from pleasantly nostalgic to seething and back down to some neutral happy-sad horizon between, and in such quick succession. And he knew that her strange powers hadn't abated.

    He added, "We picked rings out for each other. The biggest ones we could find, so we'd feel like tomb raiders. With big ancient jewels on our fingers."

She only smiled at this and, miraculously, he couldn't decipher the nature of the gesture. She could have been unaware of their conversation's secret language and therefore vastly a different person from the girl she'd once been. Or maybe she was silently hurting like he was.

They ate a brief lunch of cheese burgers and grease-moist fries while marvelling at the expansion of the mall. New stores, new halls, renovated signs and floor plans, among the scattering of classic monuments; those staples of malldom: the Coles book store of many years duration, where he and she had perused the fantasy and science fiction novels excitedly every mall visit; the Hallmark gift shop still supplying its myriad displays of greetings cards and gifts for all occasions; the old Zellers transplanted down the length of the central corridor to its new residence with greater floor space but its same old eatery, where the burgers were always greasier and the cola invariably tastier than from any of the various food court concessions which had sprung up over recent years.

They took their paper cups with them and wandered. Feeling rejuvenated with the icy cola going down their throats. Content with the fast food meal cramming their bellies and surprising them with sudden burps. They went in circles which led nowhere, traveled old sections and new alike. Getting the feel. Reliving the touch of past wanderings.

Samantha was as eager for tiny adventure as she once was, and accompanied him readily to the secluded portion of the mall when he suggested it. A short hallway opening off the central thoroughfare, without stores or ATM machines. Useless except as a nook for shopping-weary customers to rest on the single wooden bench. Or for teenage boys and girls to sit close and kiss behind the shiny emerald camouflage afforded by the potted plastic plants located alongside the bench and hiding them from view of passing mall traffic. Useless but for these things, and one other.

The machine was still there. A hulking mass of ancient construction, its false wood-paneled siding dating certainly from the 1970s if not the decade prior. Its face-level mirror besmirched as ever, the fingerprints of a million girls and boys readying themselves for the flash of the hidden camera spotting its surface.

He touched the stiff curtain, pulled it aside to reveal the narrow space within. Its single bench and dark walls. Its aroma of musty ancient days drifting out to their nostrils and bringing them backwards to distant mall days.

Wordlessly, Terrance deposited coins into the machine's dark mouth, more coins today than when a younger version of his hands had fiddled there. Wordlessly, she stepped inside and he followed. Closing the curtain and realizing only afterwards that they'd neglected to check themselves in the mirror the way they once would have.

Like teenagers again, they were inside the warm claustrophobia of the photo booth. Like adults, their limbs felt awkward in the tight space, lost adults inside a magic carnival compartment designed for children.

They watched the blank plastic face of the screen with strained grins, saw the dot of crimson appear in three quick consecutive blinkings, and knew that the old magic still ticked inside the ancient metal and plastic walls. The series of four blinding flashes while they took the old familiar poses: one with big grins, one silly face-pullings, another of exaggerated seductive pomp, and one final picture left open-ended. Any face, any expression, often the most telling of the photographed person's mood.

They waited outside of the machine and the open air felt good on their skin. A minute and then another passed and finally the strip of black-and-white squares dropped from the silver machine mouth with a small whirring.

They looked themselves over and chuckled. Samantha said with a laugh in her voice, "This one's great. We both look crazy rather than happy. Let's try again."

And they did, another depositing of coins into the hidden confines of the machine and then clambering helter-skelter into the cramped murky booth. Assuming their positions before the dark screen, she whispered quickly, "This time will be better."

He startled her, his words a breeze of heat on her cheek.

"I have something to show you."

He watched her eyes widen, caught the flash of fear

appear there once more. Now it remained, and with these new eyes she watched him silently. Lips set together into a narrow line, her pale skin ethereal in the murkiness of the photo booth.

He went on. "You're the only person I ever saw something impossible with." His words a whisper of loudness and insistence which held her rigid in the wake of their passing. Moulding her expression, setting it securely into its mask of trepidation and rapt attention. He felt it tingle inside him once more, a barely dormant anger rising behind his eyes fixed on her beside him. The soft, frightened look of her quelled its tidal pulsing a moment later, and again he eased back down to relative calm. He watched her watching him and let himself loosen, sagging his shoulders like hers and unclenching his fingers, too. Soon his breathing was normal and matched the light small sound of hers.

Silence had descended between them. The mall was a forgotten place, a million miles and years away.

"It was amazing, wasn't it." A statement put forth as a question, daring her to contradict its truth.

He saw the night as clearly as if its events had slipped through their fingers only the evening before. And he knew by the frightened look of wonder widening her eyes that she saw it plainly, too.

Like looking through a window:

The summer field, behind her strip of townhouses. Among the wild grass all spiky and quiet-noisy in the faint summer breeze. The two of them in bare knees and bare feet, being mindful of broken glass shards dangerous to their soft skin. Watchful for field snakes like the one specimen that had chased them screaming merrily the summer before, its light brown body like old leather slipping through the grass nearly as fast as their pounding feet could carry them to the safety of her backyard gate and the house beyond.

They were holding hands, an act both secret and less rare those late July nights and wee mornings. Those endless hours when time stretched strangely and they found themselves wide awake despite a day-full of adventure behind them. When their watches told them a quarter past two but two hours later only fifteen minutes had passed and the moon shone just as ghostly-bright and from its same sky-position as last they'd checked. Inventing names for constellations or star clusters which they pretended into constellation-shapes of ancient warriors and legendary beasts.

And more and more, holding hands during the inventing. During the field treks and cat-walk whispering footfalls while the neighbourhood snored and alley cats eyed them suspiciously from shadows: who were these creatures slinking about in the night? Which species of nocturnal wanderer were these, passing through the orange street light glow and into the wild country of night time fields beyond?

Another night swishing through the tall grass, heading towards the nearby river sounds. Another A.M. stretch of quiet secret talk close to one another's ears so as not to disturb the night.

Then: magic burning in the ink of the night.

Fire in the field close to them.

Crimson, and deep. By turns purple, and cold. A savage kind of flame. A colour livid and yet somehow gentle, too. Softviolent. Strange. Humbling the crickets into song-less silence and keeping cats at bay from mice-hunting. Urging their own trembling steps closer with some kind of promise.

Tentatively, they'd approached. Incremental steps, clutching each other's hands with icy-sweaty fingers. Drawn, and unable to withstand the pull. Inexorable their march towards the weirdly burning spot in the grass.

They cast glances about them: no one. No creatures stirred beyond their circle of strange light. The neighbourhood far behind them, impossibly distant and painfully ordinary. They looked closer, peering through the aura cast by the flames, saw. The grass about the fire un-singed, only stirring subtly in its wake. The area directly beneath the flame flattened, as if from the inexplicable tangible weight of the light.

Beautiful, the gentle way the flame danced. Turning slowly about, red to magenta deepening to crimson fire and purple light.

Terrance reached forward eagerly with his free hand, desirous of its touch. She did, too, shakingly though, with the tears in her eyes causing the spectacle to blur into a smear of bright. He urged her with his fervent, wild-eyed look to plunge in with him, envelop herself like he was ready to burn, too. Samantha pleaded with him silently, whimpering with her lips set in a grimace of terror. She wasn't yet ready for such exploration in the night.

They felt it graze their fingertips: coldwarm. Icefire.

Then, before their eyes, the flame in a quick shimmer of movement, danced upwards. A quietly hissing brilliance spiking from the grass and into the night sky. A rocket of fire and blood and ice into the black. Among the stars. Joining them, maybe, in their frosty vigils overlooking the land.

Then they were running.

Bolting a mad-dashing flight through the tall waving green spikes. At her behest. At her cry, he turning with her unthinkingly, only following her desire to flee and be away from the site of their recent seduction. Because of her fear at striking into the heart of their adventure. Because of the fear of the unknown which had driven her like the child she was to seek safety in knowable things.

And so they slowed only when the street lights returned and dotted the curbs. Where cats roamed alleyways, and occasional adult argument or television conversation drifted through opened windows onto the balmy air. They wandered for hours, speaking only very little, so different their mood now than before the arrival of the burning thing.

He recalled the way they'd spent the remainder of their bottomless A.M.. Like he'd wanted all their late-night-early-morning journeys to end. Entwined among the rusted skeleton of a derelict jungle gym adjacent to the field. Creaking the ancient once-shiny poles and weather-ravaged plastic child-seats with the ferocity of their tangling. She touching him beneath his pants and making him cry out quickly only a moment later. Her moment of climax just as brief but etched forever in his memory as one of awe and wonder at her secret wildness and the unimagined things her body was capable of: her legs spread wide while he filled her with his fingers and worked to make her cries louder and more insistent; until her moment of shrill outcry, startling him with its brave freedom on the still A.M. air, and the amazing sight of her wetness like a fountain shooting from the boiling place between her thighs and catching the silver of the moon as it cascaded down onto the sand below. The sputtering sound of it darkening the sand and marking this site of their quick and endless moment.

    He remembered her perfect in moonlight, perfect in his hands.

    In the darkness of the photo booth, he was prepared to show her. He murmured:

"Look."

She watched his parting fingers unfold.

Terrance remembered her look of ecstasy and the sound of her cry like a shriek making the moonlight more beautiful. And he longed for true magic again.

"I went there many times. Without you because you wouldn't come. It made me cry like a little kid, being there without you, even years later when I'd go. After you'd stopped talking to me completely. After you stopped answering your phone and your window after midnight while I chucked rocks at the glass. But I always went. I went to the field on summer nights like the one we were there, Sammy. I sat there in the Fall, too, and even visited there in the dead of Winter."

Her eyes were wide and dead in the semi-light. A flat, lost look lived in them as she watched him, allowing his words to hold her inside of the fantastic story they told. He felt peace settle over him at the sight of her so chilled, so moved to numbness. Perhaps she realized her mistake, even now. Maybe regret filled her like it did him, too.

"And then one night. I found it again. In the same place. Like it was supposed to be there waiting for us. A summer night. Perfect. A summer night, and I touched it. The redpurpleblue thing in the field. The weird fire. It came back and it was like fireworks shooting from the grass. But there was no sound. Maybe a whisper of noise but that was all. Like before. I put my hand in it and... and it didn't burn. Like I knew it wouldn't. Like we both knew it wouldn't." His smile flashed in the dark or maybe it was only a camera flashing.

He finished, "Now I have it with me every day."

He unravelled his fingers fully and saw her face coloured in crimson. He watched her raise a hand to her mouth, as if to stifle a scream or perhaps it was only some instinctive recoiling gesture which commanded her. But the longer she watched, he saw, and her eyes began to smile, in wonderment, in awe. And he saw her lips part in amazement as her hand fell limply into her lap and her breath exhaled long and slowly. Utterly captive to the spectacle of the moment. Held in place by the beauteous colour painting her and him and their shared universe of cramped musty little space.

Terrance remembered a time when he would dream her lips this way: parted and ready for his touch. She shivered him with her beauty the way she once had. She recoiled from him when he raised his hand of light towards her cheek, knocking her head against the wall of the booth. His fingers lost in the luminous crimson blaze, a torch consuming his digits and goose-pimpling her skin with its eerie beauty. An accompanying icy blue flickering in his eyes, a real or imagined river of electric current glimpsed briefly in his appraisal of her and which kept her pinned fearfully against the wall. Samantha's awed look gradually became chilled again until she noted the peace in his face, but her eyes softened completely only when the fire was extinguished and their tiny congested space was dark once again.

A silence born of awe energized the booth. The darkness still held the amazing burning, he knew it smouldered before her still. It would burn there forever, inside her memory, and the thought filled him with sadness, and resentment, too, and somewhere beyond a biting sense of vindication. And the still ignited fury, smouldering inside him. The wildly swinging array of feelings which she wrung him through as if with some innate alchemical powers of her own.

"What does it do?" and her words were barely a whisper in the murky space, the quiet bustle of the afternoon shopping mall a million miles away.

Ignoring her, he said, and felt petulant and empty even

as he did, "Now you'll never have it. You'll never ever have this." An electric shimmering from the gloom, its mood now dimmed to a more melancholy purple hue, and finally a pulsing icy blue over the walls of the photo booth and them huddled within its close embrace. A deep sadness infused his words. The sound of regret. It was all he said to conclude the reason for his visiting her that day in the mall where he once lived and pined for girls with hair like hers. And it sounded like a dual damning, of her, and her and him together the way they once were, and the waste it had all really been. Because who wanted to own magic without someone with whom to share in the great secret? Who wanted to live with the wonder of strange things licking inside of them alone? After meeting intimately one of the night's deepest mysteries, how could he share himself with an ordinary girl with wondrous hair and supple calves and lips parted for kissing?

Because some things should remain intact. The late night wanderers exploring the world of nocturnal insects and cats and the impossibility of strange lights burning in summer grasses. Some explorers should remain united in their star-lit missions.

Because of their predisposition to find the unattainable. Because of the simple fact of their perfect place in the night while the world slept.

The fire glow remnant vanished.

Darkness in the booth. The smell of ancient leather and musty air.

They realized their moment of picture-taking had passed long ago. No electric whirring sounded from within the thin plastic walls surrounding them. No hum and no flashing lights. They'd passed already and snapped them in their far-away reverie. Two time-travelers huddled closely in one final moment of photographic capture.

He stood, feeling suddenly monstrous, and left her silent inside the time booth.

He glimpsed the forlorn-looking photograph strip resting crookedly in its silver tray: a crimson rectangle with no photographed people to be found. Crimson and vivid. Violent and sad. Stronger than regular black-and-white. Mightier than simple and everyday. A strip of images showing something like wildness and beauty in each of its small frames.

He left it there for her to discover on her way out into fresh air and mall noise. Her final link to an impossible past, a proof of what she'd been too afraid to accept.

He considered his forthcoming lonely bus ride home as he walked. Its circuitous and familiar route with its many painful stops in his childhood. Its disgruntled-looking passengers with grey eyes looking nowhere, its crash of rickety metal frame tossing him around in his hard seat like so much flotsam. And he was comforted by these thoughts of these images. And he welcomed them the way one welcomes familiar little pains which remind you that you're the same person you were any number of yesterdays ago.

He saw the bubble gum machine boys at their stations again as he rounded the corner en route to the exit. He said to them as he wandered past, silencing their chatter, "You're the lucky ones, guys. Call her and make it funny." Terrance was met with expressionless stares and a trickle of laughter which grew braver and louder the further he left them behind. Crazy adult older guy with his insane words and serious way of speaking them. A conversation-piece and joke for years to come, a little legend between friends sharing special moments. He didn't mind their laughter, though, because he liked its sound, free and easy and of the moment.

Onwards!
To Memphis!

I: Anubis : The Haunted Afternoon

He drifted like a spectre through the shimmering streets of stink and haze. His steps began to stumble and a shambling gait soon marked his progress as he attained the periphery of the downtown core. He felt zombie-like, he reflected distantly, half-alive and sapped of what energy he'd begun his day with by the relentlessness of the sun, the wicked nature of the day. The thick air stifled his breathing, and his clothes clung to him like newly-molted layers of skin. A peeling jalopy rattled past, a wake of dense black exhaust pluming from its rust-festooned tail-pipe, adding to the chemical taste in the air. Its clamor seemed excessively intrusive in the otherwise still atmosphere, utterly alien receding down the desolate street.

He stared about him listlessly, welcoming his arrival in this quarter of the city, where the tall, glass-walled buildings of the downtown proper gave way to smaller, squat tenements and shabby houses whose front lawns ran rampant with wild grass and weeds. Pigeons cooed like soothing mothers from telephone wires overhead, and hidden sparrows crooned from the frail, stunted trees indigenous to the area. He grew calmer in this altered atmosphere coming after his trek through the din of the traffic- and people-teeming streets behind him, though he found that with this new serenity his melancholy deepened, too.

He stopped, feeling depleted, and oozed himself onto a wooden bench abutting a small park. He placed the shoebox he'd been carrying gingerly on the seat beside him. His throat was dry, and the lingering tinge of the single beer he'd drank hours past made him yearn for more of the same. Swallowing caused him to grimace, and he found himself envisioning arid desert wastes, sand particles drifting languidly from the summits of dunes at a zephyr's gentle behest. He removed his sunglasses and scanned the uncertain horizon, beyond the park where the river shone brilliantly in the light. He peered closely, wondering even as he looked what exactly it might be that he was searching for - A pyramid rearing into the cobalt air, the ghost of an ancient glider wheeling among the curls of cloud, or some other evidence of the day's hidden merit.

    A pretty woman passed him on the sidewalk, offering a smile as bright as her lemon-coloured sundress, sympathetic, as though she might have understood the man's haggard appearance, the weariness certainly staring from his eyes. Or else she mistook him entirely for another kind of person, a man who didn't shrink from even the most casual of interactions with others as he had for so long now. He hung his head low, his despondency manifest in the gesture. He looked the part of vacationer, he reflected, knowing all too well the accidental and ironic nature of the veneer - His flip-flops and khaki shorts and sunny hibiscus-patterned shirt; his orange-tinted sunglasses and the floppy straw hat he'd felt compelled to snatch from the doornail for the first time in months on his way out that morning. He reflected on his day's beginning, found that it seemed much more distant than was possible. He'd departed in the wee hour hush, when few pedestrians dotted the sidewalks and traffic was sparse as well. The preceding evening's chill had lingered on the air, a wakeful, rejuvenating touch along his cheeks and neck. His first encounter of the day had been curious, he reflected, and memorable: stepping onto the landing of his apartment building and taking a moment to consider which direction best corresponded to his mellow mood, he'd been startled by a giant beetle scampering across his bare toes. He'd jerked reflexively and followed the insect's progress as it scuttled past him and onto the sidewalk, moving then in a determinedly western direction. He'd went in leisurely pursuit but soon enough had lost sight of the emerald-tinted, obsidian oval shape among a nearby strip of sidewalk that was under construction, where the concrete slabs had been uprooted to reveal the dirt and stones beneath. He'd kicked about in the dirt for several minutes but no sign of the creature's sun-flashing shell like a living jewel had he discovered. And thus the mystery of his day had truly begun its deepening.

He opened his eyes into the glare, turned his attention to the flock of ghetto children gathered on the large lawn on the opposite side of the street. Some guided kites in the sky while others looked on wondrously; still others milled nearby kicking at dandelions or skipping pebbles along the curb or looking otherwise uninterested in the day's ingredients, their clothes tatty and forlorn-looking hanging limply on their bodies. A gaggle of younger children hung from the rusted skeleton of a jungle gym, looking for all the world like simians nesting among the ruins of a post-apocalyptic city.

The children held the man's concentration. Something in their loosely gathered ranks riveted him, the effortlessness with which they existed in the scene burning before his eyes. He couldn't look away. He stared and stared and at some point in his vigil the grass beneath their feet had disappeared, replaced by sand shining golden in the light. Dunes rolled away into a shimmering distance of haze. The river remained but held a character of wildness in its serpentine curvature wholly absent from the everyday waterway he was familiar with, the luminescent reflection of the sun in its every emerald wave. He continued to observe the kite flyers and stone skippers and jungle gym hangers intently. The children lifted from the sand then. He watched entranced as they drifted upwards, bright pieces of confetti mingling with the kites dancing overhead like brilliant diamonds among the scant cumulus.

Something stirred in the east, seizing his attention. Reluctantly he looked from the kite children and scanned the horizon. A golden sheen pulsed there. He watched there until his eyes fathomed the spectacle. The sun flashed iridescently from the golden host gathering in the trackless dune seas. Details emerged with breathtaking clarity, as though he were peering through a telescopic lens: countless rounded helms and gleaming cuirasses; a million brightly-coloured plumes like a great flock of tropical birds stirring restlessly; and a thicket of spears spiking into the hazy air, their keen-edged tips flashing like lightning in the desert fields. A moment later he felt the immense tremor of the army's collective tread beneath his sandaled feet.

A bluebell flitted erratically across his vision then. Its

buzzing tenacity drew his attention reluctantly and the man watched as it lighted upon his bare arm, its legs stirring anxiously among the sweat beads gathered in the shorthair there. Sunlight sparkled from its multi-faceted ruby eyes as it contemplated him queerly. Their vivid octagonal chambers held him bewitchingly, too.

Briefly, fleetingly, he forgot the presence of his old immovable companion, his immense sadness.

He blinked and looked about and the children were grounded again through the action, returned to a world of concrete streets and sidewalks and sparse plots of grass desiccating in the oppressive air. Dainty and sprightly, some of those destitute, dusty boys of summer, but held fast to the grass beneath their bare, dancing feet. The bluebell visitor had vanished too, he noticed, melted into the strange fabric of the humid afternoon. He wondered drowsily whether it had drank of his sweat, whether he had in some way helped nourish the insect for its forthcoming flights.

A voice in the somnolent stillness stirred him. "What's in the box, mister?" One of the youths had spat the words at him, having crossed the street furtively to stand interrogatively before him on the sidewalk. The boy was gangly, with disheveled clothes and alfalfa hair, both his knees enveloped with prodigious scabs like some sort of grotesque protective padding. Freckles governed his features, a million chestnut brown periods that surely would keep girls at bay during the boy's forthcoming adolescence. The boy's puckish eyes and the stealthy way with which he seemed to be edging nearer to the man suggested his desire to filch the box, or perhaps commit some vandalism to his person for the entertainment of his companions, some of whom were observing their interaction from a distance.

The man muttered, "An army of rats to swallow all of the Assyrians. Or to gobble you up, if you come any closer, pal." He frowned immediately upon uttering the strange words, wondering where they might have come from, yet also knowing in some deep part of him their place of origin.

The boy wrinkled his brow quizzically, seeming to think better of approaching the man peculiar enough to have made such an eccentric and somehow foreboding statement. For benefit of his friends watching with now avid interest, the boy snorted and declared, with no little amount of inflated derision in his voice, "Yeah, *whatever*, man. I'd watch my back if I was you. See you later, freak." The man watched the boy stomp off peevishly, skateboard tucked beneath his arm like a book.

From inside the box beside him a soft scratching came. The sound calmed the man, and saddened him immensely, too. "Ssh," he whispered soothingly towards the cardboard receptacle. "Everything's alright." He heard the incongruity of the words the moment he'd spoken them, given his experiences that day, and considering his trepidation for what awaited him that night. He considered leaving his place on the bench and continuing on his way, but hadn't yet the energy. He needed time to regain his strength, he reasoned. It was necessary for him to remain in his place, where occasional birds offered him the pleasantness of their voices, where cars chugged by less persistently than in the hectic, dirtier downtown streets. It was essential that he remain on his bench and prepare himself for what the night before him might hold; and to reflect on the clues or revelations offered up by the day he'd lived thus far, if any such knowledge could be gleaned from its mystifying fabric.

He turned again to the east. He looked there long and searchingly, but no evidence of flight or other movement he found. The fluttering paper diamonds had been grounded, and not even the mundane vapor trail beards of planes sailed the blue.

II: Ra : Endless Morning

The sidewalk patio adjacent to his place in the café window had been empty. Its tables looked forlorn baking in the morning sun, skeletal and somehow doomed. An abandoned newspaper fluttered languidly in the gentle breeze like a wounded gull seeking flight. The indolent manner with which the occasional pedestrians drifted past seemed also this way, morose and destined for sad endings at the conclusion of their journeys along the bleached sidewalks.

He sipped from his bottle, relishing the arctic sensation of the beer coursing down his parched throat. He hadn't drunk alone in years, and it felt like an utterly new experience. He began peeling the bottle's label from its surface, a nervous habit he'd exhibited since he'd drank his first bottled soda as a child. A tenacious bluebell circled his head. Perhaps it was attracted to the tang of his sweat which stained the brow of his straw hat. Perhaps it was simply curious about this solitary figure brooding over his bottle in the otherwise unoccupied café. He attempted swatting the insect into other orbits but the action only added to his sweaty discomfort, and achieved nothing. Still, the tiny, tinny buzzing clamored in one ear and then the other from time to time while he nursed his drink. His limbs felt loose and relaxed. He felt as though he might be able to squander the entirety of his day in this dim place away from the hubbub of the outdoors. He considered that he felt inclined to remain there well into the evening, and possibly the wee hours beyond, when even the most dogged and unruly bar-goers had returned home to their beds. Perhaps, he speculated, this quiet room was his destiny that night, and he should be wise to not tamper with a path so plainly laid out for him, so easily followed when compared with other, infinitely more difficult experiences he might undertake.

A cat heralded her arrival, its lustrous coat the colour of jet as it slinked beneath the window outside, watching him guardedly with its emerald eyes of mystery - She wore a bright but simple linen robe that drew his attention immediately. Woven leather sandals with curiously curled toes adorned her little feet. Her black hair was cropped short, and a lengthy side-lock swung at her round caramel cheek, while a peculiar, circular hat the colour of her tunic, bearing a perfectly round hole in its crown, rested on her head. It was pinioned in place by a thin band across the forehead which gave the child the appearance of nascent royalty. The foreign fashion of her garments seemed to momentarily alter the environment, conjuring a notion in the man that he'd been transported to another time and place entirely. Her eyes held him, enormous and like a pair of strange cerulean jewels nestled among her soft chocolate skin as she looked into the café from her place in the sun.

    They stared at each other wordlessly, she on the sidewalk like a mirage materialized before the man seated alone at the table. The man smiled, and the child continued eyeing him curiously. Then she padded around the corner, reappearing in the café's doorway and coming to rest before his place. They remained eyeing each other wordlessly.

    "The man across street is selling rats," she sang liltingly then. "He is only asking two dollars, and I have only one." Her accent was endearingly thick, her easy manner with him welcome after spending a solitary morning with only the customarily unfriendly encounters scattered throughout the hours: surly homeless men shaking their heads at him when the coins he'd deposited in their grimy palms had proved insufficient to procure them the food or drink they needed; the groups of swaggering teenagers with boisterous voices and contemptuous stares thrown him for no reason he'd been able to ascertain; those other sagging sidewalk drifters like himself, with eyes only for the cement, hiding whatever things lived in their faces from those curious to see.

    He looked across the street, searched the line of shops with their canopies hanging low as hopeless defense against the sun. He found the shop a moment afterwards, nestled between a barber shop on one side and confectionary on the other. The ancient wooden sign, presumably a relic from decades past, read simply, *PETS*. Its black-painted letters were faded with years into a dull grey hue, its wan marine backdrop peeling everywhere.

    "Are you *millionaire?*" the child ventured when the man didn't provide an answer to her initial inquiry.

    He leaned back into his plastic and steel chair, raising

the bottle toward his lips and waving it on the air in a futile effort at driving away the renewed attentions of his fly haunter. "I *wish* I was a millionaire. I'd own better sandals if I was, that don't burn my feet when I walk on these sidewalks. Do you live around here?"

She shook her head wordlessly, watching him with her jewel-like gaze.

"No?" he ventured, intrigued by the child's easy manner with him.

Again, she shook her head without words.

"Well, where are you from? Donations are most easily made to those whom we consider friends, and friends always know where they're from."

"Egypt."

Her answer amazed him into speechlessness. It bloomed a smile on his face for its frankness and unexpected manner of once again removing him from the everyday summer ennui he'd felt since waking up that morning and venturing into the familiar nooks and paths of the city. "You're an exotic bird, wow," he marveled aloud, pleased to see the look of poorly-veiled pride it registered in the girl's flushed apple cheeks.

But she only murmured, "That is funny thing to say."

"I say funny things sometimes." He waited, amused by the conflicting emotions taking turns seizing her features: discomfiture to ease to mirth and glee in a heartbeat. "Where in Egypt are you from?" he asked, genuinely curious.

"I am from in Memphis."

He ruminated on this. He eyed her warily. He smiled. "Egypt: you're from a very far-away place indeed, aren't you? What brought you here?" He heard the dreamy quality in the words, as if he were entertaining notions of the child in magical terms.

The girl watched him with a mischievous expression twinkling in her gaze, as though trying to decipher whether he was seeking to deceive her in some way. When he made no response, other than muttering emphatically at the presence of the fly incessantly annoying his ear, she again shook her head. The strange glimmer in her eyes remained, though, like a mystery for him to unravel. She only said, with meticulous enunciation, "Are you *beachcomber*?", examining with curiosity his summer clothing and relaxed manner slouched inside of the chair.

He wrinkled his brow in a show of deliberation, found that the title suited him just fine. "Yes," he admitted to the girl. "I think I *am* a beachcomber. Waylaid by the day and stranded far from shore. And hounded by pestering flies." Eyeing her suspiciously, in the same guarded way with which she appraised him, he ventured, "Are *you* a princess? Because your hat makes you look very much like a princess. Do you know many stories and legends from your country that you could tell me? It's funny, I don't know very much about Memphis, but I do seem to recall having learned somewhere that it no longer exists. I seem to remember something about there being nothing left of it at all today, except for some ruins. It all sounds very familiar but I couldn't tell you for certain, though." Images of nomadic caravans arrived unbidden in his thoughts as he watched her down turned face, winding their way among dune seas stretching infinitely in all directions.

The girl continued to examine her russet toes in silence, as if made bashful or discomfited by his remarks and questions. He regretted it immediately, and added, "I like your hat very much. I wish I had one like it."

The girl continued to fidget but remained hovering in her place. A moment passed while car and pedestrian traffic rolled by languidly in the baking air outside.

The girl interrupted the silence between them. "The man has only one white rat left. He is very pretty." Here she paused expectantly, until a bashful smile wrinkled her features and she amended her words. "The *rat* is pretty, I mean, not seller of rats. I named him Moon."

He followed the child's quizzical gaze past him. A woman drifted slowly along the sidewalk like a tumbleweed, her face shrouded within a ragged shawl the colour of earth. It took the man a moment to ascertain that the queer rattling noise haunting the air emanated from her. He peered closer and saw the large wooden rattle she beat languidly on the air as she went. A wavering, tuneless song like a dirge escaped the woman's cracked, diaphanous lips: "Anubis cackles and watches over the dead, while Isis, she heals and mends, and Ra in the city of the sun puts the sun over the heads of men."

She disappeared from view down the sidewalk and when

the man turned again to the child her eyes were unconcerned and hopeful. He chuckled and rooted in his pockets. The girl's enormous blue eyes grew wide and avid at the small jangling clamor. He flipped her a coin a moment later. It caught a stray sun-ray which penetrated the dimness of the café and sparkled briefly but brilliantly before her little hands came together as if in emphatic prayer, claiming it from the sultry air.

    Her eyes were brighter possibly than before, the man realized as she beheld him. He fell into their blue depths. Stories lay there and were shown him. Vistas vast and never before considered by the man. The great fear that had lain in him since he'd awoken that morning turned to vapor the longer he looked there and soon, his hammering heart soothed, he listened to the stories in the girl's eyes.

    Caravans wound their circuitous ways among dune seas like immense undulating serpents criss-crossing the desert. A river lit by the bright air like emerald fire snaked through the land. A rocky isthmus stretched its way into the green, where shackled men toiled, bearing great stone blocks from shore and away from the headland. Pyramids reared into the azure sky in the west, colossal and difficult to fully comprehend in their grandeur. A God in resplendent headdress looked on from his throne of sculpted obsidian, surrounded by monolithic basalt alters and all the opulence of the world and more. Naked figures turned immense peacock feather fans over him. A jackal-headed brother cackled maniacally from somewhere close, setting a chorus of birds screaming shrilly. A great army stirred in the west, overrun by an opposing host against whom they could do little – small and fleet the legions of rats infesting their golden ranks, teeming through their paltry numbers like a colossal plague. Immense wood-and-hide gliders made long arcs against the clouds, like great skeletal vultures waiting for the day of conflict to divulge their carrion feast.

    Over all, the sun hung like a circle of molten fire, etching the land and its stories indelibly into the fibres of tempestuous, ever-shifting sands.

* * *

The girl turned and appeared set to dash into the afternoon, bringing the man's peculiar afternoon reverie to rest. He shook his head, dazed, as if awakening from a siesta. He followed the girl's steps bewilderedly. In the doorway she paused, watching the air about her alertly. He waited, a little breathlessly, caught up in the beauty of her. He watched incredulously as she raised a small hand over her head and effortlessly closed her fingers, gently, as if handling some very delicate thing. She stepped one step and then another towards him and proffered her little hand. Spreading her fingers, he was startled to see the bluebell resting on the smooth caramel plain of her palm. The insect idled in its place, calmly rubbing its legs together, another mysterious and earnest afternoon prayer. "Now he will not be pest to you anymore."

He looked from the bluebell to its master. She beamed at him. He melted beneath her sunlight. He smiled wondrously. He had no more words to give her. Words were unnecessary in their final moment together. It was the most gratifying conversation he'd had in a very long time, he realized as she left his side. Over her small, round shoulder she sang merrily, "I must go home to Memphis with my rat and my mother. Enjoy your sunny day. Blessings to you, from Ra."

He watched, astonished, as the waif scampered on her way. She reminded him, curiously, of a rodent in her furtive yet quick manner. She passed through the café's open doorway and appeared a moment afterwards on the sidewalk, in the same place he'd first seen her. He followed her progress as she darted between the small space between a pair of parked cars and into the street beyond. She was more brilliant than the day in her vivid clothes, in her every energy-laden step and scuttle en route to the pet shop and her waiting rat.

The man was smiling pensively when she took flight.

* * *

He'd never considered the possibility of what such a scene might look like. He'd watched reality-removed scenarios replicating similar notions in countless films, probably read of them in books, as well. Gangsters riddled with gunfire and left in paroxysms or unmoving in the streets; cowboys settling blood money debts with noon-hour bullets, or settlers and Natives in the throes of their bloody struggles; had pored over real life black-and-white images, as well, no less startling for their grainy, antiquated look, culled from the photobooks of myriad wars of the world of which he'd read and grown disheartened by. But to learn, on a deceptive summery afternoon heralding the deep green heart of July in its every zephyric breeze and tinge of apples occasionally – impossibly - infiltrating the stink of exhaust and other unsavoury downtown stenches; to learn what it looks like when a small and frail child of exquisite beauty is run down by the familiar obscenity of a speeding car – This was a happening to alter seasons, to infuse the sun with a cancerous gloom and cast an icy pall over any hint of potential the day might have held.

The man sat rigidly in his small chair. Sweat clung to him but its touch had grown cold. His extremities felt numb, divorced from the rest of him trembling in the close air. The young black-haired bartender had appeared at his side, a small gasp escaping her when she witnessed the cause of the clamour. His stomach churned and yet his eyes, bewitched by the blood before him, looked helplessly on.

The mother had materialized then, as if from the stunned air itself. It was the rattling woman, her wooden shaker abandoned in the street beside her as she suddenly owned the scene with her strident cries, a weeping lament thrown to the indifferent blue overhead, to the mute pedestrians gathering to gape at the sight of blood in the sun. She knelt in the barren street and, sweeping her hands frantically across the concrete about her and then across the inert girl, it appeared as though she was seeking to gather the child's blood and convey it back into the burst shell of her body. The thought arrived unexpectedly in the man's head as he was held transfixed by the aching sight of the wailing woman cradling her diminutive, broken child: *That is love. There in the street, that is the love I knew.*

He, too, drifted into the street after a while, as though impelled by some force beyond logic. He passed among the throngs of gawking spectators but forced his eyes onto the sidewalk, wishing to give the mother and the shattered beauty she embraced the respect of privacy in their final moment together.

A gentle tapping came on his bare arm as he dragged himself along. He shrank into himself at the touch, keeping his eyes steadfastly trained on the sun-blanched sidewalk because he couldn't bear to look into the eyes of strangers in that moment. But then another touch softly against his cheek, causing him to flinch reflexively. Something tapped his elbow, too, and another minute contact tickled his bare calf.

He looked up into a quiet storm. They circled about him. They were all colours in the rainbow. Their wings like gossamer fluttered frantically and without clamor: a flock of butterflies descended into the street. He closed his eyes to the sensation of a million tiny wings batting gently against his body, willed himself to grow calm beneath the ghostly touch of their thousands of tiny legs and antennae probing his flesh and clothing curiously before fluttering away.

He looked about incredulously. It seemed no one else had noticed this miracle. All eyes seemed enraptured still by the scene of blood and death in the street which ruined the sunlight and blew a hushed sadness between the faceless and indifferent buildings looming on all sides like giants gathered to observe the funereal spectacle, too.

The silent squall disappeared as quickly as it had appeared. He looked after the retreating flyers wavering into narrow alleyways, putrid with refuse, and off into the thick ether in search of the sun or some scrap of foliage whereon to rest their wings.

He wished for wings, too, but could only trudge aimlessly onwards with a burden of bewilderment sagging his shoulders each step he put forward.

III: Isis : A New Night

The flower-air reeled his senses. He reveled in its headiness, a lotus-like elixir intoxicating him more the longer he remained within its thrall. He considered thankfully this oasis in the midst of miles of concrete streets and brick buildings and pollutants riding insidiously invisible in the air.

He placed the shoebox on its side in the grass and gentled off its lid. A moment later a blur of brilliant white padded furtively onto the lawn. The rat's trembling pink nose shone brightly in the dusking air. Snow on a summer night, he thought sadly, the Moon risen again over the dark, dark world. The rodent slinked off into the garden, adjacent to the stone bench upon which he sat. He watched it disappear among the lilacs nodding somberly in the faint scented breeze. He wished for it good adventuring and prosperity in its hunting. The quiet clamour of paper crackling beneath his feet sounded in the cricket stillness and he looked to find an immense beetle scuttling in the dirt underneath him. It shone blackly in the dusk light, a tint of emerald glimmering in its gem-like shell, and he considered that the insect's arrival was a lovely way of inaugurating the night. He watched it dart among the crooked dirt clods of the garden and disappear among the greenery. He wished it safe passage in the night, too.

"Goodbye," he murmured, the sound of his voice queer disturbing the stillness. "And good night, and good fortune to you."

He stood from the bench soon afterwards. He closed his eyes and drank in the night. He quivered in the muggy flower-air. He steeled himself for what was to come in the following minutes. Fear nettled his stomach, drifted a skeletal reaper's hand along his spine. It gathered beneath his arms and along his brow in the form of perspiration, and it welled in the back of his throat in nauseatingly acidic heartburn which threatened a descent into outright sickness among the lilacs and junipers.

He walked on unsteady legs along the narrow path, leaving the garden behind. The shoebox he also left where he'd laid it on the grass, like an empty house. He shuffled through the streets, feeling mounting dread with every step. He eyed his watch from time to time, feeling that its small ticking hands were somehow aligned against him, passing at an alarmingly quicker pace than seemed possible. He tried swallowing his fear but the day had left him reeling with violently warring emotions at whose mercy he lay. The course of his life in recent months had left him beaten in all ways, too, it seemed.

Minutes later, wholly shaken, he arrived at his destination on the opposite fringe of the downtown district. Silhouetted against one wall of the restaurant before him was a denser shadow. It disengaged itself from the mauve darkness and became a slim, auburn-haired woman. In the young moonlight her skin glowed wanly. Her eyes smiled at him. He steeled himself. He went to her.

He placed his straw hat over the silver nail in the wall, thinking of the long-distant morning and the endlessness of the day it had presaged.

The calendar hanging beneath confused him momentarily. He'd neglected to change its pages and it lay open to January, its facing page displaying the twenty-eight icy days of a February long since melted away. He murmured, half to himself, "What's the date today? Time seems so strange today."

"I don't know. Who knows?" The woman's voice was similarly sedate, but still its soft sound startled him, rousing him as if from the deepness of dreams. He was unaccustomed to voices other than his own between the walls of the small apartment. He turned to her, breath caught in his throat. Her languid tone and posture reclined on the primly-made bed eventually relaxed him, but only barely. He nodded at her, admiring her loose feline appearance sprawled on the bed, gleaning belatedly the wisdom in what she'd said.

The balcony doors were thrown wide, allowing the dusk to seep into the modest, sparsely-furnished apartment. A hint of coolness hung in the air, but the stored-up heat of the day past clung there still. He watched the sky framed in the door a while without words. The sound of her breathing in the murk calmed him further, like a gentle touch across his taut shoulders and neck.

He'd met her only days before, she another evening walker shirking the struggle for sleep when insomnia reigned triumphantly, and opting instead to venture into the nocturnal open air. There's had been a gentle near-dawn collision along the balding trail which ran parallel to the river, he shouldering blunderingly into her while she'd been at her usual river-watching post at the guardrail overlooking the water. They'd laughed about it, and made brief, polite conversation, and remained side by side without words for many minutes afterwards, each marveling at the splendor of the rising sun's conflagration reflected in the placid water, and no less at the serenity they were somehow able to share in each other's presence, without need for the hindrance of words to mar the perfect stillness. "Like an impossible fire," was all she'd said in reverence of the inferno burning in the river, a spectacle which grew all the more breathtaking as the sky lightened with the onset of the new day and the final stars faded like closing eyes.

One thing he'd perceived clearly from their very first moment together: her eyes, though guarded and enigmatic, had yet matched his own in the tinge of desperation they held. And he'd clung to their reckless hopefulness as she'd clung to his own.

"I'm thirsty," she purred sleepily, stirring him once more from his complicated reverie.

He poured wine for them and offered her a glass. Their conversation during dinner had been sparse but relatively comfortable. They'd kissed outside of the restaurant and it was following this brief embrace that he'd remembered: the touch of another human being, and how potent a resuscitating gesture it was. Feeling resurrected after the strange events of the day, they'd ambled to his humble apartment a few minutes' walk from the restaurant. "It's nice," she'd commented politely as they'd approached its hulking, shabby outline from the west. "It's little, but nice. I like it a lot. Like you said, it's a good place to start over."

She finished her wine in a few enthusiastic gulps. Replacing the glass on the night table before her, she reached cautiously for his hands. "Come here," she whispered imploringly. Her eyes shone in the dim air, and he shuddered beneath their light.

Their time together was the single thing he'd feared more

than any other apprehension he could recall in his life. He considered this and the true ghost of the day past haunted him again: the child, appearing in his thoughts once more as she'd returned relentlessly throughout the afternoon and night, round-cheeked and jewel-eyed and owning the unworthy sidewalks beneath her scampering, sandaled feet.

And the man laughed. The sound escaped his mouth, surprising him with its boldness, and he watched as a smile likewise touched the lips of the woman beckoning him with her hands on his, observing him meditatively him from his bed. He trembled everywhere, hands and buckling knees and a quiver inside him, too. The man shook with the laughter of relief as through the parted haze of his collective fears and confusions, he understood.

Their faces had arrived in his mind's eye, each detail heart-wrenchingly precise: their hair and eyes, the distinct ways which each smiled, the sounds of their voices filling the rooms of a life he'd once lived blissfully oblivious of his fortune.

He'd never known loneliness until nearly one year past, when Death like a tempest had torn through his life and left only ruins in its wake for him to sift through helplessly, despairingly, and utterly alone.

And then the child and her golden presence, like a sacrifice delivered into the middle of another burning, bloody daytime so that he might finally see that thing which he needed most; revealing to him that purpose for which he'd risen and strode into the new day burning outside of his home the way he hadn't been able for one year of his life and more; stepping into the fearful crowds of unsavoury humanity and cars, beneath the languorous blanket of the summer heat seeping the energy from everyone except the children who, through the innate power granted them through their youthfulness, were able to last out the sun with their unquenchable enthusiasm for living. Like sunlight shredding the cloak of the night beneath its fiery might, the golden child materializing in his day like an inexplicable vision conjured by the heat and illuminating for the man the necessity of keeping his much-feared rendezvous that night despite the fear consuming him, and beckoning him to remain secreted in safer, solitary places.

The softness of feathers ghosted his quavering hand: her lips caressing him gently. Through the veil of his tears, the man gave the woman draped across the bed his full attention. Her legs shone in the clammy air, long and supple and like water for his red-rimmed eyes. Her hair clung to her in the humidity and her eyes remained wide for him to examine as he wished. They welcomed him and held the same fear he felt pulsing in his heart.

"It's okay," she soothed, gripping his fingers tightly in her own. Her eyes were sad, too. They shone with empathy. "It's alright," she promised him.

The man breathed deeply of the Egyptian air, and found that he was able to believe her. And he said to the woman, "Thank you. You make me so lucky. To be with you. You – You're beautiful. A treasure. Every golden inch of you."

The woman laughed, not unkindly. A timbre of curiosity infused her exclamation. She looked as though she felt mildly sheepish in the wake of his saccharine confession, and more than a little pleased. She continued scrutinizing him, patiently, without words, without moving from her place on the bed. He watched her, too, until his eyes had cleared and there she still was, looking entirely the part of a goddess descended from the heavens to grace him with a renaissance of good fortune in these strange days of his life on Earth.

He cast a final glance through the window at the purpling twilight sky in the east. Its cloud walls were limned with lingering sun-fire. Perhaps he'd spy birds there if he chanced to look later in the night, or winged seraphs wheeling against the claret of tomorrow's dawn like a promise of potential lying in wait for the man fortunate enough to observe their flight. Perhaps she'd find them with him, too, or accompany him on the journey seeking their indelible beauty.

He turned from the window and the sky it held. He lowered himself onto the bed, and into the chalice of the woman's arms waiting for him.

The Prison Hulk

With occasional narrow slat-cracks and portholes like sad vacant eyes, our bobbing house of pain stares forlornly at the night sky reflected in Thames waters. Peering through a gap in the hull, I watch the stars suspended there, shifting in the dim depths like a wavering dream-picture. The liquid mirror rivets, engages my eyes when I should try for sleep.

Behind me, a man groans, and then another, and the dull hollow thudding of bodies maneuvering for some scrap of space. The clank of chains, heavy and like a knocking from some place far, far below our feet.

But only fishes sail there, in the unseen depths. Bass and eel. Salmon and countless nameless swimmers.

Lucky, free.

Poverty plagues our dear girl England these days. So many of her children penniless for years, it seems. The result a sad one: a race of destitute criminals stealing through her streets, bread loaves tucked inside coats, biscuits held anxiously beneath petticoats while the roar of policemen in pursuit grows to raucous dins. One hundred years of our dear girl ridding her shores of these criminals, sailing them away like waste removals to Australian or New World colonies. North America, with its great promise of incarceration.

I'd heard of their distant American rebellion. Independence, and they no more stood for our dumping of prisoners like garbage upon their shores. So what was she to do, our dear lovely girl, with starving convicts gathering into the arms of police like confetti on some sad day of acknowledgement? With the gaols and bridewells filled to brimming capacity with the land's new breed of petty yet unforgivable criminal?

I was hungry, too. Like so many others I knew and know now, and with whom I share these conditions of squalor. My crime had been simple and atrocious. The loaf of bread for the children and a snuff box for my wife, filched from the general store countertop when all eyes were elsewhere. Until the hand of authority upon my shoulder, as if a shop-owner's tall, stocky son should ever wield such power, and then a quick descent into this life of iron fetters and green-moulded biscuits and rats nibbling my toes in the darkness.

England gave her answer, and her thieving children shuddered at the portent it held: convert those silent old merchantmen, those relic naval vessels from their disuse since past times of war on the water. Transform them, and give them new loads to hold in place while the world continues on its daily course. When New World colonies have no further desire for them, confine those law-breakers in the bellies of boats and anchor them firmly in our harbours and rivers.

Floating dungeons. Prisons-at-anchor. Deplorable buoyant prison-houses which have come to be known as the Hulks, wearing inappropriate names like glorious celebrations of past victories and pageantry:

Warrior.
Retribution.
Discovery.
Success.

Names which carry great weight and suggest vastness of vision and high hopes of achievement. Hollow titles in our floating prison town, where cries or curses to God and death-moans are the language of necessity. And my own bobbing hell's name: *Justitia*. As if inside this large, cramped room any brand of justice is meted out to this crew of skeleton men.

I listen chilled as a soft splashing sounds where a man rolls onto his side. The water has gathered in the bilge once again, a new hole which might be patched in several days' time but then perhaps might not. If the red coats can be bothered from their stations above. If we don't wake with dirty water in our mouths and in our eyes and then the endless fate of drowning in darkness.

The thought arrives in my mind quietly, seamlessly gliding into my awareness as it always does. As though it's never very far away at all: 1841, the hungry year of my criminal act. The first day of my new unimaginable life. And how long has it been now? And how much of my time on this Earth has slipped away from me?

From the shore, the hulks bobbing in the river seem a derelict shanty-town, and we the men file towards them like ghosts returning to inhabit their hollow rotten bellies.

Another endless day behind us. Non-life in the Woolwich Warren, that awful labyrinth of warehouses and work shops. Toil in the machine shops, many of us in the foundries and dredging along the river. Twelve-hour days stretched to an interminable length amid the fire and racket and sweat and tears. The guards drift by on all sides, alert with cutlasses drawn and aimed towards our dragging ranks, as though any of us possessed any scrap of strength after the punishing labour behind us. As always, with the sun sinking in the sky and setting the opposite shoreline on fire, the great weight settles upon us. The depression from which not one man among us has ever been able to try for his break towards freedom. A weight of mountains.

The mere sight of her drifting idly in the dark waters offshore. Her wood paneling old and decaying. Her mass of boards and nails and limp, soiled sail, while rats scamper through her insides among our waste and refuse. Our hell, our *Justitia*.

I hate her. I dream of burning her into the river. Sending her boards helter skelter to the river bottom for fish to drift among and wonder over.

And we're guided across the narrow wood plank and ushered inside of her once more. Stooping, we enter the thick atmosphere, our heads brushing the ceiling only four feet from the floor, midget's quarters for grown men. We collapse because we can stand no more, vying for what little space we can secure. Soon enough, we are all gathered here once more, our strange, silent, aching family. Three hundred half-starved, unwashed men living skin on skin, among their disease and shit and slop. Our stink suffocates us and is a rank fetid breeze along the shoreline for miles.

Minutes pass like days and then another mouthful of mouldy biscuits and my supper is done. I drift soon, only dimly aware of the sound beside me, the man urinating where he sits against the wall. His warm flood reaches me, envelops my thigh and stirs me from my almost-slumber. A reminder, and I let myself go, too, enjoying the small relief of pressure in my bladder. We don't speak of such things any longer. We are one among all this refuse and degradation.

I awake in the deep morning to the roar of a new agony.

Two fools have tried for escape, and their cries from the shore are inarticulate and inhuman. Some of us peer through portholes and spy the scene in its gruesome unfolding: netted like a pair of fish, our brothers flop amid the reeds while the uniformed men beat downwards into the tangle of ropes and limbs with their short wooden clubs. Dull thuds and wallops without echo. Flat and moist the racket, amid the grunts and screams of the would-be escapees.

I watch as if mesmerized until the pair is dragged off, still entangled in the fishermen's netting, surrounded by men with cutlasses gleaming in the moon glow, and rifles in hand, too. Towards the gallows, where another kind of rope awaits them. And I think of how it might feel, that tight grip around my own purpling throat while my body swings wildly in semi-freefall, and I wonder whether our captured brother fish are lucky in this way. Free, at least, from the anguish of the Hulks.

The year, and time at large, eludes me in this place.

Perhaps September 15, 1841 had only transpired one week or one month before, with all its fateful events. Maybe the bread loaf

I once held trembling beneath my coat is still edible, and an officer somewhere is now buttering a slice cut from its round body. Maybe he pinches sprinkles of snuff from the ornamental box I once held nervously, while visions of my darling's eyes alight with unexpected joy washed over me. Maybe very little time has elapsed and my wife and children still weep freely over my fate as they did the day they came to see me. The day of darkness and sentencing. The final day before this life inside terrible, terrible *Justitia*.

Many of my brothers think him mad. The Mad Pirate Prophet, they laugh scornfully, an old sailor and merchant with missing teeth and a history of illegal trafficking behind him. He's sailed among whales and seen the distant shores of the world and where has it got him? Always promising us cataclysmic salvation, this has become his self-proclaimed duty among our clan. Another day of toil and then our forthcoming night of reward. One final night and then we will be allowed rest once and for all.

I play a game with this man while the others curse him in the dark and spit in his direction each time we're taken ashore. We are of similar temperament, and something in his vigorous soliloquies reaches some deep part of me every time he rails in his darkly comical way. Arms waving, always wagging his hands in the air, towards the shadowed roof of the *Justitia* when we're nestled close together in her hold, or thrust upwards towards the early A.M. moon and stars just beginning their fading from the sky as he beseeches us all to listen, and hear him out. Ours is a simple game: he rages, and I listen, his sole audience.

There must be an end to this. Some day, brothers. There must be an end. Man should not be made to endure this purgatory. The apocalypse nears. And what awaits us afterwards?

I make no answer, only give him the gift of my attention while curses fly from the cabin darkness.

Shut up, old man.

Mad Hatter, I'll be watching you at the foundry come tomorrow, with the hot tongs in my hands.

You'll meet your end soon enough, my word on it.

We are not all friends, nor are we one another's enemy. Simply family, with its own particular hatreds and occasional camaraderie. He is grateful, and offers me surreptitious winks from beneath his bushy old man's eyebrows like two ancient centipedes keeping guard over his eyes and the things they see. We are silent allies, seasick with the gentle endless bobbing of our claustrophobic nights spent together in this prison house of wrecked men.

    Usually we lie anchored alongside the southern shore, and the dreary sight of the factory district close at hand keeps our eyes away from the cracks in the hull and the few small porthole apertures. The din from the machine shops drifting to us, and the picture of those other unfortunates like us rests before our eyes. The great river holds many Hulks, each with her own cargo of skeletal corpse-men, slaving differing shifts in the deathly foundries.

    But tonight we lie anchored along the northern shore, with the murk of the Essex marshes hulking ominously before us. Mist hangs over the shoreline, and the intermittent cries of water fowl or tree owls sound grotesque in the uncertain light. This is where our Hulk has been towed, and upon this shore, among the wild grass and reeds, our punishment meted out.

    The cat-o'-nine-tails returns to touch us, licking the backs of each of us in turn, and two dozen of our number especially severely, those with the loudest voices of courageous or foolhardy protest. These whips make the sounds of hard and quick slaps upon the skin and send ice sweat drizzling down my back, beneath my arms. I fear their scorpion-sting in the moon-lit darkness along the shoreline. In the dark, everything is worse. Our punishment for two of us fools who've tried for a futile escape into the dreary maze of the Warren and the slums beyond. And the *Justitia* serves out her justice.

    When it's my turn, the rags are torn from around my body and my feet kicked out from beneath me. Grass fills my mouth as I topple to earth, and the lashing begins. From beside me, through the tumult of my cries and my pain and the jeers of the guardsmen delivering the agony, I glimpse him watching as if entranced, and hear his own cacophony of words. *Worry not. The end nears. The end nears and salvation will be ours. Apocalypse will save you.*

Apocalypse will save you.

When it's his turn the beating lasts exceptionally longer than for the rest of us. Poor mad, brave Pirate Prophet, wailing and railing and finally silent among the reeds in the silver moonlight. Invisible frogs croak their throaty night calls from their secret grass nooks, sounding loudly and like a dirge for the dead.

The stars flicker like nervous eyes, he whispers to me through grossly swollen lips. *Something stirs there.*

And the Pirate's trembling old finger, like a twisted birch branch, points through the crack in the wood towards the moon and her celestial children winking frostily in the black. I follow his gesture but the vastness of the sky taunts, its immense free stretches where I wish to be able to fly away into, lucky bird-man with Pegasus-wings. And so I cast my gaze again to him, frowning at his own anxious eyes, white and wild-looking in the moonlight slashing through the miniscule hull cracks and small round porthole; surrounded by deep purple bruises where the guards' sticks and lashes found him soft and unprotected. He has become my friend, among our ragged clan, and I hush him softly when his voice strains too high, stirring semi-sleeping men with their own bruises to nurse. But even they leave our Mad Pirate Prophet alone this night, having witnessed his flailing by the water. The atmosphere this night holds some shred of humbled silence, amid the usual congested, putrescent stink.

I nod at his words, touch my fingers gingerly to my swollen cheek where the cat-o'-nine-tails struck me despite my cowering with hands over my face. I hurt, but then this is nothing new. His words, as always, are a comfort. Escape, from the endlessness of this existence. A glimmer of movement between constellations. Hope, even if frail and tenuous.

And he turns to me and the silver beads rolling down his cheeks are his tears, and his whisper is coarse and desperate and truly frightening to hear. *Friend, I can't continue like this. It must end. It must! The pain...*

He trails off, pathetic and small. Stunned, I let him sob gently into my embrace. I've never seen the Prophet this broken, so reduced from his usual vigour and passion. A man undone, unraveling in my inadequate arms.

We hold each other and drift, bone-weary and without hope, our ankle-shackles entwined like our bodies.

I awake and the sound has followed me up from my fitful dreaming: a hissing, as of some great burning thing.

The pain in my shoulder is the vice-grip of his fingers, and as I stare bewildered upwards from my place curled on the planks, I see that the Prophet's face of old has returned. Set ablaze, a crimson glow flickering over his riveted, unblinking eyes like moons, his tight-lipped grimace as he stares fervently through the porthole and into the night.

His words are strange to me, and like a magnetic force draw me into their mystery: *There are lightning birds in the clouds. An angel army circling.*

And slowly I grow conscious of the scene about me, of the others wakeful and anxious on all sides, straining their eyes to similar windows or tiny apertures in the walls; the deep crimson glow permeating the entire drab hold which imprisons us. And the fiery hiss, again and again, of an unknown spectacle my mind can't begin to construct without benefit of witnessing it myself.

Unfurling my numbed limbs from the floor, my joints stiff and sore as I stretch, I pull myself upwards along the rough paneling of the wall. The old man stands aside so that I may take a turn at his spy-hole, his eyes alive, gap-toothed smile broad and coloured in light. Anxiously, I place my eye to the circle of window, and I see.

The sky on fire.

Crimson shapes descend in wide arcs against the illuminated cloud cover, trailing fiery beards in their wake. The great river is violent with its new reflection of fire. My mind makes harried attempts at rationalization and I nearly whisper the question aloud: are we under attack, are we witnessing cannon balls shooting across the water, the British and French meeting once again? But my eyes digest the wondrous and terrifying picture as they can, and admit to me that these are no cannon balls. No man-made missiles fire the sky over the Thames, quaking us in our filthy dungeon. The scene mesmerizes, awes with its power and calamity.

I dreamt this, or something like this, I tell him, amazed as my senses drink their fill of the spectacle. He turns to me briefly, and with a twinkle in his glaring eyes tells me that perhaps our brothers have been wrong all along, and maybe it is I who is the prophet among us.

Our brothers are watching, too, riveted. Some cry out like children, cowed by the violence and immensity of the scene. Prayers howled to God, they cup dirty hands across their mouths and let their eyes flood. *Dinner plates,* swears one man like an oath torn from his throat, noting the odd saucer-like shape of certain of the descending fires. *And we the feast. And we the feast!* And his descent into gibbering and mewling places him amid the rats skittering nervously along the tops of our feet in the bottom of the boat.

The lightning birds. Angels above.

And the Pirate Prophet's tree-finger paints an invisible circle in the clouds for benefit of my frantic eyes to follow. I look searchingly, and see them: shapes among the clouds, nimble and fleet in their darting motion behind the cumulus. A flock of enormous shapes illuminated through the blazing luminescence of the fire plumes plummeting all around. More of the arcing fires, or another kind of movement, ordered and intelligent, purposeful and fluid amid the chaos of sight and sound.

A cacophonous noise, part explosion, part rush of water deafens us momentarily. A fire object striking into the river close at hand. We scramble for a clearer vantage, and I'm in time to see the geyser of Thames water spout into the air in aftermath ricochet. I hear the creaking racket of dozens of men who have begun tearing freely at the boards along the southern side of the hold, dismissing any thought of the guardsmen above. I can hear the Red Coats' cries of alarm, too, the loud stamp of their boots as they dash panicked to and fro throughout the cabins. *You scurry now, too, like we down here with the mice:* I think this thought somehow despite the astonishing scene unfolding before me.

Another dense explosion and we're thrown helter skelter as the river rocks severely. We clutch at one another, crying in terror, a tangle of sweaty limbs and rags, a single moist mass of creature. The creaking becoming a low bass groaning at the opposite end of the room, and then high-pitching into a final screaming of splintering wood and the men have succeeded in pushing through a single long panel in the hull. Water splashes in where the Hulk lurches in the wake of the last concussive collision of fire and river, shocking me with its icy touch.

Look! An unseen voice rises over the din. *To the Warren!*

And we fight each other for a glimpse, those fortunate enough to see letting the rest of us know with their booming cries like shouts of victory. *The fires have struck in the Warren! The foundries burn!*

The joy in the speaker's voice fills me with something, a sudden arrival of fulfillment, or maybe it's only the words themselves which cause this, and what they mean to me. I'm suddenly inspired or brave or foolish, and without thought lash out forcibly with my hand against the wall directly before me. The wood is firm and cracks my knuckles, and though I wince at the stabbing sensation I strike again, and then again. The Pirate Prophet begins to help me, wordlessly, wrapping his ancient tree-fingers into the aperture in the wall I've helped to widen and tugging with what strength he has. Together, we pry a strip of boarding loose while the floor quakes and groans beneath our bare feet. Water licks at our ankles and the crimson sky-glow colours us violently.

Peering into the night, we see the sky, painted crimson in its criss-crossing of flaming lines. To the east of us, another Hulk burns, casting thick black smoke columns into the air. *The Retribution,* and I relish the feeling behind my chest as my lips curl in a grim smile aimed towards the frantic Red-Coated forms dotting its curves. Vindication, even if one or two or three hundred helpless men must die like rats in their below-decks dungeon. And I look away only when the sight of men on fire becomes too grotesque for my already churning stomach.

The northern shore is close at hand, its mass of treacherous foliage and swampy terrain illuminated vividly. *Witch lights,* breathes a man close to my ear, his body hot and moist where he's pressed up closely, while others whisper of will-o'-the-wisps smoking and shimmering over the mysterious marshland. I stare a moment, hearing the weak attempt at rationalization in their words, when any eye can clearly discern the foreignness of the thing we're witnessing.

And we recoil instinctively at the sudden flare of light which casts our tight, claustrophobic space into clarity as the fire plume drops from overhead and directly into the swamps. Like a mountain plummeting from the sky and into the wilderness, the roar deafens. The concussive tremor ripples forth from the mists, throwing us to the floor once more, sending river water into the hold in waves. A small flailing thing in my lap is a fish sent inside with the water, a salmon, and its scales glimmer silver-pink in the violence of the fiery light. Instinctively, clumsily, I wrap my shaking fingers about its narrow body and hurl it from me back through the gaping space in the wall and into the churning river. I consider following, but something halts me where I crouch, feet set wide apart in the gathering water, knees buckling in strain and fatigue and terror.

His hand is returned to my side, gripping my own fingers tremblingly. His words are soft but loud at my ear. *They are sailors from afar. Just look at them, in their glory. Who knows where they might come from? Just look at them burning. Burning so brightly. Nothing ever burned so brightly. And the stars of Heaven fall unto the Earth...*

I make no answer to my friend the Pirate Prophet, and can only stare at the spectacle of the night sky. My eyes grow dry and sting with the dedication and fervour of my attention, but still I watch the burning lights shooting over the river. The river water burns where the fires drop like enormous blazing stones. Fire on the water. Fire against the stars. As if the constellations had descended and lit up our existences in our filthy prison squalor. As though the stars have descended to offer us respite from our miserable lives, through a mass incineration of our fetters and chains, and the hulking monstrosities which box us up tightly and without hope.

What a fireworks display, shouts a man beside me in a gust of fetid breath, his perfume of sweat pungent and potent, assailing my olfactory senses stingingly. *What a glorious fireworks night!* he cries. *The best I'll ever see!* And though he shambles past me, making for the space in the hull, he halts at its threshold as I have, letting the water engulf him up to his knees.

And the Pirate Prophet at my side, clutching my hand tightly, whispers, *If this be the final night, if the end looks so pretty to my eyes, then I welcome it, brother. Oh, I welcome it.*

Hearing his words, I think of astronomers and their riddles in relation to the stars and the things beyond our world. The Greeks with their tales of meteors like mountain ranges hurtling through the void, and comets traveling the universe on journeys much longer than our small lives. And then I ponder the shapes of the flyers behind the clouds, and the inexplicable nature of the destruction looking so utterly beautiful in its descent down to Earth. And I wonder what these scholars might say of the picture before me now.

No, I tell my brother the Mad Pirate Prophet with a hard knocking of my bloodied knuckles against the wood planking. *No: maybe this is the apocalypse. Maybe the Justitia is the name given to the end of man. Because look at us. Look at us here in her stomach. We're not even men. And maybe they* – and I point towards the beauteous sight of the lights shooting arcs across the sky, and I am lost for words.

A new beginning, finishes the Pirate Prophet for me, his words a rush of warmth against my cheek.

I nod along, in rhythm to the descending fire comets, or meteors, or harbingers of God's will sailing in their divine ships like gigantic electrified creatures behind the clouds. Burning the swamp before us. Burning the Warren maze with its horrible foundries and barracks. Burning the Hulks, and setting the guilty or un-guilty free.

Maybe we of the *Justitia* will be free come tomorrow, and begin our new life together among the smouldering remains of the land beyond these walls. Sharing the world with the flame birds. Burning away our terrible memories of where we've been and the things we've seen. Or maybe our own fiery meteor awaits us yet, and we'll burn this night too. Because we the filthy might not belong here in a new, cleansed world.

A tremendous groaning begins, tensing us all, and we know that the *Justitia* is reeling. The river is filling up her belly. Fish swim with us skeleton crew members. A canoe-full of Red Coats paddling away from her close by is engulfed in a fiery wave, their screams cut short beneath the torrents of burning water. The river rocks us violently in its chaos of electrified waves and foam. I press my palm against the *Justitia's* wooden side, feel her trembling beneath my touch. Once she'd been a lady of war, but no more. Gone are her days of warrior-prowess, leaving her a derelict relic, old and in a state of disrepair, fit only as a cage for us criminals. I watch dozens and dozens of my brothers scramble through the gaping maws in the hull, disappearing instantly in the foam and waves. Their faces as they stumble past me and into the churning river are pale masks of energized terror, and I silently wish them luck in their swimmings.

Time passes, while others scramble for freedom from the rocking Hulk, blind shambling forms diving into the roar of river and light. Gradually I sense the queer calm settle around me. The remaining men cease their tearing at boards, their kicking in of walls. Laboured breathing becomes even, mellow. As if we have grown resigned to whichever fate is destined to be ours. As if we are too enthralled with the great clamour and chaos to stir any longer. A humbled family gathered together for a viewing of some great and significant thing beyond our comprehension. Falling into silence, we several hundred free men watch the night from our trembling prison queen, like awed revelers on an eve of great fireworks and celebration.

> I wonder, as I occasionally do, as to the passage of time. When is it? 1842, perhaps? And a hope for rebirth? 1850, maybe. A new, free world.

The morning dawns, and we stir and peer eagerly through the cracks in *Justitia's* hull. The swamp horizon smoulders, blackened trees against a sky of spoiled milk and intermittent clouds. Not a thing stirs on the far shore. No man, convict or Red Coat, in the grass, nor bird against the clouds. The foundries are silent and no racket issues from the machine shops to the south, where only smoke billows like grey forlorn ropes leading languidly into the sky. There is only the knocking sound against our hull where drifting pieces of trees and nautical flotsam bump gently in the mild current.

We've stayed here through the night. Several hundred emaciated survivors of we might never know exactly what. Of a night of retribution. A night of fiery warriors wreaking havoc and offering freedom. A night of beautiful fires.

I realized when his fingers began to grow stiff and cold where I clenched them between my own. He'd died in the wee hours, silently, and at peace. His expression conveys it, his serene eyes staring upwards, lips parted casually, revealing the faintest of toothless smiles. His weight comforts me still, and I'm glad of the circumstances surrounding his end. A peaceful departure, into a freedom he well deserved.

Maybe it will stay this way forever, I think. A silent world, but for the energetic noise of men freeing one another from leg-fetters with the banging of sharp stones against iron loops. Maybe no guards will return and bring us forth from this sinking, skeletal Hulk and into another form of darkness. Maybe we are accidental survivors of The Great Sky Fire, the missed, who should never even have been allowed the chance to see this first morning in the reborn world. Maybe the *Justitia* is at last truly dead, and we must only pry apart her remaining boards and seams and flee into the new day while she flounders and falls in the great Thames, bringing all of her chains and other evidence of pain and barbarism with her.

But none of us stir. Despite the icy river waist-deep in the Hulk with us. Despite the fish swimming freely between our tightly-wedged bodies. Not a man remaining of our giant, strange family stirs from his scrap of space, although the way lies open through the disassembled hull, and the swampy shoreline beckons beyond. I wonder what might lie there, over the singed horizon-line of tree-tops to the north, and I shudder. Because I can't fathom that spectacle at all.

And so we wait, our remaining rags drifting languidly in the current, fish tails making small splashes among us. As though waiting for a sign. Some word of direction. Some utterance, from somewhere, of absolution, or the asking of our forgiveness for a wicked life delivered upon us. Maybe a troop of red-coated guards with down turned eyes and apologies in their words. Maybe our families with incredible and good news explaining the science or divinity of the thing we witnessed in the night. Maybe the peering through the clouds of the dawn sun, like a signal of a new day or year.

A new age, good for living.

- Although initially only developed as a temporary system of incarceration, England's deplorable Prison Hulk penal system lasted 80 years. It was finally abolished in the year 1857.

"What ghosts walk these paths?"
– Unknown Hulk prisoner, circa 1840.

Gladiators

in the Sepulchre
of Abominations

They are the fields where he learned to walk.

This scorched country of dying corn and sun-ravaged wheat, where he learned to walk and where as an adolescent he once dropped down from the power of the sun and had woken up with a broken ankle and a dust coat on his tongue. His father had carried him through the shimmering heat of the day and laid him in bed for his mother to pray and worry over and nurture back to health, so that he could toil alongside his father among the rows once more.

Billy squints into the savage sky, savouring the warm dirt browning his ankles with dust. He repositions the sunglasses over his eyes, and feels the transient illusion of coolness cover him. His Ford Meteor is resting beneath a slowly descending dust cloud a hundred metres away, its mechanical insides still clinking from the long drive through the county. Bending to one knee, feeling the old tension needles like heat waves in his wounded ankle, he scoops a palmful of dirt clods and breathes with great labour at the process. Despite the shooting in his ankle bones, he remains there a while, close to the field. Dust sprinkles through his clenched fingers and a small cloud begins to rise about him. He closes his eyes and imagines it settling on him everywhere like old layers from the before-years.

After a moment, he stands with a wrenching ache in his bones and staggers towards the wan promise of the derelict farmhouse and its adjacent barn looming dark in the distance. The horizon lines in all directions are uncertain, shimmering ghost-points heat-miraging in the silence with no sign of habitation visible anywhere. The nearest farm, he knows, is several miles to the east, and a sense of his great solitude settles over him like the inescapable dust of this place. Only the crackle of grasshoppers and crickets like electricity in the corn husks follows him. The uneven earth slows his progress but he doesn't mind. He walks with care, tentatively, gingerly side-stepping the larger dirt clods for softer, crumbly-looking spots in the field. Side-stepping also the occasional black beetles and earth-coloured grasshoppers stirring like dried leaves amid the dirt. He stops often, squinting through his plastic lenses towards the brilliant blood-coloured late day sky. He takes his time during this perusal, as if waiting for something to appear there among the scant clouds, among the blinding red of the burning air. Maybe an image half-formed or partially suggested among the stray clouds hanging like ominous cottony shrouds in the air.

It's an old feeling of nostalgia which creeps inside his awareness then, filling him and following him as he shambles on towards the decrepit buildings. And he no longer feels the heat of the August sun on his skin, as though his backwards-looking thoughts of ancient days have chilled the air and him passing through it.

The house is a skeleton picked clean by the elements.

Walls and roof sunken inwards by rain and snow and years. Windows shattered by children-hurled rocks. Porch and interior floorboards parted at the insistence of weeds and wild grass. Birds own its eaves, mice and rats its rooms. He creaks a loose section of floor in the living room and disturbs a brown garter snake from beneath the dust-blanketed, tattered chesterfield. He jerks his foot away, a cry strangled in his throat as the serpent slides past him. He follows its progress down the hallway, dimly illuminated by the stray sun-rays slashing in through the ruined ceiling. He catches the creature's volcanic stare as it lingers at the far end of the hallway, the quick and chilling flicker of movement that is its darting tongue. He senses somehow that it is a dark gesture, menacing and mocking, and then the snake disappears around the corner, in the direction of his old bedroom and his parents' room. He shivers at the thought of it coiling in those places, beneath the beds and dressers, around the legs of his old desk where as a boy he'd worked diligently and with great patience to lay out his warring toy armies of doomed cowboys and Indian braves. Late nights, with such great rewards for his work each morning when he awoke and he saw them lined up along his shelf in their plentiful ranks, the hour late and his father's harsh rebukes ringing his ears and the pictures on the walls.

    His hand brushes a lampshade, crumbling it into its base with a dry groaning sound that startles him. Dust flies into his face, tickling his throat and nostrils. He sneezes, the loud jarring quality of the sound irritating him. He stands tense and alert for a moment, listening to the scratching of some unseen rodent inside the walls or beneath the floor. He turns and heads towards the kitchen, wincing at the groaning of the ancient floor beneath his boots.

    He sees them right away, a stark obscenity against the dusty pale counter-top and peeling floral design of the wallpaper. Massive and crudely sculpted, the pair of square cement blocks. Lying end to end they are maybe a metre long, their outer edges rough and notched. He approaches them slowly, feeling a quiver along his spine at the sight of them. Revulsion in the form of acid rising inside his throat when he notes the dark stains showing through the stones' film of dust. He reaches forward gingerly, stealing himself, and nudges the rigid brown leather straps protruding from the slabs. He runs a finger along the worn interior lining of leather drilled into its cement foundation, shivers. He envisions how it might feel to slip his hands inside those straps, past the wrist and midway up his forearms, and heft upward with all his strength, raising the blocks from their counter place for the first time in decades. To wear them ashamedly, and to wield them on the air, a pair of colossal cement fists. Gloves for hurting, the evilest of man-made tools he's ever laid eyes on.

    The fists carry memories in their stained, notched hides. He sees his father lumbering in from behind him, ambushing his son in the barn where he'd happened on the strange objects lying among assorted tools on the work table. His father's harsh words and quick hands, swatting him in the face and drawing blood from his lips. Offering no answer or comment to his son's questions and protests, only further reprimands from his mouth and blows from his hands.

    Billy sees himself in another time, young and frail yet strong enough to have been able to carry the great cement weapons in his arms, hugged against his chest as if in some grotesque embrace. Staggering from the barn and up the porch and into the relative cool of this very kitchen, depositing them with a crash to the counter-top where they've rested for twenty years. From where no curious children's hands have dared to remove them despite their unique and bizarre appearance. Perhaps their weight and unwieldy size prevented such acts, or maybe only the black stains bled into their rocky skins.

    He sees himself, and swallows with great difficulty: young Billy, wheezing with the exertion it had taken, limbs trembling, his youthful strength sapped. A coat of sweat glistening his arms and face, and salty trails winding from his squinting eyes and making paths through the dust on his cheeks. Shaking all over, a boy-sapling in the throes of a gale, recalling the screams of terror and pain he'd left behind him.

    Without too much conscious deliberation, perhaps to avoid losing courage and changing his mind at the very last, Billy reaches quickly for the giant blocks. He hefts them from the counter with a groan caught between his teeth. They're very heavy. Only a very strong man could lift them without difficulty, hoist them onto the air like a child wearing a baseball glove.

    He thinks of his father again, of his brawny arms and the damage they could do. He'd been a strong man. The strongest and most frightened man Billy had ever known.

    Clenching his jaws with the effort, he grips the blocks by their ancient leather straps, one in each hand, and groans the floorboards tremendously on his way out of the skeletal farmhouse and into the fiery afternoon.

    He stands in the burning patch of shade thrown by the barn towering over him. Its hulking form chills him despite the moisture beneath his arms, running trickling beneath his shirt. His proximity to it unleashes all of his old fear. Its walls are ancient and worn, its once-red skin of paint long since flaked and fallen away, replaced with a grotesque ashen colour. The mark of fire scorches the walls everywhere, a flat, deathly look. Dilapidated and dead, another husk amid this stewing stretch of corn country.

He listens and there is no wind. There are no scrabbling sounds of chickens in their rust-caged pens, or squeal of piglets wading in mud or snuffling about in food troughs. No horses whinny nervously in the stifling air, swatting flies with their tails and snorting foam onto the dirt. Only the crackling of locusts scuttling through the fields and heat-ravaged crop-husks. Only the electric buzzing of cicadas in secret shelters among occasional trees and bush skeletons.

He is enveloped in the silence of windless air and shudders. He remembers suddenly a wind from the past and its cacophony has not waned despite the chasm of years. The roar of fury and agony rides with it on the stifling air.

The barn is a baking shelter, diminishing none of the afternoon's furious heat. It does little to hide him from the naked stare of the summer sun high above, just as it had nothing to shelter him some twenty years before.

An afternoon of baking much like this one. He a boy, deliciously naïve and eager for the adventuring which a summer day might yield while his father toiled in the fields and his mother hosed down over-heated cows in their stables. Abandoning his afternoon hour of school work in answer to the adrenaline surge of excitement inside him. He and the crickets rustling through the corn. He and the invisible insect colonies and flying v squadrons of occasional geese sailing in the August sky. A young boy amid his animal companions, discovering a secret revealed beneath volcanic sunlight. Beneath the soil, deep inside of the earth where he'd believed only ants and night crawler worms squirmed.

As if it had been there all the while. As if it had always been secreted there alongside him and the world of his parents, the horses and cows and roosters. Among the fields and wood lots of his rural county home. Hot and savage as the air. There with him always. Maybe there in the earth from the beginning of time, or as long as evil deeds existed.

* * *

His father's role in the horror was the single act which Billy had never forgiven him for. He feels his presence there as he explores the old stables, the barn corners with their intricately-wrought web mansions and mammoth spider denizens. But then this is to be expected. This place of wood and dust has been a country of ghosts for many years now, and their presences all around him shiver Billy in his tentative steps.

His father's eyes had spoken that fateful afternoon even if his words provided no explanation to his young son at all. A mouthful of impassioned rationalization, but with eyes of far-distant, awakening horror. *It is an abomination, son. The boys are only working off the strain of their hard lives. They are good men. Believers in God's will. Don't fret, son. Turn your eyes from it if you must, but do not hate the boys for this. It is an ungodly thing that they battle.*

Billy fingers the crooked rusted teeth of the handsaw hanging from a nail in a blackened wooden beam. The minute motion stirs a large spider the colour of dust to cross nimbly around the corner of the pillar, disappearing on its opposite side. He prods the battered, sloshing canister at his feet, kneels beside it and removes its cap: miraculously, the sharp stench of gasoline wafts to his nostrils; seemingly the sole lingering trace of moisture in this place of relentless heat and humidity. His eyes scan the upper reaches of the barn directly over his head, its roof lost in deep shadows. Stray sunbeams slant in through slat cracks, spotlighting newly stirred dust mote legions in their drifting lazy movements. One far corner of roof is gone entirely, victim to the fire which had climbed the long wooden walls and collapsed it into the belly of the building itself. His booted toe nudges an old tin milk pail with its bottom-full of webs, and its tinny din echoes its rattling song into those invisible ceiling reaches. The noise freezes him in his place, eyes wide and staring into shadows, ears seeking to pierce the newly-descended silence and detect some other noise. Nothing stirs, though, and he imagines a million spiders turning their many eyes on him in the centre of the barn floor, he, human trespasser in this world of little sunlight and drowsy arachnid life.

It is an abomination, son, his father whispers from the shadow-corners, shivering his son even twenty-plus years after the last moment they'd looked into each other's eyes before the moment of divine reckoning. Before the mist of choking black smoke. Before the tumult and roar of fury and pain and wind.

Billy steps gingerly around the overturned pail and tangle of thick, frayed ropes lying coiled and discarded on the floor beyond it. He makes certain to avoid brushing against the stout rusted chains lying limply across the gates of the stalls. Peering through the boards of each stall he passes, he finds large blackened blocks which had once been hay bundles, massive objects congealed long ago from fire and smoke into these baleful, grotesque slabs. Like headstones, and the stalls, crypts of the dead. He spies destroyed food troughs there as well, splintered and ruined with time; occasional leather tethers and saddle gear; dark grey nuggets the size of stones which he knows are petrified manure piles; hills of pale bones amid the dirt and hay and crumbled walls; and the prevailing lonely look of the compartments devoid of animal occupants.

Suddenly, an arrival of stagnant air into his nostrils, close and rank. Familiar and powerful. And he halts mid-step, unable to breathe.

He'd made his way to the secret hole unintentionally. Having wished perhaps to prolong the inevitable in his barn wanderings. Knowing the entire while that he would find it again, in its old secret place, and that it was of course his true purpose for roaming this farm country today. Its wooden double doors have long since crumbled with the ravages of time, leaving only scattered splintered fragments in the dirt, and two long scorched hinges jutting forlornly at odd angles. The long rectangle of black beckons Billy, chilling him simultaneously. It gapes towards him like the hideousness of an immense black mouth leading into the bowels of the earth. A wound in the ground, and in the very fabric of this moment in which he sweats icy rivers beneath his shirt and trembles in his place, while ghosts speak compellingly to him from his haunted past.

Quaking at the threshold of the hole, his eyes follow the crude stone steps descending into darkness. He wavers there a moment, on the brink of it, the flashlight he retrieves from his back jeans pocket illuminating the narrow shaft and its distant bare floor of dirt and stones.

From the black mouth, his father's voice, like a spell luring him down: *Ungodly, the thing they battle.*

Steeling himself, he descends into the maw, with the touch of ghost-flames licking at his heels with every quaking step.

The roar of the arena assailed him.

The vulgarity of masculine shouts like declarations of war. Vindictive and violent. Vindicated by the power of the spectacle which they witnessed unfolding before them. Blood and thunder inside the bowels of the earth, beneath crop fields and daylight.

Young Billy witnessed it, too, that strange day while the world baked outdoors and hid terrible wonders deep in its earthen belly. A strange day of lesson-learning and astonishing discovery, when the young boy had first grasped a little of the huge mystery which was the world of which he was such an infinitesimal part. A dust fragment, a mote-boy drifting by chance into a scene of impossibility. It was also a day, as far as the boy was concerned, of learning about men, and the black pits which they carried inside of themselves. The first day he'd truly seen his father.

Knees buckling with excitement and the fear of his father's fury if he discovered his meddlesome boy trespassing into the forbidden barn and its strange and enticing secret hole in the floor, young Billy descended into the roar. Removing his dusty shoes for better stealth. Creeping barefoot and silently down the large stone steps, peering carefully beyond the perimeter of wavering light at their base. Whispering down and down in his seemingly endless journey to the basement floor. Padding unnoticed to one side of the staircase. Concealing himself there like another earth bug snug in the ground. Peering with amazed eyes towards the circle of men occupying the furthest corner of the room, their backs to him hidden behind the steps. The sight of the torches trembling in wall sconces around the room, illuminating the men with their raised fists spiking into the air. Their shouts made him incredibly anxious, their violence was a thing that he'd never heard before, hadn't guessed that it could live inside the bodies of the farm hands who he thought he'd known. Tacit and melancholy, most of them, with eyes only for the hoes in their hands or the sky and promise of rain.

After a while of anxious spying, he glimpsed it.

Through the tangle of the men's arms and legs, and their heads jostling for clearer vantage. In the orange-lit corner space of the stuffy room, surrounded on three sides by the jeering, shouting on-lookers, backed against the basement wall. Harassed by one man in particular, it seemed, who darted within the ragged semi-circle, too, fists raised into the air and gripping or maybe sheathed within some large, misshapen objects. Brief snatches of some enormous living thing which held the throng's attention: an immensely long arm or leg, pale and taut, rippling with muscle; a rounded curve of shoulder or large tangle of hair tufts.

The dull flat thud of some hard object striking flesh from within the crowd of men caused Billy to wince. The sound of blows landing, dull wallops without echo. Quick and sharp and awful. The constant clanking clatter of chain links being dragged across the dirt floor as some imprisoned thing vied for purchase in the dust and rocks, or swerved to avoid some vicious hand of punishment.

And then it reared up, induced in a moment of pain and fury to lash out madly, savagely. Fully three heads taller than any of the more than dozen men boxing it in, its enormous head scraping the rough ceiling and sending clouds of dirt cascading downwards. One massive shoulder grazing a wooden support beam, bending it askew and creating another storm of earth debris making clouds in the small room. Its fur was a wan off-white colour, spotted with dark circles edged in a raw pink flesh tone. Its eyes were huge and moist-looking, obsidian ovals casting back the torch-light like some visible reflections of its inner fury. Its bovine facial structure could not be denied no matter how Billy's senses reeled at the sight of it, resembling in most ways a massive cow-like animal. Hornless, a female, with flaring nostrils and giant jaws dripping blood beads like red rain in the glare of the torches. Standing somehow, inconceivably, on its hind legs, brandishing its hooves into curled fists like some alien boxer or gladiator.

Billy watched awed as the beast delivered a quick blow with one of its legs, crushing the head of its antagonist and hurtling him through the air into the closely-gathered wall of his companions. A flurry of scrambling activity among the farmers and their hands, the dull clanking of chains across the bare floor where they pulled the creature's reins tight. Billy noticed the chains encircling the thing, the thick loops around its neck and ankles and hands, pulled rigid by its tormentors, holding it tremblingly in place while a man stooped beside the fallen farmer at his feet. Standing a moment later with the enormous objects in his hands and lunging towards the animal: his father. The meaty crush of the objects into the thing's chest and skull where his father relentlessly delivered blows while his companions held the creature helplessly in place.

Billy saw her then, and his stomach lurched sickeningly at the sight: his mother, with different eyes, holding her treasured silver cross high into the oven air. The look of flames in her gaze as she shouted her voice hoarse like the men gathered there with her. Urging them onwards in their purpose. Basking in their meting out of punishment in the secret room.

The sound of meat being pummeled savagely, relentlessly, filled the congested space. Young Billy crawling back into a corner, behind the staircase, among old wooden crates and discarded pieces of furniture, blanketed in shadows. Huddling into himself. Plugging his ears futilely with trembling fingers. The pained lowing of the thing's suffering filtering through and quivering him. And eventually Billy slipping away into an unconsciousness haunted by the terrible clamour he was unable to leave behind.

Awaking into silence and darkness, Billy thought he was dead. He didn't know how many minutes passed of him scrambling frantically, blindly about the base of the stone staircase. Scraping his knees and palms where he scrabbled, stumbling and bruising his shins. Making his uncertain way up the steps, feeling the hammering frenzy of his heart when his hands pressed on the wooden door at their summit and met with unyielding resistance. Pushing with all his strength, but the wood holding firm while disturbed dust particles rained into his eyes. His breathing anguished and panicked in the inkiness, frightening him all the more.

From the room below: a quick crackle of sound. A snort, a snuffling in the dark. Of some breathing thing.

He was alone with the thing. Alone in the world, at that endless moment. His father and mother above, in the lit world of sunshine and farm animals and tractor-roaring. They had left him behind unknowingly, foolish curious trespassing son. Tears flooded from his eyes, the taste of salt trickled in at the corners of his mouth.

From the black, a hoarse grunt. A deep and harsh throat-clearing sound.

Young Billy's knees buckled at the noise, a high whimper escaping his lips, brief, terminated sharply in his fear at being heard by the thing. He listened intently, shuddered at the husky grunting which issued from below. He noted the threatening quality in the sound, felt it in his bladder like a hard and insistent pressure. The raspy growling came again, amid a clanking of chains and fetters.

A moment of endless silence. Billy's breathing constricted painfully in his throat, his ears ringing in the huge quiet, his skull threatening to explode with pressure. Then, a mournful lowing from the blackness. The sound of pain and lament like some awful funereal dirge. The sound of self-pity and agony in every timbre of the voice below. Billy became unravelled at the sound, unsettled in every way. He trembled within its cacophony reverberating in the small space of the room. His eyes welled suddenly, and he cupped a hand to his mouth as the wailing rose and reached its terrible crescendo, amid the tiny whispery sound of dirt and small dislodged stones spraying from the ceiling and onto the floor and stairs.

The sudden desperate urge to see coincided with the memory of the single renegade matchstick hidden in Billy's back jeans pocket; whispered surreptitiously from the kitchen table while father had left to answer the milkman's calling and his mother had her head in the cupboards over the sink, stacking newly-cleaned dishes. Plucked from among its companions in the matchbook and slipped into his pocket, quickly and efficiently and with no little amount of fear throbbing Billy's temples anxiously, because father may have smoked like a chimney during winter but would hear nothing of his son fiddling with that sort of habit. The experts said it ruined the lungs, and young boys playing with fires only ever led to trouble besides.

  Without thought, with only the pounding behind his chest and in his head, Billy padded down the staircase. Negotiating it easily with a hand ghosting the rock wall as he descended. His other hand holding the matchstick between tightly-clenched fingers, vice-like. Fear returning once he'd touched bare-floor bottom, and the snorting sounded from the dark once more. Only this time closer. The imaginary touch of spittle grazing his forearms where he stood tremblingly, stray sprays from the enormous snout of the chained thing. A short rattle of chains, the dull sound of stout links dragging along the dirt, tapping against stones.

  Steeling himself, Billy edged to the wall directly before the stairs, felt along its rough, uneven surface. Moments later, his fingers slipped onto the cool touch of the iron sconce. The small knocking noise of the wooden torch rattled in its place as he clumsily mishandled it. Silence from the rest of the underground chamber. The silence of listening, while his fingers quivered towards the torch. The gathering of his will, as Billy counted himself into the brave or foolhardy act of striking the matchstick against the wall and plunging it straight away into the blackened tip of the torch.

  A moment later, torchlight flared the stone wall before him murkily, dazzling his eyes. He shook and waited anxiously for some great roar or rush of enormous power to assail him, eyes clenched tightly together as he shrank against the wall. No sound or touch came, though. He turned apprehensively into the orange glow and looked into the secret room.

  It was a pathetic rendition of a once awesome creature.

  It cowered in the flickering orange glow. Huddled into itself, it was still massive. A mountain of sinewy flesh, awkward where it sat upright on the earth with its back against the rough wall. Its arms were long, corded with muscle despite their relaxed posture in the thing's lap. Its hands were hoof-like, but stouter than any animal's he'd ever seen. He stood awed at the agility and dexterity he glimpsed in those large digits, and at the power evident in its enormous hunched shoulders and stout legs. A mane of thick white hair hung along the back of its neck, spilling across those shoulders. Its short coat of wan fur was besmirched with dirt, its skin criss-crossed with scars and fresh wounds, mottled with deep blue and purple-black welts and bruises. Its gigantic skull was similarly battered, scabbed over and crusty, with grossly swollen jaws and eyes squinting through puffed-out mounds glistening wetly. Its large udder stood out starkly between its thighs, bright pink and soft-looking, like some inflated dirigible.

It turned its black-water eyes on the boy and froze him into a ball of fearful tension. It came to life then, and began to beat a savage din against its breast with one and then another pounding hoof-fist. The sound which it emitted was an awful din of mewling and hoarse lowing. Each blow resounded loudly within the small claustrophobic room, and young Billy was acutely aware of the force contained in the thing's curled fists, in its stout legs like tree trunks knotted with thick veins, underground blood streams pumping beneath its leathery skin as it kicked furiously at the dirt. With a grunting effort doing little to disguise its natural grace, the beast rose from its hunched position and towered over the shaking boy.

It was at that precise moment, while enshrouded within its great shadow, that young Billy realized he was looking at a goddess.

A goddess, a strange and special thing. A beautiful and remarkable living thing unlike any other thing the regular world of men and women and the weapons they fashioned could possibly contain. He knew in that instant that it would remain the most awesome sight he would ever lay his eyes on in his life.

Then: the knocking rattle of thick chains, the squealing of straining door hinges, the echo of boots along the stone staircase and the grotesque shadow thrown against the wavering torch-lit walls. And Billy's father with malevolent and woeful eyes at the base of the stairs, fists sheathed in cement squares. Lifting one monstrous fist on the air, beckoning his son forward. The roar of the bovine thing filling up the chamber at the sight of him, dropping stones from the raw ceiling in a tapping rain all around, shaking its cross-hatched framework of wooden support boards. Billy scuttling beetle-like to his father's side, cowering still beneath the shadow of him and his new hands.

His father looked down on him with strange and distant eyes, unreadable. Then he spoke.

I discovered the thing myself, son. Roaming the ranges. Stealing chickens and goats and grazing on farmer's crops all around. I found it in the night, covered in moonlight, like an obscenity in the corn rows. Eating entire ears whole, stalk and all. Watching me with its black eyes. The look of evil, son, watched me that night.

Billy shivered at his father's story voice. Far-away and different, detached from his regular coarse speech, yet matching his miles-away gaze.

It loped off, disappearing in the fields. I waited for it every night with my rifle and ropes and, eventually, it returned. Months later, on a full moon night. A Devil's night. Some say that a farmer's cow birthed it. A freak of nature, a freak among God's creatures, that should have been put out of its misery. A skull filled with lead, son. That farmer made the foolhardy mistake of not shooting it that night. But I believe something different. Most people here do, son. This is a small county, and a good place, with good people. That thing was birthed somewhere else altogether. That abomination comes from Below.

Here his father gestured towards the earth with one gigantic fist. Seeing his son's wide-eyed appraisal of the block, he nodded. *Beautiful, aren't they?* He hefted it up closer to Billy's face, and he shrank away from it. *You're ready to know about them now, son. I made them myself. After I saw it murder a man. And that man was my own father, ten years ago. Waiting up with me night after night. Waiting for it to return the way we knew it would, and then finally standing up to it bravely.* He paused a moment, rubbing the enormous fists together with a sharp scraping sound. Then, *The Devil's hooves must be combated with strong weapons, son. Your mother wears her cross well, and I fight with my hands. Like my father fought before me.*

Billy shuddered at the awful import of his father's words. He saw the distant glimmer in his eyes, like a man only barely present in the room with him while his thoughts drifted in far distant places. A madman's eyes, burning savagely in the torch glare. And when he swept the room with that gaze, Billy shook all the more, noting the hateful look which fell upon the captive cow goddess, chained pitifully among its refuse of feces and blood, displaced from its rightful place overlooking the small doings of men and kept in a den of pain ten years long.

Billy couldn't suppress the sudden flood of tears at his father's words. The way he hurled them spitefully at the stricken bovine deity huddled pitifully into herself, shrinking from the sight of the rock fists gesturing in her direction. *We feed it, son. We feed it hog slop and chicken bones and rotten vegetables, and it takes them all. It longs to eat our children but we deny its awful hunger. We feed it and keep it alive so that the Devil knows to keep his hauntings away from our town. This is a place of good people, who fight back against the meanness and evil in the world. We have a warning chained up and ready for any comer who wishes to haunt us again.*

His father approached the cow goddess slowly. Billy, watching the two confront one another, realized the small size of his father in relation to the thing before him. His father was a large man, lean and muscular, and yet the deity towered over him. Billy noted also the new attitude in her posture, a resigned kind of fearlessness as she gathered itself for this next fight in her seemingly endless existence of combat with hateful madmen. She flared her nostrils, set her giant hooves into the dirt, curling and uncurling her hoof-fists threateningly, the wheezing sound of her laboured breathing raising the flesh along Billy's arms and at the nape of his neck.

Billy's father wavered at the bristling fury he saw before him. Glowering in the thing's wild eyes. He faltered, took one and then another step backwards. Billy wondered at the great fear he glimpsed in his father's eyes in that instant, something which he'd never seen there before. Muttering under his breath, like a curse of his own faltering fortitude, *The Devil is a dangerous evil, son. We must make certain to be cautious in our dealings with Him. In numbers we must find our strength. We cannot be lured, deceived, into the Devil's hands.*

With great reverence, his father removed the fists and placed them, side by side, on the earth. He squeezed Billy's shoulder roughly, said, *The boys are in the fields. We will be gathered here shortly. Wait here, son. The time has come for you to see, and understand. The Devil has finally tried to lure you into His clutches, too. You're old enough to understand now. We will protect you, and make you understand.*

And he turned and ascended the stairs towards the light above. And Billy was alone with the goddess once again. He turned to her, saw her tense posture loosen, her muscles relax. He sensed her instinctive trust of him, and watched her helplessly. A moment later she was sunk once more to the dirt floor, cradling her head in her hoof-hands. A low, quiet burbling drifted to Billy's ears. He ached for the goddess. He wished earnestly to be able to take her pain and bury it in the dirt. His ears rang with the sound of her mournful crying. He felt it gather somewhere inside him and tug away there. An unrelenting pressure like some internal furor threatening to unravel him in that moment.

The deity raised her watery eyes to him then, and a moment later dropped her gaze to the giant fists resting on the ground at his feet, and began another percussive beating of her hooves upon her chest. A dull, flat sound, of bone beating meat. Forlorn and hopeless. Pitiful and horrendous. A sound to break a boy's heart.

Acting on instinct, Billy lunged for the cement fists.

It took all of his strength, and though his arms grew numb with the effort he succeeded in dragging the weapons along the floor and towards the shackled cow goddess. Unlike her violent eruption at the sight of Billy's father, though, she only raised her head curiously at the boy's slow, effortful approach. Her eyes widened in excitement or wonder when she saw the boy edge one enormous stone slab and then its companion close to where she lay huddled against the wall.

Eventually, a light of understanding shone in her black-pool eyes. She reached one and then the other hoof-fist towards the proffered blocks. She hefted the block high on the air a moment later, and brought it down heavily onto the loop of chain trapping her neck to the wall. She repeated the action several times, sweat beading her bruised face as she went about her difficult work. Eventually, a quick cracking sound, and the loop was severed. Again, she repeated her efforts on the chains connecting her ankles to the wall brackets, and then on one of the two chains shackling her wrists. Billy trembled as the goddess freed herself of her remaining bond, ripping the chain from the wall bracket with a single violent wrenching of her two powerful arms. He cowered as she loomed over him hugely, brandishing threateningly the ends of the chains in her hoof-fists. He wet himself in his sudden terror as the savage strength of the animal returned into its massive frame. But she only lingered there over him, snuffling and snorting on the air, sniffing her new scent of freedom, offering occasional raps of her hooves against her breast while her black eyes watched him fixedly. Waiting, even as Billy gathered his courage and rose to his feet, and scrambled towards the staircase, thinking madly about the good or bad thing he had done. When he reached the base of the stairs, he dared to cast a wide-eyed look to the goddess and was startled immediately by the immense dull thuds of first one and then the other of the two cement fists crashing into the dirt near to him. His eyes locked tremblingly with the deity's. She bowed her massive head to him in several short motions, accompanied with a swinging gesture of her hooves towards the discarded fists.

Billy understood, and took hold of the giant cement fists by their worn leather straps and, as best as he was able, began dragging them up the stone staircase.

Behind him, he noticed the heavy silence in the secret room: no more cracking of iron chain loops. No exerted gruntings of the goddess freeing herself. And the sad drum dirge of minutes earlier had ceased its beating, too, and silence had descended in the room like the anxious calm before a great storm as the goddess awaited her final bout in the arena.

With a searing pain in his back, young Billy pushed first one and then the other of the cement fists up from where he held them to his chest and clattered them heavily onto the counter. Through the open kitchen window, from across the yard, the roar of great commotion issued. Farm animals rushing panicked and headlong from the barn, whinnying and squealing and lowing; the screech of relenting wooden beams; the sizzling sputter where wood had caught flames and been swallowed helplessly; the screams of men in rage and pain. And the roar of a goddess bellowing all of her years-collected fury as she fought back, unchained in her combat for the first time. Free.

And over it all, a newly-risen wind roaring furiously, tenaciously.

Billy would never learn exactly how the great fire began. Perhaps during the violence of the fray in the secret chamber, a torch was jostled from its holder and set fire to a wooden support beam. Perhaps the battle had simply made its way up into the hold of the barn itself, where hay bales were plentiful and a dropped torch spread quickly into unquenchable, un-containable fire. Or maybe the sky witnessed the battle from on high and let loose one or more stray, jagged arms of redemptive lightning to strike at the barn, scorching to the ground the terrible prison it had represented for one strange and wondrous creature. The great wind had surely helped to spread its fury, and had perhaps aided in the collapse of the roof as well. Whether any men survived the great conflagration, Billy didn't know. Nor did he ever hear whispered stories of strange and incredible animals glimpsed in the fields, or roaming the ranges on star-lit nights.

He would never know the truth behind the incident, or its aftermath, but would take turns considering each scenario many times during the coming years. And though he spent many years away from the county of his youth – drifting and learning about the world and growing finally into a man – in his dreams he often saw her, bathed in a nimbus of supernal light, striding boldly in the night, cutting swaths through corn fields as though they were hers for the taking.

He stands at the base of the stone staircase, looking out into the rubble of wooden boards and dirt mounds. The cement fists lie on the step beside him.

Peering closer, he spotlights a section of dirt floor with his flashlight beam. He nudges a wan white object with his toe, turning it out of its half-buried position in the dirt. He's uncovered a bone, grimaces while he examines it at a distance, judging from its size that it had belonged to a man. Somewhere below this dirt, he knows, lies a small silver cross which belonged to his mother.

He reaches behind him, hefts the stone fists by their worn leather straps. He holds them swinging heavily in his hands a moment, looking out into the rubble. Then, together, he rocks them backwards and forwards in his hands, his swings gaining great momentum and breadth, and he lets go and they soar and drop with a hushed thud into the dirt of the secret room. He exhales heavily at the labour, and with something like relief at the grisly drama completed at last. A final burial, of a shameful piece of the past.

Billy sees his father coloured in torchlight, raising high fists of his own sculpting. He sees his father's misguided blows inside a room like an arena or grave below the earth, and he cries for him, and for what transpired those many years ago.

Reaching behind him, he gathers his flashlight and ascends the stairs.

In the barn, he moves towards the gasoline tank he'd discovered earlier. Uncapping it, lifting it easily, he marches slowly around the barn, making a meticulous circuit of its far rubble-strewn corners. Making sure to douse the ancient hay bale lumps and wooden walls, the wooden stall gates and the hay-littered floor. He marvels at the amount of liquid it contains, an anomalous wellspring in the evaporative temperature of this desolate stretch of county; considering anew as he completes the task the seemingly preordained nature of his having found it among these ruins at all.

When the tank is emptied, he lets it slip from his fingers onto the ground. He stares around him, gathering his breath. He wishes silently for the barn spiders' and mice's forgiveness, and strikes a match and lets it fall, too, into the gas-wet hay. He steps into the dusty yard and takes some time to admire the fury of the burning barn. Like an angry beacon reflecting the vengeful summer sky, it sends its flames licking upwards, and a great plume of black smoke. Choking out the beauty of the late day where it snakes upwards, marring the purpling dusk-coloured sky and looking just right, too, somehow, like an evidence of and protest against some un-guessed wickedness in the world.

He steps away from the flames, turns, and walks into the day. The tears lingering in his eyes make a wash of the sky, and everywhere he looks is a fiery grandeur.

Night Symphonies

There were two spiders spinning their webs beside one another in the night. One said to the other, "Hello there, friend. A loud night it is, isn't it?"

"Indeed," answered his companion. "What's all that racket below?"

They strained their many-faceted eyes and saw fire beyond the trees. Plumes of smoke billowed up into the moon-lit sky. Screaming rang out from the opposite side of the woods.

The black spider laughed sardonically. "People. So loud. Always so loud and violent."

He turned downwards and shouted at the crickets playing their night serenades, "Quit your racket, cricket musicians, or we'll come down and gobble you up!"

The crickets' symphony stopped right away, mid-song, and the night was silent but for the distant screams and rifle reports.

The two spiders finished their new webs and settled down for an evening of patient waiting and moth-eating, a little uneasy at the growing clamour on the other side of the woods. "People," muttered the red spider, hoping for a treat that night, maybe the rareness of a giant pale moth, or a swarm of jittery June bugs to make his waiting worthwhile.

The spiders looked down upon the sight: two men wearing big coats and helmets and carrying rifles chasing after a fleeing man and woman. The man staggered, stumbling on his way on shaky, uncertain legs. His face looked exceptionally haggard, pale, and there was a smear of blood around his mouth. An inarticulate gibbering escaped his mashed, frothing lips when he tried to call out to the girl, causing her to scream in concern for him. It also caused the spiders' fur to stand on end and chilled them in their high buoyant perches.

The girl was young and pretty in her colourful summer dress. She screamed over and over the same words: "No! Leave him alone! He's my brother! He's my brother!"

But the two men only laughed at her and continued harassing her shambling, befuddled brother. At last, one placed his rifle close to the brother's head and fired. His skull exploded and the rain of blood and brains and other assorted bone and fleshy gore flew everywhere, a few fragments even reaching the spiders' webs overhead. The pieces shone crimson and wet and unappetizingly in the moon glow.

The spiders didn't move. They remained motionless in their webs. They were frightened of these people and the things they were doing. They would clean their webs of the humans' mess later, once they'd gone away into the night. They watched the scene below and didn't understand what they were seeing.

The men laughing at the fallen brother with his missing head. Then dragging the girl onto the grass and removing her dress and then first one and then the other of the two men taking turns lying on top of her while she screamed shrilly, making acorns drop from the branches of the trees around them. This went on for many hours until the men grew tired and the girl's crying had become only a whimper. Then one stood over her and shot her in the head, like her brother. They walked off into the night, leaving their mess ruining the grass below.

Many minutes passed and the red spider called to his friend the black spider, "I don't understand these people. And the loud things that they do."

"Nor do I, friend," answered the black spider. "Nothing ever changes with them. They're always the same. I feel I've lost my appetite tonight."

His friend agreed silently. They listened to the stillness of the night. The clamour from the other side of the forest was silent now. Everything was still and heavy with something uneasy, something like foreboding.

Then the black spider had an epiphany, and called down to the grass below, "We're sorry your grassy homes have been ruined tonight. But might you make your legs squeak for us, if it's not too much trouble? Make your music and let's all just listen tonight."

The crickets did. Their songs that night were long and mournful. They played and they played until their leg-instruments became sore, while their new spider friends above lolled easily in their sticky beds. And the rest of the night was peaceful, and when first one moth and then another, and then a crew of un-careful mosquitoes got caught up in their webs, the spiders untangled their quivering wings and let them all fly free into the moon-lit air.

The Burning Sadness of Crash-Landed Sleepers

They found the smoking hills during some bottomless wee hour while the stars still frosted and the sun still lay buried over the horizon of trees. The darkness was potent, it reminded them how far away the street lights were, and their secretly abandoned bedrooms in their distant houses.

The hills, as they'd named them on their walk past thirty minutes earlier, were giant mulchy hay-like bales of grass and turf, and they smouldered before them. The smoke misted from each in turn and ghosted like phantoms in the stillness of the chill air.

The hills hadn't smoked on our way through here earlier, Christine thought, chilled doubly in her too-light Fall jacket on this wintry October morning. But she only commented on the noise of crickets or cicadas electrifying the hour. "It sounds like a million of them," she whispered, and her voice contained an unease which her friend Sharon heard clearly. Of course she heard it, they'd been best of friends for just over five years: they knew all of each other's secret communications.

"I know," Sharon whispered, clutching at her friend's jacket sleeve as if they were still only very young girls. "It sounds like it's going to explode."

Christine nodded silently. Her friend had meant the noisy insect music, but her words could have addressed the feeling the dark morning itself held. Maybe there were no crickets or cicadas at all. Maybe it was too early for insects to sing songs and it was only the deep buzzing of the early hour which they felt crackling in their ears and humming in their throats.

A snatch of breeze gusted and drew the phantom smoke

from the nearest mound towards them. They stood still, shivering as the mist smoked about them, shrouding the surrounding trees from sight, dimming the helpful reassurance of moon shine above.

They waited until the earth no longer smoked before they un-clutched each other's hands and dared to show one another the look in their eyes. When Christine looked at Sharon, she saw terror watching her and it frightened her all the more. Why were they always doing foolish things like adventuring after dark? And why had they chosen tonight to explore the night again, when the world smoked mysteriously, when their parents' warnings still rang fresh from weeks past: the middle of the night is no safe time for two girls to wander: it's a godless time when only bad things can happen to you.

Because it's so quiet, neither of them had truthfully answered their fuming parents when they'd caught their daughters creeping in through bedrooms windows left ajar. Because it's dark and like deep water or a deep mystery waiting to be solved. Because looking out from windows past a certain hour was like looking into a dare, because the world outside after midnight was no longer the same place it had been during the safer hours of eleven or ten, or the boring regular old times of eight or five o'clock. They hadn't told their parents these things either, they were often dishonest with them about certain things they knew mothers and fathers were never able to understand.

They turned their eyes back to the mound of smoking earth towering before them. Sharon braved the darkness when she said, "They weren't smoking before." And she shivered and cowered into herself when Christine only nodded, neither refuting her claim nor offering Sharon some kind of her usual reassuring comforts. Sharon added: "They look…angry. Steaming away like that. Or, or maybe sad, just smoking away like that."

A moment passed during which the night bugs or the deep morning maintained their steady heady rhythm.

Christine was fearful but also felt the renewed tingling of excitement which had allowed for her initial enthusiasm for exploring the A.M. with her friend. Her whisper was fast and electrical in Sharon's ear: "Maybe – Asteroids!"

Sharon's eyes widened at the prospect and with the realization that their shared mood of fear and dread had suddenly changed. They could be excited again and like paranoid paranormal or UFO specialists in the night. Their secret unspoken mission to solve the night could begin once more. Sharon's own excited suggestion was a little more frightening: "Alien spaceships in disguise!"

Christine was nodding and scanning the smouldering hide of turf and grass with its million embedded stones and bits of twisted branch. The earthy smell of exposed dirt filled her nose as she breathed deeply of their new atmosphere. The cicada-song or night hummed and thrummed like the loudest electrical buzz in her ears. She felt it in her hands now, too, and trembled her friend's hand where she gripped it tightly.

The strange look of the smoking mounds inspired the horror of the idea in her and she gave it to her friend in the darkness about them like some anticipated gift: "No, not aliens in their ships. But the actual alien beings, sleeping right in front of us!"

They'd stumbled onto the answer. They stood in awe of the sleeping mounds, no longer daring to whisper or budge fingers or toes. Confronted with so startling a solution to the puzzle, they could only stand and stare in something like reverence.

Christine thought: they're sleeping. They fell to Earth tonight and look at how good their disguise is. Camouflaged like pieces of these fields and forests. No one would ever guess!

Sharon was thinking: they landed in this field and now they're smoking. They weren't smoking earlier and now they are... They're waking up!

She'd whispered it aloud without realizing that she'd done so. "They're waking up from their sleep!"

The time for jacket-clutching and hand-holding had passed. They stepped into each other's arms and held one another in silence, never once taking their wide eyes from the mounds burning before them. They waited and the smoke billowed up towards the stars. Sharon followed it with her eyes and searched for the most mysterious shimmering speck. It took her only a moment and once she'd found it she pointed and whispered: "There."

Christine followed the direction of her hand, staring

searchingly a moment. Then she nodded. Of course. That one up there. The bright frosty shimmering in the east, this star was the home-world of the smoking hill creatures. Her friend was smart. She knew a lot of very interesting thing. She could figure anything out.

Something cracked or crackled in the darkness, or maybe it was the sizzling sound of some piece of earth loosing itself from one of the sleeping hills before them. Christine peeked from the corner of her eye to her friend, saw Sharon's quivering bottom lip. She was very smart, Sharon, that she'd discovered the meaning of the waking hills and the place from which they'd fallen. Christine saw the renewed fear in her eyes and wanted only to offer some bit of knowledge in return. Maybe another something solved or just something good and smart to pass on to her wise friend.

A moment passed. The night hummed and sang and smouldered. Christine looked past the hills and into the shadow of woods beyond, and then she had her good idea. A squeeze to her friend's hand and her finger to her mouth: Ssh, Sharon. Because Sharon, like her, loved secrets, especially during secret moments like this one while their parents snored and dreamed, unaware of happenings in the night or morning.

A gentle tug on her arm and Christine was leading them through the maze of mulchy misting hills and towards the forest dark and frightening in the near distance. Sharon went only hesitantly, because secrets were delicious to share and keep between you and your best friend, but sometimes shadows got the better of you, especially when you were already very spooked by sleeping travellers from that most mysterious of stars winking over your heads.

But she allowed Christine to lead her, and they wound their way past this hulking hill and its ashen-smoky companion; on and on until the gathering of mounds, like some alien world's equivalent of a graveyard or pumpkin patch, were behind them and the wall of trees towered black and foreboding before them.

Here they both faltered, but only briefly. They had, after all, explored these same woods at least a half-dozen times in the past few months. They were, after all, two girl specialists in the weird happenings of the fields and bushes behind their town home neighbourhood, night experts and best friends, too. They could handle these dark trees and sweeping shadows covering them all over like some deadly black blanket. Especially when a promise of a secret lay at the dark heart of it.

They wound their way through the thicket, scrambling over thorny shrubs that caught in their shoe laces and stretched their hair like clutching twisted fingers in the dark. When the roof branches became too thick and scratched out all the star and moon glow, they removed their flashlights from their bags and lit their way.

Christine felt Sharon's fear in the way she gripped her hand, crushingly, hurting her fingers a little with the force of her hold. So she made it better for them both, their walk in the dark, because her excitement was turning a little into fear now, too. She whispered: "We're like a pair of fireflies out here."

And she led them on determinedly, sure of the way because she knew this stretch of forest pretty well. It was where the prettiest things lived, and Sharon remembered, too, once they'd scampered like squirrels over the thin trickling brook and pushed their way through the final wall of brambles and bushes with their falling berries like tiny little ornaments dropping on their sneakers as they went.

And they stood in the glade and no longer needed the help of flashlight beams because the tree roof was gone and the moon and stars coloured everything. The star-reflected surface of the small pool shimmered, its array of pale floating flower blossoms bobbing buoyantly. The flowers were ghostly and unreal and very beautiful, as Christine urged them forward towards the water's edge. She was trying to lean precariously over the water but saw Sharon removing her sneakers and socks and rolling up her jeans to her knees, and so she did, too. She was so very smart, her best friend Sharon, always with such good brave ideas.

Sharon understood now, too, she got the idea and took over leading this part of their expedition. She waded out into the shallow pool, apologizing to the croaking from somewhere near at hand where her clumsy foot had disturbed a frog sleeper on his heavy lily pad bed. A firefly burned suddenly beside her cheek and she laughed and saw several more flaring up about them. While slipping through the pool, she saw the night sky reflected in the gently-stirring water: all the stars bobbed in their shaky orbits, and she searched a moment and picked out the world of burning hills, like a bright flare in the eastern quadrant of the pond.

They drifted into the centre of the pool, where the most pale blossoms bobbed, being careful not to splash. The frogs deserved their rest, and they didn't want to spoil the peace of the fireflies' lake, either. Surrounded by the flowers, Christine plucked one, two, then half a dozen of the wan water lilies from their watery places. She held them out to Sharon and whispered, "For you, my lady." And their giggles sounded hushed and gleeful in the stillness.

A short while later the water became too cold and they were making their way with a fistful of lilies each, plentiful bouquets with their tendrils of vines dripping droplets down their hands as they went. When they cleared the woods and stood looking out towards the still-smoking hills, they paused.

Sharon said, without looking to her friend, "You're a very smart UFO expert."

Because she was thinking again about what Christine had taught her weeks ago, when they'd first stumbled on the secret watery glade that one deep black night of exploring. The knowledge she'd disclosed was so amazing and magical and, best of all, it made such good sense. Sharon knew the moment she'd been told that she'd never forget. Not ever.

Ancient people thought it, and now some people still believe it: water lilies represent innocence, and stars that have fallen from the sky. Like a textbook, Christine had recited it to her friend, the best lesson she'd learned all school year, and it had taken place well outside of classroom hours.

Sharon repeated it: "You're very smart, Christine."

To which her friend responded, with a flickering gleam in her eyes as she held the bouquet on the air: "In case they fell here tonight by accident. To show they're not alone."

Sharon nodded and they walked into the hills to leave their message of peace and sympathy. Around them, the night hummed with power, and they felt it like a tremor everywhere inside them.

* * *

It was with huge excitement that two weeks later Christine and Sharon stole forth from their parents' houses and met up at the edge of the big fields. And it was with even bigger excitement that they found their way into the secret hills and discovered no smoke rising from their hunched, squat forms, none at all.

They peered closely with the help of the moonlight and the strength of the stars. Sharon pointed. "Look!"

Christine saw them. In the same places where the two friends had left them weeks before, with their tendrils wet and dripping into the steaming crust of each of the hulking mounds: the lilies.

They were still there, only now brighter, their long petals more vibrant in their pale, ghostly luminescence; their tendrils embedded now into the soil and earth of the mounds, like the rocks and twigs and tufts of grass. A further camouflage, or a sign of something much nicer.

"Crash landings," Sharon said. "All of them. You were right. And they only want to go home but can't." She turned to Christine, awed with her friend's vision, with the miraculous sight of the lilies alive and verdant without water, a new part of the landscape of the mysterious hills. "You're very smart, Christine." She paused, and then said, "Maybe they'll be a little less sad now."

Christine nodded. "Together," she said, liking the look of the transplanted and impossible and beautiful lilies growing abundantly like a tangle of pale moths all over the hills. And that was all she said.

The two friends walked on into the wee A.M. darkness. The sound of the night went with them, as it always did, humming and thrumming like some giant generator in the earth or some alive thing calling out to them as they travelled. They felt it in their ears, and throats when they whispered, and it tremored pleasantly all through their chests, too. They no longer feared it in any way, and didn't pretend that it might only be the song of crickets or cicadas or some other night creature surely as awed of its might as they were.

Or maybe they only carried it inside themselves, and brought it as a gift of music into the night, for all the night bugs who played their songs, too.

And they returned to explore the wee A.M. world many, many times after, two specialists of the secret, hushed happenings of the sleeping hours. They walked through the stillness and crept through foliage and glided through pond waters, and they sometimes stole long glances into the eastern A.M. sky, where a light burned forlornly but prettily in the blackness. And they on occasion travelled to the very special pumpkin patch, where the hills ran amuck with pretty pale blossoms stirring in the breeze.

And every time they visited this sleepy plot of field, they found the hills just this peaceful and quiet and undisturbed. And the hills, as far as the girls knew (and they were, after all, experts of the night), the hills never ever smouldered fitfully again.

Tara of the Wine Cats

I tell them all the same words: I'm wires and circuits and a hard shell and a December heart. Some of them laugh and say robots aren't so poetic. Or so sexy, they always say that as they're reaching tentatively for my breasts or thighs. I never bother telling them that I hate poetry and failed through school, and that my mirror tells me different things. I see the verdict every morning: you're the ugliest woman in the world.

And I believe, but I end up tasting their tongues every time.

His name had been Kelsey. I could tell by the way his eyes bugged out and the way he bit his lips as he stared at me naked on the mattress that I had been his fantasy for a long time. Whoever I was. A woman he'd picked up easier than he'd ever believed he could, just like that. And it had worked out for him: miraculously, his callow, tawdry words had kept me talking with him in the book store aisles, flirtatiously, while he marvelled at his adept techniques or luck. You're tired, as his eyes watched my thighs, sounds like you need a good, thorough foot massage.

That had been his thing: feet. Mine, like rare treasure in his hands as he pulled my boots off and began smelling me and administering lickings and kisses along my heel, between my toes, biting my nails. Then he had me, briefly because he tired quickly, but then he had me a second time shortly after and it was moderately better.

He grew angry when I refused to give him my number. Why not, we could do this every night, and his eyes were pleading and growing more livid and wide as the idea made him excited again. I left quickly, before he had the chance to grow violent, which happens with them sometimes. I've had my share of slaps and punches, one kick in my stomach even. Having one's fantasy crushed as it's seemingly realized brings people to that. Angry actions in rooms supposedly made for rest and something referred to as love.

I hurried from the motel, a short stay hole on the city's west side which existed only for those like Kelsey and myself, and I got into the man's car three blocks east and repeated the process. His name had been Bill, and afterwards he'd only cried softly into the pillows as I left him forever. People are all different.

His question made good sense, and it made me smile at him in an honest kind of way. I regretted it right away. He'd come and stood beside me at the table and said, "Do robots enjoy wine as much as you do, Tara?"

It's true: I'd been licking the moisture from my lips and sniffing the mouth of my glass for the lingering smell of grapes. It's something I've always savoured. I wanted to be bold and ask him directly but he beat me to it. "You don't remember me, right?"

I shook my head. He pulled out a chair and seated himself beside me. "We were together a few months ago. I took you to my apartment. You left and told me that machines don't give out their phone numbers. I remember you had wine on your breath."

I didn't know what to say, so I said, "I have wine on my breath now."

He said, "We're in a bar now. Before we were in the grocery store. We met there. In the cookie aisle." There was a little accusation in his voice, but not much, surprisingly. They usually always accuse me of something. I'm always responsible for their aches and pains.

I changed the subject, but not really. I said, "You look good in those pants, Robert." He watched me evenly and said, "My name isn't Robert."

"I know," and I waved at the waitress and she refilled my glass.

He took me home after I'd had another. Hours later, as I was leaving his apartment, he told me that he agreed with me, that I was a robot. He must have seen the cold metal gleam in my eyes. I was happy that someone believed me. "Thank you," I said to him, and closed the door behind me and never saw the man again.

Jennifer had been entertaining and had commented on our dual penchant for wine. Love cats, wine cats, that's you and me, baby. She'd been one of the more sentimental and too-romantic types, a rare find among the bars and coffee shops. She wasted some good water our one night together, pouring some Spumante Bambino between my breasts. I watched her lap it up and eventually grew aroused, but only mildly. Oddly, it took a very long time of kissing her on her mouth and rubbing her between her thighs for me to grow wet myself.

Towards the end, right before she came in my mouth as I worked my tongue into her, I remember her cries: I'm so lucky I found you, I'm so lucky I found you. As if I was a rare species of animal among the wildlife of humanity. And I smiled as I licked my lips and fingers, because the girl on the bed in front of me was right: she'd been very lucky that night, because I was indeed rare, and there was no one like me in the world.

I'd tried the experiment only once, and the sight of the red inside me had me gagging into the toilet after only a short while.

I'd been very drunk that late night: grapes in my mouth, in my churning belly, behind my eyes making my vision a wash of blurriness. Grapes were my world that night, and the naked razor blade was popped from its plastic shaver and in my palm before I realized what was going to happen. I only kept seeing their faces in front of me, losing sight of what I was doing with the razor, knowing only that I had to find something inside of me. I never learned their names, just two tall men with dark complexions, maybe Italians or Cubans, and they'd picked me up on the sidewalk outside of the bar and taken me to the apartment they shared. I thought it would never end, the way the turns kept coming: first one man, then the other, then the first returned on top of me, and then his friend, and on and on, different positions as I was tossed about every which way on the narrow mattress. Hours. The night was endless. It never stopped feeling amazing between my legs. I was crying the whole time, and heard them laughing at me for it while catching their breath.

When they'd finally let me go, I must have hailed a taxi or stumbled the twenty minute walk to my apartment. I don't remember the trip, but then the razor was splitting my skin finely, very finely, first around my wrists, then into my palms while I flexed my fingers around the small silver rectangle and watched blood gurgle thickly everywhere. Like oil, but undeniably red. I gashed my knees horribly, and then my stomach and chest, but my search was fruitless.

I found no wires. There were no gleaming casings exposed beneath amazingly-replicated and -constructed skin tissue. No electric sparks when I held the strands of hair between my pinching fingers and sawed through them with the razor. No winking lights behind my breasts, no whirrings in my red-smeared wrists: only the old deceptive pulse, making me wonder at the genius behind my creation and manufacture. Only the persistent pulse in my wrist and the hammering in my chest, putting tears in my eyes.

I knew it then more than ever maybe: I must have been made by a master, his ultimate masterpiece sculpture. Walking with my fellow people like I belonged there among them, though I really didn't at all. Humanity part two, and only occasionally when I caught myself in a mirror or reflected in a window did I stand revealed: that distant blue spark like machine electricity in my stare, like a cold light in the night.

When I woke up in the bathroom the following morning, blood was everywhere from so many minor cuts and a few deeper ones. I was thick semi-congealed wounds and red-brown smears and in need of a thousand showers which felt like they wouldn't clean me anyways. The red look of the linoleum and porcelain made me vomit again. The taste of acid was in my mouth the whole day, and the lingering atmosphere of grapes stayed behind it all, too.

    It only takes to stare a fraction of a second longer than seems appropriate and they believe you need them. And that they can give you everything you've ever dreamt of while lying sleepless in your bed. The grocery clerk was the same.

    It had been this morning, after stumbling out of bed and barely dressing for any activity outside of my bedroom, when I'd first seen him gathering grocery carts in the parking lot. It's where I looked at him a fraction of a second too long.

    Five minutes later he was trailing me indiscreetly through the aisles. I reached upwards for the snack-size pack of cookies and peeked from the corner of my eye. His eyes were on my bare legs where my dress hung mid-calf. A minute later I was leaning over for a bag of potato chips and I felt him watching me appraisingly. By the time I was in the frozen foods we were making worthless small-talk and he knew it was a grand day for him. He didn't care about his boss and was fucking me in my bed twenty minutes later. He was eighteen, what eighteen-year-old wouldn't throw his job away for a good lay with a woman whose eyes beg him for his body in hers?

    We sipped wine in bed afterwards and then did it again. I decided to keep him for the day and most of the night, too. When I told him to go home to his parents, he hung his head and asked shyly if he could come back tomorrow. I told him to look for me at the grocery store and left it at that. Maybe he's been fired already, but what difference does it make – He gave me what I needed and he'd lived his greatest day and night.

       *   *   *

He made the mistake for the both of us: there was a gentle tapping at my door two nights later and I opened the door to find him there, pale and frightened-looking. He asked me timidly if he could come in, and the old earnestness was in his words as he spoke. He was like everyone, only younger, and so maybe a little more eager and reckless.

He was basically begging me soon after. I relented, feeling sorry for him, and I let him have me twice in one night. When we were finished and he could do nothing but lie beside me breathing heavily in the darkness, I told him to never come back again. He didn't say anything for several minutes, only began dressing himself sheepishly by the light of the bedside lamp. Then he muttered sullenly, "Why not? We both like doing this."

I watched him sadly and said, "No. I don't." He waited for me to explain and I heaved a sigh because I'd never tried to explain before beyond the usual cursory words meant to ward off the attentions of emotionally clinging men, but felt somehow that I needed to then. I said, "I'm not like you. I'm not like all the men I spend time with." This made him worry, I could tell by the creasing of his brow, but I reminded him that we'd used protection. He reminded me that he'd given me oral sex twice. I feigned insult at what his words suggested, but dropped the act a moment later.

I said, "Listen to me: I'm a robot, boy from the grocery store."

He watched me strangely, not understanding. I repeated my words and watched his confusion grow. I said, "I do what I do because I have to. I don't know why. I only know that I have to do it."

"Are you just maybe obsessed...with it?" He was a little frightened still.

I shook my head. "No. I...It looks that way to you, I understand that. But no. Just, no. I mean it. I'm not like you. I have machine parts. I'm not exactly human. Except when I...You know. Then I feel alive."

He told me he was going, and left through the bedroom door. I listened and knew he was lingering in my apartment, I hadn't heard the front door close. He returned a few minutes later. From the doorway he looked at me naked on my bed and he said, "We met in a grocery store. You drank wine tonight. You're a woman."

He left unhappily and I heard the thud of the front door resound through the apartment. I heard his words like an echo in my head. I reached to the night table for the bottle of Spumante Bambino. Cheap white wine, clean and easy slipping down my throat. I'm a machine, I thought to myself, no longer brave enough to say the words aloud. I'm a robot and I can't remember who programmed me in this way, no matter how hard I try. I was feeling the beginnings of lust returning between my legs and regretted sending the grocery boy home. And I began to cry and the taste of wine in my mouth and the smell of grapes on the air of my bedroom made me dizzy. I felt uglier than I've ever felt before. And I felt very rare, like I always feel, a rare catch for all the people in the world fortunate enough to cross my path, and the proof of my humanity on my breath kept tears wet on my cheeks long into the lonely night.

In the City where Dreams Wander the Sidewalks

People who were once my friends scorned me and laughed: *Your eyes tell you strange things.*

But I know something about the black centre of this everyday Southern Ontario city. About the man who takes the teenagers from their place in line outside of the Salvation Army Youth and Rehabilitation Centre. Who filches them from the sidewalks and alleys like candy from a store dispenser. And I know this: he's the closest approximation to the Devil we've got here in Windsor, Ontario. Because when they come wandering into the dead Sunday morning streets days later, the girls and boys have un-living eyes that look past you a million miles when you stop them on the sidewalk.

I've spoken with them, before and after their transformations, and I've seen their eyes and the deep things that always seem erased from them when they return from the man. And that man is a terrible legend among these homeless, old and young alike, while the children fear him most because everyone says the same thing about him: he frequents the streets and makes circles of the blocks until he sees one he adores, it's always only a single one chosen each night; and then the passenger side door of his forbidding car is thrown wide into the evening and despite the rumours and fear riding the air in that sector of the city's downtown, they slip inside as if enchanted and close the door.

And they drive off together, the terrible man and his newest candy girl or boy.

And the new wee hour morning streets are always checkered with slow-moving children with eyes looking nowhere, shuffling down sidewalks and filth-littered alleys with no destination anymore at all.

*   *   *

I saw my first abduction on an early Friday evening in September. I'd been staring from my third floor bedroom window, blowing cigarette smoke through my window screen and into the chilly air. Absently, I saw them, two regular walkers of downtown sidewalks, the giant tattooed woman with limp and cane, two blue-ink tear drops ugly and sad running down her left cheek; and her daughter, or the girl I'd always taken to be her daughter because why else would this biker lady with ancient wary eyes always shuffle along with the Downey girl ever at her side. I remember fixing my eyes on the girl, trying to discern from my high vantage those details which made her a different kind of human than the rest of us: the strange heavy-lidded eyes, the perpetually blank expression and the webbing between her fingers. Of course, I could not see at that distance, but I knew they were there, these alien attributes. Because she, like her unsightly mother, were fixtures of the city's downtown country who I knew well enough.

When the long navy car pulled alongside them, I figured it was one of the regular johns. One of the sicko demented fucks who paid cheap money to rape a retarded girl while the hideous mother supervised, waiting until it was over to collect their money. I'd been hearing the stories about the two for years, the Twisted Two, I'd always thought of them, hating the world a little more every time they crossed my mind.

The picture three floors below was old and awful and I was stamping my cigarette out and preparing to vacate my place at the window when the biker woman began wagging her cane in the air. It caught my attention, that flurry of activity from a usually slowly waddling mass of poor motherhood. I watched, saw that the Down's Syndrome girl was already seated in the passenger seat, and that both she and the driver, whose face I couldn't make out in the dim interior of the vehicle, were both gesticulating for the mother to get away from the car. Then, in puzzlement and mounting horror, I watched as the girl slammed the door closed with a quick, flat thud. I heard her mother's anguished scream perfectly through my open window as the car rolled away down the street and beyond my view.

I sat watching the shrieking mother, waving her wooden stick in the air, and the picture of her sobbing regretfully made little sense to me; because hadn't she been offering her child up for cars to swallow for years?

I watched her for several minutes as she waddled back and forth along the sidewalk, an enormous panicked penguin, crying, confused, apparently unwilling to leave the site of her daughter's abduction for one reason or another. I felt horrible. My stomach became queasy and I considered waiting beside the toilet for my dinner to resurface. I stayed in the window, though, until the tattooed woman vanished in the darkness, and when my eyes became sore from staring into the night I went to bed and waited for sleep that didn't come.

Two days later I was walking briskly to work and the world became half normal once again: there they were, the biker lady and her retarded girl, coming slowly towards me half a block away. I could pick them out at any distance, their familiar silhouette and odd, shuffling gait. But when I neared them, the woman's eyes were watching the sidewalk, not raking passing traffic for signs of prowling johns. And I never realized the consciousness that lived in the faces of the mentally delayed because when I looked into her daughter's eyes I saw that they were dead, and they hadn't been this way before at all. Behind the usual blankness there was something deeper, something more vacuous and un-alive than I'd ever thought I'd seen there. There, or anywhere else I'd ever looked. Pit eyes, hollow and fathomless.

Those eyes have haunted me from that morning on. I see them when I'm rinsing dishes at work, and they watch me from the inside of my eyelids when I'm trying for sleep. I'm haunted, and the worst part is now that I've seen it once, I see it everywhere. Signs of darkness slipping through among the lit world. All around me, right in front of us all, the same car drifting like a spirit down our streets, curbing the roads with passenger side door wide and beckoning to young men and women traveling down their sidewalks.

I try not to see, but I always do: maybe I'm running late for work or leaving the movie theatre with a girl, when a teenager with nothing at all behind his or her stare drags past us like a resurrected cadaver on the street. And I shiver – a profound tremor quaking through the deepest parts of me – and I know sleep won't come to me that night.

Two months after that first awful abduction, I sat chatting with a fairly well-known homeless man identified locally as the Fisherman, for the fishing hat he sports during all seasons, brimming with seagull feathers, like some strange grubby peacock with no permanent residence but the sidewalks down which he travels. We were seated midway up the long concrete steps leading to the upper levels of the Ouellette-University corner plaza which houses the theatre and coffee shop and small deli. We were talking about the weather because what better subject to discuss with a man of the outdoors while he doled out the small Ziploc bags of marijuana to his regular Friday night customers. My own stash, a half bag bought at sale price because he liked talking to me, was already snug in the breast pocket of my jacket.

Then, right in front of me, and I couldn't believe my perfectly terrible luck in happening to be freezing my ass where I was when I was: the waif was pretty, for all her thickly-caked eye make-up and tattered fishnet stockings and faded blue-dyed hair like some vision of post-apocalyptic Mad Maxian Australia. Petite and evidently cold with her arms wrapped around herself in ineffectual defence against the chill air, she appeared altogether doomed leaning into the open maw of the long car hulking predatorily alongside her, its engine purring smoothly in the night.

I wanted to do something. Call out for her to stop. Urge the Fisherman to snare a hook in the girl's fishnet-stockinged legs and pull her to safety. But all that escaped me was a muttered, "Fuck" as I

In the City where Dreams Wander the Sidewalks

sat helplessly captivated by the spectacle. Beside me, the Fisherman thought he understood, and he laughed. He said, "I know, my friend. I'd like some of that young pussy myself tonight. Lucky bastard."

We watched as the girl clambered into the seat and closed the door after her with a small thud. The car drove through the green light, turning left and heading west; heading, I knew, to some awful kind of night for her. I murmured, "I think that might have been the Devil in that blue car, friend."

To which the Fisherman replied in a subdued tone, following my stare and gazing off westwards, "You're right. I've seen him, too. I didn't want to say. In case it might ruin your night."

I stared at him then, watched him carefully while he went through his stash of dirty dollar bills under the amber street light glow. I asked him, "What do you know?"

And I watched him as he didn't answer me, only continued counting his money, and then he got lost and had to restart at the beginning of his count, with a disengaged look in his eyes making his task difficult. He stood a moment later, his business done or maybe unfinished on the corner that night. And he nodded at me wordlessly and wandered off down the street, headed northwards, towards the river icy somewhere in the night.

I thought: what plot is this, unravelling in the night every night under the city's unseeing eyes? And I wondered where it was, what dank sweaty place exactly was it that served as the place of transformation for all the children of the night; who returned to wander their old haunts like ghosts called back from graves. Darkness and chains and ropes and locked doors perpetually guarded this terrible site in my imaginings. I envisioned cluttered back rooms of small convenience stores or confectionaries where unspeakable pictures play out under dim hanging sixty watt bare light bulb light. I imagined the second or third sub-basement level of a years-abandoned factory or warehouse where only mice and echoes live, in some feebly-lit corner space, on a mattress stained ugly, marked with atrocity. It could be there, too. It could be anywhere at all in this small-ish city, so big, really, when you're seeking to pin-point the nesting place of something shitty and black to the core.

And what was it exactly, I wondered in something like

awe, what was it that happened during the endless nights and what was doing it? Was he a crazy john strung out too often and riding jolting highs from inhaled cocaine lines or from peroxide cans held close to his mouth? Or was he an archetypal family man, a community figure with pressed suits and perfect radiant smiles for all those looking up to him? Or was he somewhere in-between these portraits on the endless spectrum of terrible chameleon humanity? Or was he simply badness incarnate? And this possibility somehow always made more sense than the others, although I was never certain why. I only knew that it felt awfully right, seeing it that way; like a thing risen from deep places where there's no light until the indefinable city glow catches it within its nocturnal radiance and there it is, finally, seen. A secret revealed. A long-festering malignity manifested in the playgrounds and alleys and wherever else we allow our children to become lost.

  The Fisherman said it best, maybe, by not saying the words at all. By avoiding my eyes because probing into some things is best left undone. But it was a girl that summed it up for me, a girl I worked my tedious job alongside and who I began to know more and more over the months. It was wise Martha who said something huge and revelatory apropos of nothing while we sat watching the river from her car one sun-plashed day, our fast food lunch remnants stuffed back into the paper bags in which we'd received them.

  I remember how it looked that afternoon. One of the rare days when the world looked lit perfectly, almost so powerfully illuminated that it seemed as if you might be able to figure everything out. Decipher long indecipherable problems, slip puzzle pieces together so that larger structures lie revealed. Because it's always easier to find answers when you have a reliable light source peeling away the murk and brightening the corners of the world.

  Just like that, in the easy space of silence following a quick meal, while the cholesterol attacked our bodies and we swished Coke around in our mouths to help dislodge the bits of French fry and hamburger meat from between our teeth. Just like that, as I sat there pondering the world only very distantly with sunlight in my eyes, with the Detroit River sparkling the way it does only on afternoons like this. And she said: "I've been having crazy dreams lately. About there being something…About that there's an evil living in the world." And she looked at me then, which I was hoping she wouldn't do because of the fear in my face, but she did and didn't notice, I guess, because then she added, "A pervasive evil. And it scares the Hell out of me, those dreams."

    And she was done, and so was our lunch hour break from dish-washing drudgery, and I sat in numbed silence as her revelation confirmed for me my own nascent knowledge. Like a verification of my sanity in a world reliably growing more savage each day passing. I shuddered, watching the magically deceptive sight of the dirty Detroit River looking beautiful in noon hour sunlight. And Martha started the engine and we were driving back towards work and more dirty things to scrub clean.

    My friends often laughed at things I told them.
    Your eyes tell you strange things.
    I stopped saying those kinds of things, ideas that would lead them to softly ridicule me, their steadfastly paranoid friend. But I knew about the black centre of the city even if they wouldn't allow themselves to acknowledge it. I knew about the hard dark little pit at its core which finds its mirror a thousand times over in the eyes of our most unfortunate children.

    I discovered the clue years before, but hadn't made any sense of it. I'd made no connection between this clue and the new brand of street life I'd been seeing, the avenues and alleys teeming with walking dead children. My epiphany arrived unbidden, and I recalled the memory of the clue as I was passing through the rear exit of the restaurant and into the rat-plagued alley, having just completed my evening shift. I walked eastwards without hesitation, knowing that it would still be there, in the same place I'd found it years ago, ruining the down-trodden neighbourhood behind the deceiving splendour of the casino even further.

    I stopped briefly at the casino and used a payphone to

call Martha, the girl who dreamed of evil in the world. When she picked up I told her to come meet me. She asked whether I was okay, I guess there'd been a tremor in my words as I spoke to her. I said, "Do you want to see a clue? It's about the evil in the world that you dream about."

We hung up and I walked to the place we were to meet, in the semi-enclosed park wedged in between three surrounding walls of town homes. I sat on a peeling bench and waited, listening to the incessant vibrant chatter of ghetto children from the see-saw and sand box, sounding as if they didn't know yet about the sad truth of how the world is. There was an overturned Big Wheel on the small narrow front lawn near me and it made me sad. It only added to the feeling of everything becoming worn down and useless, forgotten in the endless march of one hopeless day into the next.

Our walk to the site of the clue was short. We didn't say much as we walked. I think Martha sensed a little of my trepidation. I sensed dread coming from her in waves, as if she knew something she'd witnessed or suspected was about to be confirmed, suspicions validated.

Minutes later we were standing alongside the decrepit hulking building. It sat low to the un-cropped lawn, near to the traffic-teeming Riverside Drive, yet unnoticed too, for all its proximity to the machine hustle and bustle and stink of exhaust. It had once been a garage of sorts, an automobile repair shop gone bankrupt in some distant decade. Its windows were striped with rusted iron bars, and the scratch-pocked glass beyond them was filthy with grime.

I pointed to a spot in the window, partially obscured by a rust-flecked bar. Because it was still there, as I knew it would be. My friend leaned forward and with a crease in her brow read the message written in faded ink on the sheet of time-yellowed paper and stuck up to the inside of the glass. She read it aloud softly, an awed kind of murmur in the settling purple dusk.

"'Hey kids: are you sick and tired of living at home and listening to everything your parents say to you and claim to do for you? Do you know more than they do? Do you know everything you need to know and do you want to get out of there as soon as possible? *Get out:* you don't need them anymore. You know everything you need to know to live in the world. You'll never need them again. *Get away from them now.* The world is waiting.'" She stopped reading, and I gave her the time she needed to re-read it again and then a third time, and then I let her mull it all over and wonder what it meant. Whether it was a twisted message directed to runaways in the area, attempting to lure them into service as prostitutes or dealers; or whether it might be her dreams made tangible and masking taped-up to a grimy window of a deserted and squat building in the centre of a poverty-riddled neighbourhood, a corporeal message in front of her eyes revealing her worst suspicions to be true. There was no contact number on the weathered-looking paper, no address even, and somehow this made it worse, the absence of any trace of human connection in the enigmatic message. A communication from the depths of some unfathomably and eternally dark place to the innocent girls and boys destined to hear, those weary children lost enough in their own awful lives that they would find their way into its black heart regardless. Or who could do nothing but wait for it to come for them, a dark pre-destiny purring its spell-like motor-rumble through the streets of poverty and loneliness.

 A moment passed and when she finally was able to speak, Martha only said, "It's awful. My god, it's so awful."

 We held each other's hands fiercely then because what else could we do when beneath the pall of something so seemingly insuperable and embedded like a tumor in the fabric of the world. But even then, even during the comfort of gripping each other that tightly, and though the vacant building was squat and not very much taller than we; it yet seemed to loom larger than that, seemingly dwarfing us in the certainty of our powerlessness.

  We don't talk about it. We haven't since that night. We both know it's there, some kind of incontrovertible proof of what we've known for too long to live and breathe in the nooks and crevices of the place we live.

I see the car, deep navy and in the night it might as well be black, with its shotgun-side door opened wide like a mouth for swallowing the children living on the sidewalks. We both see it, and the teenagers themselves, returned days later but never the same, the touch of humanity gone from their stares, with their new wan faces like chalk powder. And we huddle ourselves inside of movie theatres and we eat dinners in restaurants facing away from windows overlooking the sidewalks, and when we talk on the phone we keep it brief and remain inside topics of how's work and what movie do you want to see next weekend.

And when I see the Fisherman with his scavenger birds' feathers pluming straight into the congested downtown air, I bid him a good evening, and we chat briefly about the weather changes and how the rain makes the air cool even if it's still muggy. And we make our regular exchange, dollar bills for clear plastic baggies of weed. And we say good night and wander away down the street in opposite directions, our eyes watching the cracks zig-zagging the pavement, as if all our steps weigh a ton and look at the damage we do whenever we walk in the world.

I Humbly Accept this War Stick

The sun's as bloody this morning as last night's rounds.

I found and followed him again and it's for certain now: he knows that I'm there every night, a skulking thing in alley shadows, a man-size rat among the overturned garbage cans, the walker ghosting the streets where few people roam on cold awful nights like these when the wind off the river cuts through you like a knife. He's known for weeks, I'm certain, I'm not always as tidy in my trailings as I seek to be. Too close to the garbage cans and a rattling lid stirs a rat and a sleeping homeless woman, or maybe just the slap of my clumsy heel onto the rain-wet cement as I hurry too quickly around a corner to keep pace with him.

But last night the moon was low and monstrous in the sky. It hugged the bellies of the clouds and clothed the city in silver, and I was utterly naked when he turned from her and looked into my eyes where I crouched behind the stacks of ruined cardboard boxes. I neither blinked nor budged from my place despite my racing heart, and I think it made him marvel a little. I hope he admired it, that huge courage I showed in the face of my terror and uncertainty.

And he'd turned once more to the twitching woman lying on her back before him and bloodied her further like she deserved. He raised his arm high and the wooden stick – is it a boat paddle with its end shorn clean or some piece of timber sculpted to suit his perfect hands? – his stick came down another time, and then another and another as he repeated this wide arcing choreography, so practiced and easy and beautiful in the moon glow.

The woman had been dead by his second blow but he kept at it, in order to be certain or merely rejoicing in the task at hand.

The thuds of wood into her face and body sounded softly on the cold air. I imagined the mush of her features and I grinned in spite of my fear. My excitement was huge, as consuming as it's ever been while spying on his work.

When he was finished he turned again and found me still peering from behind my weak shelter of boxes. He held my gaze for a moment, his eyes through his lint-pocked ski mask fixed unwaveringly on my own. Then he strode from the broken woman, his shadow a gargantuan saturnalia spread across the tall rough-hewn brick facades of the buildings boxing us into the narrow alleyway.

After several minutes I rose and edged towards her. I glanced around me to be certain we were alone, she and I and the rats. Then I looked on her: ugly whore, I thought, and I whispered it quietly, wishing I had the courage to give her the title louder, proclaim it to the denizens of the putrid alley world. I hate you, whore, and I dared to whisper that, too. I lingered a while, admiring by the lunar light the indentations the hero's piece of wood had made on the whore's face. It was fractured in many places, her jaw misaligned and causing her to look as if she'd been caught in death while in the midst of some bout of maniacal laughter; her forehead was crushed inwards, a ruined landscape of altered bone and lacerated skin, and one of her eyes was a pool of grey milk oozing from its socket and down her cheek.

I hate you, I told her, and I felt strong.

Then I turned and walked briskly homewards, because no more could be done that night.

Tonight I'll call out to him. I'll find him in the dark city armpits and cesspools as I always succeed in doing and I'll call out to him and ask him to allow me the privilege of watching him more closely at his work. His *good* work: I must remember to compliment him on his technique as well as the ethic behind his noble crusade, the endless striving for peace in a city only as dirty as the people who roam its streets.

I'll try to keep my voice even, casual and un-fawning

while I yearn secretly to become apprentice to him in his career of cleaning the city. The garbage collectors are the neglected heroes, I might casually mention if we find ourselves in the vicinity of trash, which one inevitably does upon wandering the streets. I'll say it easily, an impromptu commentary on the urban sprawl around us, small talk between professional and adoring admirer. But we'll speak a while and soon it'll become apparent to him: no mere fan, I, but historian, too, and chronicler of just exploits in this mid-sized southwestern Ontarian city, an expert in matters of cleansing.

Your December 19th show was grand, I'll reminisce, a veritable classic: she was an ugly one, deplorable in her actions the way she'd leaned in close to the college men twenty years younger than she who had followed her from the bar and taken her number while promising to call. She was disgusting when she told you in her hoarse drinker's voice to leave her alone once you'd cornered her in the alleyway, her tight dress like black oil clinging to every curve of her body, as if she knew the power those curves held and wanted to manipulate the pulse of the city with that awful alchemy. You were efficient and quick that night, a single swipe with your board and like a sickle it clove her face in two, one bright red river down the length of her artificially-tanned features like cured leather. I examined her afterwards, and have the records at home. Her picture turned out perfectly, one of the best I've taken of your work. My collection of photographs is extensive and the overall quality, I'm proud to admit, is superb.

The hero will watch me, astounded, and lower his streaked stick. He'll smile beneath his mask and listen intently as I describe another exhibition in loving detail. One of my favourites: the man in suit and tie who'd stumbled towards his car after he'd left the sordid strip club on the city's poverty-stricken west side. His fingers must have smelled dirty from the places he'd slipped his American dollar bills that night. I checked his identification and found only ten of his American dollars in his wallet and a single condom squeezed tightly into a leather slot all its own. He'd been a big fellow, burly around the shoulders and wielding fists like hams. He worked out regularly, I think he must have to have been so heavily built. But you were magnificent with him, and exceedingly clever the way you snared him in your trap: what was it you'd called out to him – Oh yes: "Here's your money, you dropped it, sir." And the fool, he shook his head in bewilderment and crossed right towards you, following you as you back-pedaled just enough, just enough distance to place you both around the bend of the building and into the first few feet of shadows beyond the alley's mouth. Then a quick and hard blow with the stick to sink him to one knee and then you were dragging him forcibly into the deep darkness – That was the night I first realized your strength. My god, sir, it was tremendous. And you didn't stop with him for at least ten minutes, if not longer. You were relentless as you hit him and hit him, pummelling the giant filthy man into the concrete in order to keep him pinioned where you wanted him. And when I sneaked a glimpse at the remains some fifteen or twenty minutes after you'd slipped away like one of the many shadows in the alley, I was overcome with awe. I was moved deeply at the sight of the sprawled man's smashed mouth and the scattering of his broken teeth all across his chest and littering the concrete about him like confetti celebrating your masterful work. You must have caught him square in his yapping mouth, probably wide open in a futile effort to say pitiful words beseeching you to stop the just falling of your stick. The papers in the days afterwards said he'd been a pimp in the area, and I laughed and said good riddance to bad things.

  The hero will be very interested in me now. He'll enjoy my accounts of his justice, and will ask me to continue. And I'll say this: my first time, as many initial experiences in any area, stands as my favourite, of course: she was old, a ragged old whore who'd surely sucked thousands of cocks in her thousand years of whoring her sagging body on the streets. I knew there was AIDS running rampant in her veins the moment I spied her lingering near the corner where all the johns pick up their prizes. I trailed you as you followed her, to the small vacant lot behind the convenience store beside the massage parlour. I hid in the trash hold and peered through the wooden slats of the fence and saw everything that happened. It changed my life. You did that. I watched you watching her smiling at you with her black teeth and deep wrinkles like dry rivers in her sickly, weathered face. I remember thinking that she'd probably assumed you were trailing her because you wanted her to put your penis into her mouth so she could suck it for some small fee. But I could see in your stance, and the way you looked at her – as if you loathed her and every aspect of her character which made her so sullied – that you'd do better than that. And then you'd clapped her one hard across her stupid mouth. It sent her flying backwards, that open hand. She looked so foolish staring up at you in her shock, as if she'd only then realized her own worthlessness. And my god, but you gave it to her then. It was the first time I saw the stick, the board, your instrument. You'd had it hidden beneath your long coat but then there it was. You brandished it like a sword in the small space behind the store – some might liken the place to a gladiatorial arena, and you the victorious combatant standing over your stricken foe – and by the weak light from the street lamps just barely finding its way there, I saw the notches in that wood, and the black streaks where I knew you'd done other good and admirable deeds, too. I'd never seen a human head explode, but hers did. It was a shower of red beads. I remember it well. And the sound of your stick hammering into her chest and face, the soft mushy flavour of the noise, remained with me all night while I tried hopelessly for sleep.

And I thank you, hero, because here I am.

This is what I'll tell him, and when he raises his eyes in question, I'll explain. I'll thank him all over again, for his encouragement, his reassurance that I haven't been alone all these years in my hatred of all people capable of sick thoughts and depraved deeds. And I'll thank him most of all for his inspiration. For guiding me in my own pursuits, a novice in the art of cleansing but dedicated to my craft still, because how could I be otherwise with so wise and elegant and passionate a mentor.

This is when I'll reveal to him my own achievement, so recent that I'll be barely able to contain my pride and jubilation: I'll pull the photographs from my coat pocket and show them to him like a badge proving me to be the man I say I am. The dozens of snapshots of the dead boy, the one I'd followed home from the convenience store only several days before, his transparent bag of penny candy dangling in his small fist while he asked the elderly woman feeding breadcrumbs to the pigeon flock on the sidewalk his dirty question – Do you have a smoke? And when the gentle woman shook her head, the boy with his filthy language had branded her a liar, an old fucking bitch liar. Too young to suck cancerous smoke into his lungs, this failed boy, too young to know let alone speak such vulgar words to more gentle souls.

The hero will look through the photographs, examining them closely, in great detail with his master's eye. He'll nod in admiration as he sees the damage a man's hands – a man other than himself – can cause to the flesh and face of another human being. He'll see the swollen purple mounds blemishing the chubby boy's doughy features where my fists pounded downwards with all my strength. He'll smile appreciatively at the work of my sharp nails where they'd parted the skin of the boy's neck while I took my time squeezing life from him. He'll see the clean holes where the blue eyes had been cleanly scooped out first with thumbs and then with the small travel-size lint brush which I always carry in my coat pocket, which just barely squeezed its way into the boy but I managed besides.

And he'll reach out his hand, the hero will – he'll do this tomorrow night or the next time we meet in the moonlit alleys – and I'll feel his fingers squeeze my own tightly in admiration.

And then we'll turn, together, and walk into the rest of the night.

The moment was arrived.

I stood in it, revelling, chilled, frightened, brave and proud and disbelieving that at last it had come for me.

The night held its breath. Time ceased its passage. The gibbous moon painted the scene ethereally. Only the two of us were alive in that rarest of moments. After trailing him closely, and watching his expert's hand work its beauteous magic once more in the hushed A.M. – I'd revealed myself at last, trembling in every part of me, cowed beneath the fearlessness in his wide stare. Falling to my knees before him, the cache of pictures held out like an offering, I felt the energy of the moment sizzle about us. The cleansing-energy. The fresh-kill moment.

I waited in reverence, silently, my eyes watching the deep

red pooling across the concrete between us. Thrilled by the vibrant look of it in the moonlight, the way it made lonely islands of the weeds and cigarette butts and other refuse of the alley floor like a thick and flowing tide. Time elongated while he examined my amateur's work and I shook anxiously at his feet.

Finally, the hero passed the photographs back to me and looked me in the eyes as he removed his mask. His eyes were large in his gaunt, ashen face, and sweat shone in glistening beads where his hairline had receded. Wisdom lived in his smoky eyes like clouds, experience lay gathered in their brackets of crow's feet. His face was creviced with deep wrinkles, skin-fissures in an ancient landscape. He wasn't what I expected. He was much more than that. He was the cleanest man I've ever met. He watched me closely and said in a tremulous voice, "It's been so long, my wait. I thought you'd never come. But you have." His eyes softened, and his lips curled upwards in a wondrous smile. "You are an angel." And he cast his eyes skywards, and I noticed how the moonlight shimmered the tear beads on his cheeks into small diamonds. To the sky he said, "Thank you. You've sent an angel at last. Finally, I may rest my weary bones."

And he looked to me, crying silently, his eyes ecstatic, while jewels glistened on his cheeks.

And he held out his streaked stick of war for me to take from him.

We stood facing one another for I don't know how long, but it must have been a very long while as I let pride swell my chest. It was incredible, the brightest moment I've ever known. I shook anxiously in my place before the man I admired most in the world. I nodded at the hero – my hero – and in near disbelief at what was happening I took the stick from his hand, and watched as he turned and walked away from me down the black alley corridor. He'd never wander there again, I knew, a hero retired in elegance and reserve. Dignified.

We were alone, the slaughtered prostitute and I. A boy, this one, young, maybe in his early teens. The johns called these children *chickens*, and as I looked down at his shattered features, I was glad the animal was dead.

A glorious show it had been. A suitably grand finale to

an astounding career. A final night of elegance and red beads raining through the air and onto the cement. A night of crimson tides and torch-passing, veteran angel to apprentice. The reddest-wettest night of them all.

But there was a loneliness everywhere, too, lingering in the stifling alley air and in the streets beyond, among the maze of convenience stores and massage parlours and piss-smelling parking garages and bars and strip clubs and crumbling crack houses with their filthy, zombie-like tenants listlessly haunting the porches, and all of the other old places I knew so well. There was something missing, I sensed acutely, and it was the old presence of justice riding the wind. I could only stand rooted to my scrap of cement and continue to recall that most significant moment of my life, his hand held out and the stick glistening in alleyway moonlight. I examined with reverence the tool I'd been given, running my fingers anxiously over its dark-stained surface, across its notches and grooves where it had sacrificed little pieces of itself for a greater good.

    Like a gift, from one angel to another.
    Like a calling to renew the world.

Lost in the Penguin Tunnel

The first place I caught them spying on the world was at the penguin exhibit.

They had their noses smushed against the thick glass, and their eyes were fixed on the birds within, doing their penguin things.

I said to my small group of tourists, but I was really saying it to the twins at the window, "Penguins are found in Antarctica but not the Arctic, a common misconception, and they're not restricted to only the frozen sea and land. There are different species of penguin that live all over the world, such as those who live along the coasts of Africa and Australia and South America."

I watched them from the corner of my eye. Eventually, I was certain they were listening to me, too, because first one and then the other turned their eyes on me. She turned first, and her brother a moment later. Ghostly skin, pale and unreal-looking in the eerie luminescence thrown from the water in the penguin tunnel. Both had identical tawny hair, hers pig-tailed and his a mushroom-mop hanging into his eyes, a classic portrait of twin siblings if I'd ever seen one.

I went on. "With the emperor penguin, the Adelie is confined to the Antarctic and neighbouring islands. Other sub-species, such as the gentoo, chinstrap and macaroni penguins, inhabit the fringes of the continent and certain of the islands."

I made sure to sneak a glance at them when I said 'gentoo' and 'chinstrap' and 'macaroni', because I wanted to be certain they weren't ghosts. And like all children, their eyes lit up and smiles appeared like magic on their faces when they heard those funny names.

I had to smile at that, and I went on. "Penguins are flightless birds, whose wings evolved into flippers. They're superb swimmers, of course." My audience of tourist adults nodded along to my rehearsed words, looking from me to the exhibit guidebooks and back. I turned, motioning for them to follow me along to the next stop on our tour of the zoo, and I checked over my shoulder to see whether the penguin children were coming, too.

But they were back at the glass, noses making smudges on the clear surface, eyes locked on the rotund birds waddling or swimming on the other side. And they looked so right there, so pale and diminutive that I thought how cute and funny it would be to dress them up in tuxedos and take them field tripping into the centre of a rookery somewhere, just to watch them become lost in the crowd of their brothers and sisters.

I made a sighting the other day.

There they were, those by now familiar apparitions, gliding this time from the monkey house and along the thin paved trail into the adjacent area of outdoors foliage. I lost them there, amid the swaying, sighing green, although I could hear them: just barely audible snatches of quiet laughter and sing-song chatter, elusive somewhere ahead of me, and then to my rear and now again off to one or another side.

Eventually I gave up and retired to the refreshment area, where all kids wind up at some indeterminate point in the lengthening afternoons to gulp sodas and suck on popsicles, but they never appeared and I wondered again at the unreality of their pleasant little voices among the stirring leaves and branches.

Finally, there they were, back, of course, inside the gloomy penguin tunnel.

I sidled up exaggeratedly, hoping to make them laugh at my penguin impression. They didn't even turn at my approach. I cleared my throat, feeling foolish, and said, "You two missed my penguin impersonation."

Slowly, they turned to me, first the girl and then the boy. They watched me silently with unwavering eyes and I wondered what they might have been thinking. Feeling a little uneasy, I smiled encouragingly and said, "You two seem to really like those tuxedo-wearing birds."

I waited. Eventually the girl smiled and said, "That's what I said. They're always wearing tuxedos."

I nodded, and told her it's because they're always going out on the town and eating at really spiffy fish and chips restaurants. It won me another smile, bigger, and she even laughed a little. Her brother only eyed me suspiciously and didn't say a word.

"What are your names?" I asked.

"Martha, and he's Marion." She gestured to the boy without looking at him, watching me as she spoke.

I nodded, thinking how funny that she owned what I'd always considered to be an old lady's name, and the boy so elegant a girl's name. I said, "I like those names. They suit you two." They did. Martha and Marion, devoted friends of the flightless birds, emperors of this man-sculpted rookery. Watching them there in their nearly identical outfits, white shorts and blue t-shirts and her red sneakers and his black runners, it made me feel the stiff, starchy uniform tight over the paunch of my belly and a little constricting around my shoulders. I wished I was young again.

We stood there, looking at each other in the dim, watery luminescence, with nothing else to say. I said, "We should get some better lights in here. I can barely see you."

"I like the dark," Martha said. "It's better."

I liked that. It's better. The dark is better. For the birds and for us gawking people, too. "Maybe you're right, Martha. What do you think, Marion?"

But the boy only watched me silently, peering just around the back of his sister's wispy-haired head.

I checked my watch, realized suddenly that I'd been chatting far longer than seemed right to my mind. Lost in the penguin tunnel, I thought, and I said the words to the kids, I said, "Lost in the penguin tunnel," with a silly shake of my head and then some muttered excuse to leave the security of the dim, smooth-walled passage-way.

I left the same way I'd entered, and I didn't check to see whether they'd returned their attention to the world of their birds because of course they had, of course they had.

The familiar smell of fish and the sea, except where were they, those little connoisseurs of tuxedo-species of bird?

"Hello, penguin expert," from behind me. I jumped a little, turning at her voice.

They were standing along the opposite wall of the passage this time, watching from a distance. I was about to ask, but she said, "We're back here because we want to give them privacy."

I liked that, and I understood it well. "I know what you mean, Martha. All the animals must get a little tired of getting looked at all the time."

"Especially penguins," she said, and she and her brother were a vague, ethereal shape before me in the wan uncertain light.

"Oh yeah?" I said, intrigued. "Why especially penguins?"

I heard her listening to Marion whisper urgently in her ear, the first and only time I heard him make any noise in the tunnel at all. Then she said, "Because one of them is sick today."

It took a moment for me to digest it. Sick? My smile faded and I walked to the viewing area, pressed my face to the glass. Birds waddled about the rookery, an emperor stood guard vigilantly near the icy water's edge, watching his family members hurtle through the murky depths below him.

"In the back. Behind the rocks," Martha's voice said from behind me.

I scanned the distant horizon of jagged rock and spotted him. The bird lay on its side, motionless, huddled downwards into itself, removed from the others. It looked miserable, and I watched it for a few seconds, taken aback. Then I left to fetch someone, our resident penguin specialist, thinking as I went that maybe we had them right there already, those experts so attuned to the world I always found them scrutinizing.

"Boogie's gone," and her voice was so sad.

I nodded. Boogie's gone. Swimming somewhere in penguin heaven. I suggested this to Martha and Marion. They whispered between themselves.

Then, "No, he's flying in penguin heaven."

It made good sense to me, and I was nodding again. You learn something new and thrilling every day if you're lucky. Quick-time holy reverse adaptation for any bird with a good enough heart. And what penguin, I thought while watching them all going about their bird business behind the glass, doesn't have a good heart.

We watched in silence a while, a little reverentially.

Then I thought to ask, and I said, "How come Boogie for a name, Martha?"

"He liked to dance at the edge of the water before he dove in."

I thought about this a moment. "He liked to boogie," I said, understanding.

"Yup."

We watched a while longer. A group of birds sauntered to the edge of the water and set themselves and a moment later dove in, slicing the icy surface of the pool and shooting through the deep marine blue, sleek and swift and suddenly very beautifully to my mind.

"They're like torpedoes," I said, and I could hear the awe and admiration in my voice.

"No," Martha murmured beside me. "They're not mean at all." And I listened, because I could sense that she was going to tell me more, and I was rewarded for my patience. She said, with a light tapping of her fingers onto the glass, "It's the world in there."

I heard, and thought that I had no place there at the zoo, conducting tours through every area of the acres-long facility, knowing as little as I did about things.

Two kisses to the grimy glass wall, one each from her and him, and I felt the momentousness of it on the chilly fishy air.

I didn't say anything. I stood there in the comfortable gloom where I'd made such strange and good friends over the past weeks, waiting.

Then, "Goodbye, mister zoo expert. It's been a good summer here."

I said, "Will you visit us again?"

"Mm-hm," from the shadows in front of me, or some such barely audible answer barely in the affirmative.

And I had to ask, so I did. "You were here so much this summer, you two. In this watery tunnel, mostly. How come?"

I heard the hushed whispering from the shadows, a mini-conference in the subterranean marine light and smell. I waited, anxious somehow.

Then, Martha said, "We wanted to be with Boogie before he died."

And they turned and I watched them leave the penguin tunnel, silhouetted in light as they went, arm in arm, and I never saw them there again.

The Lilac Perfumes Between the Stars

I've left three provinces behind me going to meet them. It's been a journey of over one month, living in my little blue Pinto with fast food meals of grease and trillions of calories. A backseat bed every night parked along the shoulder of some side road or cutting a swath through corn rows and listening to the giant grasshoppers bouncing off the windshield all through the night en route to tastier pastures. Treating myself to the occasional cheap motel room with mice in the walls and yellow stains in the centres of the mattresses, always too-dim with feeble lamplight, a disconsolate sixty watt glow that keeps me from being truly happy despite the significance of my journey and the great excitement it brews in me.

Driving hard through these last days, goodbye Ottawa, Toronto, and countless small towns whose names I never knew. All left behind like the dust in the wake of my passage. My eyes squinting ahead of me along the straight trail of the 401 stretching on into forever. The radio off, always silent despite my love of music, I couldn't imagine life without it except now other things crowded out all my usual thoughts. My cell phone at all times plugged into the lighter socket beneath the dashboard, always inserted therein so that its tiny corner power button will glow its comforting green shine while I wait for the intermittent calls; always tense all over until the ringing throughout the small space of my car and only then am I able to relax, knowing that our ties haven't been severed. That they haven't changed their minds, or found a worthier and more compatible comrade to aid them in their plight. They know I'm coming and mean to keep me set on my route. They're anticipating my arrival as much as I long to meet them. They've remained as faithful to me as I've been to them.

Clues and directions and a renewal of hope marking the miles all along the way: this is what their calls are, leading me, guiding me, coaxing me onwards beyond my great anxiety and the next few thousand miles of highway towards the greater truth and salvation I've always known to exist.

Only this morning, in fact. Their first call in days. Still rubbing the gumminess from my eyes, nursing my bad shoulder where I'd hunched too hard into the plastic side of the car door throughout the night. The sharp little electronic ringing and my hand reflexively snatching the telephone from its place on the passenger-side seat, excitement awakening me instantaneously and making my movement sure and precise. I listened, saying nothing. There was no need. No one else would care to be calling me. No one knew where I was. No one knew who I was.

Static at the opposite end, wherever that was. A hissing of distance and poor connection, an echoing crackle like patch cords missing inputs and knocking against steel.

Then: *Where are you, Clem?*

Her voice was golden. It always was. Sunlight in my telephone. Hot and fiery. I wanted to live inside the receiver with it.

I wasn't quick enough for her. She repeated it and I languished in the sound: *Clem, where are you?*

Passing through Hamilton, I whispered, my voice hoarse from sleep and embarrassing coming after hers. I waited and listened anxiously to crackles and pops in my ear.

Then: *You're coming fast, Clem. Good. Good. When you pass through the city, look for more flowers. There's a turn-off, a few miles past the city. One service station past and then this turn-off. Take it. There's a forest at the end of the road. A little grove, with a clearing in it. Wild flowers grow there.*

The voice paused and renewed hissing filled my ears. I murmured something in the affirmative and waited for her again.

Finally: *Bring some to us. Bring us some of these wild*

flowers.

Yes, I said. I will.

A small click and then silence, the hissing of miles ceased in my ear. I was getting closer.

I would. I'd bring them anything in this world.

Because they'd give me everything in return.

I found the grove by mid-afternoon, a little bald patch ten minutes into the scraggly bush.

The sun beat down tenaciously. The heat was relentless. The thought helped to drive me on, imagining them waiting for me at the end of it all. After the stifling and bright air. After the sweat clinging my shirt to my body like a second skin. After my life until this point, like a lacklustre prologue to my impending rebirth. I looked around, wiping my face with my baseball cap. The site wasn't very extraordinary, thin trees like black stems against the milk sky. Tall grass crackling underfoot or maybe it just crackled this way all day, baking under the fire sun. I toed around near the tallest areas of grass, hoping for some sign of petals in the verdant depths, but I only disturbed a small green snake. I thought initially that it was a garter but then saw the weird markings on its bullet head, tiny obsidian circles matching the bottomless black in its eyes as it flicked its tongue at me as if delivering a curse before hissing away into the bramble.

I looked around me, a little bewildered. Perhaps I was in the wrong grove, or maybe a little bit further in is where I'd find – I spotted them.

How could have I been so blind. I blamed it on the heat and the sweat it beaded down into my stinging-dizzy eyes.

They were dazzling in their clusters at the base of the trees on the opposite side of the small grove. Pale and pure against the lush grass from which they sprouted, virgins burning calmly in the stifling air. And one other, a single deep blue specimen residing at the centre of the patch, large and hooded and sad-looking, distinctly the ruler of this flower realm.

I kneeled among them, plucking several very gently from

the earth and depositing them into the water-filled plastic pitcher in my hand. When I had a fat bouquet arranged tightly inside the pitcher, I stole a sniff of their perfume. It was lightly fragrant, I hadn't ever smelled flowers like these before. In fact, inhaling their perfume there in the grove, I considered the possibility that maybe I'd never smelled flowers before in my life, at least not of my own volition.

It was good, smelling their smell. It was good, picking the girls another gift. Because one who bears gifts is sure to receive them plentifully, too.

The horizon was the deep orange of the sun-setting late afternoon when they called again.

It had been an entire night and the better part of the following day since I'd spoken to them last. I was quick to tell them: I picked your flowers, but I'm scared they'll wilt before I can deliver them to you.

Don't worry, her sun-voice assured me through the electric hissings. *They'll live. You're close now.*

I nodded. A smile bloomed on my lips. She was right, of course: they looked pristine, the entire bunch where it fluttered in the wind thrown from the open window, more or less secure in its sloshing container resting on top of the plump pack beside me on the passenger seat. I waited obediently, knowing there would be more from her, detailed directions to the next obscure retrieval site or simply the sweet song of her voice bidding me goodbye until our next communiqué.

Through the crackle of miles: *We want one other thing, Clem.*

She paused, and I relished the memory of my name on her voice. No one had ever spoken it so gently, so easily. I waited. My smile lingered.

Then: *There is a patch near to where you are now. Just outside of the place you call Belle River. Along a short road called Green Valley. It's near the lake, this road, and at its end is where you'll find them.*

She paused and I listened anxiously, the paradox as clear to me as ever: I felt calm inside the atmosphere of her voice, despite the air held up in my throat and the hammering in my chest and temples. She would take me away. She and her companion. They would take me away from here. We would come together as planned and abscond together as fate had decreed. I could leave this rusting clunker behind, abandoned in the middle of the highway or laid to rest among weeds and infrequently-traveled farmers' roads and cow-paths. I could forget it, and every other disappointing thing I knew, too. And everyone who had already forgotten me.

Her voice returned, a ray of gentle light soothing my racing thoughts: *Yellow.*

I nodded, envisioning their ranks now, stirring idly in the hot air, barely perceptible breezes touching them ever so slightly. Rows of yellow heads, clustering off into infinity. I said, Yes. I said it into the receiver at my mouth and savoured the acquiescent taste of it there, of filling their needs as they filled mine.

Yes. I said it again.

In my ear, the tiny click of my saviours severing our connection.

I swallowed the lump of tension in my throat and accelerated the car, stamping the pedal down hard with my foot. Only for the time being, I consoled myself. Only a very short while, this cut connection. Soon we would be together like we'd planned. As we were meant to be.

Sentries.

Rows of them, erect and proud and more vibrant than I'd imagined.

It was a beautiful place, serene and still, where sunlight burned inside the flowers.

I didn't know the names of these specimens either. They never told me and I never asked. I took what they asked me to procure and would deliver it without any questions. Picking this bouquet, one of so many over the past several weeks, I thought how lucky I was: to have found them the way that I had. To have decoded their veiled message on the computer, just another evening of boredom in my basement, frittering away my time while waiting for an end to the night and the beginning of another tedious and meaningless day.

Then, my prayers answered, it seemed.

Yes, we are who you are looking for, it seems. We can take you to places you never dreamed. We can take you higher than anything. Contact us. Sybil & Jenny.

The memory of the glowing screen in front of my nose, the machine's humming comfort as I realized with slowly growing astonishment what it was that I'd stumbled onto. I'd found it. After so much hopeful watching and doubting of myself: I'd found it, in the form of a pair of wondrous, wondrous girls.

Plucking the sunny flowers from their place in the soil, I recalled my joy that evening just a little over one month ago. Sending my response immediately to Sybil and Jenny, my fingers dancing crazily across the keyboard while I romanced the sound and taste of their names in my mouth, what quaint little monikers they chose to assume.

Waiting without sleep the entire night through, missing work the following morning, the headache from screen-watching the night away stabbing into my eyes.

Then, mid-afternoon, the beeping clamour from the computer and the new message received, the most important I've ever been delivered.

Clem: It's simple. We tell you because we trust you. We need energy to return home. Only you can bring it to us. Because you are like us. Because you alone understand. Bring us what we need, and we will take you with us, like you've always wished to be taken away. We will be yours.

My fingers danced that afternoon, oh how they danced: what energy? What *energy*?

I waited for their message to unfurl itself on the screen in front of me. I squinted at the revelation as it appeared.

Flowers.

I stared at the word for a moment, was about to respond but found that they weren't finished.

We're stranded here just outside of the place called Windsor, in the province Ontario. We're sisters. We know the area through which you'll be travelling. We travelled through it once before. A very, very long time ago. We'll guide you as you come to us.

Their story was fantastic. It was as incredible as they were, to have the courage to ask me for my help, to entrust me with their secret. It was the beginning of our strange friendship, our extraordinary adventure. I would bring them anything they needed. I was theirs. They were mine.

We were going to leave all of this behind.

I was wiping the sweat from my face with my baseball cap when the rustling came from behind me. Startled, I jerked my arm and twisted a flower in half, snapping it mid-stem. I turned and found the wide-eyed boy watching me, a grey steel bucket in his hands. His bare knees were scuffed, dust powdered his cheeks, and his hair was a dishevelled mop scratching out his eyes as he blinked down at me squatting in the grass.

I was in a bright mood and said hello. He asked me what I was doing and I answered that I was in search of flower energy. He frowned and watched me a while. Then he told me that he was out here looking for frogs, had I seen any.

None hopped my way today, I said to him. But I'd keep my eyes peeled for him.

I was finished collecting the bouquet and dusting the grass bits from my knees when the boy, still observing me curiously, said: I call them sunflowers even though they're not real sunflowers.

That's a good name for them, I assured him. It's perfect. I was happy, so I stooped down and plucked another one, this particular specimen housing a sleeping June bug among its soft-petaled folds, and slipped it into the breast pocket of the boy's striped t-shirt. He didn't thank me, only continued watching me strangely. The June bug he was wearing remained where it was, looking as serene as ever. Then he asked whether they're for a girl or something, all the flowers, his voice bored and sounding very unimpressed.

Yes, they are, I told him. They are indeed. I was turning to go on my way, and answered his frown over my shoulder: maybe one day you'll understand. Maybe I'll see you around.

And I left him staring after me, with little things like frogs and June bugs on his mind.

I'm close. I'm this close. I can smell salvation, and its scent is intoxicating.

I received their call this morning, at the precise moment the sun had cleared the horizon and brought dawn. Meticulous directions to their whereabouts. Headquartered in the bush, in the centre of a conservation area called Ojibway Park a mere half day's drive from where I was.

I pulled into the smallish parking lot over a half hour ago. I've been staring at the walls of trees enclosing me on three sides, trying to keep my breathing even. I'm here. They're here. Out there, beyond the tree walls. Out there with the raccoons and squirrels and snakes and mosquitoes.

I hear their last words to me, an echo from our morning communication.

One last ingredient, Clem.

Her voice soft, like silk or cloud or something better for resting my head against than either of these.

One final ingredient: a single one. From a patch just outside the park's entrance. We can't go out there, because if we're seen... If we're seen.

I understood. Anything, I told her, and listened to the crackling static in my ear for what would prove the last time as I waited for her voice again.

Then: *One only. It's all we'll need, Clem. One. From the patch by the entrance. Blue. A blue one that wears a hood and looks mysterious. We think you call it by the name... Lilac. You'll find us in the centre of the park. Beside a statue of a kneeling boy. An angel, we think it's called.*

Then, silence in the receiver at my ear.

I've since unplugged the telephone from its cigarette lighter power source. I'll never need it again.

I've checked and re-checked everything a dozen times while waiting for the parking lot to thin out. I have my oversized backpack and it's stuffed to brimming with everything my girls want. My girls. Just thinking about them like this makes me giddy: *my* girls, and in my great anxiety I look to make certain, for the hundredth time: they're still here. They haven't gone anywhere, and neither has their beauty diminished throughout the long journey.

The flowers, each bouquet arranged neatly in its own plastic container, I'd scoured the entire house for them before setting out and had to make one extra trip to the hardware store to ensure that I had enough for our purposes. The wheel barrow's tucked into the trunk, and with it I'll wheel the flowers in their watery homes out into the park when it is time.

There are very few cars left now, only a couple, and they'll be leaving soon enough, I think. I spy a family of four making their meandering way into the lot even now, blankets and baskets in tow. I open my door, leaving the photographs of my parents stuck up to the dashboard underneath the window, and the wallet-size snapshot of my brother, too. I won't need reminders of where I came from when I arrive at the place I'm going.

But the others, these I'll take with me. I look them over, the thousandth time since I received them over the computer. Documentation of a surgical procedure in progress, and the urgency in her voice comes back to me and I can't help but quiver: *Hurry, Clem, please. Jenny's been hurt in the accident. I'm trying to fix her, but it's hard. I don't have the means out here.* The picture makes me cringe every time I examine it, though when I do I find myself unable to look away. Poor Jenny, strapped down onto what appears to be a crude makeshift surgery bed, surrounded with the myriad strange and alien protuberances and devices of which I have no knowledge, wires and tubes assembled like a ghastly, intricate web in an effort to prolong her life if not heal her completely. The room in the picture is dark, lit only with one bizarre-looking light source which illuminates poor stricken Jenny, frail and diminutive and unreal-looking on the bed, helpless with the foil-like covering over her bare chest, casting its eerie sheen in the dark. Her head is thrown back in seeming agony, her blonde hair a tangled mess spilling over her shoulders. Her face is swathed in shadow which I know to be the ashen remnants of her features, another by-product of her accident. Sybil, she's lamented this often over the weeks, how beautiful Jenny had once been before the fire stole her old face, and could I hasten my progress because it was difficult to determine under the conditions how close she was from the end.

All of them are coming with me. All of the photographs. Into the woods, to wherever I'll wind up at the end of my journey. They represent a record, of what it was that helped speed me along in my journey, giving me the added impetus to drive like lightning across Canada with no backwards thoughts of family or job or other fragile ties.

I retrieve the wheel barrow from the trunk and load it to brimming with the flower canisters. The water within them swishes softly and the gravel of the path crunches under the stout wheel as I push it along.

I'm coming, I mouth silently to the trees surrounding me on all sides.

I'm coming, I call out silently to my girls.

Sybil. Jenny. I'm coming at last.

Excitement and anticipation merge with fear inside me and awaken a surge of nausea that leaves my senses reeling. I'm dizzy with the smell of everything I've ever looked and longed for, finally so close at hand. I march onwards into the green.

Stan was just like me except he fought against it.

Where I'd given up trying for unattainable things like a career after graduation and girls on the telephone, he remained persistent. A glutton for abuse, I'd always scoff at him, though I was always a little bit jealous of his tenacious ambition. How was he alive still when I'd died so long ago? We were only a few years apart in age, did it make the difference, would he realize the fruitlessness of life and his place in it by the time he was thirty-five, too?

Always like Stan to colour his days too hopefully: that girl from Chem Class? The blonde one with the bouncy boobs? She talked to me: I think I caught a *vibe* from her.

There were no vibes, I wanted to tell him but always felt too cruel even thinking the thought, let alone announcing it into his hopefully helpless world. And that about summed it all up, him and me and every day we drifted through, together in the basement while our parents shook their heads upstairs and wondered about us: a helpless kind of shared existence, circling the familiar place of same-old and unhappy. With no hope for tomorrow yielding anything tangibly better for us while we only continued to languish together as we always had. Hey, Stan, wipe that dumb smile from your lips, you have nothing to be happy about. You have nothing to hope for anymore. I know. I *know*. But of course I never shared with him these difficult truths.

Hey, Stan: there are no vibes coming to you from anyone, except possibly bad ones.

And mother and father sitting quietly upstairs while we rotted away the days, loving, doting in their clumsy ways, and maybe a little responsible for the awkward children huddling mole-like downstairs in front of the television, surrounded by magazines and books and movies and other distracting detritus of un-reality purchased for them whenever they needed; these ingredients that took them far away from a reality that they'd consequently never learned to face. Children lost in the bodily prisons of listless, purposeless adults.

I'm sorry, Stanley. Truly, I'm sorry. I wanted to tell you, you're the only one with whom I'd share the secret. But I saw your eyes. I saw them every day. You were as hopeless as me but you just never realized it. You wouldn't let yourself believe it because to you tomorrow existed as firmly as the basement floor under your feet.

Now I've gone away, and I'll be going even further away than that. Further than you could possibly believe. I'll miss you, Stan, and if you ever change your mind and I have the chance, I'll come back for you. And then I'll show you where we belong. Where we've always belonged. Where it always smells like flowers and the something moving on the air is their invisible vibrations as they breathe out oxygen to keep us alive like we never were, to give us the strength we never had, like boys emerged from their embarrassing shells as Titans.

They're pale, like I'd imagined them. They wear their hair long, like I thought that they would, Sybil's silvery blonde and silent Jenny's a deep tone of burgundy. They're young and astonishingly pretty, as I knew they'd be.

They look exactly like girls. Their disguises are admirable. Not only their plain summer clothes, a flower-patterned summer dress hugging Jenny tightly, and Sybil's cut-off denim shorts and tight-fitting white tank-top; but their long hard legs, their swell of breasts, and their faces, too. Their eyes, as they watch me closely, scrutinizing their saviour standing in the path before them. The guarded gaze with which they appraise me, tense and inhospitable, unnerves me, but perhaps it's only their natural reaction to encountering me firsthand at last, a denizen of this hopeless world. My nerves jangle and my breath comes with difficulty, I suddenly feel awkward in their presence, too much like my old self in the midst of what I'd envisioned would be the finest moment of my life.

I shrink at the sound of her voice, a wilting man in the late afternoon light.

You were wrong. It's Sybil, spitting the words in my face, making me confused. *You were wrong about us: you're not dealing with beautiful creatures from wherever-the-hell-you-thought. We're just a couple of Earth girls out to steal a little something for themselves, you crazy son-of-a-bitch. But you can remember us as your lovely UFO girls if you want to.*

There is an angel resting calmly beside them, his stony face obscured by the tall stems and billowing petals growing in profusion in this area of the woods. The branches of the trees tangle over our heads, dappling us all over with sunlight. There are birds up there, I can hear their chirps, and the flitting occasional shadows along the forest floor are agile squirrels leaping from emerald tree to tree.

I'm so confused. Nothing makes sense. Their laughter and cruel eyes. Little Jenny's wheeling of the wheel barrow and toting of my pack toward Sybil, where she stands poised with the gun in her hand. I stare along its barrel, dazzling under the sun rays penetrating the trees and touching its metal skin. An ordinary pistol in the hands of my liberator, Sybil. And where are Jenny's burns, those horrible disfigurements I looked on with equal parts sympathy and horror in the photographs? The scars that urged me frantically on my way across provinces and city after city and town after town, because if they could help me I was certainly going to do everything in my power to help them. And when did she have the opportunity to dye her hair this Autumn colour during the course of her extensive surgeries and convalescence, poor girl, having to suffer so.

It's Sybil again, and her laughter is a barking sound as she scorns my confusion. *Clem, what did you think, you crazy bastard. That this was real? That Jenny and me are your space age girls come down to rescue you if only you'd bring us our secret fuel source?* She laughs and twirls a flower in her free hand. The lilac. It's the lilac that she's toying with as if it's all very silly and meaningless. The special flower. The final flower before salvation.

I feel myself beginning to shake but can do nothing to quell it. Jenny remains silent but Sybil can't seem to stop herself in her delight. *Did you like our story, Clem? We loved thinking it up for you. We thought it up while we wrote it to you. No editing on that one, Clem. Flowers all along the way. Your whole trip was flower-picking and daydreaming. We knew the area you were driving through*, she said derisively, barely containing her glee, while Jenny counted the wads of money tucked neatly into the pack at her feet in the grass. *We've both lived out west. We moved around a lot. We just made it all up as we went, Clem. I guess we're just nostalgic enough to remember where the prettiest flowers grow.*

She kicks casually into the grass at her feet, sending the doll flying. A simple Barbie stripped of its clothes, its hair shorn viciously, one side of its plastic face charred black, the product, it appears, of being heated to an extreme degree. I recall Jenny's face from the photographs, its ashen, artificial appearance, and feel a lump turning about in my stomach.

I'm astonished: my girls are wicked. Not even girls at all. Sadistic creatures from who could fathom what nether region. Some cold, cold gulf between the stars, surely, because where else, where else.

You were easy, Clem. Easy as pie, as you Earthlings say.

Jenny, finished examining the bags, nudges Sybil from behind. A whispered word or two reaches my ears, a plaintive tone colouring Jenny's words. Sybil turns to her sister – and they are sisters, without doubt, one can see it in the identical way that they move, lithely and with ease and grace, unlike regular clumsy people – and lets the fire in her stare ebb, nodding and offering a hand in hefting the packs back into the dusty wheel barrow. The canisters of flowers are still there, some of the stems becoming flattened hopelessly by the weight of the bags.

I watch Jenny wheel the ungainly-looking mound of goods away into the shimmering depths of the woods. I hear the sloshing of water and the crunch of the wheel barrow's wheel overtop dirt and tiny stones and branches. Sybil turns to me and raises her pistol level with my eyes. I wince and cringe back, certain I'm going to die in this forest three provinces away from my home and its basement sanctuary where I should have remained burrowed alongside my wiser, mole-like brother. In that breathless instant I think of my car forlorn in the vacant parking lot outside of the park; and of the pictures I left behind baking underneath the window, mother and father looking happy together because at the precise moment that particular picture had been snapped their son hadn't yet liquidated their entire savings account for some equivocal purpose and gone chasing celestial salvation on the opposite side of the country; and of my brother, Stan, with his foolish, naive grin like a much smaller echo of my own great gullibility.

And I realize: the fool that I've been.

I'm a clinically disturbed fool with my juvenile head circling in the stars as always, a child of romance in this adult's awkward and ridiculous body, brother Stan proven right all these years in keeping his clumsy feet planted firmly on our basement floor. And I prepare to die, and then the explosive blow to the ridge of my nose and then blackness.

    Shimmering green.
    An emerald curtain stirring faintly in summer breeze. Brilliant light above and birdsong chattering and loud from somewhere.
    Then the birds' voices coalesce into a single strident chorus, in time with the shaking of the trees and falling branches all around me. The scrabbling sounds in the underbrush are squirrels and rabbits scurrying for shelter as their world quakes and trembles. Acorns rain down from the sky and pelt me hard on my arms and upturned face.
    Pain. It stirs me nearly completely into lucidity. I blink hard and strive to focus my vision. Details shimmer into view from the vague ephemeral shapes and colours all around me. I watch the scattering flocks of birds whipping like Frisbees through the trees near ground level for fear of the thunder ruining their sky. I see a snake twirl by near my foot, a whip fast on the move in the grass, and then it's disappeared in the foliage. I try to raise my head but the pressure in the centre of my face as I do so is as a blow to my skull, and so I let myself lie motionless. I touch my face gingerly with a hand, bring it away and look at the smear of red across my fingers. Blood. A shattered nose. The metallic soup in my mouth is blood pouring down from my broken nose. I spit and spit but swallow mouthfuls of it anyways. Its flow is too strong. The memory returns, of a pistol grip crashing into my face and then blackness, and now here I lie with stars in my eyes as usual.
    I think fleetingly of a sack filled with money, and what it had all meant, what it could have possibly meant to two girls like these. A ruse, a premeditated trick meant to make me perceive them in a different light, meant to crush my beliefs of romance in the stars? A final deception to ensure that the secret energy of flowers remains un-guessed among the gardeners and scientists of the world, because

my new beliefs should revolve around much more mundane scenarios of greedy human beings exploiting their naïve counterparts? I don't know. I only know the guilt in me, and the shame, and the sickening pounding-throbbing in my face and head and all through the confused world.

But I lie here with stars in my vision and watch the ship lift from the trees, and I know the truth about some things, as it trembles the earth and shakes the branches around me loose of acorns and squirrels. I watch it hover on the air a moment, I can make it out like a gigantic shadow through the dappled rooftop greenery, blotting out the summer sky of deepening dusk above me. How big is it exactly, does it erase everything above or is it a two-seater silver dart like some sleek robotic dragonfly? My senses reel, I can't be certain of anything. Is the humming in my ears and temples its heartbeat engine or my thoughts pouring out through my broken face and onto the forest floor? I watch the nebulous shape rest there and feel it shake me to pieces, and then it jumps away like a tick into the deep purple heavens and is gone as if it never floated like a god or nightmare above me at all.

I cry.

I cry in the mirror over the awful sight of my crooked nose. No girls anywhere will look at me now, now it's utterly hopeless and I hate loneliness, more weary of its tenacious presence than ever. My life was spared, but maybe a bullet in the face would have served me better than a pistol grip knocking me down while the forest shook all around me and salvation streaked away forever.

Mother and father visit me but Stan refuses. I'm a nutcase, a whackjob of the highest order. I tell them, and I've tried to tell Stan: I only ever stole in order to help someone. And myself, too, I admit it, but that was secondary. My concerns were foremost for two poor creatures stranded in a lonely, hostile place without friends. With only enemies all around.

I'd do it all over again, in the exact same fashion, in a heartbeat. I tell them that, too. And close my eyes to these drab white halls staffed with faceless uniforms of the same cold colour.

They let me keep flowers but I've been tending them poorly and they're inclined to wither and die within days. Unlike before, when flowers were made from magic. When their lifespan seemed potentially infinite. But I savour their perfume when I'm able, if I'm able to bear the terrible nostalgia their scent carries and will always carry for me. And I smile sometimes, when that awful nostalgia doesn't get the best of me, because I know a secret concerning certain of their species: the yellow sunflower sentries, the rows of virginal white blossoms like giant moths speared on plant stems. And the mysterious lilac. I know all about its mystery. I saw it solved and carry its beautiful secret in my heart.

Take me away, too, I whisper to my flowers.

Take me away, too, and the words are like a desperate prayer to their fragile bodies and haunting scent.

And when I water them – sometimes with salty drops fallen from my eyes, sometimes from the plastic dispenser I refill from the washroom tap – it's kind of like watering the stars, I like to think. Or at least the spaces between them. Or maybe it's only a tenuous connection at best, between their soft scent riding the air in my room, and the vastness of any given night sky.

But they wither, my flowers, as I've said, and they die. And I'm left alone, as always. A wilting man sagging through this difficult and unfair world.

And so I tremble and I cry and I'll tremble and cry very often from now on, I think. Most especially when the weather's like fire and the skies outside these caged windows wink down at me like unfulfilled promises.

Dreams of the Rocket-Boy

I told that girl, I told her twice, three times, a million times a night.

If there was a mile-high praying mantis praying to its space god out in the far quadrants, and if that big bug was towering over the lush hills and heading down into the valley where she lived and where she slept snug as a bed bug in the dead quiet night time, if that picture was moving in real time and not in fun-time reel-time, I told her this, the most important and biggest thing I've ever said to any girl:

I'd be there to intercept that rickety emerald walking stick skeleton, baby-girl, me in my silver underwear and goggles and laser pistol in fist and rocket pack upon my back and then look out, unholy insect beast, but you're in the deepest peril because you just do not pose a threat with your pincher-clamp-hands to *my* little sweetie-pie.

I told her that. I said it just like that. And I said: No need to worry a wavy-blonde hair on your perfect little head, darling, because that creature feature from Saturday matinees would be rushing back home with some cracked razor-edged forearms, if it could move at all that is. If my laser pistol didn't get him, well me in my rocket pack would spin circles into his million-faceted eyeballs and then it's a bunch of thermal detonators like a finger of bananas dropped right inside those champing jaws, and then check it out baby-pie: it's your champion of the galaxy riding high in your starry sky, it's me and I'm smiling and holding out my hand for you to take us both up into all that Wite-out-splashed night sky, with a broken bag of sharp green sticks all helter skelter and blending in with the green hills left behind us.

I told that cutie-pie these things, and I told her this: I said: Hey: you know what? And she said what? And I said, listen up starry beauty queen, but you're the sexiest little chickie in gold locks and knee socks that I ever saw. And you know what else is up, besides this here picture of stars and planets and comet-tails flashing like wispy cotton candy tufts across the big black? I said, this is what's up, sweetie: me in my space goggles and pilot's cap, hips criss-crossed with laser pistols in their bandoliers with extra extra extra packets of energy pellet ammunition, that's right. But check this out, too, let's see the other half of this perfect picture like an ancient Greek equation: yes indeed, there you are up there in all that shimmering-blinking frosty-time black, wrapped all around me like a good good vampire girl, and just so you know, yes indeed, you can drink from my neck anytime any night and we can sleep right through the morning and afternoon following, and live and love like two undead in love forever, yes indeed.

Wait! What's this? A super-sized radioactive lobster swimming in from the salty seas and there isn't nobody in this world going to salt and butter him for dinner? And what's this here: a mean-spirited, Earth-crashing host of man-size flies with smart minds and sharp claws for hands and green hellish slime from their spitting mouths all for us, all for us? Well, keep your faculties, beautiful girl, so beautiful that if you were a goddess in ancient Greece's mythos you'd be called Beautificus-Chickie-Dee, keep your wits about you because check me out: I'm wetting my lips and sharpening my cutlery because I dig digging in to some salty sea food and boy oh boy is this crab going home with a headache tonight. And these flies, well my super-sized cosmic swatter'll be painted good with gore, and genocide of the world of the flies sure was a messy but quick affair.

Because no one raises a hairy-sticky leg to my little girl, or a pinching pincer and I'm not mincing any words now am I, prospective invaders of our little lush valley? Don't you dare, because I just don't care, and you won't be wanting to make no angry boy out of me with my outer space arsenal and dedication to the great cause of keeping every silky-blonde hair neatly in place and smiles big in those big brown eyes.

I said these words to her and I made sure she heard, and

the drive-in movie was a grand couple hours of flickering bugs and soldiers in black and white and me and her all tangled up and hot in our cheeks in the back seat of my star cruiser love craft. I said the words like they were some sort of secret formula or spell and she was in love with me, and this little spheroid this little planetoid our home our valley town was safe and sound and secure and serene with us kissing the matinees away, and the long nights with no end in sight, them too. Them too.

    I hope it all works out tomorrow afternoon at the Thirtieth Annual Celestial Invaders Among Us Traveling Science Fiction Convention, because if I'm going to meet her and if it's going to work out my way, that Martian Queen with red sand-royalty flowing in her veins and the favourite past-time of sailing dusty red canals all through the wee hours, yes, that girl will be there surely, perfect and romantic and like a satellite signal for me only, and if I'm fast, and clever, and the luckiest man in the cosmos, just maybe I'll be cruising home with her beside me in my space love craft.

    And we'll head straight for the drive-in in my little green valley town, and we'll get there quick because when we travel, me and my girl, we'll be traveling at lightspeed.

"Who would I do this for? Hey, me or you."
– Glenn Danzig, from *Astro Zombies*

Love, Death, and Monsters at the Drive-In

The movie was *The Moon Creatures Attack!* and the boy and girl were Johnny D. and Monica, respectively. The drive-in was a landmark in their modest little town, and it held memories dating back countless summer nights like this. Perhaps it's always been here, Monica's father, who was very romantic at heart, would often say to her with that familiar distant look in his eyes. Perhaps it was here before us, all of us, before people and their less wonderful inventions like the automobile and cigarettes and other stinky gadgets, revelling in the fiery grandeur of a billion sunsets, basking beneath the winking of how many star-speckled nights time could no longer recall.

Monica loved her father, but thought he was a little bit funny sometimes. A little bit funny with his dreamy dreams.

"Listen to the crickets, Johnny," sighed Monica, nuzzling her petite chin against the leather of her lover's jacket. It made that creaking, rubbing sound she'd grown to love so, that now made her think of only bliss and star shine and love in seats of cars that sat parked before flashing movie screens on toasty warm July evenings. Daddy's little girl, she thought with a frown on her face, but only a tiny one.

"Yeah, sweets," murmured Johnny D. with uncalculated ease, so cool and reposed, the picture of composure. "Them buggers is always makin' a racket, but it's a good sorta' racket, huh?"

"Mmmm," Monica purred, feeling like a kitten, gliding her hands across Johnny D.'s firm chest. Nights like these were endless, and just so fantastic. She cast starry eyes up through the T-Bird's immaculately shined windshield to the giant pictures moving over the colossal screen towering above them.

The hero of the film, played by a strikingly handsome actor whose name Monica couldn't recall, had only just learned of the hideous Moon Creatures and their malevolent scheme to ruin his grand apple pie American world. A close-up cast his brows, gigantic, to wrinkle in brooding intensity above the assembly of motionless vehicles in the lot beneath.

He'll stop them, Monica reflected. With that oiled wave of gorgeous blonde hair, and that strong square of a chin, set so determinedly, there's nothing he can't stop, probably.

Casting her gaze down to her hands, which gently clasped Johnny D.'s larger, more capable hands, she felt the corners of her lips curling up into a content smile. That oafish blonde hero up there on-screen, handsome though he was, strong and self-reliant, too, was not the equal of her real star in the sky: Johnny D. That man moving overhead, stringing together a desperate plan to vanquish the invaders, he was only a picture star. But Johnny D....

Johnny D. He'd stop them, alright. There was nothing that he couldn't stop from harming his girl. Nothing in the big-big-and-endless-as-her-father-would-put-it universe.

"Johnny?", sweet as candy.

"What is it, sweetsies?"

"What if Moon Creatures landed here tonight, right in the middle of the drive-in, over by that baby blue clunker?"

Johnny D. smiled handsomely. His lips moved, like his lean hips, lithely, and with a curled, sidewise grin he said, "They'd be dead meat, sweetsies. Totally dead Moon-meat." He clenched his girl's hand a little tighter as he said it.

Monica giggled. "And then, we'd get sodas?"

Johnny D. nodded easily. Yeah, they'd get sodas.

"And we'd sip 'em?"

"Oh yeah."

"With maybe a cigarette between us." Because she wasn't *all* daddy's girl.

"Oh, oh yeah."

Monica basked in the comfortable silence between them, snug in her Johnny D.'s arms, the leather of his jacket and of the seats beneath them more soothing than the most comforter-layered and fluffed of beds her mother had ever made up for her. She felt relaxed and sleepy-drowsy, and more than a little pretty in her new sky-blue Poodle skirt. She kicked off her saddle shoes, then peeled off first one and then the other of her bobby socks and curled her toes in the evening air. "And then?"

Johnny D.'s eyes remained closed as Monica scrutinized him. He looked so serene, completely at peace, her tough, rawhide-clad, fist-wielding drive-in champion, concealing a heart carved of tender scarlet Valentine love; youthful face topped by a slick shock of black jet, so deep the colour, like certain evening skies, so filled with promise.

Monica smiled at her dreamy thoughts, she was always making poems in her head about her Johnny D. Daddy's girl, she thought, not at all scolding herself. Because she liked thinking in poems and in other dreamy ways.

"And then, then we'd go cruisin'."

"Mmmm…" and Monica wasn't worrying anymore at all about Moon Creatures and their wicked implements of war; only drifting wonderfully away atop a summer cloud lined with race car flames, smelling of comfortable leather, and full of security, and promise, and unknown magic.

The screen hero loomed over them, wearing a face of great sorrow as he listened to the leader of the Moon Creatures and learned the aliens' sad history. Their planet dying, they'd had no choice but to strike out into the unknown and make a new home on any hospitable world they discovered. They'd spent one hundred years living inside the craters and canals of the Earth's moon, but their scarce resources grew insufficient and the lush green and blue world beyond which they orbited beckoned. Thinking of their families, and of survival, they'd done what they had to.

The Moon Creature's leader, a tall pale humanoid with black eyes and a cluster of tentacles like a grotesque flower bouquet sprouting from the lower portion of his face, raised his laser ray gun menacingly in a four-fingered hand. The screen hero tensed, his heroine cried out, and the Moon Creature's leader proclaimed himself the new ruler of the Earth as his finger closed on the weapon's trigger.

Monica felt herself relax, despite the terrifying film climax unravelling on-screen, the kind of scene which always sent tremors along her spine and made the small hairs on her arms stand up. Except, of course, when her Johnny D. was close at hand, touching her, as he was then. Let them come, she thought with tranquil boldness, as her lover turned to her with a creaking of car seat leather, his large blue eyes staring deeply into her own. Bring them on.

Bring them all on.

Johnny D. leaned in close, touching his lips to hers. They kissed and they kissed, running their hands across one another, and through each other's hair. Monica felt buoyant, felt herself lifted up by her darling's strong kisses. She felt dizzy and sleepy and yet very alive, too. She felt just right. She felt just right with the moonlight colouring everything all silver and frosty. She felt good and safe and tingly in her fingers and toes. She felt luxurious as she moaned little moans and felt her Johnny D.'s kisses peppering her neck and collarbone.

Mmmm, like a kitten falling into dreams, mmmm....

He, my darling, is a mandrill.

Her father was the smartest man in the world, a secret scientist when her mother wasn't looking, predicting the course of events in evening skies and future days on Earth. He also knew his animals, all their exotic names and the far-away places they came from. She loved his big textbook words, and his big romantic heart, silly old boy that he was.

I like his beard, little Monica said. *It's so white and bright compared to his fur. And his bum is so bright, too! And his tail, it's so stubby!* But she stopped her giggling and added, in a small whimper, *He's the saddest monkey in the world.*

She saw this in the animal's dejected posture among the tall grass spikes, the half-hearted way it picked at its brown-furred body. But mostly Monica saw the mandrill's huge sadness in its eyes, watching the sky forlornly, except the sky was scratched out everywhere by the zoo's steel mesh fence. Poor moping mandrill, who couldn't escape his little caged nook and search for some trees good for climbing.

Monica's father used his professor-voice to tell her about the creature's unhappy eyes. *Every thing that lives with a heart beating inside of it feels some kind of love for its home, darling. It's what binds the structure of the big universe in place, my darling, into its funny order rather than its brother chaos, who is so different. A sense of place, and home. If you take a handsome mandrill like our friend here from his native African forests and plop him down in the middle of all this concrete and fences and people gawking at him all day every day, well, then you'll find a very unhappy mandrill.*

Monica felt hollow watching the animal, and said, *He misses his family, I bet. Maybe he has brothers and sisters.* She thought that she might have the picture of the trapped monkey embedded across her eyes forever and ever.

Brothers and sisters are often just like home, too, Monica. And beautiful daughters, especially. With a small squeeze to her elbow which made her smile despite her blue mood. Her father could always make her feel better, no matter how blue and sour her thoughts.

Monica sensed her father turn to her, the purpling dusk sky settling everywhere behind and above him. *But I agree with you, my darling girl: his beard is very impressive. Regal and kingly. He's only longing for his lost empire. A true king, even with his stumpy tail and colourful bum.*

Little Monica liked her father's funny words like poetry, and turned to him and asked, *Will he ever be a king again, do you think?*

Oh, I know it, my dear. I absolutely know it.

They left the unhappy mandrill watching his scrap of sky, and went in search of the soda fountain. When they couldn't find it, Monica's father suggested they try first one way and then another. After several more minutes of fruitless wandering along several different zoo trails, he threw his hands into the air and cried exaggeratedly, *I thought for certain that this was the right path! Shows how much I know.*

Everything, Monica thought to herself. *You know*

everything in the whole big universe.

Monica heard her father's laughter, low and rumbling, like distant thunder in the night, and they'd found the soda fountain. But she would have been just as happy to have kept wandering through the zoo grounds, because they'd been holding hands all the while. And she felt very much at home.

And in the drive-in, curled in her lover's embrace, Monica smiled in her sleep.

Her swim up out of dream country was fast and sudden and jarring. And the world was no longer a tranquil place.

"Monica!!! Oh god, Monica!! Sweetie! Oh, Monica!"

"Johnny, oh my god Johnny!!! What's happening?!!? Oh god!!!"

ZZZZZZZZZZZZZZZZZZZZZZZZZZZZZ-BBBZZZZZZZZZZZZ!!!!

"What is it, Johnny??!!"

Z Z Z Z Z Z Z Z Z Z Z Z Z Z Z Z Z Z Z Z Z Z Z - BOOOOOOOOOOOOOOOOOOOM!!!!

"Monica – Stay down! Keep your head covered!"

"What, Johnny??! Johnny???!!!!" The smell of burning meat was in her nostrils.

"I don't know, baby! Just keep down while I get us out of here! Can you do that for me?!"

ZZZZZZZZZZZZ-BA-BOOOOOOOOOOOOM!!!!

Monica couldn't hear her own voice over the incredible din. "Yes, Johnny! Yes!"

"AAAAARRRGGGHHH!!!!"

Screams all about them, of people in pain, and confusion and terror.

Johnny revved the reliable T-Bird's engine, adding minutely to the chaos of light-flashes, smoke plumes, explosions, and terrified screaming. Monica stared upwards from her position sprawled against the car seat, and saw indistinct, enormous somethings hovering overhead, dark shapes whizzing quickly through the noisy air. She followed their fleet flights, catching sight of their sleek, curved bodies and dark shiny skins, and she screamed shrilly. The organic shapes of the flying objects brought to mind gigantic metallic insects, along with the strange protrusions and sharp leg-like appendages hanging downwards from their bellies. She was frightened of all creepy-crawly things, even the common household ones, and a tremor of terror coursed through her as she stared into the swarming sky.

It was from these enormous soaring things that death was raining, as sharply defined lines of white light fell from their black bellies and burned the night away, leaving cars in flames and their passengers burning and screaming. Monica watched petrified as a hailstorm of debris cascaded from the sky and fell crashing against the T-Bird's hood: pieces of metal, clods of dirt, the blackened remains of a boy or girl which fairly exploded into ashen fragments upon impact. The interior of the car was suddenly blacker. Something flashed past the vehicle, it took a moment of peering through the dusty windshield to realize it was a person on fire. Monica screamed again, thinking of her father, wishing him away to safe places.

"Oh, Johnny! What are they?!" She was thrown roughly to one side of the car as Johnny D. swung them around wildly, narrowly avoiding a thick plume of fire which suddenly flared up in the gravel road before them.

"Airplanes, honey!" he roared into the ruckus. "Some kind of weird airplanes or somethin'!"

He floored the T-Bird and sent them bumping along the winding road which led away from the drive-in grounds. They jostled about in their seats, and plunged up and down roughly where pot-holes came too fast to be avoided in time. Soon, they found the open county road, and the tumult of sizzling and screaming and explosions fell away behind them. Trees flew past them on either side and, casting a quick glance behind, Monica saw a great glow burning the horizon of trees. She watched as if entranced, until the sudden flaring of light, like a gigantic fireworks display. And she knew that the drive-in movie screen was burning to the ground, concluding its million-year run.

She turned away from the sight and wept, letting her huge fear overcome her.

They drove in silence for a time, until Johnny flicked the radio on and Bobby Darrin sang to them as they sped through the moon-lit country. So sweet of him, Monica thought, always playing the radio for her because he knew how much she liked love songs.

Johnny D.'s voice bellowed over the roaring of the engine and music. "You're my girl, Monica! You know that, huh sweetie?! I'm here, sweetie, so don't you worry! I'll get us away from this mess! I'll fix those flying creeps real good! You're my girl, sweets! Okay?!"

Monica didn't answer, only held on dearly to him. And that was all she needed to do.

That's how Johnny D. and Monica, in love, fled the strangely perfect arrival of the virtuous and sad Moon Creatures, and the terror and death-rays and bloodshed they brought with them; in a billowing red cloud of county road dust, inside a careening, leather-seated T-Bird that they both hoped would carry them far, far away, to a place of safety and sanity, where their kisses would awaken each other every morning. Despite the fire and ashes putting out the sun. Despite gigantic steel insects buzzing through the summer skies and crawling all over their world. Despite the sizzling death raining down from above, ruining the dreamy look of the stars and moonlight, and the romance which they once held in their frosty shimmerings.

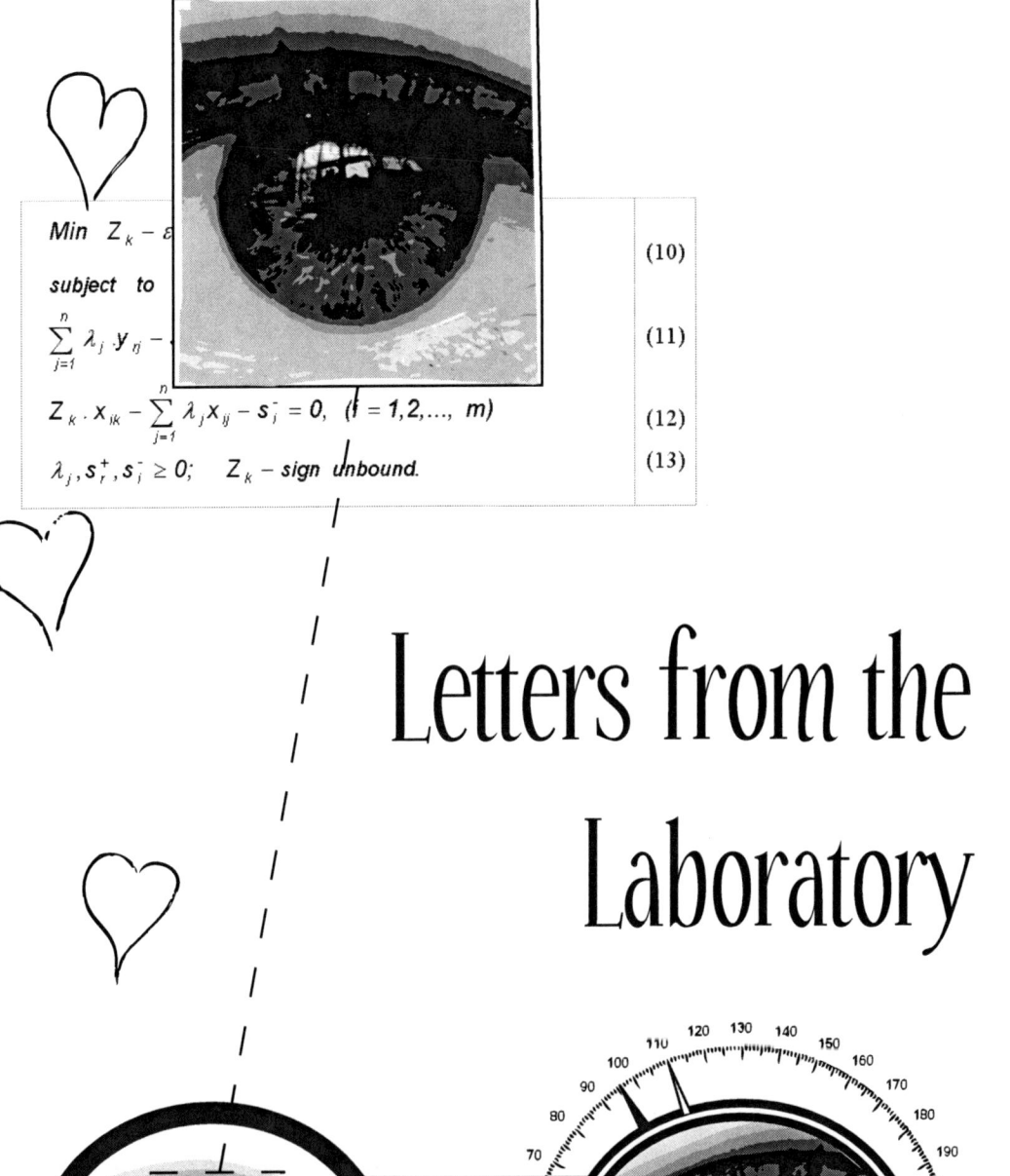

$$\text{Min } Z_k - \varepsilon$$
(10)

subject to

$$\sum_{j=1}^{n} \lambda_j \, y_{rj} - \ldots$$
(11)

$$Z_k \cdot x_{ik} - \sum_{j=1}^{n} \lambda_j x_{ij} - s_i^- = 0, \quad (i = 1, 2, \ldots, m)$$
(12)

$$\lambda_j, s_r^+, s_i^- \geq 0; \quad Z_k - \text{sign unbound.}$$
(13)

Letters from the Laboratory

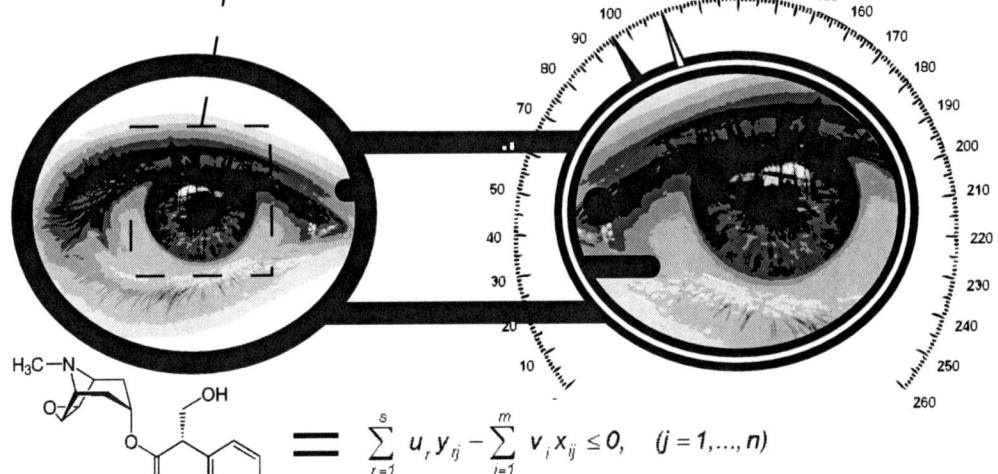

$$= \sum_{r=1}^{s} u_r y_{rj} - \sum_{i=1}^{m} v_i x_{ij} \leq 0, \quad (j = 1, \ldots, n)$$

I never knew the man who wrote these letters which are really entries in a diary, and I guess I'm sad about this. I just came across them by chance here in this school laboratory where they were conceived.

I can only guess why he left the papers behind, but I won't take that liberty because wherever he is now, it seems to me that he deserves more than that. I guess what I mean is that after reading these words, I realized something: he was full of truth, this mystery journal keeper, and these letters are full of him. Whoever he was. Whoever he is today.

Maybe I'm wrong in feeling envious of this man who I've never met. But then I've always thought of myself as unlike most people, in most ways. I guess that's why coming across these letters was such an amazing find. Like finding treasure by chance in a school lab. Like notes from a perfect pen pal for me, and I guess the sad part is that I'll never meet him and be able to tell him how much all of this means to me. I don't know. I'm only leaving these appended thoughts with his letters in the hope that whoever comes across them in the days ahead will feel a little bit of what I felt when I first read them, and maybe be as touched as I've been, and also that they might realize this: they're not alone in their loneliness. Which these very letters prove, chronicling a very remarkable narrative, and a very remarkable man, who struggled for us all.

I'll never forget these words and what they mean.

My eyes see much clearer now, and I'm very grateful.

Best wishes.

Anonymous & Lonely

The Andromeda[1] Letters

Letter 1:

I must write these letters, so here I begin. Everything begins some place, from some spark or infinitesimal glimmer of life. So, bending to the compulsion to set this continuing chronicle down, I start here.

My watch tells me it is now quarter of three in the morning. What a time, bottomless with potential. And what a place, up here in 1120: laboratory, home[2], haven[3]. It is dark, but for my small lamp, which makes my little work space warm and yellow. Outside, it is very terrible. Inclement to a violent degree. I can hear the wind screaming, and the thunder tolling as if seeking to summon me forth into the bedlam of lashing rain, but I am not leaving just yet, so I have little to fear from this fierce weather. I yet have a great deal of work ahead of me here tonight.

It is odd - everyone wonders what it is that I am building here in 1120. Professors, students, mice white as doves with their curious red eyes watching me through walls of bars. I am usually relatively reticent in providing answers for them, which invariably leads to some interesting postulates from these curious acquaintances. Some have put forth the notion that I am building a device of some kind, a new technology I am afraid to disclose for one reason or another; others more specifically, and curiously, believe that this invention might be somehow malefic in design (a 'killer robot', as one wiseacre and macabre-minded individual suggested, a student of the sort beloved among peers for his constant classroom diversions and likewise destined for academic failure); and one other, a colleague of

---

1 M31, or Messier 1, or the Great Andromeda Nebula, or the Andromeda Galaxy; spiral galaxy located in the Andromeda constellation, and one of the most distant objects visible to the naked eye; the eternal girl of my everlasting boyhood dreams.
2 A place of origin.
3 A place of refuge; home.

old, strangest of all, who believes that I am building a friend. This fellow even went so far as to offer his advice: 'Stop now, you'll create a monster!'

A monster.

Fools, and their trifling, idiot theories.

The soft, white-furred mice, they are different. They keep silent, only wonder with crimson eyes at the work of my hands beneath lamp light.

Calculating and mixing new portion distributions. Heating the resultant solution. Cooling and sculpting the solid state form into micro-thin leaves, concave and convex. Shaving off the excess liquid residue of scopolamine[4]. Applying leaves within lenses, meticulous and painstaking labour with laser. Fitting lenses inside cylinders. Tinkering with the focus, uncertain at best. Cursing under my breath at the unsatisfactory results.

Donning my latest model and scanning through windows and where I wander along frosty campus lawns and sidewalks. Peering into the faces of passers-by, glimpsing minutiae of emotion watching me in return, most often a tremor of unease or annoyance at my intimate perusal, occasionally the suggestion of fear in their eyes. The results mixed, closer to improvement than in past weeks and months, yet true success nowhere to be seen.

Rubbing at my eyes awash with strain and fatigue, seeing the world around me in distorted ghost-image long after concluding my experiments for the evening; everything microscopically finite and threatening. Finding solace only in my mice and their reliable red gazes. And of course in the presence of my steadfast companion, my lamp, lighting my journey each endless and hopeful night.

---

4 Drug, ophthalmic usage to induce mydriasis (pupillary dilation) and cycloplegia (paralysis of eye-focusing muscle); flying ointment, expeditionary usage to traverse/navigate great distances/geographic obstructions.

Dreams:

It is not strictly a dream of course, as the scene revisits me during all hours of the day as well, during varying degrees of semi-sleep and deep slumbers both. Again during the late afternoon hours today, the old haunting memory consuming me while I drifted and forgot time in the middle of another day; while teaching my fourth year students with eyes more inquisitive and eager than their younger counterparts. Their hungry look of intellect devouring my words and their meanings, following the dancing chalk nub in my fingers as I progressed rapidly through today's formulae and theorems, leaving blackboard squeakings and chalk dust in my wake.

Only the old scene replaying itself loop-like behind my fluttering eyelids. My R.E.M. sleep-haunting companion of over three long decades. A brief snippet of remembered silent communication: the way he had looked at me, his regular debasing appraisal on a long-distant late after-school afternoon which I needed desperately to remain un-ruined. The clear focus of unwarranted malice in his stare, the senselessly hateful fire examining my clumsy steps, waiting to relish my usual discomfiture and awkwardness. My weakness as a thin boy like some hastily patched-together doll of straw for him to easily topple as he always did and feel perversely proud in the defeat.

Finding the portal[5] in his stare. Understanding once again the hopeless place to which it led. Glimpsing the real person through his black pupils like holes into his soul. Beyond my revulsion at him, the seething fury with which I gazed upon him, returned the logic of my hypothesis. The cool touch of the scalpel in my fingers where I gripped it inside my jacket pocket, like a test procedure set to determine the future course of my life.

---

5 A doorway or entrance, esp. one that is large and/or impressive; Lorentzian traversable wormhole, allowing travel from one mouth to opposite mouth; as antithesis of portal type described above: that thing for which I've searched my life entire.

And then today's group of fourth year students, looking sacrificial in their virgin white lab coats, wearing yet more grave expressions as they watched their unreliable professor return from yet another daydream journey right before their eyes.

Letter 4: Importance

I am in need of a thousand-year respite because she makes me so, so, so deliciously tired. She is also my impetus for doing all of this. The reason that I pursue every avenue that I do, pushing onwards despite perpetual experimental failure. Because she is my proof, and validity of my ventures: there is something perfect[6] for all of us, if only we are fortunate enough or destined to find it.
Monster. Fools, fools.
The day we collided changed weather patterns for all time to come in this microcosm that is my existence. It was a world of ice and wind outdoors, and the first true beginnings of belated warmth for me.

Venus Loving Psyche:[7]

It was the first of October, what feels like a million years ago. I had been walking aimlessly for quite some time, wracking my brain for some new idea or approach by which to circumvent the old obstacles[8]. Something to send the skeletal framework light years forward, as it were, an illuminating source by which to work unhindered. As was common during this fairly unproductive period, such breakthroughs had not been coming. My repeated failure to find a means by which to successfully merge the scopolamine and thiopental sodium[9] into a solid substance of suitably malleable

---

6 As in 'perfection': a portal, again; that thing for which I've searched my life entire.
7 Venus, only begrudgingly, forgave and loved Psyche; as the envious world cannot help but relent and love a creature descended from infinitely better places afar.
8 My nemesis, shape-shifter of countless forms.
9 Truth-key; barbiturates which decrease higher cortical brain functioning, thus suppressing the "complex" act of lying.

texture had been keeping sleep at bay for days. It seemed that only the limitations of technology inhibited me, while my mind spun on in its endless cycle of offering new and untried - and un-attemptable - experiments.

    The night air was chill, and Halloween could be heard in the crackling of naked tree branches overhead, like wicked laughter goading me on to some brash mistake. The season could be felt on the skin, the beginnings of a time of dying. I felt it acutely, on my cheeks burning with cold, and my trembling hands buried futilely in my coat pockets. The chill had begun its persistent seasonal nipping, hungry, though not yet completely voracious. I wandered across the campus lawn, beneath the lampposts' orange light, my shoes shuffling through seas of crisping brown foliage.

    Oh! I remember my dismal mood as I followed alongside the meandering concrete paths twisting through the heart of the university grounds. Sounds of revelry drifted to me as I trudged past the school pub. I remember thinking: There. They've found it. Whatever it is. It lives in their voices, boisterous and free. While I wander the shadows like a fool in dreams, lost in circular thoughts, moving fruitlessly around and about in a cerebral cul-de-sac, ironically alone as ever in my walkings.

    I had been working in 1120 for several months by this point, with little to show for my long, long, long hours. I doubt anyone resents me more than my loyal little lamp there in the lab, whose energy I use with neither respite nor apology.

    But I was desperate, and forsook sleep in place of toiling at my work table. I am still desperate, more now than ever before, of course. There had been times up there in 1120 when I had come close to something. So very close that I felt a great chill of anticipation snaking all down my arms and legs, and I no longer required the aid of caffeine and nicotine and my nervous habit of cracking individual finger joints to maintain my alertness. I was in every corner of 1120 at once it seemed, calculating formulae, re-calculating them to make certain, fiddling here, fastening there, crying softly into the collar of my lab coat in frustration or anxiety or hopefulness and sometimes all three emotions simultaneously, and grinding my teeth in fixed concentration through it all.

But always, events wound their way to the old, familiar conclusion: nothing. Every new path the same, epiphanies barely glimpsed in my work before me but mostly only felt, invisible tauntings leading always to naught. And the intermittent interludes in the abortive wall of monotony, when the cluttered world in my head appeared lined with the optimism of yet-untried formulae and procedures, those radical ideas like tall trees bearing abundance of fruit, these too wound their ways invariably to nothing.

These wrinkled thoughts occupied me that night, and it was approximately thirty minutes or so into my distracted evening wandering that I turned the corner of the Science Building and collided softly with that which I had nearly resigned myself to believe I would never find.

A chance[10] encounter. A gift of luck[11] in the midst of my darkest time.

She was the answer. She was right there. She was simple and elegant in her black coat that looked so warm to me. And her breath puffed from her startled mouth onto the air because it was that cold, a wasteland inhabited in that moment by her and I and no other. Stunned, she laughed to herself, showing me a mouth full of shining perfect teeth. It was this smile which held me. I did not require the aid of my latest model to see the inherent nature of her expression: sincere and involuntary, the unmistakable contraction of the zygomatic major and inferior area of the orbicularis oculi.[12] This, and some other indefinable aspect which I had never before encountered, except in dreams. And, thus smiling, she offered apology for bumping into me. An *apology*! The irony urged a smile from me, as well, huge and foolish, and with more determination than I can possibly convey in my writing here, I made as if I was not facing something very possibly fallen from Andromeda herself. With what I thought to be great composure, I offered my own flustered apology.

Then we spoke, and time stopped[13], and our deceptively simple but physics-altering conversation went something a little like

---

10 The unexpected ~~or random~~ element of existence.
11 The ~~random~~ fated occurrence of good ~~or adverse~~ fortune.
12 In opposition to the insincere and voluntary contraction of *zygomatic major* alone, or, Pan American smile.
13 Anomalous event; death/rebirth in the span of seconds in direct reaction to collision between seemingly identical elements.

this:

She said: "It's just so cold, I had my face buried in my coat and scarf, and I didn't even see you coming."

And I said: "I've just been wandering out here for so long and I haven't seen anybody, and so I suppose I just didn't think to be...careful?"

And she said, with a little laughter in her wavering voice: "Yeah. Um, anyways, sorry again. Have a nice walk."

And because I sensed that she sensed the cessation of time, too, I said: "Where are you headed?"

And she said: "I work at the radio station. I've got a show in fifteen minutes. I kind of have to run."

Then I said: "May I come?"

And she paused, for only a second, but when time stops in the rest of the world around you as it had then, you really can feel the lifetime of a single second. And then she said: "Yes, you can."

And because I was not yet willing to set the world in motion, I added: "Where are you from?"[14]

And she said: "You mean, where do I live?" There was a little tremor in her voice which I was certain came not from the chill air.

And I said again: "Where are you from?" And I waited, and I hoped so much, and I recall thinking how I could bear disappointment no longer. That something had to change in the world for me. It simply had to.

And she smiled, and shrugged, but provided no answer.

I exhaled, and my lips quivered as eventually I regained enough composure to tell her triumphantly: "I don't know about myself either." And I began to walk, and she to follow, even though she was really leading us, to her warm little radio booth and her selection of soothing nocturnal sounds. I took her by her elbow, and told her: "Wait. I have to stop by the lab upstairs and lock up. I won't be long at all."

I slipped through the infrequently used side entrance of the building, climbed the darkened staircase up and up to the

---

14 Origin; derivation (determined even at this early stage to be of an extraordinary nature, as evinced by the anomalous event noted above).

third floor; I wished a good night to my lamp, putting him to bed in sudden darkness to the chorus of nervous mice, and locked the door behind me. I remember feeling strange as I descended the gloomily-lit staircase and left the building, and very excitedly nervous, as if I stood at the edge[15] of something very vast, looking into blackness.

Outside, our conversation resumed.

She said: "So, what are you working on up there?"

"It doesn't really matter tonight," I told her, and I no longer noticed the nip of the wind on my upturned face as together we went into the night.

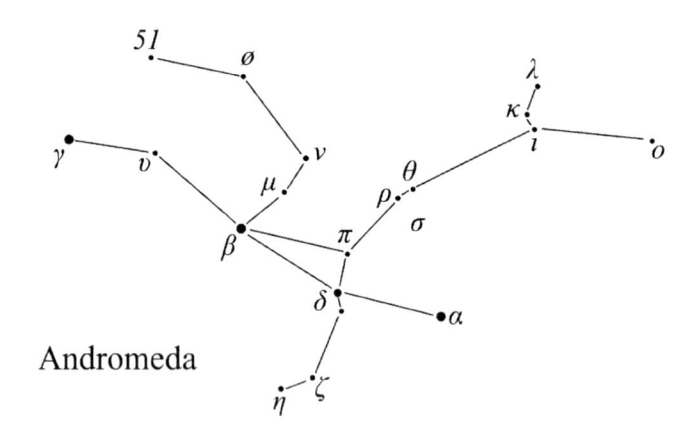

---

[15] Point at which one place/experience ends, and another begins.

Letter 5: Hope

The next morning woke to find me hurrying about 1120, checking this, adjusting that, and feeling oddly perplexed. My confusion, it soon dawned on me, grew from the uncharacteristic way with which I was greeting this new day.

The previous evening had been marvellous. The Andromeda creature's name, I learned, was Lucy Darla[16], and she and I had spent the entire morning in the campus radio station's cramped broadcast[17] room, speaking in low voices. She had intermittently paused in order to announce something into the microphone before her, but for the greater duration of our time together, the device remained shut off.

We talked, we talked.

When we had collided outside of the Science Building, I had been struck by Lucy's beauty, but sitting across from her in the dimly illuminated broadcast booth, it grew all the more. The electric glow of orange and green radio band light playing over her soft mellow features: I was held by the picture. And my words came. And it was not simply the perfect aesthetic of very large and round eyes ideal for midnight swimmings; nor the fact that the tip of her stunning head ended in exactly the most ideal place in space; nor even that I could imagine fairy tale scenes unfolding in the thick black of curls that was her hair. Beyond these striking facets of her, culled from my most delirious adolescent's daydreamings, lied another, much more wondrous element.

It was her mind.

She opened it up to me, easily, and with great assurance. And I was left aghast. It was all I could do to keep from rushing into the wintry world outside and crying like a romantic in a paroxysm of

---

16 Portal and new country both; the unattainable found if not yet wholly attained.

17 I'd been receiving her transmissions as far back as I can recall; their potency then created a new microcosm, hermetically sealed; a fortress to withstand the gathered nemeses of my existence.

joy to the sky: "I've found it! At last, and what a discovery it is!"

I saw the paradox clearly then. I could neither budge a finger on my hand nor raise my voice above its low whisper. I could not shout out to the world the greatest discovery ever to have been made by this dabbler in scientific pursuits. I knew with certainty only that something had opened up before me. And it had continued to open up to me, as I sat pleasantly helpless and staring, dumbfounded, all last night through.

And this opening thing was Lucy.

Rooted in place, like a tree undeserving of the light shining upon it, the realization slowly crept over me. Not in great epiphany, but in slow, incremental awakening knowledge within me. It crept so slowly that when I perceived the thought it seemed very much as if I was remembering something long forgotten.[18]

She was the ingredient.

She, the one I could project ahead in my mind, and see in three days, in three years, in a thousand centuries, as pristine as ever. Perhaps strolling through summer gardens at my side, plucking plump fruits from overhanging vines and drinking their waters in a life far removed from any I have known, or perhaps nestled perfectly against my arm in a bed I have yet to lie down in.

She, my happiness[19] ingredient.

The reason for my being so stricken with this revelation, of course, became apparent to me.

It was the trust she put into me, there in the orange glow of the broadcast room, as her opened mind easily, politely, charmingly, sweetly invited me inside her. Her eyes were clear and gentle, and through them I spied her deep parts, as though she was offering them for me to examine the way people tend never to do. It has been often said, and perhaps more often romanticized, that the eyes represent the window to one's soul. The pupil the black hole through which light passes onwards to the retina, enabling us to see and be seen. I detected no suggestion of concealed emotion or thought in her wide-

---

18 I'd interred the corpse of my dreams in a grave; and then: Rebirth, and climbing upwards through the earth and worms.
19 Essence of my search fulfilled, as well as the model from which my work may unfold.

open appraisal of me. No deceptions or subtleties of hidden motives lurked there. I required no man-made means to decipher her, to pick apart her seeming perfection and analyze its purity. I have been a loyal disciple and student of Ekman and Friesen's Facial Action Coding System[20] for many years, steeping myself in studies dealing with the microexpressions biologically inherent in human beings; and no transient flicker nor attempted concealment did I glimpse in Lucy's serene features the entire evening through, and an expert in such areas I surely am.

I considered asking her to send a signal[21] home for us both from her broadcast booth, and request a ray of light from another solar system to beam us from our winter place and into bright light. But this was too much to ask of her. We had only just met.

As if through a dream-like haze I remember walking Lucy to her apartment, only three blocks west of the radio station, bidding her a good morning and wishing her pleasant dreams, and not expecting good fortune to shine on me still. I did not dare to hope that she would ask to see me some other time, for dinner and more boundless conversation.

When she did, my pulse quickened; the romantic youth of old seized control of my smiling lips; I sputtered 'of course'; and I do not remember anything of my walk back to 1120.

---

20 (FACS): system to taxonomize human facial expressions, originally developed by Paul Ekman and Wallace Friesen in 1976; represents the common standard to systematically categorize physical expression of emotions. Using FACS, human coders can manually code nearly any anatomically possible facial expression, decomposing it into specific action units (AUs) and their temporal segments that produced the expression.
21 Confirmation of mission's completion.

The Gorgon's Ugly Hair Between Us

By ~~***** ****** ******~~ (Age: 12)

My dearest ~~**** **~~,

You, beautiful as Andromeda...
I would swim like Perseus to you on your
   rock
And vanquish Cetus with my knife
I would bring the Jaffa rock away
And choke Poseidon with it
For sending his big fish your way

And if the Gorgon stood between us
I would close my eyes and with my sword
Walk to her bravely
And I would strike! And strike again! And
   strike again and again!
Until her ugly head of snakes hissed no
   more
And no more venom spit my way

And I would turn to stone the world
If it dared to try and take you away
From me, my love
Making my every day the most perfect day
You, beautiful as Andromeda in the
   North...

—Even then, the precocious romantic struggled forth from my awkward boy's frame in search of the goddess' eternal perfection... If the child had only known of the good fortune awaiting him after the trial of those hard years, a wealth beyond his most fevered dreams...

Letter 6: Breakthrough Collisions

It seems only apposite, after all, that a new glimmer of hope became illuminated following my chance encounter with her.

Another handful of A.M. hours given up to the tediousness of failed tinkering with the solution. Then the scopolamine/thiopental sodium synthesis[22] cycle completed yet again, although yielding this time a startling revelation. Upon cooling, the thin leaf flexible in the bottom of the Petri dish, its ends curling upwards visibly before my eyes in the wake of its steaming transformation. The slice of hybrid solidity suddenly malleable between my fingers as it never was before.

The mice squeaked and scampered excitedly, rattling their tinny prisons, sensing the breakthrough significance of the moment.

Success, and a step forward for us all.

---

22 Process which combines two or more pre-existing elements resulting in the formation of something new – Oh, the parallel paths we sometimes tread with our labours/our loves!

Letter 8: Dinner, Do Not End

Dinner had been unbelievable. Lucy had been more than that. Both seemed to have gone on infinitely, and I am so happy about that.

Time moves differently today.[23]

Broken Hands

The tyrant lies beaten
Awed by the might of two
unable to fathom another pair of fleas
wielding everlasting life

They chuckle at his confusion
together as one as they are
surrounded by dead chronometry,
tearing watches like shackles from their wrists
while quiet clocks like pendants
hang from around their necks
as a reminder of where and what and when
they've left behind...

---

23 In the wake of Death/Rebirth event: a new era. Former temporal laws are skewed.

Dreams Again

Her eyes have followed me into my dreams.
There is the old scene, now replete with a new conclusion.
The ground about the boy as red as his face, the dripping orbs like giant oysters in my trembling hands as I stand over him.
Then, the unexpected turn in the old story:
Irises like oceans shot with hazel-almond shores. Pupils like inviting portals to wondrous places perforating these watery geographies, leading into her deepest parts.
Lucy-eyes, and a doorway into a realm of joy.
A beautiful vision sweeping the skyline of my dream, catching and holding me day-dreaming my time away, leaving my work untouched, the sixtieth prototype failed and useless on my work table before me like all of its predecessors. And me waking into lamp glow slowly, luxuriously, revelling in the refreshing feeling of a restful snatch of slumber, only to drift off again not too soon thereafter and repeat the entire vision once more.
Only the final, and very fleeting, sliver of that succeeding dream-vision unsavoury. Jerking me from semi-slumber and into agitated wakefulness, haunting me through the remainder of my laboratory hours and succeeding only in inhibiting progress.
That final fleeting scene, showing my hands deftly plucking my darling's eyes from their perfectly-formed sockets in a riot of blood

and vein. My hands moving quickly and slipping the eyes inside my mouth, one after the other in quick succession like a pair of blood-soaked olives. Devouring them, voraciously, to the most awful of accompanying cacophony: my Lucy's anguished screams crackling my eardrums and jarring me wide awake and frightened in my tense laboratory station, and sending a beaker toppling from the table and crashing into shards on the tiles.

My violent reemergence into wakefulness frightening the red-eyed mice who rattled their plastic wheels and tinny cage-bars. The yellow-orange glow of lamplight soothed me, though, as ever, and eventually I retraced my train of thought and fiddled once again with the lenses in my hands.

Letter 12: Obstacles Again

The application of scopolamine/thiopental sodium leaves has resulted in highly unreliable micro-recordings. Blurred images and a frustrating lack of focus, with resultant severe eye fatigue and recurring headaches. I am plagued with fevers and nausea, and a queer stench of death – as of rotting onions and vegetation - seems to permeate every corner of this laboratory. The path ahead appears as fruitless and uncertain as in months past.

I must remind myself of her, and thus retain my dedication to these pursuits. I close my weary eyes and her lovely gaze floats there in my mind, like a silent and infinite muse to my discouraged energies.

When my lamp glow burned away to nothingness in the midst of my experimentation some hours ago, I saw those eyes hovering in the newly descended darkness as well, like a pair of celestial bodies materialized from the ether to oversee and inspire my renewed efforts. And I was quick to remove the drained bulb and replace it with another, and then the reassuring return of yellow-orange warmth and generous light by which to toil on into the morning.

Letter 16: Lovely Months Leave Little Time For Letters

It has been long since I have written. It almost seems to me that my friendly lamp and 1120 as a whole are slowly divorcing themselves from me, despite my compulsion to proceed with my work. Paradoxically, it's almost as though I no longer feel compelled by my pursuits the way I once did, which perhaps illuminates the anxious and frantic way with which I approach them now. I feel as though I am working against time in some sense, as if I must utilize quickly every final ounce of concentration and dedication remaining to me. As though these elements of my spirit are somehow waning exponentially in relation to the growth of my great contentedness.

Things seem to have unfurled strangely, strangely. My work propels me night after night, and sleeplessness and poor eating habits while I work inside 1120 contradict the happiness I feel outside of its walls. Times change like seasons sometimes, nights of deathly cold wither and perish and we face a brand new risen day afterwards, aglow with sun and warmth. In the Era Before Lucy,[24] I had been consumed by my research to the neglect of all else. And now I am faced with the final ingredient every day: she, the successful result of all my personal searchings.

I forge ahead in my work now only for the sake of those others in this world who are like me. Those silent brothers and sisters hidden beneath their own proverbial rocks, sequestered in their own laboratories and houses and lives in search of their own joys. I cannot be selfish now that destiny has delivered me my own happiness. I am a man of science and will always serve the ideal of beneficial discovery, so that we might all one day be content.

But I am frightened. Like a silly boy with his heart on his sleeve, thumping like thunder in his throat every time he is near to the thing which makes his dreams sweet and his life worth living.

---

24 An unimaginable realm; characterized by cold and feelings of despair and futility.

I treasure Lucy with a profundity I have never before known, and I am almost certain that she reciprocates. But sometimes, when she asks me about 1120, I do not want to explain. Not because she would not understand, but only because it is too tiring to put it all into words. Words are simply inadequate sometimes. My time in 1120 weighs too greatly, on my mind, chest, hands and eyes, on everything that is a component of me.

Occasionally when Lucy asks me these old questions and I answer her in deliberately meandering fashion, I glimpse something a little like sadness steal over her beautiful features. Or perhaps it is defeat, or maybe these things are the same.

I cannot bear that kind of look upon her face. I have always hated ruining good and pure things. Six months have passed since I began my education in things perfect and far removed from my lonely world of old. And because I spend every waking and dreaming moment of my new days with Lucy - in a state of contentment so all-encompassing that I can only liken it to paradise - I have made final my decision to ask her.

That was five minutes ago. I am on my way. My heart is thunder in my chest, an exposed puzzle piece of myself which I wear pinned to my shirt sleeve for her to examine as she will.

Letter 17: Every Single Joy Ever

Lucy said yes! Lucy said yes!
I am happier than all the rest!
Lucy said yes!

Together, we will go, our long journey begun.

Joining Andromeda in the cradle of her spiral arms...

Letter 24: Rapture is a Girl

The last few weeks have proven exceedingly busy. Lucy and I have been planning and planning and planning, a life of blueprint schematics I rejoice in perfecting. In all honesty, Lucy has been handling most everything, while I simply follow her about in a comfortable daze.

I delight in watching her do things. Anythings. She makes the mundane amazing to behold. She speaks with her plants. When she levels the pitcher of water to their outstretched fronds, she chats amiably with them, and never in the same manner with any two of them. Likewise, she knows intimately and caters her speech to the respective personalities of her two cats, and spends equal amounts of time holding each in turn curled in her lap. She speaks to me softly when my shoulders slump after a long day behind me, and remains respectfully silent when my eyes stare into space in search of answers to experimental quandaries new and old alike. She knows who is who, and what is what in her world.

As I sit here in 1120, I know that an order of things has nearly come around, a circle draws closed. Now when I open my eyes into early morning half-light, I understand continuity. The only disarray greeting me is the state of others whom I encounter during my occasional and professional forays into the world, and perhaps the dishevelled state of my hair in the bathroom mirror. Now, I only finger the last rendition of my project which I had worked on, months past, and wonder at the absence inside of me of my old passion. My fingerprints smudge the lovingly-crafted lenses. The ultra-durable telescopic cylinders housing the delicate lenses extend and retract in my fingers, but I leave the model on the table. Feeling distance towards it, and a bitter-sweet tinge of nostalgia for a thing once significant to me but no longer. And I recall the feeling, like a companion of old, now gone away, and it takes my mind a moment to recall its name: loneliness. And again I find myself awed with my good fortune.

Lucy's sweet voice awakened me this morning, birdsong

in the plastic telephone receiver at my ear, and how could I have refused her request to drive into the county to pick up the ceramics set she has had imported from afar. Another infinitesimal ingredient of the life we are building together.

The air smells delicious. Its taste is on my tongue, in my throat. I cannot help but revel in its splendour.

I know that soon I will have to bid goodbye[25] to 1120 forever. I will be with Lucy, and we will remain here no longer. A much greater future awaits us than one bound by lingering, inconsequential ties to this life of old. This is exceedingly wonderful, a quest completed. Yet it seems to me that there remains something yet undone. There is something with which I must leave this laboratory. An explanation, perhaps, or…What?

I do not know.

I know that on the one hand of dream-like optimism I see only rainbow colours and endless days of happiness and discovery unfurling like a golden road before us; while here in this cluttered little familiar space, amid restless pangs of guilt and half-abandoned projects, some greater thing remains unfinished. It mars the continuity that otherwise permeates my days and nights.

I have always pursued knowledge, and yet in the end I have only chanced to collide with it luckily. It is truly wondrous, and quite droll, as well, how life proceeds. I am a man of science, and so perhaps what such a man requires in order to leave a sanctuary such as his place of work is validation. Quantitative evidence, that the path opening before him represents an objective choice on his part, rather than the influence of his jumbled and fluttering emotions.

I believe that she is my key to joy. And so I must test my theory as a hypothesis must be so tested. Perhaps this is the only way that I may truly leave 1120.

I will wait, and hope everything becomes clear.

Now, in this moment, my simple mission lies in the pleasant monotony of county landscape and dusty roads.

And that is perfectly okay with me.

Maybe the birds will sing for me as I drive.

---

25 The growing-apart of long-standing friends/colleagues; bitter, this little taste of sadness in an otherwise paradisiacal existence.

Letter 25:

I cannot contain the shaking which consumes me. I do not think it will ever leave me. Nearly an entire day has passed and still I quake with it. I am unravelled. Oh god.[26] I must write, and think, and write, and think yet more so that everything will solve itself in the end, like another formula waiting only to be deciphered. This journal is my friend and confidant, after all, and in it I can confess as I always have.

But I am certain I do not think it was my fault. No. It was not. I am innocent in the wake of this random and abominable occurrence.

It had been the first time I'd seen the man, and he was already dead and smashed all across the windshield of the car. I never actually got to see his face, thank god. But there was too much blood. People do not have that much blood inside of them. They cannot. We are much more beautiful within our fragile shells than that. Much more immaculate to behold when we lie dead. But this faceless, wholly exposed stranger was incontrovertible proof that we are not, the crimson ocean of his spillage haunts me still. The new man of optimism and romance inside my skin vies for control of my faculties, but the scientist of old maintains in his cold rational textbook voice that I must return to logic in examining the ghost of this ruined man on the windshield.

I am thankful that his snapped neck situated his face so that it stared off ahead of me and down that dusty Essex County road. Otherwise, I am not certain I would have been able to gather myself sufficiently to ease the car into a gentle roll away from the site of death and trauma. The sunlight was too bright, and caused the spray of blood on the window to shine like fire as we drove, the broken man and I.

Soon I was speeding through the country, green farmers' fields ripening on both sides of the road, the man's body not far enough

---

26 Invocation of deity - Indicative of personal regression in the midst of new despair.

behind me. The windshield wipers only worsened my view of the road before me, and I remember thinking how much more difficult it would have been had some ornamentation or piece from the man, such as a necklace or sliver of skin or strand of hair, remained behind, plastered amid the red liquid gore streaking my car window.

My mind had been reeling with Lucy, of course. Because it always is. Adoringly. Happily. Contentedly. But I had not meant to run him down. I have only ever sought to aid my fellow man in this strange existence we share. I have not yet divulged this afternoon atrocity to anyone, and I do not think that I will. I am frightened, as never before. An encounter with Death will breathe this fear into a man, and leave him stricken.

But I obtained Lucy's ceramics from the quaint souvenir store. My mission this day completed.

God: why? Why me as a component in this occurrence, and why now? Who has orchestrated this? Who is manipulating the strings of my life?

I am so sorry for what has happened. I truly am.

And yet, despite my revulsion at what has transpired, the horror of the deed imprinted indelibly across my eyes making my spine quiver; yet I find my thoughts drifting to her, again and again, and I feel a good and comforting warmth stealing over me, despite the tragedy of these present circumstances. As though the forthcoming sight of her smiling eyes will save me from worrisome thoughts clouding my mind, tugging at my heart.

Yes, I have done good today.

I have Lucy's ceramics with me now, a neat bundle swaddled in tissue paper within its little gift box, resting on the desk beside me. Two kittens sculpted together, connected upon a base of summer lawn, hand-painted July green.

More dreams:

I have never seen this scene flickering behind my eyelids before tonight.
A snippet, an excerpted memory, a telling portrait.
I saw myself, the young scarecrow boy of straw: burying a scalpel in the soil. The sun rays reflecting from it blindingly. Like a treasure for future excavation.

Letter 56:

I have been secluded in 1120 for three days and three nights now. I have not eaten well and neither have I bathed. My body odour is foul, and mixes with the overpowering stench of vegetable rot which lingers between these walls. Together our stench creates an abattoir's atmosphere of slaughter and death. I have cancelled all of my classes and seminars, and locked the door to this haunted room. My thoughts are contagion, and the armies of caged mice are nervous, and they have been eating very little of what remains of their tiny brown pellet-food. Lucy is more than a little perplexed. I could sense the hint of worry edging into her voice earlier this afternoon over the telephone. I am not myself.

I finger the products of my old work which lie scattered about me in varying states of assemblage, recalling my great search, and winding my thoughts always back to a soft and fortuitous collision outside of this very building and what it all means.

I am going to tell Lucy of my violent encounter in the county, in the dust, in the brilliant sunlight.

And I will present her with a small gift of ceramics.

And her eyes will smile despite her new knowledge of the thing I have done. As they likewise smiled when we made our decision to embark together on the strange and extraordinary journey before us.

Letter 57: Thank You

I am sitting in my car as I write these words.

Not ten minutes ago, I found myself looking down into Lucy's remarkable Andromeda eyes. And inwardly I smiled, rejoicing, because I had at that precise moment rediscovered the centre of the universe relative to my place in it. It was where all her smiles begin, in her deep ocean pool eyes, cascading down like summer rainstorm to her lips.

Lucy's eyes, the portal for which I've searched without respite.

I delivered her two kisses: one for her, another for me, and none for anything else in the world.

And then I was smiling outwardly and she asked me why the sudden sunshine and I only laughed and caught her up in the mightiest hug I have ever bestowed. Because no deed done outside of my new universe of perfection can ruin these bright days of ours now. In that moment of becoming immersed within her great and wondrous warmth, I understood this succinctly. And I held my tongue over matters of disturbing and unhappy discourse, because I no longer needed to think about such things at all, let alone introduce them into our shared golden-aired world. Dust and blood parted like vapour in her sun-like presence.

Thank you, Lucy. I am now on my way, to make certain...

A final experimentation, to satisfy the lingering man of science dwelling inside my frame. Like a treasure unburied and held gleaming in my fingers, sunlight flashing from it and lighting the path before me so that I might see.

Letter 58: Time to Pack

It is approximately one hour since my last letter.

In that time, I have accomplished much. I wound my way back out into the heart of the dusty county, a serene Essex stretch of corn rows and bright sun. I found the boy strolling absently along beside the remote dirt road, stick in hand like an adventurer or explorer, his jeans dusted at their knees. I pressed down with great insistence on the gas pedal of my car, and ran the boy down. A cloud of dust followed my progress, and passed beyond me as I rolled to a stop. New gore decorated my vehicle, more this time devoted to the lower portion of the old, dented hood and hanging silver fender than to the windshield.

I peered cautiously from my window and found nothing stirring in the road behind me but a settling rain of dust particles. To make certain of his condition, I reversed, rolling slowly backwards toward the motionless broken boy.

As I drew parallel with him, his blonde-tousled head gleamed wetly red in the sun. It was like fire again, this human spillage, only this time brighter, more beautiful to look upon than it had been earlier. His striped t-shirt had been pulled upwards and his dusty belly looked very bloated, as if the merest contact with it would pop him wide open.

things opening[27]

I donned my latest model with quivering hands. The sun flashed from the lenses and reflected its light against the trees bordering the road like some sort of secret signals. Leaning from the window, I examined the boy closely. His features were serene, his facial muscles relaxed. He might have been sleeping if not for his blood as evidence of his state.

I swallowed hard, and backed up twenty metres or so beyond him. Then, satisfied that we were alone, I repeated the procedure, and drove over the small form. The car lurched sickly,

---

27 One mouth to another, the tunnel easily traversed.

and then it was over.

Once more I craned my neck and examined the child. From the settling dirt particles he materialized, bloody and dusty and small. His look of peace remained.

No moral or scientific error is mighty enough to topple me today. The power of my joy is boundless. She is my energy as I revel in my new life. I am unlimited. Together, we two are forever.

Thank you, Lucy.

And thank God[28] for you, Lucy.

As I drove through the day, the songs of the birds in the trees were soothing to my ears. I added my voice to theirs, and sang their songs of joy, too.

---

28 This design is too precise, nearly too beautiful to behold: a Maker's outline lies revealed against the summer's sky.

A Dream of Flying

I was swimming in the sky of her eyes. Flying in her beautiful gaze. I swam for hours. I swam for days. I made my way lazily to her hazel shorelines. And there I slept.

Until morning woke me and, refreshed from my long slumber, I smiled at the sight of my darling still dozing beside me in bed. Coloured warmly in the orange dawn sunlight.

Beautiful.

Mine.

Letter 72: Peace

I sit here, and write here, here in 1120, for the last time ever. When I am finished, I finally get to begin the long journey towards which I have toiled for so long. In a new place, far and far from this realm of old whose fabric can no longer contain me.

I have learned so much from her. Lucy has shown me what it means to collide with something and have it open up before you and thereby allow you to do the same. Courage and reciprocity and a gate parted to places idyllic and unimagined. Everyone in the whole wide world wants exactly this. Love is life and life is this right now, all over me and all around me, in this once weak shell of my body and I am so grateful and happy!

Murder on a sun-splashed day. Joy abounding.

A hypothesis proven. A scientist content.

And to you 1120, old friend, you and I are done. But I will not leave you without an explanation. And here it is: It is all right. It really is. We do not need to build much of anything. Not a monster, not a fiend, not a friend, nor a bed. Maybe some things cannot be created, sculpted, moulded. Maybe some things simply are, while others simply are not. Maybe we must each tinker with our own ideas and dreams, and conduct our own explorations for happiness.

I am going home.

Postscript: And to you, little faithful lamp, my deepest thanks.

Additional Ingredients List (updated): October 24:
Version #67:

- *Plastic and chrome-fitted frame, including two adjustable eyepiece cylinder units*
- *Tri-Optic lenses, including one-quarter portion microexpression recorder – successfully records involuntary facial expressions lasting duration of quarter of second for later study & analysis*
- *micro-video recording unit - one-quarter size of dime*
- *Pupil-focusing filter, model 009-C – allows focus of up to one Angstrom*
- *Hybrid serum: Scopolamine & thiopental sodium solution (solid state form) – used to enforce optical lenses' analyses - unreliable results, requires extensive further study*

- *My hope, undying.*

"If a Minkowski spacetime contains a compact region Ω, and if the topology of Ω is of the form $\Omega \sim R \times \Sigma$, where Σ is a three-manifold of nontrivial topology, whose boundary has topology of the form $d\Sigma \sim S^2$, and if, furthermore, the hypersurfaces Σ are all spacelike, then the region Ω contains a quasipermanent intra-universe wormhole."
- from Matt Visser's *Lorentzian Wormholes.*

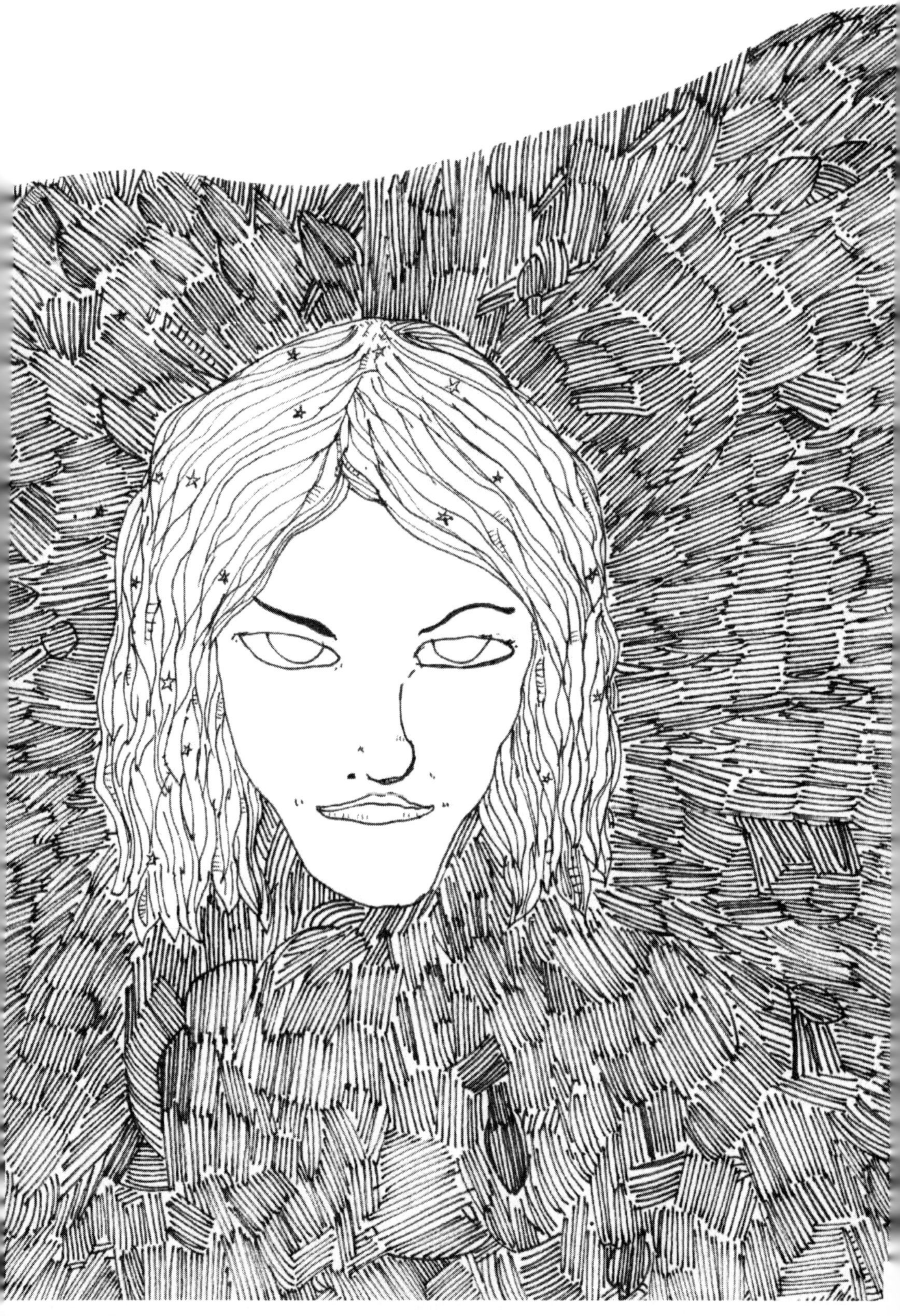

A New Dream, Recurring

I see myself from above, and I am pacing our moon-washed bedroom. Something gnaws at me, keeps sleep far away in the wee hours. A creeping doubt nestling inside me, gnawing at my certainty. Awash in troubled thoughts, eyes frantic and large in the darkness. How truthful have I been with myself, and to my work, and to 1120?

I see myself as if it is a different man drifting through the dream bedroom, although it is most certainly me. Face taut with anxiety, donning and removing and then slipping on once more the strange glasses. The gleam of lenses flashing with moon rays like a glimmer of epiphany in the darkness.

Drifting to her side of the bed, where her head of black fairy tale curls nestles in pillows. And this man with moon-flashing eyes stands over her, watching her sleeping. Hands poised, fingers reaching outwards towards her serene face, lit in moon glow through the window pane. His fingers tense, drifting closer to her features. Brushing her exquisite eyelids, which flutter a frantic dance in her dream-sleep. His fingers hanging there motionless, taut, waiting.

And her eyes open (a window, a portal), and the dream is done.

The Snow Robins Fly Between Heaven and Hell

The snow robins fly between Heaven and Hell.
My hopeful mantra while I wait to die.

    The door's open before him. Sunlight pours in through the window, its silk curtains – a wedding gift from his parents – thrown wide to the summer outside. There's no warmth despite the golden light colouring everything.
    From the doorway he looks into the room and feels as though everything is in disarray, although nothing's been touched, no single thing's been disturbed from its usual neat place. The long oak desk sits in the yellow glow, its array of papers and books and the blue glass bottles fully stocked with pens and related stationery all in their old place. The étagère with the myriad figurines and knickknacks and curios we'd collected over the years displayed tidily as ever on its shelves. The tall wooden bureau in its place beside the walk-in closet, too, all of its drawers and smaller central doors shut tight against the still air of the room.
    No motes of dust twirl like ballerinas through the yellow light. Only Montgomery, our Boxer pup, cowers in the room's centre, whining nervously and watching him with mournful, watery eyes.
    Our bed lies before him, coloured golden. He's thinking: it's the place we first laid down together naked. It's the first place where we made love in the house, under the silky sheets and rich comforters, gasping and groaning and howling like animals in ecstasy. He thinks this too: it was his favourite place in the world once. It was

the best place he'd ever woken into un-alone. The bed, our place for once resting our tired, content heads.

Its pillows are as they'd always been, stacked two to a head-place, neatly side by side. It's his mark, always the obsessive-compulsive in him neat-freaking – the term, coined by me in fond astonishment at his meticulous ways, turns something inside of him – the rooms of our house. The plush comforters are immaculately arranged, precisely aligned at each corner of the mattress and tucked in just so, tidy and patted flat. His eyes fix on the spot in the centre of the bed, and that's where they remain for a long while. He stares there and ponders a great many things: the ways of the world; invasions into guarded places; and the fast, inexorable movement of changing things.

He considers that he's held the hands before him a thousand times in the two years since he'd married his wife. He remembers back to the day when he'd slipped the shiny golden band over my finger. The afternoon had been golden, too, he recalls, and random details of the outdoor ceremony flit into his thoughts: the birds singing their choir songs in the park trees; the plump bees like lazy striped zeppelins whirring through the air everywhere and making the children giggle and scamper; our small gathering of friends and family turned out like we'd never seen them before, wearing their best suits and dresses and faces; the sense of serenity merged with the celebratory atmosphere among the paradisiacal park gardens.

He's a romantic, has always been, and he remembers all of these things and more from his place at the threshold of the bedroom, a potent brew of random memories assailing him like a blow to the senses: the first kiss we'd shared while tipsy and swaying to rock and roll songs inside my garage, was it Hendrix or the Who playing on the little, battered radio and who cares, really, because the kisses were what mattered, much more than their soundtrack no matter how much it defined the days then; the countless afternoons idled away by Little River, close to where I lived with my own parents, sitting on the break wall as though we were teenagers with our jeans hiked up like makeshift clam-diggers while we stirred the warm green water with our bare feet, laughing and starting whenever a dark shape of fish slithered too close and grazed our ankles; furnishing our home and laying out each room according to our childhood fantasies and adult inclinations, the television room – his most favoured getaway – located deep in the basement in order to preserve theatre depth and darkness year round, while the kitchen windows we draped with ferns and other long-leafed flora because we both enjoyed lush reminders of summer during winter's death-air days and nights.

And then the romantic in him conspires to crush him as he returns from his reveries and is brought back to the tragedy in the bed before him. He thinks of me: dear Darla. His dear darling Darla. And he asks himself, his quixotic inclinations becoming overwhelmed with the reality he faces: what happened here? When did the world I always feared invade here, to remind me of its terrible, vindictive ways?

He shambles forward on uncertain legs. The golden light covers him, too. He feels cold beneath its false summer's touch. He entertains – fleetingly, very fleetingly, because as hopeful as he can sometimes be, the realist always, always resurfaces to ground him in the context of the world – that every aspect of his day has so far been an illusion. His unreliable proof of this lies in the summer light so incongruous with the icy air. But then he pauses at the foot of the bed. He stares down into its soft plain. He reaches a quivering hand forwards, wishing to stroke my cold fingers, blue and coloured strangely yellow in the sun-rays pouring through the window. But he only stands there, unable to move, staring fixedly through the sudden blinding wash of tears to the exquisite hands of his beloved wife resting motionless in the centre of the bed we'd shared. The congealed crust of my blood gleams blackly around the raw edges of the members. The blood has formed a wide pool in the centre of the mattress all around them so that they appear to float there like alabaster islands. My blood, he considers distantly, has soaked through the layers of comforters and blankets and bed sheets and deep into the mattress beneath. Perhaps, he thinks, it's seeped its way into the wooden frame of the bed, as well, and now drips onto the carpet beneath.

He's searched the entire house and its surrounding grounds and found no sign of the rest of me. Neither did he perceive any indication of disturbance, other than the misplaced brush laying discarded on the linoleum in the drawing room. Only this small but telltale indication of the world as he's always feared it having infiltrated the fortress he'd built for us. And there, too, in what was once the warmest room in the vastness of our house, our stronghold, as he'd always considered it. With a shudder he thinks of the woods bordering our county home on all sides, and regretfully considers his brief but fateful trek into their verdant twists and turns in pursuit of our wayward runaway Boxer puppy, Montgomery. And he ponders which piece of that old world – the one before marriage and our new and untroubled life together had dulled his former vigilance – might have stalked boldly forward from those deep green depths and claimed his most reliable source of happiness.

Then his veneer of composure collapses. He can no longer think at all. He reaches forward blindly through the stinging wall of salty water muddling his vision, and brushes the familiar tips of my fingers. Eventually he becomes brave enough to slip his hand through my stiff fingers, and the icy touch of this small, cherished piece of his beloved urges from him a loud sobbing. It wracks him. He shakes within its violent grip, and it's this paroxysm that makes him suddenly aware of the lightness of his darling, the near weightlessness of my severed hand in his as if we're engaging in some perverse and grisly formal farewell. I shine like a sculpture of ivory through his tears. I always have, he liked to remind me of this often, admiring my pale complexion while tracing invisible designs over my skin with his fingers and whispering into my ear that I was the only beautiful ghost he'd ever met.

He screams, inarticulately at first, and from this chaos of his pain a single word emerges. He cries the question, to the bed, the flimsy walls surrounding him, the lifeless hand in his own: *Why?*

And he collapses on the blood-darkened bed, where he weeps and weeps and weeps, hating the hugeness of the regret filling him up more and more as he ponders the recklessness of his having chased our disobedient puppy into nearby but far too distant places; leaving behind things he cherished, even for the mere thirty minutes or so that it had taken to track down and snatch up our much-loved pet in the woods, while the covetous world – laying in wait as he'd always worried over – had seized the chance he'd given it.

And this: I'm certain of this. He's my husband and I know him well: in this moment of despair he takes a second to look to each upper corner of the room. He does this fearfully, tensing his muscles and narrowing his eyes in anticipation of what they might hold. And though the walls are clean, he examines these lofty upper reaches scrupulously, making certain that they're devoid of fleet, hairy life. He's always hated them. He's always feared them greatly, for their many watching eyes and quick sharp legs: the spiders. His loathing of them nearly as neurotic as his obsessive way of keeping his surroundings clean, tidy, well-ordered. Almost as if they represent some very essential thing he's always feared. *Life is full of waiting things* – a long-standing mantra of his, and I'm certain that he mouths these old words while surveying the ruined room around him.

I believe him now, too, and understand his fear: life is full of waiting things, and they're ever vigilant.

Clutching this piteous remnant of me in the illusory golden air while weeping and marvelling at the seamless insidiousness of the world: it's the first day he truly realizes the weakness of sunlight.

The snow robins fly between Heaven and Hell.

This I remind myself over and over again each years-long day and night. I think this while I draw aimless lines in the perpetual powdering of dust on the desiccated wooden floorboards about me. I think it while pissing and shitting in the corner of filth which is my scrap of space for these things. I tell myself this while he's sharing this ragged mattress with me, so that in this way I might hold on to the idea that here – in this unimaginable place – I still have the companionship of old friends. This is my home now, this constant dust and this stained mattress and the chain around my ankle binding me to the rusted ribs of the heating vent from which only cold winds blow.

Time passes strangely here. Months are years in this shack. The floorboards creak like sad music in my ears. I see the sun only in pieces where it shines through the grimy window glass – so muted and far-away-looking, like the now-dead hope inside me. The light is sallow and unhealthy through the film of dirt, through the cracks in the old cardboard wings and between the strips of grey electrical tape and the time-yellowed newspaper pages plastered across the glass and telling me old stories. It's through these impoverished slits looking into the old world that I watch the boomerangs in the sky. They circle over the trees I glimpse between curling newspaper pages. They hang like ancient gliders in the blueness I'm able to discern through the perforated cardboard strip obstructing the lower portion of the window. Sometimes I'm able only to hear them, their muted cries sounding forlorn, lost, like the wailing of distraught children. They're the raucous cries of scavengers, impure white-feathered gulls like miniature vultures waiting for their chance to feast. They fly there every day, a mad mob of them etched against the sky, as if they sense decay and death in the vicinity.

    I look to the immense wad of bandages engulfing the end of my wrists. They give me the appearance of wearing giant gloves or mittens, but of course if ever I was a gladiator I long ago fell. The numbness emanates from them fiercely. Like a continual encroachment of ice it deadens my arms more each day passing. When I move too quickly knives of pain embed themselves deeply, muscle-deep, bone-deep, and spasms grip me writhing on the floor. I examine these sodden, ragged gloves and my mind reels at their reality, and the fact of my wearing them at all.

    The terrible sound, as if cued by my weak, self-pitying musings, is here again. The pained squealing of un-oiled hinges from above. The clattering of the wooden door in its frame. The heavy thudding of his boots descending stairs, and then clomping across the floor. The groaning of wood near at hand as he seats himself in his chair in the shadows like a king come to examine his chattel. The deep sound of his breathing from the darkness, growing louder and more livid-sounding the longer he watches me. Minutes, hours, years of his growing fury touching me and then the scraping of wooden chair legs across wooden floorboards. The immense sound of his footsteps coming to me again. I don't know why this misplaced fury. I don't know what it is that he thinks I've done to deserve his wrath and I don't think that I'll ever learn. I know only that the pain ritual will go on, unabated as it has for these past thousand years.

But they come to me each day, too – the avian cries. I listen hard and hear them now, beyond his huge breathing enveloping our cramped shared space. And though their mocking sound belongs unmistakably to that of the gull family, I know to which group of bird I must convince myself they belong, if I'm to preserve any shred of strength in this place; my only friends left to me in the world, like ghosts from yesterday: my snow robins.

I remember the robins rustling the trees.

They seemed my soundtrack throughout all childhood in our small southern Ontario town. Their songs I loved, and urged me to seek out their small vibrant forms in the leaves and copy them as best I could in my child's hand, filling drawing pad after drawing pad with their portraits. They seemed even to follow me into the golden era of marriage. They'd made the park trees alive on the sunny afternoon when I married the man I knew I couldn't live without. Hearing their voices on the balmy air I looked to the trees and found the little fiery birds perched there like ornaments. He told me after that it had been the first day he'd noticed the colour of sunlight on the world.

Before he kissed his bride's waiting-wanting lips, he puckered exaggeratedly and nipped quickly at my hands, first one wrist and then the other. It won him chuckles from everyone gathered, and scattered applause even before the real kiss and our walk down the aisle to our families waiting to congratulate us. His private joke with me: his little artist girl.

He told me once that he'd fallen in love with my hands first and then the rest of me soon after. My hands first, because of the places they gave him to walk into and leave behind his everyday concerns and more deeply personal worries. I'd been teaching at the community college for nearly a year then, different classes covering different media, pen and ink studies of the human anatomy in all its possible amazing contortions; mixed media of any variety of styles, stippling paint onto pieces of found art to yield anything from a blue-coated garbage pail with russet flowers adorning its warped lid to a long narrow vase made more striking by the photocopied pictures of the artist's favourite A- or B-list actor glued onto its curved, sleek sides and resulting in a Marilyn Monroe or Lance Henrikson gazing outwards from all sides with physiognomies queerly elongated and seemingly following the viewer everywhere. And my favourite lessons, the painting classes in which students were instructed to throw their emotions onto the page in front of them, whether the long brown rough-sheets torn from their immense upright spools, or the higher-quality art stock, or for the prodigies of the group the coveted handful of canvases the department allowed us to work with during any given semester.

    He'd been a student of mine, trying his hand at brush strokes and pencil rubbings while apples blossomed in his cheeks every time I caught him watching me. Shy, charming in his timidity, and hopeless with his paints even for his passion: I grew to adore him in a matter of weeks.

    I'd wondered over his main interest in his studies: spiders, or in the case of his awful portraits, eight- and often ten- and twelve-legged amorphous blobs meant to represent the arachnids he admitted to have always feared to a nearly phobic degree. Why bugs, I'd asked him one afternoon, watching his face flush with embarrassment as he mustered his reserve in the face of the woman he was so clearly smitten with. He came up with: They scare me. They have for as long as I can recall. They're too quick, with all those legs. And their eyes, well...And the *hairy* ones…He trailed off, making a sour face that made me laugh. I pointed out that if he hated spiders for their many legs and fleetness, then he surely must be terrified of centipedes with their trillion digits and speedy locomotion. He only chuckled and kept drawing his spiders.

    We laughed about it later, the contrast in the subject matter we focused our artistic efforts on during class time dabbing at canvases, and becoming stiff-necked with long hours spent detailing away bent before the easel. My fixation with birds perhaps as uncanny as his own, though our reasons for these respective obsessions seemed wholly opposing. Always in flight, your pictures, he remarked one day while flipping through my sketchbook, and he was certainly right; whether illustrations of the animals themselves or their man-made winged successors, the airplane, the helicopter , the colourful hand glider like some man-made minimalist interpretation of the exotic parrot. And like an antithesis to my attempted expressions of freedom: his queer arachnid fixation in his own painting – his eight-leggers, as he referred to them with a candid levity that seemed always to seek to hide his unease in contemplating the creatures – always repugnant, horrid, and imbued with an indefinably threatening aspect. It was his distinct style with paint, I learned, and soon enough I glimpsed the part of his personality that harboured those ghosts too: his deep-rooted paranoia, which his eyes revealed to me early on even if his words didn't for fear of frightening me away towards less peculiar men: you can't trust the hidden corners the world has to give you. There are always things waiting to snare you if you're not deft and quick-witted and prepared for their inevitability.

    He once asked me, while watching me work over my shoulder after class, whether all birds flew in murders. I remember frowning, being uncertain, telling him honestly that I wasn't sure and that we should look it up. He pointed to the piece before us with an oddly troubled expression, a group of pencil robins I hadn't yet begun filling in with colour. They formed a compact flying squadron against the blank canvas sky. He told me that they should, strength in numbers, making me laugh because how just like him to say something like that, something so defensive and secure-feeling. It was one of many classroom moments when I'd felt an incredible surge of affection for him, and as strong a need to comfort him: I answered that robins flew together, and that I knew this for a fact, though I didn't. It worked well enough, because he smiled and his mellow mood seemed restored when he leaned down and pecked my earlobe with his lips, nuzzling me for a moment before letting me get back to my work.

    We'd had good times: there was the house and paying it off and making it our own. Engineers – especially those as skilled and sought after as he – earn good money and so we were quick in sculpting out the perfect cubby hole space for ourselves that we'd always wanted. I had my own room for my work overlooking – for inspiration's sake – the bountiful backyard garden, because I'd never grown bored of still life pieces when the right contours for wingtips and dinosaurian avian toes weren't coming to me. He was good to me in this way, always catering to my needs without my ever needing to voice them too loudly. We both were this way, living to make the other content. And so I feigned enthusiasm when he tenaciously sought out the finest equipment available to keep us safe, the top-of-the-line security systems, the myriad burglar alarms and trip wires, the motion detectors and tall, extravagantly-expensive wrought-iron fence with its spear-tip summit to enclose our prodigious property on all sides. I'd never understood the need for these precautions, not really – his skewed vision of the world seemed only a fictional re-working of those things it might hold, a paranoid inversion of sunlight and birdsong, where imaginary spiders dashed over ceilings of rooms we inhabited and spit their webs at us.

I joked about this once and never mentioned it again after I saw the hard stare looking out at me from his usually soft eyes. I said: My god, are you hiding from someone with a price on your head? Is there someone after you? You're the most paranoid husband in the world.

His stare fixed me. He became a different man as he said curtly and solemnly, as if seeking to edify me on a very grave subject: there's someone after everyone.

I made no answer to this but thought about it a lot afterwards. It was only shortly later, a few months perhaps, while in the middle of the same portrait I'd intended as a gift for his forthcoming birthday, that – sensing an alien element in the drawing room's air, or seeing the shadow darken the canvas before me – I turned and faced the image of his great fear, personified and corporeal and suddenly inhabiting the world in which I lived, blissful and wholly unprepared for such an encounter. I hadn't listened intently enough to him, after all. My great regret was born inside me that very instant of confrontation. The brush in my hand clattered to the floor and stained the tiles the deep red of the murder of robins I'd only partially embellished against the sky of ocean blue that they were supposed to have owned with their fiery brilliance.

*   *   *

It's the first day he realizes the weakness of sunlight – the day I disappear and my hands are all that remain of me in his life.

He comprehends this as – numbed and trembling in the centre of our bedroom – he chances to stare through the bedroom window and spots the fleeing shape. It speeds across the field between the house and the forest looming beyond. It flees in a queer manner, quickly despite its awkward shape and lanky frame, galloping yet not exactly, loping in the manner of a wolf but not quite. Perhaps a combination of these two forms of locomotion and some other difficult to define. But there it undeniably is, a hateful black shape ruining the lush green of the grass over which it moves, carrying over its shoulder a bundle which is unmistakeably me. Fleeting, the scene, and then the obscenity has disappeared through the wall of trees, lost to the depths of the woods where, in his heart, he knows that it can never be found. Trackless, those woods, where only deer and squirrels might know their way, and farmer's fields beyond them, and the monotony of county geography: the countless scraggly bushes and dense thickets dotting the endless expanse of countryside, with the many small towns interspersed among the bucolic miles, and the larger cities glittering beyond like their noisy, filthy younger siblings.

And though he's only just confirmed the bedroom reaches above him to be devoid of webs, he knows better. He knows more than ever before that now, from somewhere, from some gloomy place, eyes watch him in his colossal sorrow, waiting for the opportunity to cross the landscape of his life and wreak havoc once again. He seeks to come to terms with his knowledge that he'll never again hold my hand as we walk together in the world, but of course this kind of resignation is impossible, and he can only weep.

Life is a nest of spiders, he thinks, and the old idea is validated in this moment. They're nimble, and fearsome, and their feather-light touch as they dance across you in your days is reason enough to build yourself a fortress. And to hide there, hide there as best you can while hoping madly against their trespass.

He'll remain hidden in the fortress he now rules alone. He'll from this day onward – more so than ever before in his life – turn a wary eye always upwards when he enters the rooms of his life. He'll search their corners, and look for eyes like fire glowering out at him, and listen always for the imperceptible sound of loathsome forms scuttling quick as life about him.

And he whispers, and Montgomery cowers nervously on the carpet at his feet, and the words are something like an oath or confirmation of his old beliefs: we must beware, beware the stickiness of their intricate design, like traps for our peace, waiting, waiting.

I'm a ghost in this rancid air.
I'm a cloud in this inclement sky.
These things he's taught me over the months.
These things he conveys to me in the wordless, heavy breathing which carries like some demon Wendigo-wind through the grey atmosphere of this shack. I have to squint for him, straining my eyes through his rank smoke into the shadows where he lives and smoulders. I know he's there. He's there once more, draped in shadows. I can hear him and feel the uncannily tangible touch of his eyes as he examines my pale, emaciated captive form on the mattress on the floor. There's a glaze over my eyes, it seems, which turns this place more unreliable. Maybe it's only the constant murk, or the wet ash he paints like mascara into my eyelashes every evening as if he's preparing me for an evening out to dinner. I close my eyes and feel their gummy weight on my eyelids, thick and gruesome like tarantula legs caressing. They cause me to think of the man who feared spiders on my behalf and who paid great money to secure me from their traps. I think of him and see his adoring eyes and the pain tearing behind my chest is my agonized heart awakening all over again to my plight.

My stomach throbs with a vicious pain, stabbing and unremitting. It's been days since he's brought me food, and even then I'd only succeeded in tearing at the meat briefly before nausea came and convulsed me, forcing me to spit up brown water and phlegm.

I don't know whether the Devil hunts with rifles or with traps or with his bare hands, but I know that this is how we survive: he's the hunter and oppressor, gathering the freshly killed bodies of rabbit and fox and deer and mouse and feeding us as he does every few days, uncooked meat with a washing down of rusty-tasting water. I know this, too: this place is like regressing to Hell, this shack where the Devil presides and I always think that I can't possibly bear any more and then the raw new light of another day filters through the filthy glass and I marvel at my un-splintered self. When will I unhinge? When will the growing numbness in my arms – punctuated with the knife-cutting periods of pain – engulf me entirely? When may I finally die and join the fate of my hands?

These things are all I know about him with certainty. The rest I can only conjecture, but I've decided on this vision to define my Hell: we're hidden in the bowels of a deep, deep valley, in a dead bush of desiccated trees and mazes of thorny bramble. Poisonous, fishless creeks trickle from those dismal depths. Deadly vapours rise from stretches of dank, un-navigable fenland. It's a place where people don't walk, and have never walked and nor will they ever. Here there are no animals, making of this place a land so barren it's as if a great fire had razed it to the ground long ago and from which inferno its trees never recovered, remaining dry, bald husks, flaking with ash and breaking apart in the wind. For meat he must visit the green places beyond the borders of this domain of which he is sole ruler, to rural spaces where jittery and nimble deer roam, sharing their trails with quick-flitting rabbits and squirrels and black bears with their deadly teddy bear cubs. To town- and city-places where people dwell together in their homes oblivious to the routes taken by hunters such as this, so close to their lives, grazing their children at play digging in sandboxes or swinging in swings and causing them to turn and wonder at the sudden gust of winter air stirring their clothes and hair. I sense that he may on occasion bring back a single creature to inhabit this place and rule its bleak stretches alongside him: with his large, filthy fingers I envision him plucking spiders hanging like dark marbles from the branches in the thickets where he hunts; wearing them like onyx jewels on his person, in his filthy beard, and bringing them with him to spin their elaborate web designs between the rotten trunks of this underworld land.

I've never once discerned people-sounds through these walls and black windows. If it weren't for my brave winged friends infiltrating the air spaces of this cursed place, I'd be truly alone.

The wood-groaning from the shadows, as if awoken by my rogue thoughts and reminding me of my isolation and helplessness. His steps like those of a giant's over the floor. The rotten stench of him growing more pungent as he draws nearer. It's a wind growing in velocity as the floorboards groan, always the signal that he's coming for more. Last night and the thousand nights before haven't been enough to sate his hunger.

I hate his hands. They're the worst two things I've ever met in my life.

Second only to his eyes – there could be no worse touch than theirs. Sometimes when he's having me and a stray moonbeam or sunbeam colours his livid face I'm not sure whether they're two black wells without bottom.

My thoughts are invaded. His putrid breath is mine again as his tongue like sandpaper finds my cheek and slithers a moment later across my forehead, making a circuit of my face to my other cheek and downwards to my chin and from there drifting finally across my clenched mouth. I can only close my eyes once more as it begins all over again. I wish I was brave enough to bite down and tear this tongue from its awful pitmouth and spit it from between my teeth to writhe and gush blood like a severed snake on the floor. But I'm not so brave. New marks will surely have appeared on my skin by the time the ritual is over, the renewed red lines and welts like a perverse map over my pale legs and arms and all down my breasts and across my shoulders and neck after he whips me for no reason that I've been able to fathom other than because he's the Devil in the guise of a man with small obsidian beads for eyes. I continue to clench my eyes tightly, knowing that new stains are appearing in the fabric of the musty mattress even now. These will dry into semen continents and add to the horrible geography mapped out in this mattress; with its crimson fringing and spotting, evidence in this sad mapscape of those times when he's become exceptionally violent. Even now, the mattress shifts beneath us from the vigour of his thrustings; the chain squeezes my ankle mercilessly where it's drawn taut; the great bulk of him crushing the air from my body; and I think as I always do of this mattress serving as a stage for the most appalling spectacle in the world. His stink is intolerable and I gag at the acidic taste rising inside my throat. Spikes of fire radiate from beneath the dirty gloves I wear and prick into my shoulders and neck.

I've tried everything and given up on all such futile attempts of escape: pleading with a reason completely dead inside of him; threatening him with the logic of missing persons searches and his future behind bars; lying to save my splintering thoughts, first lies to him so that I might gain his trust, a weapon I could somehow exploit; then lying in order to save myself, but I always see clearly through my feeble attempts at sanity. I never was good at that sort of power, lying. I hear myself in the rotten aftermath, amid the new stink of our sex and sweat and filth, and I cringe and cry at the memory of my awful lies urging him do the things he does harder, harder, more violently than he's ever done them before; telling him that I love these things and never want them to stop because these are the things that I've always wanted from the world. I once dared to question him, seeking to appeal to an absent humanity in him. I asked: Who are you? What happened to you? You must have been hurt very badly, too...Of course he didn't answer with words. He only unwound the bandages from about my wrists, revealing the grossly distended, mottled blue-black stumps wrapped within. This is where he concentrated his fevered attentions that day, and long into the night. I've never spoken to him again.

My awful attempts at deceit have only ever proven transparent and insincere to his ears. Here I still lie, waiting each day for the master of this world to return from dreams of smoke and black glazed eyes turned inwards to horrid places. And then more evil deeds and the memory of them will be mine again, while I look down at them as if from high above because this is how I've taught myself to see this world: from above, where I feel divorced from what was once me and I'm able to bear the sight of the enslaved woman below. This is the only thing that I can savour here, this brief sensation of drifting like smoke in this air.

When this latest raping is finished I lay unmoving,

numbed but sensing distant points of pain touching me. These grow steadily in intensity and I await their manifestation fearfully. My body is flaccid. My skull throbs. My eyes are thick and itchy from a mire of tears and ash-mascara. I lay inert and listen to the blessed sounds of his departure from the mattress and me; the rustling of clothes over his limbs; the metallic chinking of his belt buckle being fastened; the clod of his steps taking him into some other dark corner of this place. I wait a while and crack my eyelids – and feel revulsion at the actual cracking noise of my lashes parting – a fraction, only ever a fraction for fear that if he's still watching from the shadows and notices that I'm still alive it may awaken his fury with me once again. And I can't contemplate having to suffer his attentions again in my beaten state. So through slitted eyes I watch the splashes of wan white where the daytime peers in at me through the gaps in the cardboard and duct-taped window like a subdued sign of Heaven. I watch earnestly for the boomerangs that I know are wheeling there in the sky, arriving and then flying away but always revisiting me at some time. I strain through the rushing clamour of blood in my ears: I hear their cries muffled through these walls and I know that they're there for me again. I paint my visitors, the only way I'm able to paint now: concentrating with my narrowed-eyed, secret stare I see them exactly the way I need to see them. Golden- and red-feathered, like a sky deepening into dusk, my birds have a look of fire about them despite their frost-tipped wings and the slivers of ice creaking in their plumage as they glide on their way in this wintry place. The landscape over which they soar is an inhospitable one, frozen and marked everywhere with death and putrescence. Their soft feathers suffer the penalty of flight here as ice forms and creaks along their wings and drips into long stalactites from their small sharp beaks. But they fly on, unhindered, strong. They've become my masterpiece, bridging the gulf between this Hell and the golden place where I once lived. They beckon me to return, and await my fate patiently.

    I remember the look and feel of sunlight from long before, and it was never so sad as the feeble wintry glare that penetrates through the paltry slits and gashes into this slave room.

    Every thought I own saddens me now: these chains and the recurring varieties of pain that make all of this like some kind of incredible fiction. And so I construct long lists in my head meant to distract me from this place. I have until the end of time for tasks like these and so such lists may be thorough. I begin now to compile bird species according to how often I tended to paint each in turn. I begin with my favourites and move in descending order of preference through the endless variety of families: robins, my magical snow-white darlings with feathers like fire; the beautiful Blue Jay with its lavender blue plumage and prominent royal crest; the modesty of the small Vesper Sparrow, its sprinkles of white like snowflakes among its tail feathers; hummingbirds of all kinds, tiny vibrant motion-blurs needling violet and crimson flowers; the Raven like a flying speck of night against cloud backdrops, a wan and melancholy vision, yet serene and comforting to observe, too. The end of my avian list is comprised of those sad flightless creatures, the emu and ostrich and dodo, like unfortunate regressions compared to their brothers gifted with aerial mastery, destined to tread their lives forever overland with the rest of us less endowed animals. I have until the end of my life for living inside of lists such as these. If luck is with me then maybe that won't be long now.

  He returns to me. The thought of him returning for more so soon stabs inside me. In my panic I open my mouth and nearly begin to beg for respite. But he only grips my face in one large hand, steadying my shuddering body, and with the large callused thumb of his other draws on my face. The smell is of soot, of burnt things, and I imagine the wicked mask he's giving me. He's done only after several minutes of rubbing his fingers over my cheeks and chin and eyelids and forehead, and then he lets me go and walks wordlessly into the gloom from which he came.

  I'm a ghost in this place. Does anyone remember me from the old world, I wonder. The blonde-brown has long faded from my roots and my premature grey shows through everywhere, though I can't be certain because when was the last time I saw myself in a mirror? I don't know but I'm certain I hate mirrors now. My thirty-first birthday has surely passed, although I can't be certain because calendar-markings scratched into the chalk-dust plains of time gathered on these wooden floorboards are easily blown away by careless strokes, by the back of his brute's hand after it strikes my cheek or mouth or stomach as punishment for daring to track the passage of time. His hands are colossal, and long-fingered, and hard as iron colliding with my lips and teeth and nose and eye sockets and cheekbones and temples and breasts and thoughts.

And I think of my hands. I hold aloft the withered, bandaged remnants. In the uncertain half-light, they have about them a disturbingly monstrous aspect: their enormous medusoid shape, with loosened dressings trailing from beneath like the tendrils of some strange marine creatures. I can make no arcs of colour across canvases with ruins such as these. No longer can I build worlds filled with birdsong for my lovely man to wander in, pleasantly lost. My hands severed and left in the centre of our bed back home like a mockery of his dedication to keeping me safe – I have no way of painting for him anymore and this is the thought that makes me saddest.

I re-live my darling's darkest day through his eyes every day that I'm chained here, because I know what happened inside of him. I know how the reality of our empty house validates his great fears of the world, and I know how he must feel now that he's alone again in that world. The meandering lines I etch on the floor are few, one trailing into two becomes three and then I have no room left in my little space where I'm tethered like a dog. I have to wait weeks or months for the dusty rains to fall from the ceiling above or from the skin of my body and his when we're connected like snakes in the filth and stink of the soiled mattress, and only then will I have my rotten mocking canvas again.

I'm broken again, withered arms burning, black thoughts weighing like mountains on me. I consider that I may somehow – for some reason I can't fathom – deserve all of this. And I think of the flood of guilt that drowns my husband every day, and this – this more than anything else – causes me to weep and weep again.

A visitation in the night, from a high place.

A crunching at the window, stirring me from my daze on the mattress.

I listen intently and discern no breathing from the

darkness. I smell the air and his stench, which hangs over this place always, is less pungent than when he occupies his throne in the shadows overseeing me. Stealthily I crawl from the mattress and to the window. I place my ear to the obscured glass. I hear:

The strong sound of wings flapping on the air, like a blanket being beaten out and freed from its coat of dust and dirt. Through sleep-befuddled eyes I see: the robin like a gift of fire against the window glass, a sliver of brightness through the cracks in newspaper and cardboard. The crunching-crackling sounds are the ice flakes splintering and falling away from its wings as it beats them into a small wind at the glass, hovering uncannily in its place in the air before me. A tiny blizzard dazzling my eyes as I watch, spellbound.

The ice and snow showering downwards on the air, small flakes and large, unveil the grand splendour of the crimson animal clothed inside. The robin. The fire bird. Like a miniature beacon of salvation, my personal Phoenix risen through the quagmire of all of this and blazing for me in the shack's black window. A breath of cinnamon touches me, a spicy tingle in my nostrils. I grow suddenly calm.

I fix my eyes on its black unblinking stare watching me through the dirty glass. I see the entreaty in those black circles. They're a spell and they've bewitched me. In their depths, I glimpse: Summer. The season grows there. A sky-blue pushes away the black and owns the eyes. Their gaze is new, but familiar. I was disarmed by those eyes long ago, and following my heart found happiness with him. My darling, finding me in my black pit of loneliness. They sing, those eyes. They sing a song of lament. It tears me inside to hear: my sweet Darla in webs – Forgive me. And it's the thought of him like this – and the tangible sight of him before me – anguished and broken with self-loathing and regret, that hurts me more than any other pain I could ever suffer here.

And then the song is finished: fly with me, bid his beautiful eyes.

I smile. I haven't smiled in I'm not certain how long, but I smile now. The bird beats its wings once more, and disappears into the night.

I return to the mattress. My head swims. Thoughts careen from one another until a single thought surges upwards as if through depths of sleep and dreams until it's arrived here in this place on another endless day huddled in Hell. The epiphany pulses in me like a second heartbeat. With it there, my smile grows. After a moment I recognize the emotion filling me: hope. And I know: he must be told. The Devil must learn how I feel living in his world, after he stole me from mine.

Most of all, he must learn that I know what he is.

I awake from my delirium of semi-sleep as if from the deepest of dreams.

The beating of wings echoes in my ears as I gather my voice and my courage. After several minutes, I'm able to call out to him in the darkness:

I hate you.

My voice is hoarse from disuse, crone-like and strange in the immense stillness. It wavers, but I feel strength returning to it. These are the words I choose, and the clarity of the solution they represent makes me feel foolish for not having realized it a thousand years sooner. It's as easy as this. *I hate you.* I call it out again and hear the hateful, rhythmic quality in my words, as if I'm rejoicing in putting them into the shadows.

Then a knocking from deep in this place. A screaming of rusted hinges, followed by a tense and waiting silence. The knocking again, familiar, the measure of his strides descending the groaning staircase. A loud clattering from before me as he sends the chair toppling away from him across the old wooden boards. The violent thumping as he moves his gargantuan feet across the floor. The quick rolling sound is one of his bottles careening away from his place of vigilance and knocking dully into the wall.

I keep on because I have a new mantra like a weapon to wield in these exhilarated final moment of confrontation: *I hate you.*

I hear the buckles of his belt knocking together as he loosens the leather around his waist. I wait anxiously for the touch of lashes to descend across my bare chest and shoulders but sing my new song without pause. He waits in the fringes of darkness, watching me, contemplating me, relishing the thought of devouring me again.

    I give him my song.
I hate you, spider.
I hate you, spider.
I hate you, spider.
    Like a spell, my words summon it. I see the spider materialize from the shadows. It unfurls itself from the darkness. Its many legs drift nimbly across the floorboards groaning beneath its bulk. It's gargantuan. It's hideous. Its breath is putrid. Its eyes smoulder like torches in its head. Its fur is thick and sharp, a black thicket of hackles bristling in anticipation of the feast to come. Its fangs champ together eagerly, too, as it nears the fly snared in its web. The Devil is no man. The Devil is the immense, grotesque world which my darling always feared, hanging in its giant web while devouring its hapless captives.

    I laugh, madly, and sing the spider my hateful song. *I hate you,* spider.

    I'm stronger than I've ever been, in this moment. Soon I'm numb to the stings savaging my flesh. Their bite is like raindrops on my skin. It becomes refreshing and I laugh and sing my song with greater fervour amid this storm.

    Then the congested feeling in my chest and the cloudiness in my eyes and skull as the squeezing at my windpipe is the iron grip of large fingers working in deeply, securing a relentless hold. It enters my mind suddenly, fleetingly: the distant recollection that these are the hands that ruined my final painting long ago, disrupted me in my eager, loving work; these hands that pummelled me into unconscious submission and mutilated and blasphemed my body and then dragged me away into the forest of ice and death from which this man had come and slipped into our home; perhaps through a window thrown carelessly ajar in welcome of the clean air of the new season, or through the unlocked rear door because I never had shared my darling's paranoid passion for safekeeping our lives. It's gone in an instant, the thought, a fleeting sliver from the past, but it imbues me with strength. Through the red pounding in my skull I can make out his raspy, laboured breathing and so I shut him out again, gasping the words out hoarsely through his white-knuckling grip.

I. Hate. You.

I'm winning: the world is swimming with murky deep water. Fire consumes my arms. A heartbeat begins its violent rhythm at the end of my wrists. It grows to a hammering sensation. I imagine geysers of fire erupting from them like torches throwing back the dank darkness of this place. I feel something fluttering inside me. Long-dormant wings stirring. I feel them blooming from my shoulders like a gift from angels to take me from this great web.

I'm prevailing: the Devil doesn't know his own strength, and he never guessed mine like a secret sac laden with venom inside me. The air has left this place. I feel buoyant, tranquil. There's no more oxygen for me to swallow. I'm evaporating into the ether, becoming air myself. The web is turning to dust around me.

I'm flying from this pain: my eyes see black.

Nothing.

Nothing.

Only a chalk sky with delicate summer clouds in the distance. He's there in the field watching the horizon, his hand over his eyes to shield himself from the brightness he's grown so unaccustomed to. It's the first day in a very long time that he's dared to venture forth from the house and brave the outdoors. The cool air is refreshing on his skin. He smells of it deeply: a hint of cinnamon rides the breeze. A scent of renewal in this season of flourishing life. He spies something in the east. Its shape is familiar. It comes closer. A sensation stirs him. From deep inside him, something awakens. Long-buried, a once-familiar peace begins its blooming. He feels warm. He keeps his eyes in the sky as they approach in the great stillness and quiet.

He's smiling when he lets his hand fall to his side. He looks quite the way he did when he kissed my wrists in a park to the backdrop of trees brimming with life. He sees them now over the spruces and a question forms in his thoughts: do robins fly in murders, he asks himself.

And then he remembers that they do. They do, and the sight of them, like little flitting pieces of fire against the sky – like friends long-lost but revisiting after a migration into the darkest of dreams – allows his breathing to come easier as he watches their wheeling flight across the firmament, as if nothing could stop them from going where they wanted.

The Silly Significance of Running with Soda Fire

I'm pursued by impassive, nameless men who – true to their cliché television and film counterparts in this if no other way – wear their plastic sunglasses in the deepest night as well as by day. My photograph is an image seen in outer space via satellite and transmitted back down to secluded rooms in clandestine headquarters on the planet upon which I run, placing a tenacious crimson dot like a beacon on my moving body. I can't stop, given my circumstances, and I have no hope to survive; but the doom of everything I cherish and loathe is a soda pop can snug in my left pants pocket, and so I'm committed to run onwards. I make sure to place loose change in my right pocket because the small clinking of coins onto the sleek steel surface of the cylinder makes me nervous and I must remain calm if I'm to remain free. Calm is my only vestige of hope in these harried, dour days, and it's small, small. Wavering like candlelight before a storm front fast approaching. Fading with every aching step I put forward like light from a sky darkening with dusk.

I've always hated responsibility, and sought to shirk it when I could. My mother's open-handed claps to my ears taught me that if little else throughout my childhood and adolescence: I resented being made responsible for something someone else should have been made to suffer through, like my negligent father, leaving the burden of caring for my mother with me, and she and I growing more antagonistic towards each other each day passing because of it. Always a distant man, my father, muscular of frame but weak with disloyalty to her and to me. My limbs have never been strong like his. *Weighing down the brain scale, but where's the boy's brawn* – my father's words of old when critiquing his disappointing son. And yet I run. I plod on through another endless night and it's all really the same monotonous stretch of black now, while death ticks precise machine-time in my pocket, making each painful step a little gesture of hope for those I hold dear, and everyone else too. Default in a world where those few who know of my plight don't sympathize with it at all, and you're all lucky to even have me running this stupid race on your behalf.

I stop now, panting among scraggly road-side underbrush, longing for old, reliable comforts: my childhood bed in Ohio, the ceiling directly overhead covered with the diorama of plastic model rockets suspended among hanging plastic planets positioned to approximate a crude replication of the solar system; my dormitory room during my first year foray into University, adorned in much the same ebulliently youthful manner but with the added element of occasional female companions sharing the cramped quarters with me; and also for the hot embrace of my favourite hooker, Aimee, Dayton native and frequenter of all the most sordid trash bars, with her thin legs and disgusting yet riveting way of bending to my every lustful command. That a human being only as little and unimportant as myself should wield such power over another person. But then the tiny tick-ticking in my pants pocket is a reminder in the dark, and I turn my thoughts away from bitter-sweet reminiscences and gulp down the remainder of my tepid coffee, purchased one hour before from a donut shop off the turnpike. And I jog off slowly into wheat fields and darkness, the most important man in the world.

Or even Janice, wherever she might be tonight, who I left almost three years ago, discontented wife with all of her boyfriends and doting devotion to our daughter, Tasha: even her arms would suffice tonight, maybe. And little Tasha, magic hugger with stars in her eyes and big questions falling like something pristine from her pouting lips: *why is your work in the middle of all those sand dunes? What kind of work is it, anyways? Why can't you bring me there, too?*

And the glimmers in her eyes like signals for impending

bad weather each time I gave her no straightforward answers, and then the tears, that worst rainfall of all.

I dreaded those open innocent questions and the eyes that implored quietly for answer after the words hung heavy in the air between us. And so I left the questions. Only briefly, in order to complete our work, clandestine happenings in the desert, sequestered just like little Tasha said, making it poetry, *in the middle of all those sand dunes.*

Only that one project became two and then many and many, and weeks became months and calendars were discarded whole and replaced and Tasha's mysterious father was still buried beneath the sands beneath Gobi heat beneath the close scrutiny of an elite group of men who understood his genius in matters of electronic code-breaking and all of us there in those series of underground complexes and everyone else in the rest of the world, too, we all were and are still living our fruitless lives like ants beneath the close scrutiny of those greater by far than we can ever hope to be.

Those men in those bunkers and complexes ordered the father of a good little girl and the ex-husband of an awful wife and better mother to crack the mysterious soda pop can open, wide open to expose secrets of travel and communication in the most foreign-distant places. Because that father, that ex-husband, that fool me, had mistakenly spoken aloud his epiphany when it at last became clear beneath powerful lights and infra-red goggles and the whirring instruments in his trembling hands.

I said: *If we open this soda we call them to us. We'll call by breaking this seal and letting them know we have half-intelligent brains in our skulls and they'll come and it'll be over if we do that and so we mustn't do that. We mustn't do that.*

Or something like this. I said something as grounded in logic and steeped in disquiet and sincere with concern for our species as this and I was speaking to a silent room filled with important men wearing insignias of myriad size and shape and design along their collars and shoulders and an eager look in their eyes watching me, and I knew my mistake immediately. I'm only human, and this hollow-sounding excuse somehow isn't enough when I realize what I've let slip into greedy warfare minds.

I'm the stupidest man in the world, the man of hugest error.

And I'm the man of biggest regret.

Because I know. I *know*: the ticking-whirring is no purring kitten filling my pocket, but the worst imaginable event of all in our collective history, heading straight for us in our small, numb and complacent lives. Because I know. I solve codes and I often can feel their message before I've deciphered them. They call it a gift. I've known since my marriage died that it's only curse.

And so I spend my new life, such as it is, running. I run in shadows, I run beneath the cover of overhanging trees and rarely-used country paths and I travel with eyes perpetually scanning the lonely country through which I move. I drive stolen cars hot-wired in the wee A.M. hours until their engines sputter and die, or until I grow too fearful of roving highway patrols searching for missing license plate numbers, and I abandon the vehicles in ditches or farmers' fields or empty lots. I watch the skies fearfully, and the road before and behind. And I'm not safe. I'll never be safe again. And if I died now, the soda pop canister would eventually be discovered in my pocket or in the tightest of death-grips in my clutched fist and another colossal act of human foolishness would pry it from my fingers and force apart the resilient steel walls, revealing the beacon pulsing like a heartbeat within. And the strange, insistent glow inside would deepen as if in excitement, and pulse more frantically in the hands of the fool who willed to hold it.

And then fire, and then the end.

My stomach aches fiercely with emptiness. My head swims with nausea from my immense hunger, too. I spy a roadside confectionary shining its brilliant fluorescence into the night. I must go there, despite the danger to my life and to yours, too, despite my slowly depleting money supply. I'll steal when I have to. I must eat, if only because I must go on as long as my legs are able to travel. I readjust the pack over my shoulder, wincing at the ache it stirs in my muscles. I keep my eyes fixed on the bright sign ahead and in its neon brightness her face materializes. My daughter, angelic and swathed in light, propelling my steps forward.

* * *

The crouched form is the smallest tiger I've ever seen, orange-furred and motionless as it waits to pounce among the dead-looking grass growing wild among the cactus underbrush.

I watch from a little ways off, grimacing a little as I spy the tiny black lizard darting among the cactus stalks, oblivious of the kitten predator within striking range. Suddenly, the lizard stops, alerted to danger by some minute shift of air currents or of the cat itself, a youthful and inexperienced hunter in the night. A quick flicking of its long black tail like a whip in the darkness and the lizard scampers out of sight into the undergrowth.

I nearly chuckle but for force of habit, and only grin silently as the kitten, startled terribly by the lizard's fleet movement, also darts away in the opposite direction. Its dash brings it towards me, very close in its mad haste, and it only discerns my presence kneeling in the tall grass when it chances to catch my eyes watching its own. They shine an eerie emerald in the moonlight, holding my gaze evenly. I sense the animal's fear at my presence, a newly discovered hunter trespassing on its land. I wait, and let the aroma of the chocolate bar in my hand waft on the air to the kitten's nostrils. A moment passes, the two of us bathed in moon glow and staring as if spellbound into each other's eyes. Then, it edges forward, tentatively, small pink nose twitching, green eyes watching me warily.

We eat chocolate in the wild grass, one of several Mars bars I'd found stuffed into my jacket pocket. I leave little chunks of the bar on the ground which the cat tentatively edges towards, sniffs cautiously, and then eats, its eyes never once leaving me.

It's good to be cautious, I want to communicate to the animal, and when I reach forward this time, it allows me to caress the soft fur of its neck. I pet the animal for a while, relishing the contact with another living creature. I watch the sky. It's become an anxious habit of mine, watching the sky, any kind of sky, pristine afternoon blue, overcast with clouds of iron everywhere, clear evening with brilliant star fields emerging in all directions.

That's what I see now, endless star field, twinkling with potential.

I finish my chocolate and watch the kitten slink away into the bushes. I think of Tasha, and the memory comes to me suddenly from several years past: it had been only weeks before her fifth birthday and she'd been relentless in her efforts, passing the information along to me or her mother at any given opportunity: *A kitten's a really good birthday present to give someone. Really, really good.* Always with the mischievous little sparkle in her eyes which I never could help but adore.

We never got her a kitten, or a pet of any kind. Her mother hated animals, and didn't want to have to care for one if our daughter lost interest in it once its novelty wore off. The end. The memory makes me sad, and I find myself suddenly wishing very hard that I could simply wish her a kitten right now, wherever she is, whatever she's doing. But things aren't so easy. Things are always more difficult than this.

A moment later I'm creeping through the grass when I spy a tiny movement near my foot. I tense reflexively, relaxing when I see the lizard's tiny obsidian head peeking towards me from behind a particularly broad blade of grass. It sits poised alertly, eyes fixed unwaveringly upon me. By the shape of its bullet-head and its diminutive size, I think it's a salamander, though my expertise lies in other fields.

I reach slowly into my jacket pocket and retrieve the remainder of the Mars bar. I un-wrap it as quietly as possible so as not to disturb the creature and leave a small wedge of chocolate amid the grass stalks. Then I creep away, silent as a shadow.

I don't believe that lizards find chocolate particularly appealing, or that a place could possibly be made in their diet for it. I only like the idea of leaving a little something behind for the reptile, a gift, or an offering of peace, between two hunters in the night, between two hunted animals creeping noiselessly through the darkness.

* * *

I'd felt it coming, the rushing toward me of some inevitability. I'd felt it pulsing under my skin, in my skeleton maybe, like something preordained. Which is why I'd only stood there in the aisle, feeling helpless and remote from myself as I waited for the arrival of something that had finally caught up with me. I never gave too much thought to the notion of periods of calm preceding storms, but I understand it perfectly now: that pervasive stillness of life and you in it just before the rending and crashing chorus of thunder and rain. The air was loaded with suspense, and in the cliffhanger atmosphere I tried desperately to order my wildly running thoughts.

And the convenience store lit up like the face of the sun seen up close and the groceries rattling in their boxes and packages and toppling like confetti from their shelves and cluttering the avenues; spilled pickle juices lapping into shores of thickly settling ketchup, amid the ruin of spilled penny candy containers and the motionless forms of several other late night customers unlucky enough to be near to me at that precise moment. The window glass shattering and the burglar-proof bars caving inwards as the helmeted and goggled figures burst into the small store like midnight villains into an old comic strip. The violence of their inarticulate shouts and the crunch of their heavy boots across the new landscape of glass shards and other debris. The wailing of the other customers in their confusion and terror as they were passed roughly from one pair of hands to another to learn their fate for wee A.M. shopping at the most inopportune of times. The flickering of the overhead lights as if in some panicked electrical seizure resulting from the savagery of the commotion, coupled with the frantic blinding arcs of flashlight beams spotlighting all corners of the small store at once in their search for me scuttling like an insect in the aisles.

And then my final frantic dash to the rear of the small store, and my desperate foolishness as I jerked open at random one freezer door of several and quickly slipped a soda pop can containing doom there among dozens and dozens of similar others before collapsing to my knees once more. Then my thoughts reeling, and my eyes blurred and peering upwards from the sticky mire of the grocery aisle, and the freezer door lay gaping, its hinges surely fit to snap off completely, so wide was it held open by the man in military garb, all of his bulky equipment clunking insolently at his side. And my eyes lighting upon the contents of the freezer, and the laughter somehow escaping my constricted throat at that strange sight of that ugly brother, metallic grey and un-pretty, nestled so wrongly there among its pretty and appealingly-airbrushed sisters.

Coca-Cola. Sprite. Faygo Moon Mist, surely sprinkled down recently from lunar places as the innocence of its fairy tale name suggests, and luckily bottled and canned and secluded here in this happy freezer. And Pepsi with all its myriad flavourings, those new lemon- and cherry-flavoured offshoots which excite children everywhere. And death. Un-opened genocide waiting patiently for the hands of fools to pry its soda pop hide wide. And the signal will be sent. And the wait begun.

And resignation seeping into me along with the horror of the drama concluded at last, as the greatest of weights was at last lifted from my shoulders.

My last memory of that terrible night, the worst in mankind's short, impetuous history: that dull drab cylinder, no good at disguises, slipped from its misplacement among its innocent counterparts, nestled between the fingers of the military man.

I run now with freedom in my step, and resignation, too.

The hand of my daughter rests in mine every Saturday and Sunday afternoon as we stroll through green parkland and through the doors of neighbourhood ice cream parlours. I avoid crowded confectionary aisles when I can because I don't like the haunting of awful ghosts, but when Tasha's eyes shine imploringly and I know she's thirsty for some soda mist culled from moon craters (or for any other fanciful notions emblazoned in large letters on beverage containers and snack packages and which children believe in), I follow their line of vision without pause. I follow her everywhere, and it makes me feel like the only good military man in the world, obedient to sweet orders. And I rarely think of Janice, except for on occasion when I'm with my favourite hooker Aimee and I can't help the regrettable pictures that fall before my backwards-looking eyes. Or when I see her eyes reflected a little in the sullen look on our daughter's pretty face, a dissatisfied expression which I can't help but adore besides.

  I've done my best.

  I've run more miles than any man in the world, for no good reason but the few things I hold dear.

  And I spend my days waiting, living well from the money slipped silently to me, because a master code-breaker is my secret title and I'm needed on occasion in deep places in the desert when signals from afar need interpretation. My old insistence on running is a thing of the past, and is a sin that's been forgiven me by the men who need my special knowledge and expertise. I live between band-widths and among strange bleeps and scattered whirrings originating light years away and filtered through military-issue sonar and speakers to our unlucky ears, feeling their texture, determining better than anyone else their meaning, their location of broadcast, their imminence of fateful arrival. And I live an otherwise quiet life alongside more oblivious neighbours than I, with my daughter staying with me two days from each week and occasionally Aimee comes for dinner then, too, daddy's old friend from long ago. I haven't made the trip into town yet, but I think that a feisty feline ball of orange fur with a bow around its neck would make for a really good early birthday present in the weeks to come, a really, really good one for a little girl as sweet as they come.

  And I think of racks of neatly stacked soda pop cans and the image fills me with silly and deepest dread, and then I realize, and I laugh, because what else can I do but close the freezer door in my mind once again and know in my heart that I tried my very best. And when I on occasion wander just such cluttered aisles, I at least know that the small hand in mine is warm there, and as safe as I can make it.

  I idle away the long afternoon hours when I'm not needed beneath the sand. I spend the days reading newspapers in my chair on the patio and enjoying the sun on my face. I swim laps in the pool, seeking to break records I set in my youth. I have the weekends with my daughter, which I invariably look forward to. We watch movies together and I take her to the zoo to laugh at the antics of the monkeys and ponder the thoughts of the wise-looking elephants, wrinkled and grey and ancient. I look out across my lush summer lawn and I yawn often, bored, listless. The fire is coming into our skies, a violent picture soon to ruin everything. But I don't care anymore. I can't care anymore. I'm tired, and I can't ever run another mile, and I don't even want to. I'm the most unimportant man in the world, just like you.

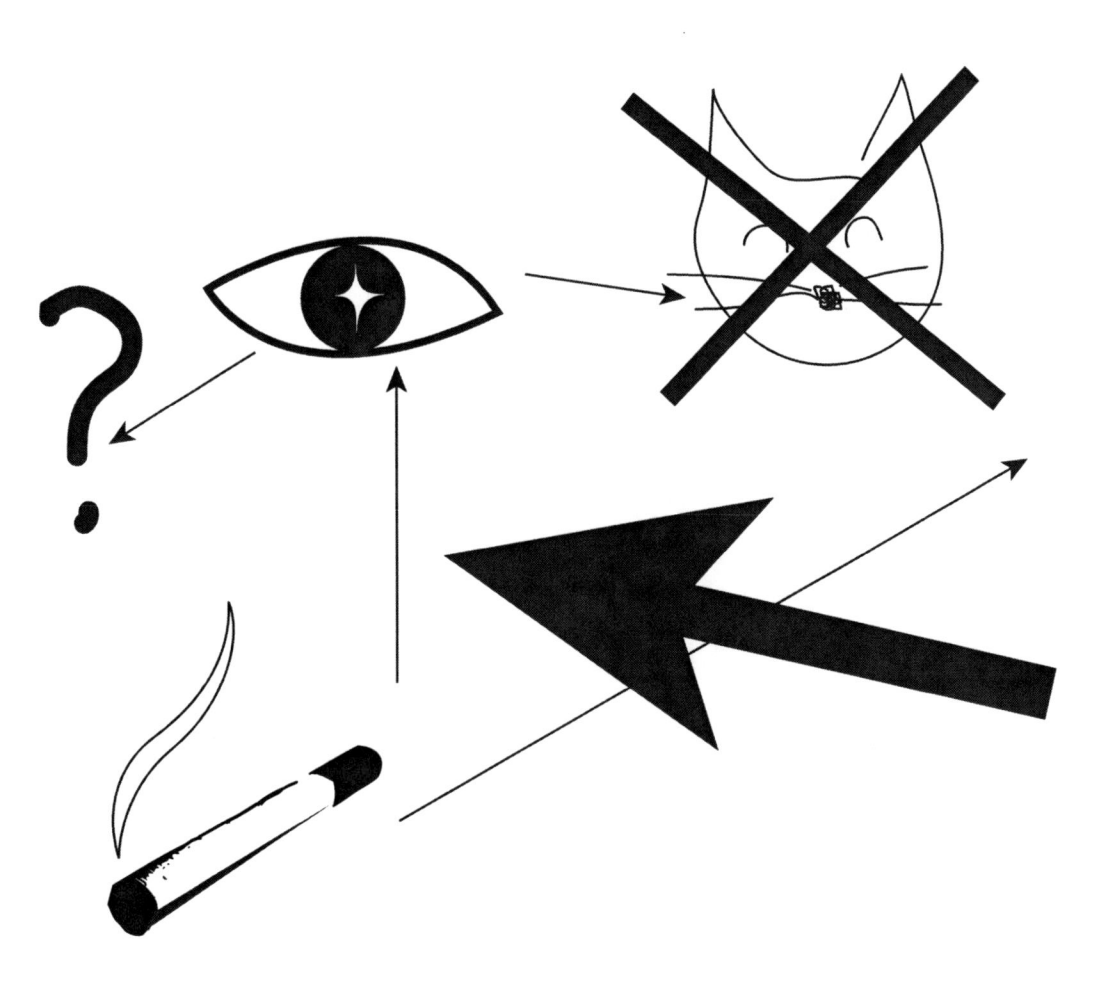

Waiting for the New Reign of the Fire Ants

That happy family of devils, I always hated them.

I hated their self-aware and confident smiles, mouths full to brimming with teeth straight and sparkling like star-shine. I abhorred their tawny heads like lions in summer, and the way they moved with hunting-cat grace through all the summer days of my youth, fooling all of the neighbourhood. Their words were nearly flawless too, over-flowing with good cheer so contagious everyone in their vicinity would feel their lips curling upwards in their presence.

Pretenders, the most expert I've ever encountered. A family headed by parent ghouls with perfect Halloween children, eyes burning with jack-o'-lantern glow and thoughts much murkier. And I hate them still, more and more with each moment of our shared past that collects and solidifies in my mind.

Oh, and there it is again, as pristine as ever, the picture: my first glimpse behind the mask.

Two boy-lions coloured in green towering a million years above the grass where I dwelled with my family of army ants. They stole my sunlight that afternoon. It was June, I remember. I remember it perfectly. I stared upwards with trepidation, suddenly chilled in my shirt sleeves and bare knees and bare feet.

In the giant silhouettes overhead, framed in fire from the early summer sun, a hint of a leering grin, times two. And from those wicked mouths, parted with practiced, perfect smiles displayed for the whole summer world to witness: "Hello, weak Neptune scum."

And their laughter, booming like rocket engines, turning the balmy air cold but filling my cheeks with new burning.

I looked at my hands, examining them fixedly while wishing earnestly for the tyrants to depart. Their laughter came again, and one of the boy-lions edged his huge, sneakered toe to my side, and before my eyes he crushed a small hill into scattered dust. I watched helplessly as a thousand, a million of my friends evacuated in long, frantic lines from the devastation. I watched them, all coloured in green, and then I removed my goggles and the tiny insects turned red again.

And from the dizzy heights above: "We aren't fooled, Neptunian filth. Remove your telltale headgear and we still see you for what you are." And the sneakered foot nudged me in my side, threateningly. I shied away from it, but it was insistent, and I was toppled into the grass with my panicking, fiery friends. I was scared then, too.

Then, the biggest affront: "Give me your weapons!" And my green-screened goggles were snatched up by rough, big hands with broken skin about the fingertips, and the overturned salad bowl with its scotch-tape-and-cardboard coloured wing-tips from on top of my head. The banana blaster, too, taken up from its place on the grass beside me. I peered upwards, feeling very young. I could feel my bottom lip begin to tremble, the first sign that salt water was threatening to flood my view of the world. One of the monstrous boys was watching me closely through the green plastic of the goggles he'd donned, mockery in his narrowed eyes, curling his ugly lips upwards, his mouth crammed with ordinary banana. The other wore the plastic bowl over his own head, and his big finger was pointed down at me, and the rolling sound on the air was his giant, loud, stupid laughter falling from the great O of his mouth.

I'll never forget that mouth. It was so big. It was bigger than anything in the world that afternoon.

And they danced away across my front lawn, wearing my father's factory goggles and my mother's salad bowl, leaving behind a ruin of rough, yellow fruit skin to turn brown and ugly beneath the sunlight; and they laughed with disdain, ruining the romance in the good words they sang as they went on their way: "Neptunian, Martian boy, space goggles, ant scientist." And they slipped away like strong hunters over the neatly cropped lawn, kicking a discarded tennis ball into the street on their way towards the house next door as a final casual display of their ownership of the day. These invaders, I then realized, were newly arrived in our green and good neighbourhood and my days of easy explorations into space and ant country were very suddenly drawing to a close.

My telescope confirmed my suspicions: they were devils from afar, landed here to crush weak boys into powder for insects to take on their backs and drag back to cool subterranean caverns, there to wonder over. This salt smells familiar somehow, but how?

And in the dust, there we were to remain, beaten.

So, with my stick of battered old silver arranged perfectly in my upper-floor bedroom window, trained downwards at precisely the right angle, I saw everything.

First it was only mildly odd behaviour. I didn't understand the kneeling postures upon the carpet, couldn't fathom the complex positioning of long, strong fingers to temples and cheeks. But then the radio transmitters appeared in those strong hands, secured deceptively inside stereo headphones. I was never duped. No innocence lived in those eyes. Nothing but bottomless places I couldn't completely understand, where only bad things dwelled which I couldn't communicate with at all. And I spied every night for an entire long, spoiled summer of my childhood and I witnessed many things boys should never have to see as their scheme was hatched: innocent walkie-talkies emblazoned with Parker Brothers insignia, surely bastardized and, after re-wiring, pressed to ears in the rooms below my far-seeing silver eye, supposed children's toys used to call upwards to those cold places between the night sky stars. I saw the red glow seep into the false boys' eyes when the lights were turned out for the evening every evening, setting the room ablaze, a pair of beacons easy to home in on. Such a vibrant red signal. Such a violent light. And other things, too, so many other mundane incidents injected with horrifying new meaning, given my knowledge: footballs contained sensory equipment and were used to scope terrain and secure data; the awful boys' parents' feigned attempts at friendship towards my own mother and father with a bestowing of home-cooked pastries, little cup cakes assuredly rigged with micro-reconnaissance devices, dumplings pulsing with detonators and which I surreptitiously bundled away on several different occasions in plastic trash bags to drown in the river; while cold looks delivered me as I sat huddled in the back seat of my parents' car pulling into our driveway indicated the intimate and secret knowledge I shared with the invaders.

I was privileged. I was cursed. I bore my burden well, for a ten-year-old.

I recorded everything, in one and a half battered coiled notebooks which I borrowed from a school friend and which I never returned. I leaf through them now and shiver at the discovery set down there in large, loopy child-scrawl so many summers past: they had come, for us all.

Many incidents stole that distant July away, shook apart my August like premature Fall breezes through the summer trees. All recorded by my young and careful hand. Meticulously-maintained observations like a cursed summer journal or fantastical yet scientifically accurate log. For future utility. For reminder in case I one day reached the age of parents and grandparents who doubted the truth in secret affairs. For proof, in case my life ended in untimely fashion, and then others might find value in my carefully wrought entries.

How could any boy enjoy the laziness of afternoon July skies when clouds might have hid electric eyes watching his movements across lawns and streets, through the dust of baseball diamonds and through the whisperings of wild grass in unkempt fields? Or those same skyscapes at night, when each shimmering star-dot was a burning eye following you unwaveringly no matter where you hurried, whether leaving the theatre with the movie's adventure lingering in your every step skipping along the sidewalks, or while walking to and from the neighbourhood confectionary for a late night snack of chips and fountain pop. When the skies watched his progress, a boy didn't notice the nocturnal symphonies of crickets in lawn grasses, couldn't be bothered to count crab apples in his parents' trees by the brilliant light of the noon-hour sun. Glittering dragonflies whirred by unnoticed, and rainbows emerged inside sprinklers' cascading waters for no young eyes to witness and watch entranced.

Taking refuge inside closet-hole nooks with flashlight glow guiding my hand, crouched beneath hanging heaps of morose winter clothes; in beneath-bed fortresses with boxes and blankets piled on the mattress above; braving centipedes and silver fish while squeezed into the narrow confines of the crawlspace with its sad bare-bulb lighting: these were the places I scratched at the pages, writing the secret history of the summer. Offering hints or clues or prophecies of the future fate of the world.

I remember distinctly the day I'd begun, a harried thank-you to the neighbor girl who'd provided me with her back-to-school notebooks when I'd discovered I had none myself. Pulling them from their white plastic bag wrappings with a rolling of her eyes and a small shaking of her head: strange silly boy, why are boys so strange and silly in the things that they do? Leaving me to my own devices, curled in my window-pane spy-hole, hunched forward with my eyes to the silver stick and pen and paper close at hand.

I saw many strange scenes through the silver eye.

The two brothers whispering through their window below mine and padding like noiseless ghosts across the grass. Pausing midway down the length of their house, only several feet from me spying bravely in my secret window vantage. Through my slightly ajar window, I heard the sound every night of their reliable nocturnal ritual: the tiny clicking noise, repeated twice, thrice and sometimes more times. Then the sputtering flame and the lighting of a cigarette which was passed back and forth between them. Their whispering language, usually never stealthy enough to avoid my keen ears. Given away by their wee A.M. schemings, the strange strings of words which I was certain were designed to maintain the subterfuge but never fooled me: *I want to get that girl. I want her so bad,* or *We have to check out the party next weekend.* I was old enough to know a little of the ways of older boys and girls, but still I wasn't duped. I pierced through their covert language tactics and deciphered the hidden meaning in their words of stratagem.

Get the girl. Check out the party.

Acquire specimens. And re-establish contact with the mother fleet hovering in the cumulus layers.

And the burning ember those two had passed between one another? The acrid cigarette stink did reach me through the window screen, but a ruse it surely had been. Some form of land-based operations signal, a burning circle among the maze of neighborhood houses for the cloud watchers to see and decipher? Or were other pairs of spies burning circles in the darkness of night also, across the street nestled in the grass alley between houses there, or briefly in a darkened window or alongside the stout cedar with its leaves rustling in the nervous night?

I once panned my electric eye into the east, managing to snatch a clear view of the neighbors' houses which abutted our backyard. And there indeed my suspicions were proven correct: a woman in pale nightgown and slippers, hair wrapped tightly with curlers like large spiders criss-crossing her skull. Cigarette between fingers, gazing serenely towards the neighbor boys whispering in the shadows of our houses. Burning circle to burning circle. Silent communication in the night.

My hand becoming numb with the frenzy of my note-taking. By moonlight I wrote, little window scientist recording the quiet invisible happenings of my haunted neighborhood.

July 23. 2:36 A.M. The invaders gathered in smoking spot. Talked about: getting girls (abducting human beings) and watching the show (unknown event, something to do with abducted girls? Scientific experiments on humans? Executions?). "Smoked," using burning object disguised as cigarette (for signaling other invaders?).

July 29. 3:10 A.M. The invaders gathered on grass. One brother was holding weird box in his hand. Box had lights that winked and blinked and made weird noises. He was aiming it into the sky while the other brother was kneeling beside him with his hands over his ears. They did this for exactly half an hour and then went inside. They didn't talk at all the whole time. (Weird invader ritual? Some signal to other invaders? Getting ready to take over?)

July 30. 3:20 A.M. Invaders were watching the sky. Both had arms open. This lasted few minutes. Had to be careful or else they might have noticed me in my window. Then something fell down from sky. Right past my window and made me jump a little. It landed on grass between them. Made noise like Poom! and was smoking. Smoked for long time. Invaders were kneeling beside it and doing something but I couldn't see, even with telescope. Went inside at 4:05 A.M. Climbed through window like they came out. It looked scary when they did it. They were really quick, like spiders. I hate them.

August 5. 12:51 A.M. The invaders gathered in smoking spot. No "smoking" tonight. Only talking on telephone (no phone cord – transmitter?) with unknown speaker. Talked about the "party" (mother ship, fleet?) in two days' time. Then changed language. Started talking in weird language I didn't understand. Never heard anything like it before. (true invader language?)

August 9. 12:32 A.M. One invader only. "Smoking" alone. Nothing else to report. But I can't sleep.

August 16. 2:58 A.M. Invaders gathered in smoking spot. Talked but I couldn't hear them tonight. A cat came and hissed at them. One brother picked cat up and went into bushes with it. The bushes were shaking and then brother came out but no cat. The other invader was holding big metal-looking box. Very long. Put it on grass and opened door. Looked like 10 or 15 small weird animals came out. They looked silver and had no fur. About as big as small dogs or big rats. Animals moved away from invaders in every direction. No noises from them. Scary.

August 16. 4:00 A.M. One hour later. Brothers standing and "smoking." No talking at all, just standing in dark. But I could see their eyes. Suddenly all animals came back at same time. Went directly inside metal box. One invader closed the door and they took box inside. (Scouts sent out on mission in the neighbourhood?) Creepy.

August 16. 9:00 A.M. Went to investigate bushes. No one around. Found cat, but not sure if same one from last night. Eyes missing and looked like all bones were missing, too. Mushy-looking and soft and flat. Like an old carpet. Gross and scary. Was leaving bushes and noticed something move above in window. I looked and there was the father invader. He saw me! Ran home. Am in closet. Scared.

August 16. 8:00 P.M. Saw something downstairs in basement. Was getting microwave popcorn for mom from shelf and saw something move beside the washing machine. Looked and saw small animal. Mom says it's a mouse and we better get traps. Doesn't *believe it had silver-ish skin and red eyes. I watched it run away from me and then it disappeared. In middle of floor...just disappeared! I picked up old hockey stick, the Bauer with aluminum blade, and nosed around for a minute but there was nothing except 2 centipedes around the dryer. Smelled weird, though. Like smoke but different. But I didn't tell mom because she'd tell me about my imagination again. (One of weird creatures the invaders had last night? Sent it here to spy on me? Kill me? Will it come back? Have to put traps all over my room. Hope they have traps strong enough and smart enough.)*

August 18. 5:03 A.M. Just woke up. Thought I heard the invaders outside my window. Listened and thought they were talking in their weird language. Went to window but nothing moving down there. Glad I'm up here and not down there. (Maybe I'm picking up their transmissions in my braces, like kid I read about who caught radio stations that way?) Weird.

August 20. 2:05 A.M. Waited and waited but nothing except one of the invaders leaving house and walking somewhere. It looked like he was holding something, maybe camera or device disguised as camera. That was over one hour ago. Nothing else to report. (My teeth hurt. Been hurting all night. Headache, too, bad one. And there's weird ringing in my ears that's been bothering me all day. I don't like it.)

August 23. 5:00 A.M. Just woke up. Thought I heard their voices again but nothing outside. I can't sleep. I'm thirsty but don't want to go downstairs alone. Trap under bed just went off a minute ago and scared me! But I checked and nothing was in it. Maybe a spider set it off but got away. Weird.

August 26. 2:50 A.M. Only one invader. Brought girl with him. Were close together on grass. Him on top and she was crying. (Human specimen being destroyed?) Thought it was finally happening, the big invasion. But then felt stupid when they were gone and dad didn't believe me. I'm scared.

    The memory is vivid and brings me from my reverie: waking my father and being reprimanded for the late hour's disturbance. Only to discover no murder being committed on the A.M. grass between our houses at all, only an empty space of lunar-lit lawn where I swore to him of what I had seen minutes earlier. The burning in my cheeks when he reminded me of my big imagination, and that young boys must sleep or their eyes will tell them strange things. Standing before him with bowed head and eyes examining my socks, shamed and furious, my ideas foolish in his eyes and the simple truth in mine.

    Mother's discovery beneath my bed of the ragged notebooks. Her perusal one afternoon of my documentations while I was away, seated stubbornly in an orthodontist's chair or doctor's office. Her dinner-time commentary on my work, shockingly unexpected and offensive: *A very imaginative son we have here. There are invaders that walk among us.*
    Their quiet laughter, mocking but prideful. Because fantastical though its meanderings may have been, my imagination certainly was an active one. Me stewing helplessly in my seat with meatballs and noodles cooling on the plate before me, bearing their innocent offences with burning cheeks and downcast stare. Mother's tender voice of concern, just in case her silent son's imagination kept reality a trifle too far at bay.
    Well, their football might *be a secret weapon, sweetie,*

but it might just be a football, too. And the walkie-talkies, too. All boys like those kinds of things. And though they shouldn't, I do fear some of them even smoke cigarettes. It makes them look cooler to the girls.

They do different things to girls, I wanted to shout at her. *And leave cats boneless and flat in bushes, and pray to the stars for weird things to fall down on the grass.* Loudly and vehemently so that she might finally hear and maybe even glean some small bit of understanding. But choosing only to maintain my armour of silence, only picking at my cold meat and unappetizing noodles, waiting for the privilege to leave their mocking table and then make straight for my bedroom sanctuary. Up the stairs in a flash and locking the door from inside. Sliding like a baseball player to the sacred spot before my bed and pulling the books out in a frenzy. Rifling through the pages until my eyes saw the familiar words they sought.

Proof, against adult logic and its wrongful sanities.

Here and there, scattered throughout the book, appearing in many entries in my neat, careful letters like some living authentication of my secret apocalypse.

Tonight: Another sighting. The invaders' eyes glowed again. Red eyes in their house. I'm so scared.

And I *was* scared. Truly and terribly frightened of those eyes and the things they might have meant for me, and my disbelieving and hurtful but still loving parents.

Red eyes in the night.

And what adult logic could thwart this terrible science and make a boy disbelieve the certainty of his theories?

And I watched for them every night, and saw them many of those nights. Burning in the darkness like miniature infernos. Hateful and piercing. Eager and intelligent. So fearfully intelligent. Shunning the warm daytime outdoors and ghosting fretfully through the halls and rooms of my house, waiting in my secret window pane shelter, for a night to fall when the stars would collapse and bring with them a million more pairs of dancing fire to teach us all about the summer night sky and the things it might hold.

I am still waiting, only now in this updated version of my old world.

My wife lies beside me, the rhythmic rise and fall and rise of her chest in the dim glow of the bedside lamp a small reassurance. I love her. She is my treasure, second to none, to nothing in this world. Even to my secret cache of literature secured snugly at the bottom of the small wooden box beneath our bed, ostensibly a home for out-of-print space exploration magazines from my youth. This literature which has followed me from young days like a haunting or reminder: that I must never ever forget.

I lie here and I wonder: has anyone else seen the fire glow in their eyes, that light which could burn away in the darkness of a bedroom until orange sunlight and birdsong returned to the early morning sky?

I wonder.

I moved from that neighbourhood years past. I have raised a family of my own. That family of devils from afar lives there still, or the handsome evil sons at least, so I've been told. Parents die, sometimes upon distant foreign soil like my old shimmering-green neighbourhood in the throes of lush summer. Some things are constant. Or perhaps it is only that some parents seek to return to the place of their birth. Visiting is good. It warms the blood once it has grown cold with distance and home-longing.

But they are still there, a household of inheritors. Two lion-sons remaining, oddly – revealingly? – in the selfsame house, an old and familiar base of operations since times long past. Sharing those rooms and spaces with their own families or fellow secret soldiers. Owners of strips of well-manicured, lush lawn and plentiful vegetable garden, of a half dozen or more rooms. Of a headquarters disguised strangely, beautifully, faultlessly, a chameleon in the country of my youth.

The tawny-haired boys have grown into men. They have matured inside and out and remember me when, on occasion, we collide in neighbourhood grocery aisles or with the hands of our children slipped snugly inside our own as we stroll slowly over park lawns. And they say commonplace things like: *it's been so long, and it'd be great to have a chat sometime.* And I seek the crimson in their hard stares and, often, very often, I'm certain that I spy it there still. Beneath the pleasant demeanors and polite greetings. From behind the eyes in the place where truth can be seen, if only we look close enough.

My wife tells me they're charming. She insists about her radar with regards to people, and that some are definitely good all the way through.

And I see the innocence in her eyes and I realize anew each time I behold that kind and naive look: I do not hate that old family of devils. Maybe once, in a different summer whose leaves have long since withered and crumbled to dust. When I was collapsed from my blissful place as ruler of insects and stopped noticing the beautiful look of the sun burning in the purity of blue skies. But no longer. I do not hate them for stealing my space glasses and helmet or for toppling my kingdom of hills because they must have their reasons for landing beside my beloved childhood home and remaining here with us. Their mission mandate. Who am I but one frightened man of Earth to question their motives?

We will never have dinner with those children from the old neighbourhood, not ever, not if I have anything to do with it. I will never have another black hole mocking mouth swallow another day of my life again. Not until I must bow to fate, and my final moment is arrived.

I turn and measure the timing of my wife's breathing. Her eyelids flutter subtly, she's deep in dreams and I hope they're a pleasant country for her to wander in tonight. I reach beneath our bed, brush the familiar wood with my fingertips. I pull the box from out of darkness and deposit it like an old gift in my lap. I feel the old excitement pulse through me and I rummage among the tattered old magazine covers and dog-eared, yellowed pages. And beneath, buried under words of wonder and dust from the crumbling newsprint paper they are set upon, I pull the old notebooks.

I turn first to the last page I wrote upon those many years ago, to the last page in case I am running out of time, in case I must awaken my wonderful wife beside me and deliver her one final kiss on her lips.

I recall that final, distant night of an August I can never forget, when the stars shimmered like eyes inside my telescopic lens, and I feared school coming, bullies in the hallways and at recess, and other much more deeply fearful fates. Marking a seasonal time when miraculous life had appeared and disappeared before me like silvery snippets of magic show terror. When the sky rained down strange smoking gifts for those with arms ready to accept them. When I scratched a final farewell to my stolen summer, and a final proof of the profound secret pulsing at its heart for adults to disbelieve and for me to know, and know alone. And I close my eyes as my fingers search easily for the familiar creases, the memorized shape and width of bent corners of the old notebook pages. And I open my eyes and I am reassured again, of at least some things. I read:

August 31. 11:30 P.M. Last day of August. May as well be the last day of summer…

…My braces are noisy. I have an electric mouth tonight…

…They're coming for us all. I hear them when they talk to me.

And I pause there a moment, as always, and with sadness and fear and a very familiar surge of huge excitement riding my perpetual secret loneliness and rushing its way like cosmic energy through my nerves, I finish reading, and the book is done:

You don't understand.

I close the pages and secure them within their box and slide everything again beneath the bed.

Outside, beneath the cool, dew-soaked grass, I know the fire ants are preparing for another day of toil in the earth. I move my lips in silence, mutely speaking from younger days of hazy summer – and from this expectant, vigilant now, too – and I wish them the best of luck.

And I finally shut off the bedside lamp, and I am cold in the darkness as I wait for bright doomsday.

Pining for the Lost Love
of the Moon Creatures

The moon was huge, a bright, low-hanging coin in the late night sky, dwarfing the stars with its luminous blaze.

Being careful to keep his gaze fixed on his hands as he spoke, Dan said, "I'm beginning to see the light."

From beside him on the top tier of the bleachers, John swallowed some of his Faygo cola. He felt the icy beverage move down his throat, quenching the dryness put there by a late night meal of cheeseburgers and French fries, and through the warm summer evening's air. "I'm glad, man. Enlighten me. I so need enlightening."

Dan poked at the jagged landscape of ice in his cup with his striped straw. "Basically, just forget it. Get up, keep truckin', the new day sucks regardless. We live, we die pretty soon."

A pause, and, "I feel better. Thanks. Wanna join me in opening my wrists to the elbow? I might have a pair of razors in my jacket pocket."

Dan was absently blowing droplets of cola through his straw at a tiny swarm of night bugs hovering beside them. The insect cloud held its position despite the cold shower. "Maybe in a bit. Listen though, man. Think about it: 'Wine in the morning, some breakfast at night, I'm beginning to see the light.' It's this simple, maybe."

"You're quoting Lou Reed at me."

"Who better to quote?"

"True. He seems to know things, that man." John could still taste the hamburger in his mouth: grease, the sharp tang of onion slivers, the harshness of mustard and the gooey melt of hot cheese.

Summer tastes, for sure, and a staple of their late nights out together. "Okay," he said. "So then...You're not too happy, it sounds."

Dan didn't answer right away. He stared into his cup a moment with a pensive expression, eventually coming up with, "No." Defeated, tired.

"See? You can't psyche yourself, and try to make yourself happy, even with inspiring song lyrics on your side. It's gotta be something bigger than that."

Silence fell between them. The crickets, a million miles below them, lost among the tall renegade grass shooting up beneath the bleachers, sang without accompaniment. There was no other sound on the air, their legs violining loudly in the huge quiet of the night.

Then, "That girl I like, from the mall?"

"Yeah?" and John turned to look closer at the silhouette of his friend in the gloom.

"She moved. Back home."

"Oh, oh," John stammered. "Well, I'm sorry to hear it. That sucks for you, man. Truly. Truly. Where did she...Where's she from?"

Dan went back to examining his hands beneath the wan light of the sky, and he said, "The moon."

Silence returned between them for a moment, the crickets doing well in their attempt to once again fill it fittingly with their electric soundtrack. Suddenly hearing the sadness in their nocturnal song, John said, "Really? She said that?"

"Yes."

Tentatively, "Is she perhaps a little mescaline addict as well?"

"She's gone. She called me last night to say goodbye. 'Bye, I'm going home, back up to the moon.' I went by her house today. Empty. Totally. Totally barren." He paused, his mouth screwed up to speak but the wrinkle of worry in his brow halting his words momentarily. Finally, "She didn't even tell me why she had to go. Just that she had to. Like there was no way around it, even though she sounded so sad telling me. Like she wanted to stay but couldn't."

John let a quiet whistle out through his lips. He didn't quite notice how pretty it sounded riding on top of the melody provided by the crickets. "What the hell, man."

"Yeah. Terrible. Everything's. Just. Terrible."

John wrinkled his brow. "She must've been planning it or something, for a long time, or whatever, and just didn't tell you." He paused, and examined his own hands. "Maybe she didn't like you, maybe."

A moment later Dan said, "She said she did. She said it last night. Except she used the word 'love'."

"That's the biggest word."

"Yes, it is…Fuck."

"That's another pretty big word."

"It's not that big."

The ancient wood of the plank they sat on, weathered and marked in a million places with engravings of the initials of boys and girls who ostensibly loved one another, creaked as John shifted his weight. Dan sat motionless beside him, intrigued by his hands still, which were now clasped weakly together as if in halfhearted prayer. He noticed vaguely how ethereal they looked to him beneath the pale light of the night sky, and wondered how phantom-like the rest of him looked seated among the old rickety, moon-drenched bleachers.

A moment passed, only the thick breathing of the night around them.

"I can't look up, man." He paused, and John saw from the corners of his eyes how he raised his head from examining himself, but then quickly let it fall downwards again. "My whole life's garbage now," he continued self-deprecatingly. "No, I can't go out tonight – it's a full moon…I totally see her up there. Crazy. Crazy. Pathetic and crazy."

Tentatively, John said, "So you believe her? That she's… You know?"

"She wasn't like anyone I've ever known." He shook his head, knowing he could never adequately convey his knowledge of her in words, and dropped an ice cube from his overturned paper cup. He watched its progress like a glistening meteor plummeting into the shadows beneath the bleachers. Look out, world of crickets, he thought absently, things are crashing down all around. Then he said it again. "I totally see her up there. I...I feel her. Like she's touching me, everywhere." He traced a slow line with his finger across the back of his other hand, feeling the moonlight in his skin. Then, "I can't even look up. I feel...I feel sick almost, even being out here. Physically sick. Like a chunk of me's missing or..." He drifted off, shaking his head helplessly.

John's eyes hung in the sky when he said, "She's probably closer than that, man. She's probably one town over. Nobody ever gets too far away from here."

"...Okay."

"She's not an alien, man...She's not Alf or anything. She's not from *They Live*. She's not that totally cute." He didn't sound convinced of his own words, but they laughed quietly in the darkness anyways.

Silence between them. Then Dan, his murmuring voice soft, "She left me a rock from the...from the moon." He batted a large white moth from its erratic orbit near his face, watched it flit forlorn-looking over the rust-flecked rear railing of the bleachers and off into the night.

John followed its progress, too, thinking how ghostly it looked fluttering in the darkness. "Can I...Can I see it?" he asked. "The rock?"

Dan thought a moment. Then, "Maybe...Maybe not. Not right now. If that's okay with you." He slipped his hand protectively overtop the slight bulge in his jacket pocket and kept it there. He sensed cold emanating from the pocket, but knew it was only his agitated imagination.

John nodded. "Yeah. Sure. No problem." He swatted away a mosquito from where it buzzed near his ear. It had startled him, its loud angry sound materializing so close to him in the soothing night. They sat a moment, and he murmured, "She gave you a piece of the moon." And it was all he said, and it said it all, really, putting it that way. He suddenly saw the somehow forlorn look of the wan, lunar-lit soccer field before them. He thought he maybe glimpsed something a little bit magical, too, in the ethereal, silvery glow.

They sat in silence a while longer. Suddenly, "She

couldn't have said she's from Nicaragua or something! Or Toronto! Any place remotely more mundane! But no, she had to ruin the man in our moon. I prefer his old face." Even as the last words left his lips he doubted them.

John chuckled softly, but his laughter drifted alone on the air this time.

Another moment of silence, and then John murmured reflectively, "The moon. The moon. It's a cold, cold place. Maybe everything's cold up there."

Dan's return murmur came quickly: "I'm not so sure about that."

The quiet descended between them again, broken briefly by the distant roar of an invisible plane rumbling somewhere against the stars. Then only cricket symphonies and the occasional tinkling of ice cubes against one another in their paper cups.

"Hey, man," John said, making his voice a little louder for his friend's benefit. "Some things we'll never know. And maybe that's okay. So look up. But look towards where you think…To where Pluto is."

"Pluto?"

"Pluto. Far away and remote. A mystery at the edge of the galaxy. Icy and dead, but then again, you never know. Pluto."

"Which way's that?" Dan's eyes remained trained downwards as he said it, a despondent murmur in the dark.

"Oh, that-away," John said, gesturing absently overhead. Then, "Good things land here sometimes, I guess. For whatever reasons."

Dan stirred the remainder of his Faygo with his straw. "…Pluto?"

"Pluto."

"And what kind of wonderfully hurtful things lie there, man?" he asked wistfully.

"You're fantastically sappy sometimes, man." But he was smiling as he said it.

"What can I do?"

John glanced to his watch, holding it aloft for a helpful shimmer of moon glow. Then he rose slowly from the wooden plank,

457

and said, "3:44 A.M. Let's break open the wine, Lou."

Dan stood, too, slowly, pulling a pair of plastic sunglasses from the pocket of his summer jacket. These he slipped on, and a moment later they were making their way across the neatly kept field.

The moon's face was full and pock-marked with crater and hill, resting low and lustrous in the early morning sky; and, like the crickets prettily noisy in the cool grass, it stayed with them as they went, a giant ghost hovering in blackness. They kept their eyes on the path before them as they walked through the lunar light, avoiding the glimmering stars overhead, but could do nothing to drown out the insect symphony around them. And this was okay, because it seeped upwards from places they understood, from grass and dirt and earth they could easily fathom; and it existed for them alone, to help soothe their murky thoughts, or for the simple reason of sounding perfect pulsing in the darkness.

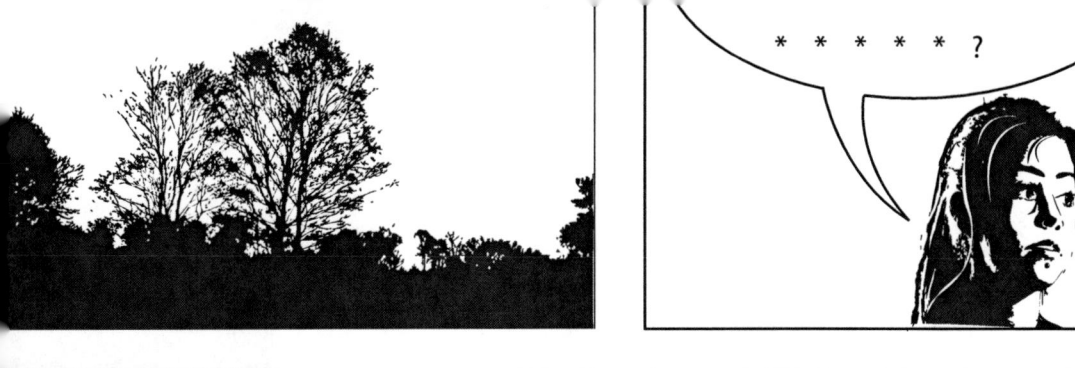

The Empty Hands
of Alvin Calvin Rourke

Hello to whoever may be reading this true documentation of my life, as written by myself: Alvin Calvin Rourke. Forgive me of any gaps or discrepancies in my narrative. Under the circumstances by which I pen this, I believe it is somewhat understandable. This you will also understand upon the completion of my story.

Let me begin with a rough sketching of my early childhood – the true beginning for us all – and subsequent maturation into a young adult. As a boy, I found myself constantly on the periphery of the regular playground activities associated with and practiced by children. Perhaps it was my timid nature which, regrettably, forced me into a position on the outer ring of most social groups. I say most, as eventually I discovered several others in whom I glimpsed characteristics similar to my own. These few became my childhood friends.

One of these, my first true 'friend', was named Mickey Lablanc. He was a short boy, and a rather thin boy, but then so was I. We found that we shared many interests, ranging from collecting comic books, reading science fiction stories and, most notably, watching horror films. This last seems to me now an ironic twist upon my strange and incredible life, laced with an overly generous amount of foreshadowing; in particular when I recall exactly what it was that Mickey and myself had always found so attractive, so irresistible and as well terrifying about this unique genre: the notion that perhaps, just perhaps, there were things in our natural world which for the most part went unseen, things not readily observed, yet there with us each day of our little lives nonetheless. Perhaps hybrid animal forms, the blood of man mixing in unholy flow with that black blood of the wolf, really could be seen loping hunched and malformed upon dark moors beneath the wild light of certain midnight moons; perhaps goblins rode down often from the belly of the moon in our sky when that moon was the colour of blood, down from those cold black spaces between the stars, upon the warm summer-night air when the world lies sleeping; perhaps wretched, rotting ghouls sometimes screamed their indignations and laments throughout the huge silence of dead night, the lonesome ache within them becoming unbearable; and maybe their cries on occasion were answered, in obscure, fog-enshrouded cemeteries, where the mad, scrabbling noises of cadaver-fingers upon the wooden walls of their coffins floated on the cool air.

And who was to say, particularly to two imaginative and naïve young boys, that it was beyond any and all probability that a blood-drinking vampiric woman could not reside next door to your very own home, posing convincingly and oh-so deceptively as the average middle-class social worker, a mundane facet of an apparently ordinary world; who fooled your parents, everyone, with her polite 'hello's' and 'how are you today's', only to retreat into the cold blue depths of her basement and sleep away the better part of each of her days hung upside down, waiting for the call of hunger to awake her once again. Who could contradict our suspicions, our beliefs that these things were?

Our mothers and fathers, naturally. But then, they did not believe you when you swore to them, perspiration beading your young brow and heart-pounding fear swelling in your chest, that yes indeed, there had been a monstrously long shadow crawling across the floor towards your naked bed, upon which you lay. *Upon which you lay!* With what for protection? A blanket? And perhaps a pillow or two? Because you, in your haste to rush to bed at your mother's insistent behest, had foolishly forgotten to carry your Masters of the Universe Power Sword with you when you had turned out your lights.

Oh really, father, it was only the wind, moving the old elm's branches across the window outside and that was all that I had seen? Why, thank goodness you came in here when you did, and informed me of this natural phenomenon that had me so frightened just moments ago. Silly me. Oh, but did you happen to hear what I had attempted to inform you of? That it had not been the shadows of a branch moving in the breeze that I had seen on my bedroom floor, because it had claws at the end of its hands, *its hands,* and the old elm outside does not have those, I am quite certain of that, but correct me if I am mistaken.

Oh, I am sorry, father. You are correct in what you say. I am getting to be far too old for behaviour of this sort. I will indeed cease my banter and go to sleep, and no longer dwell on idiotic 'child-fantasies', except that I myself happen to be a child, and if I see that crawling shadow again tonight and it is crawling towards your and mother's room, father, well, fuck you and have pleasant dreams, well, at least until it creeps into bed with you and mother and rips you both into a million red pieces. Good night, father. Sleep well. And I love you, too.

Forgive me. I seem to have digressed in my account of my life's happenings, on a more personal path of memory. But perhaps it is as well that I have, for this will paint for you, the reader, a more vivid portrait, and will, I hope, help you to understand a little of what I myself now believe to be true, at the culmination of my tale.

To continue, my friend Mickey and I chummed together for years, watching movies, visiting the mall and the comic book shop regularly, and simply keeping one another's company.

This continued until we had reached high school. Here, our paths diverged somewhat. Oh, we still spoke on the telephone, mostly about new horror films and old science fiction stories, well beloved by us, but our relationship seemed restricted to this sort of communication. Gone were the long weekends of film-watching and popcorn-eating, as were the afternoons of comic book browsing and story-telling when it got to be past midnight and such.

Mickey made new friends, and many of them. Less and less we spoke, until our friendship had been reduced to simple 'hello's' and 'how are you doing's' in the hallways at school. This is not to say, though, that in any way old Mickey had metamorphosized into the unfeeling and careless monster that so many people in this world we live in do. He never grew into something so hideous. We simply grew apart.

I was invited, for example, to attend many a social function with Mickey and his newly acquired companions, which I usually declined. I did not feel altogether comfortable amidst these others and so I remained at home weekends, secluded in my bedroom, studying and learning to become what I had always wished to be as a child: a writer.

My textbooks consisted of Lovecraft and Poe, and Bradbury and Tolkien, and Heinlein, never excluding Wells, Burroughs, Tesla, Pratt, Derleth, and the greatest of them all, Howard.

I plodded through the required five years of seemingly endless high school, arriving at a sad juncture in my life. I could go on academically to university and likely be rather unhappy, or I could remain at home working, and remain rather unhappy still.

I chose the former, on the basis that perhaps rigorous amounts of literature and writing classes might improve my poor writing skills. They did not. Midway through my third year away at school I replaced my major, which had at the time been English Literature, with Psychology. I felt discouraged with myself, and more than a little angry at my undistinguished performance. I had been writing for years at the time of this change, and my work still reeked of what appeared to be contrived Poe and Burroughs. But they were highly influential, in my defence, and so my work naturally reflected them.

If truth be known, I was less disappointed with my writing than were several publishers, who informed me that my submissions were utter drivel, essentially. Thus disheartened, I ended abruptly my tenure as would-be freelance writer, and continued on studying in the field of psychology, a decision which I never really forgave myself for making.

As worth noting here as at any other point in my narrative, is a minute fact about myself which has endured from approximately my twelfth birthday to the present. From said time as a young boy, until this very day, I have maintained a rather enjoyable, and often very necessary, habit of mine.

You see, what I do, and have been doing for these many years, involves two main components: cockroaches, as in those wondrous, resilient creatures that you may find scurrying underneath your oven when you turn a switch and flood the kitchen with light in the early morning before heading out to work; and alcohol, as in any of the wide variety of substances that have the equally wondrous ability to intoxicate upon consumption.

Now, you may find this somewhat perplexing. What, you are likely asking yourself, would these two seemingly unrelated ingredients have in common with one another? Well, I agree with your inevitable conclusion: nothing whatsoever. In most cases.

However, as an inquisitive twelve-year-old boy, I had happened upon several discoveries one cold fall afternoon while my parents had been up in town. Firstly, I had found that although it burned the lining of my young throat like hell-fire itself, the mysterious stuff within the bottles from which my father so frequently drank affected me in an unfamiliar but not altogether unpleasant manner.

In essence, I had discovered getting my twelve-year-old self drunk on my father's alcohol (always making certain to add a generous quantity of water to the translucent or opaque bottles afterwards to ensure my safety from discovery).

Alright, reader of my story. You now know of my alcohol rituals. Where do those damned roaches come into play? Let me explain. You see, after the room began to elongate before my young eyes – always the signal that it was time to move on to the next important step of the procedure – I would make my way into the kitchen, bringing with me the bottle of whichever substance I had swallowed. Once there, I would set it on the table, amidst my mother's tea cups and plates and saucers, and begin my search for the cockroaches.

Falling to my knees before the stove and always feeling a trifle silly in so doing, I would pull clanging out of its recess the yellowed bottom drawer upon which the kitchen unit sat. And there, underneath the monstrous device, I peered into a world hidden from our view, at least the most of the time. It was always under the stove that the most cockroaches were to be found, and the fattest and juiciest, too. Yes, they would see the sudden flood of light and hear the resounding crashing in the upper reaches of their metal castle and they would attempt to flee from the giant invading their realm, somewhere into the dark crannies of peeling linoleum and wallpaper. But I was quite quick. I would always manage to reach in and snatch up at least one hapless individual before he could be safely away, sometimes more than one.

Grasping my prize gently between my thin fingers, I would then make my way to the kitchen table, upon which lay the procured bottle of liquor. I would lightly, oh so lightly, drop my cockroach into one of the available and empty tea cups, and situate myself in a chair overlooking this boy-fashioned prison.

Then followed my favourite step of the procedure. Lifting the bottle of alcohol to the lip of the tea cup, I would slowly let fall a drop, and then another and another of the substance from its mouth onto the cockroach below. Then, quickly quickly, because roaches are very fleet creatures themselves, I would pull a sheet of cellophane tautly across the top of the cup, securing the insect within.

Then, I would wait, and watch the cockroach scrambling about inside the cup, probing the porcelain walls with its twitching antennae, becoming inevitably more and more covered by the wetness of the alcohol.

Soon, we would be ready to talk with one another. It usually took several minutes before this could happen, but it always did, and it was always worth the meagre few minutes of waiting.

It was always the cockroach that initiated the conversation.

"Hello," he would say. "And how are you?"

"Fucking terrible," I would usually answer, experiencing a rush of power and freedom as I spoke it. My mother and father were of the strictest belief that language of this sort was uncivilized and bespoke an uncouth upbringing. Fuck them, I had always mused, and still do, a smile upon my face.

"Well then," the cockroach would always say, so very gently. "What seems to be the trouble?"

Then a long conversation would ensue, in which I laid bare my naked thoughts and feelings to my understanding, and more importantly, listening companion. By the end of such interactions, my mind always seemed cleansed of its congested and muddy obstacles and I could return both my friend to his shelter beneath the stove and my father's liquor to its place of residence in the cupboard in the living room, with its rows of companions.

Most times thereafter, I would retire to my bedroom and sleep until the sounds of my parents' return awakened me from downstairs. Then, I would make as if I had been reading a novel the entire length of their departure, and smile at them as they passed my room en route to their own.

Now you know of my cockroach/alcohol habit. You may find it to be an odd, or perhaps vaguely frightening concept, but I assure you, my mind is a stable one, slightly overworked at times, but stable nonetheless. I have only disclosed this small practice of mine to two others in my life, my friend Mickey when we were both but twelve years of age (old Mick probably assumes I have outgrown something I had done so long ago, when we were but silly children), and my wife Chloe, who is now dead.

Ah, she was a lovely lady, my Chloe. Ever supportive of my pursuits and quite understanding of my quirks. At first she could not quite understand my fascination with my cockroach friends. In point of fact, she was revolted by them, and more so by my conversing with them. But eventually Chloe accepted this activity, even if she turned her head from the procedure. But that was alright with myself, as the cockroaches told me on several occasions that they were not at all fond of my wife.

"Get her the fuck out of the room!" they would sometimes hiss in my ear, venomously but quietly also, because roaches they may have been, but impolite they were not. Neither they, nor I, wished to offend dear, dear Chloe.

Have I mentioned to you that Chloe is dead? I believe I have. It amazes me still, her passing. We had lived through our share of difficult times and in their midst I remained firmly convinced that it would be she, and not I, that outlived the other. She had always been more resilient than I. But that is the mysterious and unfathomable nature of life, is it not, the unpredictability of its meandering ways. In order to sketch for you the circumstances by which said lovely lass met her untimely end, I must return in time several weeks.

Oh, you may have noticed, my history of my life in these pages seems to have moved forward very rapidly, overlooking many lost years and experiences. Do not fret, reader of my narrative, for I assure you I have excluded nothing that is worth noting. My life has been a rather simple one, at least until the point several weeks prior to now, which I will henceforth disclose to you.

I was driving home after work, and a long day it had been, with many a fruitless attempt to lure some signs of life from too many pairs of vapid eyes. But it was Friday, and so my spirit was more agreeable than had it been another, younger day of the week. This, despite the fact that I'd spent the better part of my afternoon nursing my wrist where Maria had nipped me earlier in the day. A strange case, that one, Maria 5 I like to call her, for the five small marks like teeth indentations along her cheek. It had been very quick, she with her empty eyes gazing nowhere as always and then, of a sudden, an intense brand of animation in her stare and a jerking forward of her head and then…The wound hadn't been very bad at all, a mere blood bubble aftermath marring the flesh about my wrist, but the shock of it, of so docile a young woman leaping into such awful energized life…Well, a long day truly it was that I'd left behind me. So, there I sat, behind the wheel of my vehicle, watching the road for any sign of roadkill. I mention this otherwise trivial tidbit in light of the fact that I, as a child of perhaps eight or nine years, was once taught a lesson by my wise father regarding such deceased animals.

"Alvin," he had delivered with precise enunciation, "Always, and son, I stress *always* watch the road for any sign of roadkill, because the more aware you are that animals like those you see dead at the side of the road, in the gravely shoulder area, are just that, dead, well, the more prepared you will be to swerve your own car out of the way when you are older, perhaps saving an animal's life."

This lesson I have never forgotten, to this day. But let me return to my story.

Yes, I was headed homeward when it had begun. I had noticed something peculiar earlier on that day, while at work, but dismissed it without further thought. But now it seemed to be growing worse. What the problem was, you see, was that I had been feeling quite poorly that day. And it was becoming progressively severe as I drove along. Perspiration beaded my forehead, although a frosty October wind howled in through the open passenger-side window, and my hands felt hot and clammy. My breathing seemed quite difficult also, as if a great weight was pressed against my chest, causing the intake of air into my lungs to proceed at a rather sluggish pace.

Approximately one quarter of the way home was when I noticed the physical appearance of my hands, as they rested upon the steering wheel before me. I nearly slammed my foot down upon the brake pedal as I looked upon the horror, a scream caught up in my throat.

Reaching from nearly the tips of my fingers of both of my hands, to somewhere past the cuffs of my button shirt, was a puffy, raised area of flesh, greenish and pinkish in colour. *Greenish and pinkish,* and this is the absolute truth! The spot at my wrist where Maria 5's teeth had left their mark was notably swollen as well, and a sickly yellow pallor surrounded this wounded area.

In panic, I nearly tore the sleeves of my shirt upwards, exposing my bare arms beneath. They were similarly covered. In trepidation, I glanced up into my rear view mirror, and gasped aloud at the sight which greeted me there. Staring back at me was a snippet of nightmare from an old science fiction or horror film. The mottled green and pink layering that I discovered upon my hands and arms had spread to my face, and peering closer, to my neck.

I sat dumbfounded and terrified. How? I asked myself desperately. And when? When could this affliction have possibly overtaken me? I had left work with no hint of any such monstrous deformity upon my body. My co-workers, and secretary, as usual, had bade me good night, and wished me a pleasant weekend. Everything had been fine, a long week behind me, of curing old fogs from people's minds. Everything had been rational. But now…No, I cursed myself. I am fatigued, I told myself. I was simply imagining, experiencing some vivid and prolonged hallucination…

No, as I glanced again into the mirror overhead. Somehow, sometime, in the twenty minutes or so since my departure from my office, this accursed thing had overtaken my defenceless body.

It simply was not humanly possible. But then, did it have to be a human condition? Need this flesh disease, or whatever it truly was, need it be of this Earth? No. Why would it? I thought of old Mickey then, and what he might say given our shared past of immersion in pulp pages and comic book panels illustrating just such astonishing scenarios.

Then, of a sudden, I had torn open the zipper of my pants, and peered with intense excitement downwards into my exposed lap. And yes, dear reader, the horror had indeed reached my cock. And my grossly swollen balls. I am sorry mother, father, you would disprove, and demand more eloquence: indeed, then, the affliction had by this juncture reached already and seized a firm hold of my manhood.

I tore my gaze away, attempting with no great success to keep my attention fixed on the road before me and my duties in operating my vehicle. I tried to lie to myself then. Oh, it is nothing, I told my madly scrambling mind. It will be gone by tomorrow morning, merely a transitory – if severe – rash or other such dermatological aberration. Except that it would not be, I knew in my heart, there was no possibility that it would be gone come morning, and hello there, Chloe, why don't you give your loving husband Alvin a peck on the rotting cheek, and if you are still interested in that promise I made you this morning before I left for work, why don't you pull off these pants and grab a tight hold of my green and monstrous cock.

Yes, I was terrified. I knew then for the first time true, *true* fear. I cannot say for certain exactly how long this inhibiting fright lay upon me, but it was surely present for the better part of the afternoon. For you see, I, in my confusion, drove about the countryside all throughout that first terrible day, a monster in his car, doing my utmost to avoid populated areas. Sticking mostly to old and disused farm back roads and such allowed me some much needed privacy, as I battled my dilemma. Then, towards nightfall, due in part to my quickly depleting gas supply, I turned the car in a homeward-bound direction and drove on.

It was at this point, minutes after turning on my headlights to help guide me through the setting darkness, that the hunger began. God, I remember thinking, when was the last time I had put something in my mouth? Noon, perhaps? I had needed something to devour in the most intense way at that moment. I hurried on my way, disregarding stop signs in my haste, a cloud of dust following my speeding car like a ghost. In the distance, over the jagged roof of tree line on either side of the road, I caught sight of several smoke plumes billowing into the deeply purpling sky. They made me terribly nervous, as though their startling presence mirrored some burning thing inside me, perhaps my hunger, or my huge and growing fear which threatened to collapse me in my already nerve-wracked state. As I drove along I glimpsed a bizarre scene unfolding in a distant farmer's field, a sight which I questioned having actually witnessed. Was my weary mind offering me hallucinatory scenarios as a means of warning me of my body's great fatigue? Was it really a group of farmers that surrounded the oddly shambling form of a man or woman set on fire and setting their small patch of night aglow with eerie luminescence? And not five minutes afterwards, was it a re-written version of this selfsame scene that I saw from my driver's side window, this one depicting the lumbering form of a man giving chase to and ultimately falling upon an older woman and grappling her to the grass amid a mad flurry of limbs? Had I actually witnessed this atrocity before the trees loomed tall and dense and took the awful sight away from my disbelieving eyes? Was it screams that filtered intermittently through the dense county thicket to my ears as I sped along, or only my own hammering heart muddling into my scattered thoughts? Was everything alright in the rest of the world, or was I completely alone in my unique plight? I did not know. Everything was uncertain and like electrical currents sizzling through my skull.

  It was only as I turned into my familiar drive leading to my humble domicile, that I remembered Chloe. Dear, lovely Chloe.

  Checking myself in the mirror, I was dismayed to discover that my condition had worsened considerably throughout the evening. Where patches of my ordinary, soft flesh had been mere hours past, now there was this puffy greenish and pinkish layering. I could hardly locate a single spot where the affliction had not spread to. And my hands were swollen. They now forced their way out through my shirt sleeves, thick-fingered and leathery. My fingernails, notably, did not alter in size or length. They remained constant, and were engulfed by the growing mass of the flesh about them. I noticed with a deep tugging sadness the sight of my wedding ring similarly enveloped by my quickly-growing new flesh, almost stolen from sight entirely beneath the awful layers, like some physical parallel of a sullied past. I did not dare look into the confines of my pants.

Quickly looking about myself to ensure the street in both directions was devoid of human life, I opened the car door and shambled up the stone stairs to the front door of my home. In the distance somewhere I discerned the wail of police or ambulance sirens, but nothing else stirred. Their sound frightened me considerably, their sound like some tragic lament out in the night. It was awkward work getting my keys into the keyhole, what with the bloated condition of my hands, but several gruelling minutes later, it was done.

Once inside, I listened intently to the sounds of the house, in the hope of locating the whereabouts of my wife. It was difficult: there was a new sound present in my ears, sharper than the tinnitus of old which I had grown used to by now. Like a distant howling, like wind breezing inside my auditory canals from some distant place and making hearing difficult. But I strained my ears, and at last I could discern faint stirrings issuing from the downstairs floor area.

Quietly, very quietly, I crept towards the doorway that led onto the flight of stairs issuing into the basement. There was no sign of Chloe, and so I continued down the steps, pausing at regular intervals to listen for the exact whereabouts of the lovely lady in the spacious confines of the room below me.

Then, the quiet sound of wood on wood, a light tapping, and a moment later the faint sloshing of water. Ah, I realized. She was painting, one of her lovely and detailed landscapes, probably.

hungry, I thought, hungry hungry hungry man

I reached the bottom of the staircase and peered around the corner, hugging the wall closely. There she was, her back to me, working indeed, on a semi-finished landscape, this particular one depicting a warm and inviting English countryside. Stealthily, I crept up behind her, being cautious of the sound my still-clad feet made on the simple, unfinished concrete floor.

Then, excitement coursing through me, I laid a monstrous hand upon her small, delicate shoulder. With a muffled shriek, she jumped, dropping her paint brush onto the stone floor.

"It is me, dear," I said into her ear, in an ineffectual attempt to calm her. "It is only me."

"God, Alvin," she breathed, relief in her voice. "You scared me silly. And where have you been? The television's filled with –"

That was when she turned her head upwards and behind, and looked into my face. A scream left her, and tore through the room, echoing from the bare, cold walls. She backed away from me, her trembling hand to her mouth, her eyes wide and staring.

"What – Oh, what's happened to you, Alvin?" she managed, through quivering lips. Ah, I remember her perfectly then, as delicate and frail and pretty as ever, an autumn leaf plucked from one of her painted trees, as far away from me as she had ever been, too.

And then it struck me. All of it, in a cascading stream that came directly from out of the past and coalesced in my suddenly acutely rational mind at that moment in my basement of cold grey walls and warm canvases. And as I looked down into the wide orbs that were the eyes of my wife, Chloe, I understood everything. Very clearly.

"Dear," I said, my words slurred and my voice croaking awfully, "I have died and returned. I have died and turned into a zombie. Or something very much like that."

This was a realization that had crept so stealthily into my mind and at such a gradual pace that I had not even realized its presence until asked the question by another.

"What?" poor petrified Chloe had stammered, her wide eyes never leaving my hideous countenance, as much as she certainly must have wished to. Oh, how sadly faithful were her eyes right then. Yes, sometimes she could be so very faithful to me, devoted as a dog. And although I knew the answer long before I had even thought to ask, I asked anyways.

"Chloe," I remember saying, very calmly and lucidly and with painstakingly precise enunciation too much like my father's way of speaking, despite the incredible circumstances, "I have died and returned to you as a zombie, and although I do not know *how* I know what I am about to inform you of, I ask you to trust me when I say that I really do know this thing for certain: that if I bite you now, anywhere, you too will turn into a zombie. And then, then we can live together, happily I hope. It will be like…like beginning anew. Perhaps this is what we need. Perhaps this is what we have needed

475

for a long time."

We had tried this before, starting over, but had found it difficult. It is a hard task to see truthfulness in the eyes of one who has deceived you in your shared past. I had tried to the best of my ability but only ever saw her wish for another man staring back at me from her lovely eyes. Always forgiving of her deceptions was I, as if it was not she who was completely at fault, but me somehow. Always relenting to the easy path of doting upon her while believing with no real conviction that my helpless adoration was reciprocated. But this new offer from me to her, this seemed different, a real and true new beginning for both of us. United like this, we could at last remain true to one another.

Of course, I knew beforehand that this invitation would be met with some skepticism, and disbelief, and perhaps utter and complete abhorrence, but I felt obligated to ask.

"Alvin," Chloe said, her words a jumble. "What are you talking about? This is crazy. We'll go see a doctor, whatever it is –"

"Oh," I had interrupted my dear wife. "I see. Let me ask you, dear…" I paused, gathering myself. It was the single most important question I had ever asked in my life and I wanted her complete attention. "Do you love me?"

"W-What?" Chloe had asked in confusion.

I waited, as I knew she had heard my question. Images of our shared past flitted before my eyes while she struggled for an answer. I saw the many masks she had worn over the years, the sincerity of the young girl giving way to the disenchanted newly-wed until finally the deceptive-furtive stare of the woman of later years watched me resentfully. All her faces falling away one to another until I saw her naked and quaking and ashen-faced before me in the basement.

Then, after a moment, she answered. "Yes. Of course, Alvin. Why –"

"No, Chloe," I can hear myself saying. "You do not. You just told me so. As you've always told me."

And so the expression my Chloe died with stretched across her lovely face was one of great confusion. Great confusion as

I took her head between my two giant hands, and jerked her this way and that, until her thin neck snapped like dry kindling. She collapsed to the concrete floor in a heap, directly before her unfinished painting. The picturesque scene, imbued with its array of lovely and deep greens and oranges, a Spring portrait of the world returning to life had, I thought, become suddenly a little more sublime with the power of death's ingredient added to the work. A winter wind through a scene of seasonal renewal.

Then I climbed the staircase and went into the kitchen, where I have for the most part remained ever since. I poured myself a glass of red wine and knelt before the stove. Pulling out the green metal door underneath with a familiar clanging, I saw with great joy that there were several brown cockroaches scuttling about in the shadows. Pinching one gently between my plump, rotting fingers, I then replaced the drawer in its nook, letting darkness reign once again in the hidden world of my prisoner's companions. Well, not so much prisoner as friend, I would still maintain. Perhaps we are the real prisoners, trapped within these fragile shells of trembling, discontent humanity.

Regardless, I placed the cockroach in an empty tea cup, as I had done so many countless times before, and sprayed him with a few drops from my wine glass, stretching taut a sheet of cellophane over the top of the cup a moment later. Then I waited. It was not a very long wait this time.

"Hello," said the voice of the cockroach. "How are you?"

I laughed. I laughed loudly, and hard, belligerently my mother would say, and it felt oddly pleasant.

"What is so funny?" asked the cockroach.

"Oh," I answered, wiping tears from the corners of my eyes, which were becoming difficult to see from, as the flesh of my cheeks had swollen a great deal, and was partially obstructing my vision. "It is nothing at all, my friend. But in answer to your query, I am doing very terribly today."

"Really?" said the cockroach. "And why is that?"

"Well," I said, "As I am sure is evident to your eyes, I have, for some reason that is beyond me, died and turned into a zombie. Like the ones I read about as a child. And secondly, I have just snapped my wife's neck. And you know what?"

"What?" asked the cockroach.

"I am hungry, very hungry, and I feel a desire to…to eat her. My wife. You understand?"

The roach paused, then, "I see what you say, however, I am not certain I understand why you would want to, my friend."

"Well," I said to my companion, "I do not know for certain. Although I suppose it has much to do with myself transforming into this zombie. Yes, that is it, for certain. All zombies do that sort of thing. Eating their wives, or anyone else for that matter."

Silence, then the voice of the cockroach: "She didn't love you, did she?"

At that, a great sorrow filled my chest. "Ah, well," I said to him. "She did and she did not. She did not want to be transformed into…this."

"I see," said the roach. "So. What are you going to do, my friend?"

"I do not know. I haven't the foggiest idea what I am going to do now. What… What should I do?"

The cockroach was slow to provide an answer, and when he finally did I quivered along my spine. "Perhaps it is time for you to confront yourself," he said. "Perhaps the time has come for you to meet the true Alvin Rourke. Awakened at last after so many years sleeping fitfully within the shell."

"But how?" I asked plaintively, desperately. "How? And what will I say to him?"

"I am sorry," said the voice of the cockroach. "But I have no more advice to give you. None at all. The next answer is for you to provide."

Around this point, the cockroach fell into a deep and untroubled slumber. Which he well deserved, as he had tried his utmost to aid me in my dilemma. That was approximately one week ago.

In that time, the roach has not awoken, and so I have no one with whom to speak. His companions are nowhere to be seen, and I am no longer as nimble as before, and so would be unable to capture a new friend in any case. Perhaps this is why I am writing this account of my life. I have eaten most of my wife, as the food in our refrigerator and cupboards is revolting to me now. Probably another attribute of living as a zombie, I suppose, if this can be called living. My thoughts have turned muddled, they become more difficult to catch as they flit through my consciousness, emphasizing my fraying mental state. How have I remained so precocious, given my eroding physical appearance? How has any semblance of rationality remained to me while I crumble and decay and spend my time cannibalizing the woman I wed so many years ago? What would old friends say, Freud, Jung, watching me in my plight, pondering the deepest questions while gnawing feebly at my swollen, rotten wrist? But then, this is beyond Jungian scope, is it not? No. No, maybe it is not after all, and perhaps the submerged iceberg of Freudian consciousness has only now emerged from the murky waters of my mind to help carry me through my unique dilemma. Perhaps I am as much of the man as ever I was, and then some. Perhaps I am as close to perfection today as I am ever capable of becoming, and dear Chloe, she truly chose poorly when it came to her last moments at my side. Maybe I am among the first of my kind, a new breed in the evolutionary hierarchy and who could guess what I might fathom tomorrow? Perhaps today I know everything.

    And still, I do not know what I should do next. Should I call a doctor for an appointment? No, I would never be able to drive. My body has begun to crumble and decay. My hands are too clumsy to operate the vehicle in any case. It is only with painstakingly slow progress and huge concentration that I am able to pinch the tip of my pencil between my thumb and index finger now, and with as legible a hand as I am able, pen this, my incredible narrative. Besides, even could I drive, a physician could do nothing for me now. I feel so cold. Cold everywhere, all over the new skin I own and inside as well. Deep inside, where the screaming lives and keeps me perpetually frightened because of the threat it poses to my rational mind.

    The television is broken. It only plays soundless blue screens or white noise and makes me wonder whether the world outside has stopped living, or if maybe everyone now owns a new skin like mine and sits huddled in their homes reliving their botched lives, too. Where are you now, Mickey, I wonder, full of spit and vinegar as you always were, or lumbering and ungainly and dead-alive with flat eyes like some figment of old pulp story?

Or perhaps I should call the police. They would lock me up, certainly, but they would also see my condition and…And what?

Again, I do not know. I am a man in trouble, and I do not know.

If only the cockroach would awaken. But alas, he is tired, as am I. Perhaps that is what I should do at this juncture. Get a few hours of sleep. It has been long since I have slept. The noise like howling in my thoughts has only grown louder these days, drowning out any hope of dreams. The cold seeps through me and leaves me numb everywhere, shaking frantically, and the tremors only go on and on.

Sleep: yes, that does indeed sound like a wise idea, even though I fear what my dreams today may tell me if they filter through the screaming. Or perhaps I shall call the authorities after all.

Hmm…No, I am still not certain. I am certain of one thing, however. That I have most certainly written enough for this day. For this lifetime. So, here is the point at which I sign off, and attempt to face the uncertainties that lie before me. This has been, and is still, my life: flowing, unfolding, like a river into some greater body of knowledge, where the iceberg peaks and emerges from the waters like an epiphany. I shall try to live it well.

Alvin Calvin Rourke

Salty Magic Balloon Trips
for the Moon to Judge

He has always told me that I am a balloon, taking him to blue places over the hills.

My balloon with green and white stripes, he always says, meaning my special striped summer dress, and with my hand in his he would twirl me through the garden behind the house. He knows I love dancing outdoors, the touch of cool grass on the bottoms of my bare feet. Especially when there is sunshine all over the garden, keeping the dahlias warm and making the golden hair on his knuckles and fingers shine. The garden looks so soft in that light, soft as big, gentle hands around mine. He is always so gentle with me. He is even gentle carrying me over the places in the stream where it becomes too wide for me to cross easily, while he hops very carefully from stone to stone like a frog, light as a ballerina on his big feet. He is gentle when he finally puts me down hours later in the deep green woods where fireflies blink like magic lanterns in the night, his finger to his lips: *Shh, because some secrets are good to keep, especially deep in the woods. Deep in the woods,* he tells me, *is where the fairies live, and we must keep quiet, in case they are sleeping.*

He is my audience as I whirl through tall grass with the flowers he gives me in my hair, under a roof of green. It moves in the wind, that roof, shimmering like dreams you wake from on mysterious summer nights.

He is my audience as green and white stripes fall away from me onto the grass and flowers are my outfit. He watches me in silence, his mouth a sharp line under his nose. I cannot see his eyes because of the sunglasses he wears at these times, even after shadows begin to stretch from the trees over him, over us both. But I know he is watching because I sometimes grow tired and begin to slow in my dancing, and this is when I hear a twig snap from the shadows, see him shake his head at me slowly: *No, go on, Adda, go on and dance like a little balloon on the wind currents.*

He always says this to me, in a whisper in my ear before we reach the special spot in the woods: *Dance, Adda, my little balloon on wind currents. But not too high, we do not want to be seen.*

He is frightened of being seen, has always been. He fears goblins that drop like ugly grey stones from the belly of the moon and land heavily upon summer grasses. He is afraid of God watching him from beyond cloud cover. He says often that they are one and the same, God and his goblins, and that He is their leader-king, directing their progress from cold, dead lunar places and downwards into warm summer night forests. This is why I dance beneath the rustling green roof rather than in the openness of the glade, only a few minutes' walk southwards. We are safest where we are alone, and his eyes behind his dark glasses I am certain are smiling in a safe kind of way.

I am a good dancer, he assures me. I should be, it has been long since the forest became my stage. My feet have grown, and my legs and arms and all the rest of me, too, while he has watched and applauded silently from the deep green shadows. *You are my favourite thing, lifting me to clear places.*

I have always been his favourite thing. His secret treasure, he calls me. Since as long as I can remember.

I remember a day, late in the afternoon and long ago, and I was only six years old maybe, when I first knew for certain that I was his favourite. *Where are you going*, breathlessly to his departing back, the dark stains marking his shirt down its center. *It is summer,* he answered over his shoulder, not looking to me. *I must make certain there are no goblins about.* And he disappeared into the rustling walls of green before me.

I waited as a six-year-old would wait, impatiently and with bare feet inching towards the spot in the trees where my father had disappeared. I was breathless from my performance, but stole forward anyways, leaving my clothes on the forest floor behind me. I crept about quietly, watching carefully for lurking goblins and God, and then I found him. I watched curiously through a gash in the tall brambles before me, watched as he stood naked among the clump of thorny bushes, his back to me again. His body was moving slightly, though I could not tell what it was he was doing. His head, I remember, lifted up towards the sky once, but with a gasp that made me frightened for him, he quickly returned his gaze to the grass before him. He has always been scared of being seen. He has always watched the ground beneath him as he walks, fearful of clouds and their pilots circling above him. And I watched silently as his breathing became louder, and then turned into a kind of panting like a dog, until a second gasp escaped him which sounded as if it had been strangled out of him. And then he was no longer as rigid, and his posture relaxed and his breathing became normal again.

And then when he turned suddenly at the awareness of someone behind him, and he stormed through the bushes toward me with fire in his eyes and his clothes in his trembling hands, then I saw the tears in his eyes. I remember the slash of sunlight which fell across his face just then like a beacon or spotlight, and how it made his tears flash like magic in the corners of his eyes. His eyes were so sad, I wanted to die.

I cried, too, as he fell to one knee before me and crushed me to him and sobbed like a big little boy in my ear. I can still hear him crying when I close my eyes.

We left soon after, but since that day, I have always been able to see the sad magic in his eyes.

I love him, and he loves me, and so I cannot help but await tonight's celestial picture with deep sadness like I have never known before.

Do not stop me, my lovely, my darling girl, I must go. Finally, I must go.

And he is going tonight, and he is taking me with him, he promises, but only in spirit, only in gesture, and when he speaks in riddles like these I love him more for all the deep mystery with which he has always been so filled. He has done wrong, he tells me, but with the same kind eyes that he has always looked upon me.

I think of old days long past as I sit here in my bedroom window, old scratched silver telescope across my knees, watching the black sky circling over the forest. There are fairy tribes asleep in that tangled maze, and hulking grey goblins, too.

His words of magic from the old days will never leave me, his mythologies will endure.

And many memories sleep there, too, among the secret paths and flower colonies and in the great shadows of trees.

And then a single thought comes unbidden to my mind: where is the lord of goblins, who might be able to put a stop to the madness of nights like this, when dear men like my father plan to sail away from their daughters forever?

And there, over the dark hulking shoulder of the woods in the south it rises: a bulbous nose big as a tree, and it lifts upwards and eases its way like a shadow across the huge expanse of sky; until it veers within reach of the wan lunar light which emanates softly from the silver sliver moon hanging still above it. And there it is, hanging against the heavens, and I want to raise my hand to wave hello and goodbye both, but my hand will not move from the telescope.

Its canvas body is striped hugely and happily in green and white which the moon illuminates in pale prettiness; I shiver, and then let my eyes drop downwards, following the imperceptible threads I know hang tautly beneath, downwards to the small wooden basket, a cylinder a million miles above Earth. He is there, with a faded summer dress from a thousand summers ago slung over his shoulder; and he does not wave either, though he knows where I am, at home in my bedroom window, and he knows I am watching through this stick of silver now to my eye, hoping madly against a night time rainstorm of goblins from the heavens which might put holes in the skin of his balloon. A cloud of twinkling lights hovers in the air near the basket, a swarm of curious fireflies or maybe an entourage of fairies with their tiny lanterns bidding an old guardian goodbye.

Now I am watching you dance, and I am smiling, because things do change in this life, like you have always promised me.

I replace the telescope on my lap. And I can see his eyes as they looked into mine only yesterday, so full with sad magic and courage. And I see his lips curl as through the ache in his voice he tries to give me a parting smile. Then: *Goodbye, I am leaving you, my darling girl. I cannot stay any longer. I am not that strong. Please try to forgive me.*

Please try to forgive me.

I forgive you, and now there is magic silvery from the moon in my watery eyes, too.

The balloon continues to rise, like a second moon, naked for the world to see, for anyone to see who might be watching.

I forgive you, for all the magic in my eyes.

The Runners Among the Stars

There goes a Runner, he nearly blurted out, starting at the sight of the fleeting movement along the jagged cliff face in the distance.

But he controlled his jangling nerves. He lowered his eyes from the bizarre sight so that Krista would not notice the direction of his troubled stare and become upset again. She'd shed too many tears because of his foolish decisions already. Her place between him and his wife, cocooned inside the sturdy sleeping bag, was the most secure she'd been able to find. He gazed cautiously towards her, saw to his dismay her large brown eyes fixed on him. Huddled down into the thick folds of the sleeping bag, only her nose and eyes peered over its rim, but he saw her fear plainly.

Reaching over, a gentle caress of her arms through the blankets did little to soothe her. Still her eyes remained huge, fearful. Still she said no words, only stared with her usual intensity and her newer accusation. He offered his daughter a wan smile, disheartened by the look she wore, borrowed more and more the last few days from her mother.

He fiddled with the radio in his hands. Its plastic screen remained darkened. No hours-long dedication to tinkering inside of its intricate system of internal wires and mechanisms had yielded any progress. He pulled apart a tangle of miniature red and green wires and re-fitted their ends in one of two dozen re-combinations he'd already tried futilely. No spark grazed his gentle touch. No colour flickered into the dark display screen. No crackle of static life tore through the device's miniature speaker, disturbing the otherwise haunted silence of their camp.

He looked up accidentally into the eyes of his wife and was held in their power a moment. She owned hateful eyes these days, his once darling Darla. But then he deserved that kind of a stare. He merited her bitter silences when he wanted so much to hear her comforting voice of old. He warranted no less than their daughter's outright allegiance to her mother over him.

A distant baying stabbed the silence. It rebounded from the surrounding cliff walls and shivered their spines where they all instantly huddled into themselves. He turned to his family, saw terror renewed in their faces. Krista sitting upright in her bag, clutching her mother, whose frantic eyes darted all around their makeshift camp. The small pocket knife she gripped in the faint fire glow dismayed him.

He'd never wanted this for her. He'd never wanted her to have to grip a weapon like this, in defence against things the darkness might hold. He'd never dreamed of sharing a camp fire such as this with the only two people he had in the world.

The cry and its echoes faded. The trickling of rocks as yet another cascade of rubble sounded somewhere in the settling dusk kept them rigid in their places. The evidence of their movement in the distant darkness. The fleet movement of things they'd all glimpsed but disbelieved upon first sighting them two days ago when they'd landed on these strange shores.

Tentatively, gingerly, he stood, and carrying his own knife in his fist, made his way as stealthily as he could towards the ever-present song of lapping waters.

Kneeling forward as far as he dared along the hard rock crust of the shoreline, he saw himself. In the still dark waters, his face looked sad, weathered. Frightened. He watched himself a while, waiting for tears to arrive. Soon, his eyes welled and he cried, softly so that his family wouldn't hear. When he was finished, he still felt helpless and the bite of the hollowness in his stomach made his head reel.

They had little food remaining. Little water as well, for the dark waters of this place seemed unimaginable to drink. Black like oil, viscous and frightening. Everything threatened here: the short spells of pseudo-daylight, when the sky purpled and faded only some of the stars from their fixed places until another long deep black night arrived without warning; the barren landscape of rock and hill, with the distant promise of jungle-like lushness always very far away among the crooked profile of the strange and alien-looking cliffs. The black waters by which they'd arrived days before, smashed along the hard cliff side, and that had been the end of their small emergency rescue craft. He recalled their frantic climb into those forbidding crags, and their precarious trek along the peninsula risen from the menacing water, taking with them what they could salvage of their wrecked boat. Meagre supplies of rations and some water-ruined equipment and little else but their own shaking, horrified selves.

From behind him he heard the muted sound of Krista crying into her mother's embrace. Darla's hushed words attempting to soothe, but even he heard her faltering voice, the tremor which ran through all of their voices now.

He shook his head at himself as he examined the evening star field overhead. He recalled the expression on his wife's face days before when he'd explained the unique predicament of their situation. *No Darla, I'm very certain of it: we are not anywhere close to the point we set out from this afternoon. We're very far from there.* He recalled her frantic wide-eyed look as she'd berated him for his stupidity, his infantile desires to play at God even while he was treating his family to a rare week of vacation, knowing as well as he that the fateful trek had simply been another excuse on his part to seek escape from the perceived ennui of his life. The contemptible father, perpetually fleeing responsibilities to his own while seeking romance wherever he might find it; whether in the beds of infinitely more sexually precocious and pliable women, or upon uncertain Ocean plains, rolling and churning with deadly mysteries. He'd only held her livid gaze and broke his resigned knowledge to her as gently as he was able.

The stars, Darla. These stars, and he'd gestured around them while watching her carefully. *These are not stars we've ever seen before now. This place is different. These are foreign stars around us, Darla. They're alien to any I've ever seen in my life. They're on no star charts I've ever seen. Just look. Just look at these* waters.

And she'd followed his quaking finger as it pointed out to her the breathtakingly strange, unfamiliar sight of the swirls of shimmering star-specks; the blatant green luminescence of the moon-like orb hanging heavily in the east which was no lunar face she'd ever gazed on before; the surreal glimmer of cloud-like dustings which stirred in the distant air like some wondrous cosmic debris. He'd asked her to show him a Dipper or a bear in the myriad shimmerings above but of course she hadn't been able to.

The realization entered her fully then, and her look of terror gave way to one of resignation and fury. Livid, her words to him had been simple and unequivocal.

I hate you, Stephen.

She'd taken Krista as her supporter as always, leaving their lop-sided relationship intact even in this distant, unfathomable place. He knew he was awful for it but he hated them, too. When he needed to feel the warmth of another's touch, they shared a sleeping bag together and left him the camp fire and darkness. When he starved for a look of tenderness their eyes offered only accusation and distance.

He wanted to die but felt terror eat his insides at the steadily growing certainty that soon enough he would have his wish. He'd always believed that he understood solitude but now he knew it truly. Staring out over the infinite distance of the still water, he discerned its horizon a million miles away. And he realized his tiny insignificance in the unfathomable vastness of the universe.

Ironically, he hadn't been thinking of himself at the outset of their ill-fated deviation from their original course. He'd only wanted to help whoever had called out to them. He'd only wished to save someone from plight, when of course his priority should have been keeping his family far from danger. A brief land-fall, he'd promised. A pick-up, a grateful thank you from the rescued, and off they'd be into the remainder of their vacation. He couldn't have predicted the sudden arrival of inclement weather and the subsequent off-shore turbulences out-weighing favourable odds of landing, and then the sudden clearing of the skies to reveal the shocking panorama of a firmament utterly unrecognizable and a placid Ocean black and deep as night. But his wife's argument had ultimately been vindicated: there really had been no way to ensure their safety, particularly in unguarded waters such as these.

The cries returned then, shaking his bones beneath his skin, crawling nervous fingers of dread along his back. Their echoes reverberated from the cliffs for several minutes and in their wake he listened to his daughter sobbing into her mother's arms.

And as she cried, the trickle of rocks along the cliffs, threatening landslide. Threatening much stranger, darker things than quick and violent burial.

He'd named them immediately.

Their first few hours cast away had been undisturbed. Then, the bizarre twittering cacophony from the heights, the distinct crashing of stirring rocks beyond the perimeter of jungle foliage. They'd stared into the distance, and there, among the vapours rising from the verdant greenery of the hills, there along the crooked-sharp cliff faces towering above the tree-line they glimpsed them for the first time:

Look at those Runners, had been his first rush of excited and alarmed words.

The words described the things well, those long, loose rolling coils of serpentine life cruising the cliffs; with their countless tendrils flailing in the air like demented octopus arms. They darted along the precarious rocks, carried along fleetly by their many appendages, and their quickness had terrified him immediately. It impressed upon him their alien-ness and the severity of the inexplicable plight he'd suffered his family to live through. *Where* had they landed? And how could a trip through Atlantic waters have led them to a place as distant and strange and inexplicable as this land?

Appearing and eventually disappearing into the lush

greenery from which the cliffs rose, the things' skin colour made them starkly visible as they scampered along the dark rock face. A grotesque smear of emerald and yellow, they looked an unreal spectacle drifting along in the barren landscape of stone and mists.

What are they, mother, a hysterical Krista had not ceased crying for several minutes. *What were they? Will they hurt us? They looked so ugly, mother.* And Darla reassuring her that the things wouldn't harm them as long as they were left alone and undisturbed in the hills and jungles, while they waited for father to repair the radio so that someone could hear their distress signal and rescue them.

But water had wreaked havoc among the radio's circuits and father's hands had never been very adept with electronic gadgets and gizmos to begin with. Father had never been very good at repairing much of anything – Those were the unspoken words which loaded the growing silences between him and his wife and daughter.

Since that first sighting, the Runners had made appearances regularly along the cliffs, and their rustlings came to them from somewhere in the flora near the cliffs' base as well. Stephen kept a fire blazing all through the long night and during the brief day as well. All three slept with their fingers curled around small knives, even little Krista. On one occasion he'd spied one of the things skulking relatively near to the perimeter of their camp. He'd discerned its tendrils idling eerily in the fringe of fire glow, and had risen slowly and determinedly to his feet, knife gleaming in his hand. Moving forward, he had frightened the thing away. He'd listened to its progress swishing through the underbrush in the distance. Then silence returned and he'd settled himself down for more sleepless hours of tense alertness and terrible fear.

He found his terror at the sight of them growing with each hour that passed. The mere thought of them thrilled him queerly, and he had eyes only for the shadows which surrounded their small camp. He mistook hanging vines and creepers for their roiling tendrils, half-glimpsed their swift movement amid the trees. Something in their character haunted his thoughts. Something in their essence which persisted in his mind yet eluded outright definition. They were large, he knew this now for certain. The specimen he'd spied and scared off had been close enough to chill him completely with its enormous bulk and the deadly coiled look of its tendrils. Yet it hadn't attacked them, none of them had ventured any closer to their camp than this one curious specimen.

He tested the sturdiness of the knife blade against his palm. It was resilient, and sharp enough to cut through wood. He'd used it only days before to strip the scales from a carp, and yet he knew with certainty that it would prove no real weapon against whatever lay beyond the fringe of campfire glow. The distant jungles rustled with life. No birds sounded from those emerald reaches yet something stirred there incessantly. He gripped the knife so tightly that his fingers grew numb and his knuckles white as bone.

His throat ached to swallow. He'd been thirsty for hours but had withstood his urge to drink from their meagre supply of water. Half a canteen between the three of them, and he was shaking his head in dismay once again. What would they do? He recalled his earlier reprimanding of Krista, having caught her stirring the dark waters at the shoreline with the end of a long queerly-shaped stone. He'd read her intentions immediately and berated her harshly. *You can't drink from these waters, Krista – We don't know if they're safe.* Her retort had been child-like and forthright, and very apt: *Nothing feels safe here.*

He whittled away at a useless plastic compartment cover from one of the ration containers they'd salvaged from the wreck of their boat. He began with only a series of purposeless lines zig-zagging the surface, but soon found himself etching his name into the plastic. Several minutes later he saw the words he'd put there and wondered if they meant anything at all anymore, given their plight: *Stephen Sicles, father, husband.* Perhaps they'd never meant anything at all.

He heard a sound and stiffened, raising the knife into the air defensively, a new reflex they all shared. He squinted in the feeble firelight, saw that it had only been the rustling of Krista in her sleeping bag as she'd turned over beside her mother. He looked to the discarded radio beside him on the ground. It looked forlorn, a useless relic from another place and time when he and his family could hate each other peacefully.

He sat propped against a large rock with the knife between

his fingers. Somehow he found a brief moment among his troubled reveries to drift and sleep.

Waking brought him Darla's face, leaning in close in a conspiratorial whisper.

"Stephen. We have barely any food left. And no water. We need to drink."

Her forwardness had always annoyed him. Now, her impetuous way with him brought fury. It boiled his veins and reddened his thoughts. He wanted only to hurt her.

"Darla," his voice a razor-thin slicing through the air. "Are you a fool? Are you a complete fool? I know what you're thinking." He got to his feet and gestured towards the shoreline. "That water is black, Darla. *Black.* Do you see it? It's black like oil, and it's alien and I haven't seen anything like it before and I'm certain you haven't either."

But it wasn't his usual wife who answered his vigorous outburst. With her eyes on the ground, and her voice low and muttering, she seemed a wholly different woman. He froze instantly, sensing that something was profoundly amiss. He leaned forward, straining to hear her.

"We were thirsty, Stephen." The pang of apology or regret weighed down her words and made her voice sluggish, a drawl he'd never heard from her before.

Realization dawned on him. "Darla," he mumbled. "You didn't..." He trailed off, heedless of the sudden twittering which began its awful song from the distant trees and cliffs. He was held riveted by the cowed, solemn look of his wife. She looked beautiful, he realized, and he realized also that he hadn't thought this way of her in a very long time. He felt compelled to tell her this, as if he wouldn't have the opportunity again because their time of speaking to one another freely like this would soon be over. But his concern was suddenly very deep, and he only asked, "What happened, Darla?"

She shook her head, trying feebly at a timid smile which didn't materialize and only left her face wan and dejected, a frightened mask of the strident woman she'd once been. He waited, watching in disbelief as she pulled up the sleeve of her jacket and revealed to him her discoloured flesh. It extended from her wrist to her elbow, a mottled layering of green and sickly yellow which gleamed wetly in the starlight.

He quivered against his will at the sight of it. He knew the colour scheme well. The striking morass of vegetation-smeared skin. Those colours had darted through his dreams even, making his few snatches of sleep wakeful and haunted. He saw the tears in his wife's eyes, and marvelled at the note of apology in her single word to him then: "Stephen…Stephen…"

He was hesitant to take her into his arms as he'd first felt inclined. He recoiled at the sight of the grotesque colour in her arm. He murmured the words, fighting an instinctual urge to retreat from her quickly. "Did you drink the water?"

A moment passed as she collected herself. From the slopes, the twittering rose in volume. Many voices cried eerily in the darkness. All she said was, "I'm sorry, Stephen."

He trembled along his spine. He shook and felt his unsteady knife-hand thrusting little jabs into the air. He watched in revulsion as his wife removed her jacket to show him her other arm, saw that the discoloured sweep of the flesh condition covered her entire arm and disappeared beneath her underclothes. He shuddered, and a gasp escaped his parted lips. He stepped away from her, then froze. He scrutinized her face, noted the greenish tinge invading the whites of her downcast eyes. Her name shuddered from his lips like the embodiment of all the great fear devouring him inside: "Krista?"

He waited, breath bated. The calls on the cliffs rose into a crescendo which tore at his nerves. The rustling noises of plants and bushes and wild grass stirring in the wake of some great mass movement chilled him and his body shook with the terror of the unknown and unseen so near at hand.

He watched his stricken wife's head-shaking of apology and heard her soft words amid the din of alien cries and crashing foliage: "I'm so, so sorry, Stephen."

It broke his spell of immobility. He turned and dashed towards the fire smouldering in the centre of their small camp. He knocked over empty ration containers in his haste, nearly burned himself in the flames as he knelt before his daughter. She lay huddled into her sleeping bag, a shaking lump of warmth into which his frantic hands sought to knead some courage, some reassurance. "It's okay, Krista. Please, don't worry. I won't let anything hurt you."

He heard the terror ruining his false words of fortitude. His nerves rattled at the din of the Runners as they approached from the underbrush. Then, his breath stopped in his throat and a lump of ice formed in his chest at the twittering voice, close at hand. It was muffled through the thick durable fabric of the sleeping bag but it shook him terribly. He tore his hand away and recoiled from the stirring lump. He toppled backwards in his fright, entangled in the bag. He watched numbly as the mottled yellow and green thing climbed from the sleeping bag and stood facing him. It was a more diminutive version of the creatures they'd witnessed riding the cliffs. Yet its mass of tendrils waved just as frenziedly in the air, stirring terror deep inside of him. He screamed a shrill din. "I'm sorry, Krista. Oh, I'm sorry."

Only the twittering crying answered him. The coiling limbs darted towards him, grazing his ankle and slapping the earth about the fire. He turned and then they were there. Surrounded on all sides by the undulating mass of the Runners, he screamed hoarsely. They screamed an awful symphony back at him, reaching for him with their trillion limbs, touching him obscenely across every inch of his flailing body. Their touch was hot, wet, powerful, a burning rain across his skin. Through his tears he noted the descent of darkness. The things swallowed the false security of the firelight. They blotted out the stars and took away his family and left him with nothing.

He clenched his eyes tightly, shrieking shrilly, and within his own din of terror and confusion he realized how very alone in the universe he truly was. The Runners hadn't taken his daughter away, nor his wife. They'd left him long before, and maybe they'd been right about it all along: maybe the blame had always lain with him.

He screamed until his voice broke, and then he screamed in silence until darkness swallowed him.

* * *

He awoke to the song of an electric grasshopper.

He let it drone its droning music for several minutes before he dared to search out its place of hiding. He looked: it was the camp, in ruins. Scattered containers, strewn sleeping bags, and strange protracted patterns along the hard surface of the ground, as of many heavy cylindrical objects being dragged across the rock. The fire was completely extinguished, nothing smouldered in its mess of charred twigs and branches. He shivered violently, noticing the clinging wetness of his clothes to his skin. They were sodden, and he noticed with slowly growing dread that his thirst seemed slaked. He heard the soft slapping of water on rock and knew he'd been dragged to the shoreline.

He didn't move. He felt numb everywhere. He turned his eyes around in his skull and his head screamed. He blinked and a lightning storm flashed inside his head. Eventually, he looked long enough and discerned the source of the electric insect sound.

Several meters from where he lay, he saw it: the radio, from the boat. Its small speaker crackled faintly, and he saw its bright crimson power light like a beacon in the darkness. Its small but distinct electric call issued from the speaker, and it took him a moment to hear its relation to that other sound he knew so well from the darkness. He knew the sound only too well, and the flood of immediate memories it triggered would have caused him to scream madly once again if he'd had the voice remaining to do so.

The cries, the eerie twitters from the shadows: they came through the speaker, shook it and rattled its internal mechanisms. They had been the source of the distress call he'd picked up while sailing the ocean with his family. The exact signal called out then from the speaker. He'd succeeded in repairing the radio after all, he mused, wishing distantly that Darla and Krista could be there then to see at least this small triumph of the man who'd always lived only to disappoint them so much.

He listened to the distant noise of the Runners in their jungle haunts and cliff crannies. He listened to their echo in the radio near him, and he became oddly soothed by the sound. *It's musical, in a way,* he thought, letting his eyelids fall again, letting himself believe that perhaps death was finally arrived to take him blessedly away from the new madness of his life.

Then the rustling from behind him. His opened eyes and the notion that maybe his descent into madness had only really begun. The stabbing pain like needles into his side where he spun about quickly to look into the denseness of shadows. He stared a moment, seeking out the thing he sensed in the near impenetrability of the shadowed foliage before him. He saw it there, a coiled mass regarding him steadily. He'd never seen the things' eyes, didn't know their method of visual navigation, if they had any. He made out the humped crown of the creature's uppermost reaches, saw the outline of its long tendril arms as they stirred idly on the air. The breeze they made wafted onto his cheeks, chilling him. He drew his arm over his face as some futile means of shelter, and saw it: the yellow spotting the back of his hand, and the green slashes of deformed skin reaching across his fingers. He swallowed, craving no more water. He'd drank more than enough. He trembled. He waited.

Then, the twittering from the Runner before him, only now different. He heard: *We are sorry to do this to you, traveler.*

He strained his voice, knowing it was shattered, and surprised himself. The twittering sounded awful exiting his body. It seemed to emanate from every part of him at once. It consumed his thoughts as he spoke to the creature. *What happened to me? And my family?*

It is this place, said the Runner to him. *This place which traps travellers like you and me, and the rest of us. I was a fisherman, you know, long, long ago. Cruising the deep Pacific when we were heard the call on our radio. We answered it, and answered for it, as you see. Others of us have come from much further away than this. Places so distant many of us cannot fathom them. We speak to one another in our new voices and they unwittingly call out to others. Some of us once called for salvation. Now some of us believe that we've discovered it already. Here, in this place.*

Stephen's thoughts reeled. He thought he'd lost consciousness but then the creature went on and he found himself following the thread of its words easily, enthralled.

One of the early ones discovered it first, long ago. Our cries, our voices carry in a very strange manner. We call to the stars for salvation from our plight. We hope for it, pray for it, and it always arrives in the form of a traveler like yourself or myself. And then this secret place keeps them here forever. It satisfies their thirst and in the quenching gives them a new life.

The Runner raised its dozen limbs high on the air. *Look on me now,* it said. *Look on yourself. We are truly sorry, brave sailor.*

It turned from him. He could distinguish its outline fading into the shadows. He reached a stricken hand out after it. The new Stephen called after the Runner: *What is this place? A different world that we – that we stumbled on? What is it?*

From another region of the darkness, from the tangles of undergrowth another voice answered. *A place of judgment, some of us believe.*

And then another voice, from the opposite side of the foliage: *A renewal. A new beginning for us all.*

Stephen stared into the darkness a while, shuddering. *My family,* he called out. *They're with you now.* It was a statement, and saying it hardened something in him, maybe resignation, maybe resolve. He wanted desperately to see them, to feel himself in their new embrace.

Those two are here, was his answer from the stirring shadows.

Stephen lay still a moment, collecting his spinning thoughts. In the distance, he heard the cries. Many of them, shaking the fronds of the trees and trickling stones from the high faces of the cliffs. He stood, with some effort of stiff and numb limbs. He stood facing the rustling darkness. He sensed the Runners moving off into the undergrowth. He took a step forward, and another and then another. He shambled onwards unsteadily but soon felt his movement grow more sure and fluid. He followed their progress into the verdant depths. He felt warm and stripped himself of his jacket, and then his shirt. His arms gleamed greenly beneath the starlight. His limbs ached less and less as he slipped through the grasses. He felt renewed.

He stopped a moment in the darkness which stirred with life. A warm touch coiled gently around his ankle. A caress in the shadows.

Welcome, spoke the Runners, their single voice touching him everywhere.

And the mists swallowed them, and their song sounded eerily beautiful in the night.

Captain of a Ship of Flowers

"The wicked flee when no man pursueth: but the righteous are bold as a lion."

- Proverbs 28:1

I ache for her.

Oh, how I long for her earthy perfume of soil and flowers. Her scent like a ghost lingering impossibly among the vacuum between stars.

I was captain once, of a dozen men shooting across the Big Black in a tube of silver. We flew to many places, saw many sights which we stored in memory for our wives and children to see one day through our inadequate retellings.

The old romance of pulsars shining like life in the darkness of endless space miles on every side. The wild ricochet spinnings and whirlings of asteroid collisions and the gigantic silence of a universe asleep. Wondrous sights exciting the child within each of us while light years away our families watched evening skies carefully, longingly, wondering which if any of the countless shimmering specks held us in its frosty care.

I remember, and I weep.

I wipe useless salt water from the corners of my weary eyes as I shoot through the cosmos, desperately racing time and diminishing fuel and the might of hugest fury licking upon my heels. My destination is locked into central navigation, and perhaps my destiny too, as it has been for the last two months. And there is only void and coldest vacuum pushing on the walls of my toy ship as I streak fruitlessly towards home, an ant alone in this life.

The romance has died.

It stopped its persistent breathing two months and three weeks ago, when the huge brightness flashed and my crew died around me. My friends and companions, men noble and wise and given to science as faith. Dead, coloured in unimaginable light. Perishing with awe staring wide from their eyes, looking out into the incredible fire.

I am recording these thoughts, perhaps my final thoughts, in the hope that if discovered, my personal revelations might open up the eyes of others seeking to follow in the path I have travelled. My sliver of wisdom in an otherwise wasted life. I have seen a million sights which sent shivers along my spine and put the flesh of a goose upon my arms beneath this old space suit. And maybe I should not have seen any of them. Perhaps it was never my business to look.

I have stared deep into deepest eyes in the furthest corners of space and glimpsed the mystery of foreign souls. Those eyes looked out at me occasionally with curiosity and often with fear and yet I always pushed forward indiscriminately, propelled by the old desire for knowledge. Like a hunger or unquenchable thirst. Like an infant's instinctual reaching for the teat.

Lucky children, we, having witnessed sights very few of our brothers and sisters could ever claim to. I have held tiny magenta-furred marsupial-like animals in gloved hands, watched them crawl along my arm and scrutinize me with wide globe-eyes as the child in me stared out happy and awed. This child, like all children, wanted to claim his discovery for himself and, with his friends, captured several specimens of the bizarre creatures, bringing them along like a prize of fireflies caught in a jar. Our jar was our silver rocket and our newest pets, like others from past journeys from past worlds, died in our care because what did children know about the caretaking of unknown life? Our vehicle, after all, was no zoo, but simply a ship designed to carry us men of science further than our predecessors had ever journeyed. We'd named her the *Success*, proudly proclaiming our confidence and courage, never doubting our steadfast faith in science or our equally adamant pursuit of knowledge.

Our computers hold records of our exploits and I spend my time now reading the sad literature this represents. What seems like an endless history of files, making me marvel at our tenacity and foolhardiness.

So many landings upon so many grounds. I search through our files and the plethora of records leaves me astounded at our doggedness. I see the file name appear on-screen, the familiar orange digital characters sad and haunting inside the dark monitor depths: 'File #7990: Circles', and I recall: the caverns of beauty. The caverns which had been miles-deep in the earth, like an epiphany after leaving the inhospitable and mountainous surface terrain of the seemingly lifeless moon orbiting the gas giant along the galaxy's rim. Our trek below-ground had taken the better part of twelve hours and had begun to seem a fruitless venture. Then a persistent heavy moisture lining the granite walls, utterly lightless the deeper we'd plunged into the subterranean depths. Until the levelling out three thousand precarious feet beneath the earth, the complex network of caverns and smaller grottoes, and inter-connecting tunnels and tributary passages. This intricate labyrinth and its soft, ghostly form of luminescence, the small fire globes like a fairy tale magician's crystal balls hovering in static orbits along the ceiling all around us.

Their beauty breathtaking as we lingered entranced among them, captivated by their eerie and lovely fire. And my accidental brushing against one of their magical number, in one of the narrower side-passages whose ceiling reached substantially lower; and I'd been struck unconscious by the minute globe's touch, a quick surge of silent current coursing through my space suit's thick skin and into my own skin and skeleton beneath. I recall my swimming return journey into consciousness, my immediate yearning to see and reach towards the ghostly alien glow once more despite the tingling in my extremities like some aftermath lightning-sizzling. A gentle magenta luminosity beckoning in the cool, moist atmosphere. The discovery had been at once exciting and startling, and had ultimately settled guilt into the deepest parts of us all: the globe had suffered, too, having crashed to the cave floor from my careless child's contact as well. Its soft heartbeat pulsing light was stopped forever. Transformation, from magical circle of floating light, to limp, lightless and lifeless husk of wrinkled leathery flesh upon the tunnel floor. Accidental murder in the caverns of uncanny beauty.

    I scroll downwards, staring into the *Success's* computer screen, astonished and disgusted by the seemingly endless number of missions so formally collected before me. So seemingly quantifiable, our awful history of wrongful trespasses. I do not need to open the file named 'File #7979: Accident 14', its memory remains potent, stinging. One of several unfortunate mishaps I remember with acute clarity because the error had been once again more mine than my peers: the small moon we called Pallus-Ardeo, with its perpetually congested and overcast atmosphere, its thick tangles of swampy foliage and endless landscape of trackless bog land. My great fear at the sudden appearance of wildlife so startlingly close at hand, the small gnomish animal rushing towards me from the undergrowth and my reflexive drawing of my laser pistol. I'd seared the creature through cleanly, stunning myself and my crew with the quick efficiency of my action. The animal's blood was a deep blue staining its virgin white pelt as it rolled instinctively into a fetal curl and expired before us. It was only days later that we learned of the race of jungle dwellers to which this creature belonged, who inhabited the deepest and most dense stretches of the marshy country. The animals' binding group behaviour was akin to that of the chimpanzees of Earth, and it wasn't very long until they'd welcomed us completely into their primitive circle as if we were their own, and in so doing broke our hearts. It was difficult to look into their eyes: I could still see the ghost of blue upon my hands.

    World after world and their collections of myriad moons, and we never satisfied our longing to witness and document and lay claim to yet more discovery. I have tripped over lunar surfaces and slid waist deep into hollows filled with ancient dust, desiccated remains of once thriving civilizations. I have floated through ghostly gaseous atmospheres and swam with the bizarre, flitting shapes of alien fishes in bottomless seas. I once explored a gleaming crystal thicket and touched its silver trees only to recoil from their startled cries, unsettling evidence of unexpected sentience. Their songs in the dark of night haunt me still, a collective wailing so mournful that even then, years ago when we were all younger and more brave or naive, I questioned our purpose among them while plugging my ears and trembling uneasily. Should we have heard those cries, so pained-sounding, so anguished, as if we were eavesdroppers on some alien rite of mourning?

And I close my eyes and the greatest ghost I have ever known returns to haunt me: because I am once again remembering her world, verdant and fertile and alive with sounds, tickings and whirrings and buzzings and unseen shufflings in the brush. A world of deep valleys and dense forests and jungles which we'd named Verntellus, a world abounding with life and yet owned truly by a single of its wondrous denizens. And tears return to my eyes and choke me because I recall my most horrendous personal crime: it was in these trackless jungles that I, with deepest guilt and backwards thoughts of home, first laid lips upon the dainty pink mouth of a creature resembling in most all ways a humanoid flower, vibrant pink petals surrounding a centre-face of exquisite prettiness, a lush stock-body undulating like a snake secured forever in the earth of a planet I still and always will consider to have been paradise. My thoughts return to her often, I am rooted there beside her forever.

I love my wife, and I blow her kisses across gulfs of black which I know will never reach her lips. Katharine, watching with dedication my invisible travels among the stars from her old backyard porch perch. Turning her lovely eyes only occasionally downwards to earth, and to her small garden of lilacs and gardenias looking forlorn in the night glow. I recall her smell, a natural scent, of soil and flower-perfume. Katharine of the Gardenias, toiler in the earth while her husband scampers among the stars.

Space does this, swallows warmth and makes the past waver before our eyes, like pictures before candle breath.

It has been long since I have held a candle cupped in my hands. I yearn for the burning warmth upon my skin. It has been long since I have been touched by home-warmth. This great void became my new home a million years ago. A million dreams ago. An ironic solace and source of warmth, or perhaps it had only been my passion which had achieved that.

But now I am cold again.

Colder than I have ever been.

And I understand and respect completely the utter power of the black wasteland all about me.

It is an angry God whose eyes watch over our insect lives if what we glimpsed in the blackness between those distant star constellations was truly divine, as I believe it was.

We came as harbingers, and our greetings were perpetually peaceful. We were men of science, with deepest faith in our machine hearts and instrument panels. They told us how to find you, wondrous denizens of alien countries. Now you must tell us how to act. No text written tells of that. We were not pirates, making landings in order to pillage and burn.

We were children, scampering across the skies as if we owned property in so much endless intangibility. Arrogant and thoughtless: Look at us, we can fly like birds! Watch us spike our silver rocket into this and that alien soil so boldly, like a salty salute back to the families we've left behind.

Men in flight through the universe. "That's us sailing through the Big Black," we would say romantically, as if reciting old verse, and somehow it had always justified our pursuits. This was our passion and profession, after all, the calling we had each answered because an inner voice so compelling could never be quelled. And then after our long years travelling and discovering together came an inexplicable contact, the eruption of heavenly light in a star-field panorama suddenly illuminated completely.

And now everything has changed.

Now I understand my insect size.

I, scientist and dust mote between stars.

I loved my companions, have kissed flowers in their presence and maintained their confidence and friendship. We discovered paradise together.

Now I alone sail these winter paths between spots of twinkling bright. I alone remain, strapped tightly in place inside this vestige component of our old rocket. This escape pod like a steel balloon fitted with all the trappings of scientific-minded man bent on survival once his explorations have proven futile or too hazardous to continue. Shooting without purpose through all of this space. No purpose other than to return to the only scrap of home left to me in the universe. Into the arms of a woman waiting with eyes riveted to the stars for signs of movement. Into the embrace of a creature deserving of so much better than a husband she'd lost to the stars long ago. A fool with blue blood and flower-perfume staining his hands.

I wonder about myself, and *Success* and what the word might truly mean given my newly-realized insignificance.

We saw the face of God two months ago, and everyone but myself died looking upon it.

I alone in the universe recall so vividly His wide open appraisal of us in our childish fright, awed and silly in our traveling stick of steel and plastic and rubber and fuel and fire and hope and pretentious spirit of exploration.

A routine reconnaissance among the moon clusters of a lifeless planet. Qasim and Rix running their usual climate and topographical scans, eyes dutifully intent on their work; Sossi expertly maintaining our altitude over the minor moon while whistling an old song from his youth; Poirier waiting for the word to don his gear and venture below, occupying himself as ever with the sketchpad across his knee and pen in his hand, doodling rockets and pretty girls against starry backdrops. Banfield filling the doorway with his heavy frame, soiled dish towel across his shoulder, his presence informing us that our supper was prepared as soon as we were ready. And all the rest of us scientists, eagerly studying and readjusting our instruments, waiting expectantly while our machines analyzed the terrain below.

And then there was the light.

The blinding radiance which stopped the dreams of my companions forever. Looking up from the screens before me at the materialization of the conflagration, I had glimpsed a fraction, only a minute portion of the fury burning in that giant stare before its brightness blinded me. The visage hanging before our craft, briefly yet lividly illumined against the shimmering backdrop of the nearby nebula. Was it truly a pair of eyes the length of forever piercing our craft and our souls? Had it been fire licking out from that light with judgement in its appraisal? I close my eyes, and I think intently, and I only see this at the heart of the light: condemnation, because yes, it was indeed judgement. This I know with certainty. It is all I know now. And the vision of my friends burning in their seats with flames in their eyes and jetting like angry volcano plumes from their mouths, with the awful confusion and terror consuming their wide open red stares: this image is imprinted indelibly across my eyes. I will see it always. It will be my ghost for the rest of my days, trailing me closely like a fixed stare from the darkness. It, and this other memory, of the visage itself staring into the deepest parts of who I am. Leaving me, solely, unscathed, to smell the stench of burned flesh permeating our rocket, and to weep for all our collective wrongs.

And then the horror which was the great fire's invariable companion, as I recall of necessity jettisoning their crumbling, blackened bodies from the ship, one by one, the most arduous and painful task I have ever committed myself to. Colleagues, friends, given up to the infinite gulfs in a harried mockery of funereal rites.

And I recall thinking, as I watched their bodies become swallowed into the huge blackness: *I asked for you to come to me, didn't I?* And I remember answering myself, as I frantically leapt into the escape bubble and strapped myself in rigid place, my body numb everywhere with the trauma that had befallen me: *Yes. I begged for you to answer my child-like, selfish cries all these years.* I am a scientist in search of quantifiable knowledge, but I have also always pondered the invisible text written between the lines of those old volumes of scientific fact and conjecture; that body of unfathomable theory slipping in and out of my conscious thoughts as it has done since as early in my life as I am able to recall: the mystery of Creation, like an impossible puzzle defying all the instruments of deduction and reason that I have always had at my disposal.

Is this why I have been spared, to sail the cold spaceways alone, a hermit harbinger of esoteric knowledge? I ponder this question and am consumed by its implications and I am deeply afraid because although I can claim no hard evidence for my theory, I feel it breathing inside me like living fact. It is faith, and it has grown hugely like a cancer in me these recent weeks. Like certainty, and I am afraid of it, and it is a fear more profound than any I have known before.

And I think back to that fateful moment, when His eyes lit the black plane with their commanding fire, and I ordered my little bubble to remove me from that scene of death and judgement, slipping unluckily away into freefall. And I spun and spun and tumbled through and through and eventually regained my bearings and managed to maintain the familiar course programmed long ago into the navigation computer's reeling memory system.

And I sped on my way, numb all over my body and in deeper places especially; and through the porthole windows of my escape pod, I yet see the burning gaze which I have sought to leave behind, following me resolutely still.

And the fire in its appraisal is its fury with me.

I think of my wife, and I wonder whether her gentle eyes watch the sky tonight, hoping for some sign of my traveling like a flea among the stars.

I am pursued, by I am uncertain what.

By small globes of crimson light pulsing like heartbeats in the darkness. By the ghosts of blue-blooded animals living a more civilized existence among their tree nests than I have ever led, far away from where I was born and raised in a small farmers' town of orchards and corn rows. By memories of flower-scented transgressions infused with guilt, ruined by its stinging bitter presence inside me. By my fears and uncertainties as I ponder the significance of pursuits in this limitless country when I am only as little as an ant.

And I wonder: is it sin to seek paradise?

As if on cue, my instruments flare up like a fireworks display and all the old terror returns. Coursing through me, I feel the cold everywhere, the vacuum of space living inside my skin now alongside my depleting courage. I watch the alarm indicators burn like small manufactured suns, seeing them as a smear of crimson through my tear-filled eyes. Their vivid warning hues, their deep

519

reds and oranges are the colours which bring to mind wrath. It is a colour I deserve to look upon through these salt-watering eyes.

For my pursuits I am pursued, and I am frightened that the anger of the universe is just. Because I recall and shiver at my star-skipping history. Because I am just me, and I am alone. Cold and wifeless. Spinning like a single mote through time and space. Faith has slept dormant inside me the whole long career of my travels, yet I plodded on with the rest of the children, reckless in our experiments, seeking, always seeking the next astonishing sight.

A great tremor courses through my bubble, rattling its walls violently. I sense acutely the proximity of the vacuum pressing upon me from all sides.

Just as suddenly: silence.

The computer ceases its frantic whirring. Lights stop their burnings and flashings and colossal quiet has descended once more in my little bubble. I exhale deeply. I blink tears and sweat from my eyes. I am alone once again.

I stare out in the vastness of the Big Black and I shiver, for among the stars I see her. I allow her constellation-portrait to coalesce within the shimmering points before me. And I feel her watching me as I have always felt her longing for my presence beside her. Back home, in a place which my pursuits have caused me to forget time and time again. And I purse my lips together and blow her a silent kiss through the miles of space and years. And I wish for her forgiveness, a gift which I will never deserve. And I name her amid those shimmering stars, and whisper her name softly inside this small steel bubble. Like a prayer. Like a wish. Like a final goodbye to a sliver of my past still haunting me among other, guilt-ridden memories.

Katharine, the Watcher. Katharine, of the Gardenias.

Watching me now as ever, with the scent of withering gardenias and lilacs haunting her porch aerie space. And the tears are rivers coursing freely down my cheeks.

And through this wash of salt water, I understand. A sudden epiphany, and my final mission stands revealed. The only good purpose, really, that I might have left.

I have no place remaining to which to return. I am a

man alone. This infinite universe surrounds me, stifles me. I will not bring my judgement with me to a place I once called home. A place of wives owning sad sky-watching eyes, content enough with their corner of garden and family of flowers. Whose dreams and goals remained earthbound, while others brought their insatiability with them to the stars. Failed gods, tiny men realizing only at the very last their folly of arrogance, and their true insignificance. I will face my judgement here, in the icy void between stars where only greedy souls live. The sole shred of success I may hope to achieve in my small life.

My final gift to you, Katharine.

You deserve so much more than this weak-willed creature by your side.

In the far distance, a comet arcs silently past. Its frosty beard lingers against the blackness, and sends shivers along my spine.

To the infinite darkness surrounding me, I whisper the words: *Show me. Teach me. Show me what I've done wrong. Deliver me Your judgement as You see fit.*

And I shut down the remaining power in my bubble-ship, and listen to the final cessation of electronic hummings and whirrings. This tiny man-made ruckus amid all the huge and humbling silence of the universe. And the stars provide the only light, an icy, frosty glow through the porthole glass.

Except for certain constellations, which burn a little warmer, a little more sadly than all the rest.

No answer has come yet, from the Big Black.

Only silence, vast and awesome.

In its embrace, I drift.

In my slumbers, I dream, and I dream often of flowers. Of holding them in my hands and breathing their perfume and their saving oxygen. And my sleep is deep. And when I awaken I wish only to return to dreams, where I am alive.

Pigeons or Ashes, and the Final Gift of Jimmy Colley

The boy held the chain away from him. He examined with reverence its small silver cross swinging pendulum-like on the oppressive air. The setting sun's light limned it bloodily. His tears blurred it bloodier and he said, "He was a *hero*. You know? A true *hero*. A hero who believed in *God*." And he gave the chain a minute tug to send its cross rocking more violently from one side to the other, sending sun-flashes from the silver like encoded signals from his hand to the mantle of the sky wheeling over their heads.

"Yeah," acceded the smaller boy standing beside him, his freckled face grimacing in the glaring air. "He was mine, that's for sure."

The first boy nodded, his tall gaunt frame lost inside of his ragged clothes. "Yours and mine, Max, and everyone's out there even if they don't know it. Everyone who's a good person." He swept the surrounding buildings with an all-encompassing derisive gesture, eyes feral and bitter. A pigeon, spooked from its perch along the steel landing one level above their own, rose into the air in a mad flutter of grey feathers like a burst of ashes or some grim confetti. The boys followed its ambling progress mutely, bridging the great hollow space between the fire escape and the adjacent brownstone tenement. The bird lighted upon some ledge or other aerie indistinguishable from the patchwork façade of the building, all grey-speckled stone set within the greater brown wall, looking quite as though it had been swallowed entirely by the brick face.

"Most people don't know anything," murmured Max, scanning the building for evidence of the pigeon, his words sounding as though they were meant to represent some sort of finality to their moment near to the sky. When, a moment afterward, his friend hadn't responded and the boy felt a lingering incompleteness to what he'd tried ineffectually to convey, he concluded with a bluntness which nearly stunned him – because they rarely discussed the nature of the people they encountered day to day – "Most people are the worst things in the world."

This his companion understood. He nodded adamantly. "Yeah. Yeah, you're right about that. Do you want to go back down, or...I don't want to go back down. I don't want to find any work tonight at all."

Max shook his head adamantly, a vigorous gesture which felt urged from him of its own volition, and began to lead a slow silent climb through the sun-scorched skeleton of the fire escape. His companion pocketed the chain and cross and – delivering the city a final baleful glare – turned and followed, the great heat and stifling humidity bowing his skeleton, as if these midsummer's conditions represented a power which beckoned him earthwards, a power which it felt exceedingly – startlingly – good to fight as he clambered that little bit closer to the sky.

They'd rationed their meagre lunch on the metal grillwork floor between them. Two crackers apiece, left over from their late night donut shop visit the evening before; a pair of Mars bars which one of them had lifted from a convenience store earlier that day while the other had distracted the sole employee, the elderly Vietnamese proprietor who seemed feverishly intent on catching them in the act of thieving and yet, for all his handful of security cameras and his wary eye, hadn't been able; and a grape juice box to share, that a kindly woman – a uniformed nurse seated on a wooden bench outside of the nearby old care facility in which she worked – had given them from her own paper bag lunch when they'd asked her for change and, seemingly dismayed that she hadn't had any money to offer, had instead thrust upon them her beverage.

The taller boy popped a cracker into his mouth, chewed disconsolately, and said, "How many ghosts do you think are out there?" His eyes, squinting in the blinding air, gazed in the direction of the street glimpsed beyond the alley. They'd come to rest several floors above the alley floor, high enough that they felt free from the possibility of human contact, though its fetid urine-and-garbage stench wafted to them still, ruining their meal.

Max followed his stare. "Out there? In the city? Jesus. They're everywhere, Steve. The city's filled with every kind of ghost you can imagine, right? The sad quiet kind – like that old lady's ghost that haunts the parking garage near the river and makes every floor nice and mellow – and the demon kind, too. I've seen those, too. You have, too. Who hasn't, right? They're everywhere. Jesus, they are."

"It sounds like something he would have said."

"He did. I stole that from him, because it makes such good sense. He said that all the time, about ghosts."

Steve nodded, chewing mechanically but tasting nothing of the stale cracker turning into wet powder between his teeth. "Yeah, I know he did," he murmured distantly. "I know. He's one of them now, too. I can feel him out there. He's there, but not the way he used to be. I can still feel him, though. Can't you?"

The tenacious heat of the sun, the languor of the day, their mourning moods: these ingredients merged into the hazy indolence which sapped the boys of their remaining energy and allowed them to sleep in their elevated fire escape aerie looking over the trash-filled alley. Steve was the first to stir some time later, rubbing at his eyes, then more frantically at his forearm where the flesh was scalded where it lay pressed to the burning steel floor.

He sat up, tilting his chin in search of a breeze that wasn't blowing. A moment later his companion, sensing somehow in his fitful semi-slumber that he was enjoying his dozing alone, turned about on the steel floor and repeated much the same manner of rubbing at eyes and arms as Steve had a moment before. He murmured drowsily, "What time is it?"

His companion peeled back the perspiration-heavy clump

of his bangs where they hung into his eyes and examined the sliver of western sky peeking through the alley's mouth. "I don't know. The sky's red in the west. Maybe seven, eight at night."

Max nodded wondrously, looking stunned in his somnolent state. "We slept for a while, eh? Holy."

From the mouth of the alley a jovial cry erupted. They turned and glimpsed briefly the trio of girls – mid-twenties, dressed identically in blue jeans and fitted black tank tops – passing along the sidewalk; the first of what would prove to be the usual hordes of weekend bar-goers seeking good times and revelry until the mid-morning hours. Max, glowering after them, spit through the grillwork. His friend followed the globule of saliva as it fell, elongating queerly in its descent into the alley below. He nodded. "Yeah, I know. I know."

"They've got it made, don't they," said Max, shaking his head, his words coming hard and fast and brimming with vitriol. "Those bitches got it made tonight."

"I know." And then his companion added, addressing his own thoughts and Max's, too. "I can't believe he's gone."

And he looked away, into the burning west, when a moment afterwards Max began a subdued weeping that disturbed the air and groaned the steel skeleton around them as he rocked to and fro in his place, as if futilely seeking a familiar embrace that could no longer come.

Whether it would prove helpful to the younger boy or only exacerbate his grief, Steve didn't know, but making his voice as casual as he could, he murmured, "The first time he saved me...I remember it so good..." He drifted off dreamily, seeing from Max's red-rimmed eyes turning to him hopefully that he'd succeeded in giving the words as a kind of gift to his younger companion. While staring off into the dusking sky directly over their heads, he went on, "Man, you can never forget things like that. Not ever. Meetings like that stick with you, you know?"

At the sound of footsteps intruding into the alley quiet he turned his eyes downwards and raked the shadows encroaching along the alley floor with trepidation, steeling himself for the kind of invader that might reveal themselves. Although they'd remained secreted among the rust-spotted skeleton of the fire escape several feet from the alley floor it apparently was not far enough to avoid detection – A lone man had entered and wandered the length of the alley, seemingly having lost his way, dapperly dressed in suit and tie and utterly incongruous with the stink and shadows mingling below. Turning his gaze upwards he immediately found the boys huddled in the grillwork like a pair of pigeons, and he watched them quizzically for a moment without speaking before turning and leaving the alley, his expression confused, and haunted with a misplaced sympathy which both boys had clearly seen etched in his features. This gave Max, frowning irately after the man, the impetus to clamber down to the second landing and – grunting and cursing in his prodigious repertoire of invective which revealed itself from time to time – hoist the rattling, rust-covered ladder up after them, freeing them in this way from any possibility of being reached in their place (what would have been the ground level of the landing had been removed for no clear reason and was now wholly absent).

His only words once he'd returned three floors up to where his elder companion sat waiting in meditative silence were, "Good riddance, to people getting the chance."

He then popped his remaining cracker into his mouth and waited for his friend's story mood to return and lead him places.

Steve pierced the tiny foil-covered hole of the juice box he held with its straw, sucked on it with a mellow sheen over his eyes. Then he began. "I was just over there. Across the street and in the opposite alley, down behind the coffee bar there. It was early in the night, maybe ten or eleven. I was on my knees for some guy, just about to do him there. The guy was talking, real low, things I barely heard but what I did was weird and dirty stuff. And then I heard *his* voice. The words just hung there. 'Stand up, son.' I looked and saw him and I stood up and went over to him. He had his arm up, like for me to come and take cover with him or something. So I did that. I went over to this man I'd never seen before, wearing his faded old poncho and a beard as long and white as his hair, and the guy standing with his fly open, he went nuts. He started coming over, calling Jimmy – I learned after that his name was Jimmy – calling Jimmy all this bad shit, said he'd kill him if he didn't mind his business. But Jimmy looked him in the face and told him where to go. He said that, and the guy listened and fucked off a minute later, even though he was a head taller than Jimmy and about twenty years younger. Even though Jimmy was an old man, even then he was old and that was, like, a few years ago or whenever. And he didn't mention a thing about that guy to me the whole rest of the night, didn't tell me what I thought he was going to say about it. He just put his hand on my shoulder and said, 'It's been a long day, hasn't it? You must be so tired.' And I was. He knew I was. He knew just how tired I was. And we went back to his place, to that little attic filled with all his stuff, all those old books and magazines and newspapers and the old cats that came in off the balcony and drank the milk Jimmy always left next to the door in the little saucer. He gave me the couch for the night and didn't ask me for anything, not even for me to give him a reason for being where I was earlier that night. When I woke up in the morning he'd put a tray with breakfast on the table by the couch. I guess the smell was what woke me. Bacon and toast and an omelet – I hadn't had an omelet in months then – and he was sitting across the room, by the window, covered in sunlight, like he was my granddad – or someone's granddad – and I knew right then that that was the closest place I'd ever find to being at home again."

He said nothing for a time, and then added, "I liked how he called me *son*. He always did that."

Max was wiping at his eyes. His nostrils bubbled with mucus but he made no move to wipe it away with a hand or shirtsleeve, the picture of the young, oblivious child. "Yeah. He did it for me, too. Called me that. That was the nicest thing that ever happened to me."

The words seemed to signal some significant thing, silencing the boy's talking. In their wake, they ruminated in silence while the night descended.

"He could have been a jazz player," Max said, reintroducing conversation between them. "He could have lived off his playing, he was so good. But he only kept it inside that little apartment of his. Sax music used to fill up that little place, when he had his mood on, like he used to say."

"The Attic."

"The Attic, yeah. I loved that place."

"Me too. We met there, you and me."

"Yeah, we did. In December, near Christmas, a couple years back, right?"

Steve nodded and his voice was solemn. "It's been almost six years. I came by his place after I got beat on. One of those kind of nights. Six years. Six years gone."

A frown of concern wrinkled Max's face. Steve saw this, and waited patiently for the younger boy to explain his troubled thoughts. "How come...How come he never got out of here? He hated this mess, this town. Jimmy named it a shit-hole every chance he got."

"He had a bad leg, right? You remember? His *lame* leg, he called it. It's why he had to use a cane. He lost his job because of it and slept in places like this for years. He told me that once. He was waiting it out, he told me, until he was old-age old and then he got old-age money. Pension money. Then he got himself his Attic, with the money. He used to say that he was too tired to go anywhere after all his years in the streets, sleeping in garbage and catching naps in motel rooms with shit people."

Max looked up, his eyes immense moons haunting the dusk air. "Jimmy did that? He had to do it, too? I knew it! He never said so, not really, I mean, but I knew it anyways!"

"Yeah. He did it for years." It wasn't exactly pride in Steve's voice. Even he heard it, and discerned in his words their timbre of empathy. With it arrived a strange feeling of maturity or fatherliness as he sought his best to keep Max from hysterics with the things he said.

Max suddenly thrust a finger across his lips in a gesture of silence. Following his gaze, Steve found the skeletal shadow disengaging itself from the greater blackness beneath them. It jangled a tune of cheap jewelry and pocket change, and a girl emerged from the night. Her eyes – they could see even at that distance – were lost inside a dense perimeter of mascara applied by an amateur's hand.

531

She craned her neck to better see them in their steel perch. Her thin lips moved in her gaunt face, and a reedy voice called out, "Hey, people. What are you, living like pigeons? What, you think you're sea gulls tonight?"

"Hey, Jasmine. Where you headed?" Max called downwards, his eyes flashing to and from the emaciated girl and finally remaining trained on the shadows beyond her, as though he feared for her. Steve saw this, and something turned in him – Max, he knew, *liked* Jasmine the way some boys and some girls *liked* each other. It was very sweet, he thought, and innocent, and of course this was precisely why it ached him so to witness whenever the two chanced to cross paths on dangerous nights like this.

"Have you heard?" Max called out to her, his voice precariously edging towards a girlish high-note frequency. "You heard, probably, eh? The bad news."

"What? What are you talking about?" she retorted peevishly, as though she disliked not knowing all things or that she perhaps resented the boys for their imminent revelation when she – much accustomed to disaster – didn't wish to hear any more terrible news. Or possibly her irritation came more simply from having to strain her voice and struggle to make out the boys perched high over her head. Or maybe she felt lonely down there alone among the refuse and shadows, naked where any passerby might see her and approach her and summon her to do the things that young people like she and the boys did for others.

When the boys, also weary of shouting their words, had climbed down to her and arrived on the level one floor above the alley floor, they kept their eyes in the shadows and Steve – the more courageous of the two when in the girl's presence – murmured, "... Colley's dead. Jimmy..."

The skeleton girl seemed to waver in her place before the boys. She appeared imbalanced in her cheap high heels, like a street performer walking on stilts, as though she might crumple to the cement at any moment. Eventually she steadied herself enough to scoff and spit into the shadows. Placing a wrist along her bare bony hip jutting from between her skirt and tube top in a gesture of practiced cockiness, she stammered, "What the fuck? What are you saying? What the fuck, man. You don't know what you're talking about, man."

"I'm sorry, Jazz," squeaked Max nearly inaudibly.

"You *seen* him? I mean...How do you know shit about..?"

"We found him," Steve explained, voice gentle. "Today, in the morning. We called an ambulance, but he was long gone already."

The girl's eyes widened, her whites appearing like risen lunar faces from her dark mascara-caked face. "Fuck you, man. You assholes don't know what you're saying. You're fucked up. I'm going to Jimmy's right now, fuck you. He ain't going to be happy with you for pulling shit like this. Lying assholes. Fuck you, assholes. This shit ain't funny, fuck you."

Max, visibly steeling himself – seemingly drinking in the sight of the girl with her cheap jewelry jangling its tinny song, her soft-looking chocolate skin, the small glinting shape hanging from its chain between the protruding parentheses of her collarbones – called out in his shrill mouse's voice, "Jazz. It's true. We wouldn't lie about it. I wouldn't lie to you about it. There's...There's room up here. You want to be a pigeon tonight?"

This invitation was met with more garbled invective from below, the abrasive clatter of a glass bottle being kicked along the concrete in a theatrical display of her wrath. They watched her stagger off, an unnerving desperation defining her wobbling steps striving for fleetness but managing only a pathetic and awkward gait in her heels and affected swaggering. She remained unsteady and tottering in her heels until – framed in the orange streetlights illuminating the alley's mouth, they saw her pause and pluck first one and then the other of the cheap shoes from her feet and then patter across the street with them hanging each from one of her hands; the gesture, this heedless stripping away of her own put-on street personality which communicated her desperation more than any other action could have in that moment, made the boys' hearts ache for her.

Max, watching the girl disappear across the street, sucked back the phlegm clogging his nose anew and began a slow, disheartened climb back along the steel staircase. Over his shoulder

Steve overheard him mutter, "Jazz could be cool," almost wistfully, but with an underlying timbre of sympathy. "She could be nice if she wasn't such a bitch all the time."

"I bet Jimmy would've agreed with that, too," was all that his companion could offer, but it sounded distantly like the most appropriate thing to have said at that moment.

A moment passed without words between them as they reconvened on the landing three floors up the building's face. Max retrieved the half-empty packet of candy cramping his jeans pocket, unfurled it and offered it to his companion. Steve only shook his head, despite the hunger pains kneading his guts. Instead he muttered, feeling a queer optimism in so doing, "You ever want to have a girl? A *girlfriend?*"

"Yeah, one day. I'll get one one day." Max seemed confident in providing his answer as he chewed a candy vigorously.

"Oh yeah? When?" Steve had tried but failed to keep the challenging, nearly fatalistic timbre from entering his words, and grew irritated at his own candor.

But his companion answered pleasantly enough, as though he'd discerned no disbelief in the words or else was convinced of a different future for himself than one owned by disaster and alley-living. "Some day, when I ain't out here, yeah. I ain't going to be here forever, that's for sure."

Silence fell between them, like a shroud steeping the alley in a blackness deeper than any nightfall could descend. An immense rat appeared in the moonlight below – Steve had initially mistaken it for a black cat – making a rustling-rattling clamour as it sniffed among some overturned garbage bags. It disappeared among the rusted grillwork at the base of the brick wall a moment afterwards when the echo of footsteps filled the narrow enclosed space. The boys peered between the fire escape bars, watched the man stumble from the shadows. He came to rest at the base of the wall directly beneath them. The distinct, quick sound of his zipper coming undone sounded in the stillness, followed immediately by the torrent of his urine splashing from the bricks and onto the ground. They watched as if entranced by the spectacle of yellow water widening about the obliviously drunken man's shoes. The man's unexpected words –

"Fuck! Yeah, fuck you, you won't talk to me!" – startled the boys, and the smaller boy's subtle shifting in his place betrayed them with a resounding groaning of metal in the night.

The man stumbled backwards several steps, very visibly startled himself, peering upwards with his flaccid dick clutched heedlessly in his fist. They watched vague, unreliable lucidity replace his inebriated look of stupidity, and he barked, "What the fuck are you doing up there? What do you think you're doing up there! Fuckin' *kids*. Go home. Come down here and I'll beat your fuckin' asses," before wheeling about and careening the length of the alley in the direction of the awakening evening street beyond.

The boys wished nothing more than to remain in their birds-nest place, as long as time or the hunger scrabbling inside their guts would permit, far removed from the filth piled everywhere below. And so they did, watching without words as moonlight appeared and covered everything in a veneer of silvery blue, making things over deceptively, as if there might actually be hope left in the night.

They'd climbed yet closer to the sky, scrabbling like rodents through the steel chutes and stairs of the fire escape, coming to rest nearly midway up the building face. Once there, panting from their exertions, dizzy from peering over the railings one too many times during their ascent, their mood seemed lifted from its earlier pall to a lighter place – possibly a result of night-climbing away from the world they knew – and their conversation was resumed.

"Yeah, Jimmy used to have magic words," Steve huffed, gobbling air hungrily. "The things he used to say."

His companion agreed with an emphatic nodding of his head. "He knew how to make you feel good. He could make you forget anything you needed to."

"You never had to remember things with him," Steve agreed. "That little attic was like a plug, the city on the outside and you safe on the flipside. With Jimmy."

"Sometimes I used to think he was the only decent person in the whole damn city."

"Yeah. Yeah. Maybe he was. Probably he was."

"I think he was. Really I do. I mean, we're okay, I guess, as far as people go, but Jimmy...He was...He was *why* we were okay. He made us better. He made *me* better."

The sound of the younger boy's nervous laughter, edged with panic and hysteria, drifted on the humid air.

Steve, seized once again by the story-mood, said, "The things he'd say...He once told me something that I never stopped thinking about. It was just another of his million theories, but this one, it stuck with me, you know? He said it that night I came to his place after the Detroit Night, when that guy took me back to his room across the river and it turned out there were five guys. So I came knocking at like six A.M., smelling like shit and fuck and Jimmy let me in, no questions asked like he never asked, only waited for you to say what you had to if you had to when you had to. And he let me in, and when I didn't say nothing he fixed me breakfast while I took a shower – scrambled eggs and toast and bacon like he knew I liked best – and then he turned on the news when I still wasn't saying nothing, and then he shut it off and got us coffee. I still couldn't say nothing about what happened, but he knew the kind of night I'd had. So he said something, I think because he knew I couldn't but really needed to hear something. Something good. Something only he could give me. So we were sitting there, on his ratty couch, and he said, really quiet and he was looking out the window when he said it: 'Look at it.' And I did, and it was the city spread out past the window that he was talking about, and then he gave it to me, like a gift for me. He said, 'Forests once grew wild here, and then people like a disease.'"

"It's like a song or something!"

Steve was nodding solemnly. "I know what he meant, too, you know? It made sense when he said it, and now it makes even more sense. Maybe I needed to think about it a few more years to understand it totally. I do now. I get it now. Man, that Jimmy, he knew a thing or two."

"He always wanted to live his dying days in the county. Remember, he used to say that a lot."

"Yeah, I remember that good. I never saw the county."

"Me neither. Jimmy made it sound pretty great, though.

He made it sound like the way we thought about his Attic. Like it was the most safe, special place in the world. Hey, is that where Jimmy was from, do you think? You think maybe he came from the county, before he lived in the city here?"

"Jimmy never said where he came from."

"No, he never did. But he sure said where he wanted to go to."

"I'd like to. I'd like to see the county."

"Me too, Steve. I'd like to see it, too."

They stopped talking for a moment, and listened to the city, fully awakened into its night-time ecstasy, pulsing from beyond the alley's mouth. The chatter of sidewalkers bar-going, the roar and chug and sputter of cars adding noise and stink to the air.

As if taking his cue from this clamour and the visions it lit up inside of his thoughts, Max said, "He used to say that there's nothing stopping you from doing what you got to do."

At this Steve turned to him. "I know. You're right. He did say that. He used to say that a lot, when times were rough especially. I think he meant that you do what you do until you got to do something different. Until you're able to do it. Like he did. He had nothing, right? He had a box back of the grocery, by the dumpster. And then he waited it out, waited his days out until he could get his old-age money. And then he got himself his Attic."

Max, putting his eyes in his lap where his fingers fidgeted anxiously, murmured, "Sometimes, when I'd be staying there with him, right before I fell asleep on the couch or in the sleeping bag on the kitchen tiles, I'd pretend that...I'd picture all the crosses he had up around the Attic, and the one he wore around his neck, and I used to pretend that the Attic was Heaven, and Jimmy was, like, God or something, or someone like that. Someone who was just all good, good all the way through. The way God's supposed to be." Max had retrieved his own chain and cross from his pocket, given him by Jimmy as he'd given such gifts to all of the children he allowed to sleep on his floor. He held it tightly in his little fist, eyes closed as if in deep deliberation.

"He *was* that way," Steve reassured his friend. "Jimmy was."

The boys sat in mellow silence for a time. The night clamored but they existed in their own bubble detached from its debauchery, like a moon orbiting the face of the derelict building like some forsaken monument in a metropolis long fallen into decay.

Then, a more immediate disturbance stirred them. They looked below, glimpsed vague movement which coalesced into another alley visitor. Eventually, this madly-gesticulating skeleton revealed itself with a resounding cursing of the boys. "Fuck off, did you have to climb the fuck up there? How am I supposed to reach you there?"

"Jazz!" exclaimed Max, and his enthusiasm at the girl's returned presence conjured a smile from his companion's hard-set lips.

"Hurry up, fuck off! I need to get up there, quick!"

The urgency infusing her voice, that rising edge of fear that she always sought to keep absent from her tough facades and words of bravado, impelled the boys to scramble to her aid. They climbed downwards as quickly as they were able, looking for all the world like a pair of gangly-limbed monkeys racing through the rusted skeleton of the fire escape. Once upon the second floor landing they extended the adjoining ladder into the alley and helped the girl clamber through the precarious barrier of steelwork. She shook away their efforts once she'd attained the relative safely of the narrow platform, though casting a wary eye behind her. Peeking between the steel slats to the alley beneath caused her to utter a gagging noise and cup a hand across her mouth. The air sounded with the tiny jangle of her thrift store bracelets at the motion. "Holy Jesus we're up the fuck high," she squeaked out before lifting her shuddering gaze to the boys smiling gentle smiles meant to calm her. A moment passed, and though she said nothing about it, both could see in the girl's collapsed posture and eyes more lost than usual that she'd learned the truth of their claims; perhaps having visited the old man's apartment and found it empty the way it never was; or maybe a clean-up crew or medics and police officers still loitering on the premises in examination of his meagre belongings or the final evidence of his life on Earth, the subtly trodden place on the threadbare carpet where they'd found him that morning, curled tightly as if in fetal sleep; or else perhaps she'd glimpsed their old friend Jimmy Colley the way they'd been seeing him throughout the long night, too, the man gone but his ghost presence left behind to comfort with its lingering lessons whispered on the air if you bent your ear and listened as carefully as you were able, past the city clamoring its old song of engines and human chatter and savagery.

Suddenly she was clutching at the boys, her heated voice freezing them into fearful immobility. "Shit, man! He followed me good! Where can we go? I don't know if I can go any higher..." She looked fearfully upwards through the zigzagging network of the fire escape ascending the length of the immense brick face of the building, while the boys watched apprehensively the heavyset form lurch from the shadows to a place directly beneath them. The malicious little eyes set deeply into the greasy, brooding pockmarked features with its high sloping forehead and receding shock of dark hair pulled back severely into the oiliest of ponytails; the kitschy array of silver rings glittering from his fingers as vainglorious testimony to the power he wielded over lost children who earned him his paltry money and jewelry and corrupt kingdom; the coarse-looking tufts of hair jutting from the collar of his lavender silk shirt making him yet more bestial; the sneering lips conveying the man's pleasure in having at last cornered the rogue girl escaped from his stable of similar such slaves.

"Come down here, Jasmine, girl," the man's feigned voice of solicitude sought to persuade her, betrayed by his lingering – seemingly inborn – vicious gaze piercing the gloom like a pair of black diamonds.

"I ain't going down there!" the girl spat, continuing to clutch fervently at her companions.

The sneering visage below melted into a mask of livid scorn. "You think I can't wait you out, girl? You and your hero boys? What, you think you can hide out on your man when you got work to do tonight? It's best you come down here right this minute, girl. I don't joke about shit like this."

She watched him a moment with loathing in her eyes before speaking. Shaking her head, she told him, "Fuck you, man. I ain't working for you no more, man. I quit on you."

The greasy, crater-faced man chortled and named her filthy names, while the boys led her away in their care; slowly, slowly ascending the winding course of the creaking, groaning fire escape; urging her to remain calm and to keep her eyes trained upwards and never behind them in the event that their increasing altitude might make her dizzy or vomit. Eventually, she grew too weary to carry on and they paused, easing themselves gently onto the floor.

"I ain't looking, but fuck tell me how high we are right now," she whispered, her voice quivering while her eyes stared directly into each of the boys' faces in turn, examining them with great care and attention, as if memorizing every detail of their physiognomies, each minute scar and pimple and pore and suggestion of nascent stubble illuminated by the moonlight; possibly because such dedicated focusing of her attention helped to push away the reality of her mid-air predicament, or perhaps because she wished to remember these rare and kind boys if it was her destiny to plummet into the alley darkness gathered below.

"We're up pretty high," Steve admitted with as reassuring a voice as he could offer. "No worries, though, okay? We're safe up here. We've been up here all day, Jasmine. We stay up here a lot. We're safer up here than down there." He accompanied this with an expansive gesture which took in the breadth of the city's downtown core spread beneath them; which suggestion of their elevation caused the girl to tremble and cover her face with her long caramel fingers until the sensation of vertigo had passed and she could watch her companions raptly anew.

They didn't question her about the nature of her night's unfolding; neither remarking on the man of filth stalking her below, nor of the exact nature of her discovering for herself the fate of their dear friend, Jimmy Colley. They let her have the time she required to regain control of her fraying faculties, to ease her careening thoughts, to quell as well as she could the great fear that surely was devouring her heart on that night of mourning, while beset by the demands of selfish and evil men prowling in the grounds beneath them like some bloodthirsty hound waiting out its prey.

Max, Steve saw with an odd sense of expectation, seemed to be gathering himself again – his lips mouthing ghost-language and his eyes flickering as if he were dreaming a soon-to-unfold scenario of some import – and when he finally spoke the question he put into the night was purposely simple, and easy for her to answer or not to answer. "Hey, Jazz, are you happy to be a pigeon now, too?"

She gave him the pretense of an exasperated look, but this melted quickly into one of relief or peace. A moment passed and – adjusting her bony legs beneath her so she too could recline in a neat cross-legged bundle between them – she asked quietly, "So, what are you doing here? What were you talking about up in this bird cage? You're damn crazy, this is so high up, but what were you doing? What were you talking about?"

They ruminated on this a moment. Max answered her. "Well, I guess we were talking about a lot of different things. We were talking a lot about the way it was. With Jimmy, and before him. And way before everybody. Like, a long time ago, I mean."

His companion added, "And about where Jimmy's gone to, and about how we're going to go there, too, in the morning."

At this, Max looked to Steve with surprise. A glimmer in his friend's eyes stirred something in some part of him, too. Something in the words moved something inside of him. He turned to Jasmine, was courageous enough to place a pair of grimy fingers gingerly on her forearm as he asked her, "Do you like trees, Jazz? You like the forest?"

The girl's eyes, hidden in the smeared swamp of her mascara, flitted briefly to the boy's face, looking uncertain, as though she was accustomed to being duped by peoples' words. She stammered, "Well, I ain't seen a forest. I like trees, though. Yeah I like trees."

The smaller boy turned to his companion, exclaimed, "She likes trees! She likes trees, too! Hey, let's climb to the roof and look to where the *county* is! The *county*, in the south. You want to see it, too, Jazz? Let's go look for the *county*, and make plans! Let's follow Jimmy Colley in the morning! I like your cross, Jazz! It looks nice around your neck like that!"

The girl was discomfited by the cryptic nature of the boys' uncharacteristically ebullient words, and fidgeted in her place, creaking the ancient network of pipes and ladders about them. Eventually, though, the boys' presence grew to become a comfortable atmosphere, and there, between them, clothed in their strange, indolent smiles, she felt peace come to her, and something which took her a moment to realize was excitement at the prospect of the forthcoming morning, when something good might – just possibly might – reveal itself to them along with the rise of the dawn.

      He cursed and damned his missing property, the runaway girl. Sweat circles marked his shirt beneath the arms and made a long strip down the length of his back. It beaded his forehead and annoyed his eyes no matter how ardently he sought to blink it away. It had taken him the better part of thirty excruciating minutes to pry apart the heavily-boarded rear door and climb the twelve stories of the derelict building – feeling his way semi-blindly in the uncertain light filtering through the dirty windows – and then gain access to the roof; having had to fiddle with the old iron door and its ancient bolt, bruising his hands and lathering his skin with sweat beneath his rich clothes and replacing his cologne-smell with the tang of his body's natural stench.
      Finally, he'd managed to splinter the deadbolt, encrusted with what appeared to be years' worth of accrued grime, and from there to climb the final claustrophobic and stuffy staircase and through the thick metal door at its summit – opened after several more minutes of battering its stout surface with first his shoulder and then, successfully, with the tire iron he'd likewise used to break down the ground floor door – to the rooftop beyond. He went furtively, low to the ground of the rough-hewn roof, eyes wide and intently scouring the area opened before him, the tire iron sprouting from his fist like a hideous, obscene flower. The flat surface left little room for concealment, yet he made a meticulous circuit of the roof, checking behind the shed-sized antennae platform and handful of brick protrusions whose purpose he couldn't guess. He peered anxiously over the lip of the building on all sides, the morning breeze rustling his clothes, drying the perspiration along his face and forearms. He dropped small and heavy stones clatteringly throughout the length of the fire escape, watching them filter through the rusted skeleton and plummet to the alley far below with dull walloping sounds as of meat slabs being slapped down with great impact upon a hard surface. He

held a hand to his eyes and combed the surrounding rooftops, and he raked the hazy morning streets and intersecting alleyways in this manner, too.

He could make no sense of the conundrum, having kept his vigil in the alley the entire duration of the night and morning, his fury growing with each hour passing while the girl remained hidden from him in the dizzying heights of the fire escape with her rescuer boys. He'd been a mere handful of minutes – five at the utmost – in gaining entry to the condemned building, and another fifteen to twenty in clambering through the darkened stairwells to the roof. The last he'd seen of the trio had been the sight of them clambering over the rim of the building far overhead while he'd paced in the alley, silhouetted plainly in moonlight and filling him with vengeful furor.

He shook his head, staring into the air, cursed vehemently. "Fucking bitch," he named the fugitive girl or the awakening day. He kicked a stone, sent it rolling with a flat echoless noise along the rooftop.

A sudden clamor caused him to cry out, fling his hands protectively about his head. He shrank towards the roof floor, staring about him uneasily.

A bevy of pigeons had erupted from some unseen perch, alongside the building or atop the antennae platform or some other secret vantage in which he hadn't spotted them earlier. He followed their flight as they rose into the bright air, limned in the risen sun's fire. He blinked after them, a rain of hoary feathers like ashes drifting languidly about him, like a patch of inclement weather for him and him alone to wade through during his return descent into the street.

The Animals have Seized the Diamond Sea Kingdom

"For what is a man profited, if he shall gain the whole world, and lose his own soul? Or what shall a man give in exchange for his soul?"

- Matthew 16:26

I don't want to do it.
But what she did or did not want meant nothing as always.

I made her do it the way I made her do all things. I took her by her hair, a big handful of blonde locks as I pushed her head downwards to smell the raw rot of it. I held her like that for a few seconds until she gagged and twisted out of my grip. It left a great knot of her hair in my fingers, the violent way she wrenched away from me and collapsed on the floor beside the bed.

I stood over her, watching her dry heave for a couple of minutes. When she was done, I grabbed another fistful of hair and dragged her back to where the German shepherd lay spread-eagled on the floorboards. I held her head firmly with both hands and pressed her crying face into the bald area of the dog's abdomen. The scar of the stab wound was fresh enough that its congealed scabby perimeter broke as I rubbed her cheek over it. She cried and gasped when she felt the wetness on her skin, and then started gagging again.

Lick it, I whispered into her ear, and listened to her wail and sob at my words. *Do it,* I ordered her and leaned over her shoulder to make certain she obeyed. She did, tentatively at first, small flicks of her tongue at the scabbed-over crusty black of the gaping scar's perimeter. *Lick it in the middle,* I told her, *where it's wettest.* She shook her head and cried and I forced her mouth towards the bloody spot. She resisted for a moment. Tired of struggling, I whispered it in her ear: *Diamonds tonight. A sea of diamonds and a sea of their faces, watching us walk down the carpet. Watching you walk the velvet carpet.*

    I watched her eyes, saw the determination slowly seep into them and replace the fear and resistance. She took a deep breath and eyed the wound directly in front of her nose. Then she plunged in. I watched her work her face into the crimson sore, listening to the lapping sound as she licked viciously with her tongue. She didn't hold back – she bit at the purpled, puckered flesh around the rim of the wound and sucked it with her lips. She groaned while she did it, first with disgust and then with something more fervent. Something like sheer willful resolve and passion.

    I pulled her underwear down from behind and slipped myself inside her.

    I was finished with her in a few minutes. I left her lying on the floor beside the dead dog, breathing in air in hungry gulps with red around her mouth. She looked beautiful, and I was grateful for her. Her eyes were glazed as she stared up at the ceiling, and I knew she was seeing diamonds there, shining down at her like a sea of promise.

    She'd gotten used to it by the time I'd begun bringing the animals into the lowest level basement bedroom with us and forced her to let them smell between her legs, more and more often during her menstrual cycle so that they would be at their most lustful. She'd cried the first few weeks of it but then only winced as the animals mounted and humped her in their mad-eyed frenzy, while I watched fixedly, playing with myself.

    She bore the acts because they were what I wanted. The thing I'd warned her about when she'd virtually begged me to take her out with me her nearly half a year ago. *Please,* she'd said, and her eyes told me what she'd do for me if I relented: anything. I'll do anything for you, those baby blue jewels promised me. Anything for the promise she saw in me, inherent in the new life I'd be giving her if I were to agree and wear her on my arm like a trophy. *Yes,* she heard me saying in her thoughts, *I'll give you everything in return for your body.* The women were always like this. They were the worst for this kind of behaviour, this dirty attitude towards life and the way I live it. As if they were goddesses and their bodies like keys for opening any man as they wished.

I was used to ignoring the types without madness in their eyes. They cringed and shrank back from the things I wanted when they realized the depths of what they were. They always seemed to figure that their legs and breasts and made-up faces could buy them free reign of the kingdom I've built for myself over the long years of toiling in obscurity through to my progressive rise to fame. They'd flaunt their bodies for me, parade themselves before me as if I cared for their shapes, only to run when their time to perform came. I'd grown tired of being violent with them, of dragging these disillusioned women across the carpet and tying them to bed posts, of holding their legs wide while the animals found them. I needed a woman who wanted to be found by them.

I knew Barbara was the one when I first disclosed to her the things I wanted.

The night was late, the middle of a wee morning following a gala event at the Saga Theatre. The Troubador, that had been the restaurant, with appetizers more costly than the finest meal she'd ever eaten before in her life. She'd been new to the world of fashion modeling, her eyes revealed it as much as her face sought to remain stern and composed: she was veritably shaking with excitement. I'd seen her huge yearning and knew immediately that I wanted her more than all the others who'd come before.

The first step had been the easiest, as it always was. She'd known me, and fawned over me, as everyone knows and fawns over me, and had left the theatre on my arm. Small talk during a twenty minute limousine drive to the estate. *The castle,* as she called it, and the way she'd said it with her eyes all lit up when she took it in – the virgin ivory portico with its august colonnade; its high walls and long winding cobblestone drive; its thousand windows lit up like eyes and beckoning us into the opulence between those walls – it made me adore her for her unabashed innocence. She'd been drunk, I'd made sure of that, and so at first it seemed to her only a small kink in a fantastic game the two of us were playing. The dog on the bed with us, lapping the wine from between her breasts where I dribbled it, it made us laugh. She giggled gleefully, as if it was the funniest moment she'd ever lived. She quivered a little when I slipped my fingers into her that first time, and then smiled and breathed the words: *Get the dog out of here.* With a mischievous twinkle of promise in her dreamy eyes. Her stare becoming bigger and a little frightened through the veil of drunkenness as I parted her thighs to let the dog smell her.

In the end, it had been easy: drunk, bewildered, sleepy, overwhelmed in my presence in my castle. It was the first night I truly realized that I was a king of something. I ruled her that night, with my dogs. My new queen and our dogs of delight.

I explained it to her the following evening, as gently as I was able: *I'll give you everything you've ever wanted. You see that I can,* and I gestured around the enormous room, with its vaulted ceiling towering into the distance overhead, where stars frosted like winter places through the skylight. The fireplace crackled warmly near us where we sat huddled on the sofa like a scene from one of my gentler films. From an alcove set into the wall near at hand, an ivory angel watched over us impassively. I offered her everything. I told her: *This life as a queen, for your service in the secret part of my life.*

My secret nights with the animals.

She agreed after considering it a few minutes. There were new diamonds in her ears and the glittering rock was a small asteroid on her finger. She smiled and said that everyone has their kinks. I nodded, smiling, and liked her a great deal in that moment. We chatted about other things, the kind of life she could expect, the trips across the world at the drop of a hat, the people and places she would soon know, the things she could now buy for herself and her family. We talked about kings and queens past, and of our place in the scheme of humanity. Then she asked about the animals: *What kinds of animals, or is it only dogs?* I made my voice gentle and told her about the horses from the ranch I owned in Texas, and of the young gorillas I often had imported from Africa. I watched her eyes widen and assured her that she'd be fine, that she'd enjoy her life of royalty. She nodded and sipped from her wine glass and thought about what I'd told her with a distant gaze. I saw the decision become made in her eyes as they hardened into the look I've known them to hold since. Anything, they said: anything for you.

We're so lucky, I told her. *To have found each other. Partners in this big, strange world.* And she agreed with a small nod of her head and kissed my lips.

When I'd shown her the first dead animal, she ran away. Literally, she ran from the bedroom where I'd removed the silk sheet from the disembowelled carcass and had left the house altogether.

I found her an hour later, in the woods of the grounds, near the thick concrete wall which surrounds the property on all sides for five miles. I held her beneath the pergola, the moonlight calming her where it slanted down through the vine-festooned trelliswork and coloured her silver. I held her while she cried and listened patiently while she begged me to not make her do the new things. I was firm with her, and maintained that this was the place my cravings had taken me, and that she should remember our bargain, and the things it afforded both of us.

She relented, although it was a few days before I forced her to engage in this new fun with me. Even then, I'd had to hold her hands down with all my strength, and smear her fingers in the animal's wet wound, deep in the place I'd plunged the knife and twisted it and jerked it around while the muzzled Doberman pinscher squealed and whined and flailed and finally crumpled onto the floor.

I'd left her on the carpet with red hands and bloody lips, a glistening belt of intestines coiled about her hips and a new string of pearls circling her lean long neck. Rescued from Pacific depths by professional divers on my payroll, the small beads glowed magically. I saw her reach for them, her eyes closed, a half-smile on her lips, but she stopped herself: her fingers were dirty – she didn't want to mar my newest gift to her.

It was becoming increasingly difficult. I tried to make her understand. I tried my hardest to make her recall our vows to one another.

I make you a queen in every way, and you make me a king by playing my secret games. The world is ours.

This evening it all came to its ugly head: I lost her, because she lost her magical connection with me.

It had been routine, nothing out of the ordinary. Mid-afternoon, hours before the premiere in the city's downtown core with its media and flashbulbs like ecstatic lightning all over the maze of sidewalks and red velvet carpets. Mid-afternoon and Barbara was preparing herself, putting powder to her cheeks and blue shadows to her eyelids in front of the immense bedroom mirror. And I brought them in, two large German shepherds, each already eager with a large pink erection dangling conspicuously between their hind legs.

Maybe it was my poor timing intruding on her daytime peace, maybe she'd simply been in no mood to entertain me. I'd had to fight her, several minutes of dragging her to and fro across the carpet while the animals growled and mewled and pawed the carpet. Finally, I had to hit her. I cuffed her hard across her mouth and she sank to the carpet and stayed there, sobbing. I gave her to the dogs then, and watched while they smelled her and clambered over her body.

When they were finished, and when I had finished touching myself and then her, too, where she lay on the carpet motionless, I gave her the box. I placed it beside her head, and stroked her smooth sweaty face and whispered to her, like a line from a film: *Rubies. Two of them. One for each of the most exquisite ears I have ever seen, and nibbled with my lips.*

Her glazed eyes watched me and I jerked at her words: *Never again. You sick animal.*

And she turned her face from the box beside her cheek

and closed her eyes, and there was nothing I could do. There was nothing else to be done: I'd lost my queen.

Summer was frying the air outdoors when I showed her into the bottom-most of my three levels of basement sanctuary. Her shirt was already open and her nipples hard and erect where my hands rubbed them from behind. She felt me hard as I pressed up behind her, urging her into the room.

I guided her to the couch resting upon the dais, felt her tense underneath my touch when she discerned movement beneath the silk shroud. *From India,* I told her, meaning the silk, and the intricately-embroidered hangings all across the walls, and the divans and bronze tiger statues standing guard in every corner. Her eyes remained fixed on the couch and the form twitching there beneath the silk.

You're my queen, I whispered into her ear, and pushed her forward with my hand in the small of her bare back. *You're the queen of all this land.* There had been a premiere earlier in the evening, followed by an art show opening reception downtown, and during the after-party following I'd promised her that from this night onwards everyone would see her with me all of the time. *Explosions of flashbulbs every night, framing your face for newspapers and magazine covers. Stars on the carpet, fallen right out of the sky – You and I.*

She nodded. Her eyes were hard and ready. I lifted the silk shroud with some theatricality. It was a whisper in the basement as it flitted through the cool air-conditioned air. The tiger sentinels watched mutely and shone golden in the lamplight.

The wound in Barbara's stomach was ripe, purple around the edges where the serrated edge of the knife had sawed and caught the flesh in its butcher's teeth. My stitches were an amateur's sewing job, taut in places and hanging loose in others, their thin white fabric stained red. The gag stifling her sobs was of the finest silk, imported from Calcutta for more money than most regular people earned in a month.

I whispered it in her ear: *Jennifer, you're a queen now.* And I waited, making sure she was listening, and then I whispered: *Jennifer, you're* my *queen now.* And I gripped her bare shoulders tightly and pushed her forward towards the couch.

I watched her stand before the couch, looking down at Barbara before her, bound and gagged with beautiful bonds, red hole gaping in her middle. I watched her lean forward and wince and crease her brows in something like fear or worry or revulsion. I saw her turn to me and then again to the woman before her, once, twice, three times in her indecision and frailty. And I watched the stern look come over her face as she swallowed down her reservations. I watched and saw the hardness in her eyes as the cold gleam of pearls stared up at her from the quivering neck of the dying woman before her like magic pieces strung together for the taking.

And I watched her lean forward and place her mouth to the blood of a fallen queen, and seize her crown. I smiled, and touched myself the whole while as the sucking and licking and sobbing sounds filled the miles-deep room. I smiled and nearly laughed out loud, because that was how invincible I felt just then. My reign would never end – there were followers to be found everywhere. I looked on into tomorrow, where a sea of diamonds glittered onward into infinity, like a promise of contentment.

The Grey Tammy and the Living

The living Tammy appeared on weekends. Friday nights she came and Sunday nights she bedded herself like a hibernating animal until her rebirth a work week away. Saturday this incarnation of my best friend lived like she never seemed able on the remaining days of the week. Something in her nature slouched her during those middle days, like gravity pulling her down and down until she crawled like the dying towards the bright light she glimpsed ahead of her.

It was the Monday Tammy who clung to her chair across the kitchen table from me. Haggard and pale, she looked as though she hadn't seen sunlight for years. Her greasy blonde bangs hung low over her eyes. Her eyelids drooped and I couldn't make out the pretty eyes they hid. I almost didn't want to see them – their vivid blue would be like a pleasant day peeking through the cloud cover of the rest of her, and this idea repulsed me a little. The skin of her eyelids held the dim stains of eyeliner, looking gently bruised. A bandage was spread across her small angular chin, looking too-big and awkward. I remembered the look of the bruise from the night before, when it had been fresh. Nothing remotely stylish about it, like eyeliner looking cinematic. You could almost see the ghost of the man's knuckles where he'd caught her a hard one. I didn't remember why he'd done it; maybe he'd been drunk or bad-tripping or both, or neither. Sometimes men did this kind of a thing to her. It wasn't that she was blind; you couldn't say something sarcastic about her, something like *she knew how to pick 'em*: she didn't discriminate among the throngs of the interested very much at all. She let everyone choose her and have her, and of course who wouldn't pick her from a crowd with a body that nice to look at, and with eyes so hungry?

The newspaper sat on the table between us, untouched. I thought of her declaration a few weeks before, that the Monday edition carried only bad news so better to forget it. She poured herself a half-cup of coffee and I noticed her bandaged hand. I hadn't known about that injury. I wondered what he'd done, the man from the night before, or some other man she'd met while I'd been looking elsewhere after our latest gathering of friends and strangers at our small apartment hole had spilled over into the trash bar midway down the block. I wondered where he'd gone and hoped he'd stay there or further away than that, which he probably would like most of them did after doing what they had to with her.

A pool of sunlight slowly spread its way into the room, enveloping her in her chair. I waited for her to notice it touching her. She cringed a moment later. "Fuck off," she cursed the new day, making no move to vacate her place, only placing a hand across her eyes to shield them from the intrusive glare. Her grey face and bandages gave her a mummy-like appearance, and I wished for her the longest sleep to deflate the bags from under her eyes. A thousand-year slumber and then waking into a new world, maybe even as a new girl.

I finished my coffee and cereal and sat with her a while longer. I told her, making my voice soft for her Monday ears, "I gotta go. Or I'll be late. So." I slid from my chair and left her hating the sunlight and the things it lit up for her to see.

When I came in after 5:00 she was the first thing I saw, curled up like a sick child on the couch. I hung up my coat gingerly, trying to be quiet, but I woke her besides. "I skipped work," she murmured from the greylight of the curtained room.

"That's okay," I told her, worrying about rent in a week's time, deciding immediately afterwards that I needn't worry because she'd find a way, like she always did. Men seemed to like giving her money. Money wouldn't be a problem, not for her. "I'm hungry," I said. "I'm going to make spaghetti. You want?"

"Okay." Passing her on the way to the bathroom she caught my wrist in her hand. I looked and her eyes were grateful and remorseful. I smiled. We said nothing.

The following morning was a rainy Tuesday. I found her at the living room window, staring into the overcast sky. I felt a little happy for her, sun-hater that she was. I said, "The thunder woke me. How did you sleep?"

She was a few seconds in answering me. "I slept a little. I feel sick. Like I'm going to puke. My throat's scratchy. Talking hurts."

I came to her and rubbed her back. She smelled like cigarettes and sweat. She was ashen. Her bandage was gone and her chin looked like fruit gone bad, green and purple and swollen. The pouches beneath her eyes were dark. They were puffier than they'd been the day before. She reminded me of someone dressing like a football player with paint greasing the places under their eyes, but otherwise not resembling a football player in any way. I thought how it looked as though her eye-pouches, as bloated as they were, might hold the tears she'd cried lately, and how if she kept it up they might burst sometime soon.

We watched the brewing sky together. Wind and rain lashed at the window glass. It felt warm and safe there in the curtained room. I wished that I could stay there in the dark with her all morning, just listening to the storm. I felt her waiting for me to say something soothing. I said it softly. "Maybe do you want to forget work today? And I'll just see you later on?"

She nodded beside me. Her hand found mine and squeezed it in thanks.

"Do you want breakfast?" I asked her. "I'm going to grab some cereal."

But she only shook her head imperceptibly, and drifted from the window. I watched her cross the room like a ghost in her white pajamas. I heard her bare feet patter on the tiles in the hall. Her bedroom door whispered closed and then there was silence except for the rain on the glass. I hoped she'd feel better later on. I hoped that she'd wake into a day as comfortably dismal as the morning spitting and crackling outside.

    I came in from work that evening and she was straddling a stranger on the sofa. The silence of the scene, two naked, voiceless figures connected in the murky light, made it a haunted kind of a picture. Then her voice came at me like a knife in the dark. Simply, she yelled, "Privacy!"

    I gave it to them. I slipped past and into the bathroom at the far end of the hall. I ran the tub and undressed and climbed in and left the water running until it bobbed past my chin. I stayed there for I don't know how long, waiting for the haunting to finish in the living room. The water was hot, almost scalding, and in the risen mist I kept seeing swirling pale unclothed figures.

    When I came out with my head in a towel she was waiting in the hall. Her eyes were searching mine, and I wondered what they saw there. She said, "Don't look at me like that. Don't give me that look." Then she turned into her room and slammed the door. Her voice came muffled from the room: "The rent money's on the kitchen fucking table."

    I knew she knew it, that I'd given her no kind of a wrongful look. She condemned herself when no one else dared, and when too few people cared enough to do so.

    I arrived home later than usual, bitching about staff meetings that didn't require menial me being there, running late and stranding me in the cold and wet with the next bus a half hours' wait away. But the smell of pasta filled the air, and Tammy's kind smile and the way she rubbed my arm made the day disappear. I felt even better once I'd changed into my around-home jogging pants and baggy t-shirt. It was nice coming home to dinner being readied, and

I told her so. "I never get tired of spaghetti. It's delicious. Thank you."

She smiled, hands on the air in a gesture showing me that it was no big deal. We ate in silence a while.

"I didn't go to work again today," she confessed to me. Then she cried. Without warning of any kind. Her eyes ran like faucets, and I went to her and tried to hold her and eventually she stopped batting away my hands. I held her, and I told her that I'd hold her good until she felt better. "Until you feel better, okay?"

"Okay," she sniffled, laughing at her nasally voice, and the pathetic look of her fallen apart again.

A moment passed and I went back to my chair. I thought that she'd had her cry and that she'd be good for the remainder of the night. "It's almost like I'm not even me, you know?" she thought aloud. Sometimes she surprised me in this way, the way she started digging into heavy subject matter so unexpectedly. She startled me like this from time to time, even though nobody knew her as well as I. She sputtered on. "Until Friday, when I can be…When there's time to be free and…"

"I know." My voice was consoling. It just came out that way, even if she might not have wanted to be consoled. I couldn't help that with her.

She went on earnestly, sounding as though she was trying very hard to convince me of something. "It's like I'm different, right? Like I'm different then than on days like today."

I nodded, smiling kindly. I drank my coffee like everything was okay. Coffee with pasta I found disgusting but I needed the caffeine boost after my long day. I needed to stay alert for her when she was in a coming-apart mood.

"It's like I'm two totally different people, even. That's what I feel like."

Her voice was pleading. Her eyes were relentless scouring mine for something.

"I know, Tammy."

She looked haunted sitting across from me in the flickering kitchen light. The single candle had been her idea. She liked the pretend-romance of things like this. She admitted that she was a girly-girl, who liked things like scented candles and colourful knee socks. Something about the admission always made me sad each time I heard her say it. The candle smelled like strawberries. Its red wax had pooled like lava in the ceramic dish it sat in. I looked through the murky air at her. Her shoulders were slumped and her voice tired. Her features were gaunt and her skin sickly. A pimple bloomed red and prominent along her upper lip. Her eyes were black and her smile nowhere to be found. I said, "Two more days. Only two more days."

There was silence for a moment. The noise of traffic shooting past on the rain-drenched street outside sounded louder then. Sleek and slippery, it reminded me of snakes hissing through tall grass. I didn't say a word. Tammy spoke then, and it sounded perfect in the candle-lit kitchen, her voice and her words.

"As long as you still love me."

I told her that I did. "I do." Her eyes were in her plate before her, as if she was frightened to look at me. I knew she heard the smile in my voice, and I knew too that she could tell it was a sad smile. But it was truthful, the way I was with her then, like I always was. I finished my coffee and lingered a while. We sat without talking in the strawberry air. I left her sitting in the candlelight a while after, heading for bed and without feeling any guilt. I felt her eyes watching me go, but she said nothing, and there were two days until Friday when she could live again.

Thursday she slept.

I left her curled on the couch in the morning. In the evening I had to search for her and finally found her sleeping like a little girl – huddled inside of an old brown sleeping bag, on the floor inside of her walk-in closet, its door half-closed. Once again, I tried to be stealthy but either I was clumsy or else she had keen ears.

"Hi," she murmured sleepily from the closet.

I leaned over her. The smell of shoe leather was on the air. It was a comforting atmosphere. I understood why she'd want to make her hideout there, in the close musty space.

"You look like a big potato," I told her, making my voice sound amused despite the tugging feeling in me when I saw her like that. So small, vulnerable. So beautiful and pure-looking.

It earned me a small chuckle from the shadows. I ventured, "I'm hungry for hamburgers. You hungry?"

Her voice carried no strength. "I'm going to sleep a while longer."

"Okay. Have nice dreams." I left her. I ate alone. I washed my dishes and then watched some bad T.V. The air grew cold and I got blankets from the basket of blankets and pillows we kept beside the couch for just such emergencies as this. I watched the news but she was right: it was all bad, or at least the parts I caught. I thought of her, huddled like a potato in the room beside me. I went to bed soon after. I hadn't seen her at all since finding her hours before. I fell asleep feeling lonely and when I woke up I hoped I'd find her at the kitchen table, looking better or still sad but at least there waiting for me. It was Friday morning, after all, a good time for waking into. But the table was empty and I left without eating breakfast, wondering who I'd find at home at the end of my day.

She looked every bit a classic witch drifting past in the hallway; jet wig catching the pale overhead light, black and blue striped stockings, mascara caked on and making her eyelashes into tarantula legs. I called after her, "You look like a witch."

She didn't answer, but the sounds of her preening herself came from the bathroom. Water ran, the bathroom mirror squeaked as she opened it on its rusty hinges. The clattering noise of her hands rummaging in the shelves behind the mirror. A protracted silence followed as she coloured her eyelids or reddened her lips or tried to fathom the young woman watching her in the mirror glass.

Party nights seemed endless. The hours leading up to them were delicious, too, when potential seemed to hang in the air. Anything might happen tonight – we used to say this to each other in years past, meaning who knew which boys we might meet and kiss, or how much beer we'd drink and how much laughter we'd let out. Anything might happen. The night might never come to an end. Our mantra, hopeful and filled with promise, and maybe a little bit pathetic now that years had passed and we'd seen the trend of those nights, too-brief and nearly always disappointing. Sad, that still we returned to those old ways, as if we were still the youthful girls of the past. As if time hadn't marched on and added lines to our faces and worry needling us whenever we thought about tomorrow, no matter how earnestly we played the part of being oblivious of its looming presence.

  Her singing voice drifted to me, and I admired her hopefulness. She was romancing the moment the way we used to, like I'd never be able to again. The song I didn't recognize but her husky voice carried the melody nicely. An upbeat song but a little mournful in her deep timbre, but it might just have been that I knew her well and sometimes the sound of her so misled really brought me down.

  Her voice came from the bathroom. "Am I the good one or am I wicked?"

  Thinking of her kind eyes and her wicked smile, I told her truthfully. "Probably a bit of both."

  She said nothing to this, but she picked up the lost thread of her song a moment afterwards. Her husky voice carried the melody sweetly, deep and light, somehow making me think of all the black candy in the world.

  It was a good party with a healthy turnout. Everybody was saying so. Arrivals began as early as 8:00 with the main body of the crowd filling our congested place by midnight and spilling into the hall a while after. This was okay. Weekend loudness and debauchery was allowed in shit-holes like ours located undeniably on the ghetto side of the city with fellow tenants welcome to pop in as they liked. Another communal gathering of friends and acquaintances and shady strangers drifted in like flotsam from the street. All were welcome on those nights of freedom. Great party, ladies. A get-together to remember.

Like always, she treated it as a masquerade, owning the spotlight in her dark get-up and weekend manners. Cozy with her man on the threadbare couch, unabashed in the way she fiddled with parts of him, clothes, hands, hair. Vivacious – she was that, and more, too, of course, although I think maybe only I saw the rest. Maybe only I saw the transformation of her, so shocking from the yesterday-her to the tonight-her. Alcohol helped the change, and the occasional acid hits, but I hoped she wouldn't inhale any more powder lines like she had on a few past nightmare gatherings.

Her cackle filled the room suddenly, another bout of unchecked flirtatious laughter. She was good at it. She reeled everyone in. She was a fisherman in this way, who could catch anyone. Or maybe she was just the bait, and she wasn't really in charge of casting the line at all. This made sense to me. She made a few heads turn with her brazen ways, and a few pairs of eyes exchange a certain kind of knowing look. Judgement on a party night, and I hoped she hadn't noticed any of it like she sometimes did. If these clowns are judging me bad, she'd once lamented on a hung-over morning, then how bad must I be? But then I watched her a while with her new man, her fingers clinging in his long hair. He was pretty with his long locks and bright eyes. Her voice came clear through the music. "I come from a long line. Of witches and other bad people." And I knew she was feeling good. I knew she was free. I thought of women riding broomsticks against lunar backdrops. I considered how good she'd look against that pale circle hanging in the night. I watched her smiling eyes and thought that the moon would bow to her beauty. The moon might even fall from its orbit to honour the passage of such a creature through the unworthy night.

She laughed again and her man laughed loudly, too. His eyes were narrow because he knew his great luck with the girl draped over him like a wet article of clothing. I left them in the middle of their prelude to other things. I went in search of another drink. Or possibly I went in search of someone to talk with, someone like me, someone that I might really luck out with and who might truly like me back when I liked them, too. Someone like her, but possibly a man to woo me like I'd once hoped to be wooed. A stranger blown in from the street outside. A knight exiting the night outdoors to rescue me, like a hopeful, naive dream from my youth.

Another Sunday night was upon us, another final escape before the world encroached as it had to. Saturday was a wreck behind us, dim and hazy through the usual party-fog. Friday was an even murkier thought, a misty notion that might have happened but then again perhaps not the way the disjointed pieces seemed to tell that night's story.

Silence and unspoken expectation hung over our greasy dinner of leftover pizza. I felt her excitement and deeper fear. She was ready to dive into the night like she'd dove into the previous evening and the one before that. She'd give it everything she had. This is how she treated her escapes. Violently, almost, as if each of these were her final night to taste beer and cigarettes and the tongue's of strangers and freedom.

We ate in this loaded silence. The pizza was good, maybe made better by the expectant atmosphere. Into it, she spoke. "I promise to find something new soon." She'd made her voice bold and brave for me. It was her way of tempering her confession, giving me vows of bettering herself like she swore to do from time to time. Starting anew, a clean slate, a remade her that we both knew could never exist. She lost jobs like friendships – her mother had said that to her once, years ago in the days when they still spoke infrequently. The words made a lasting impression on her – she still quoted her mother from time to time, when she was feeling especially self-loathing. I'd been watching the sky through the kitchen window when she said it. The rectangle I was focused on was a deep purple, rich with early evening stars. It was a perfect Sunday night sky. I said nothing.

"I *promise*, Sarah." Her voice was tinged with worry, and something deeper that we both knew was her shame. A wad of elastic-bound dollar bills sat beside her plate. It looked dirty so close to her food, but it was also a relief to exist there at all with the phone bill due the Friday before and the phone company sure to hound us throughout the forthcoming day. I didn't draw our attention to it. I made like I hadn't spotted it there at all. I didn't ask when she'd found out about her last job gone to hell like the others.

I nodded and finished my pizza slice. We sat a while without any words. I became grateful the more I thought about it, that she'd given me the confession on that night. On another of *her* nights, another weekend night like a final stand or something just as pivotal and all-important, instead of waiting for Monday morning when grave news seemed appropriate, or expected. I said into the dead air, "Are you gonna fuck him tonight? Ronnie, right? Was that his name? Is he coming tonight? He's pretty. He seems nice." I stirred my coffee listlessly with my spoon. I made my voice casual, like I was asking only another everyday thing of her, which I really was.

I eyed her where she'd been drooped like a rag in her disheveled bedclothes and tangled hair only the moment before. Her posture now was straighter. She looked healthy. *Stronger* might have been the word for the look of her then. Pale as was her natural complexion but with apples coming into season in her cheeks. Not fully bloomed but an undeniable rosy ghost. Through her bangs, I saw her eyes. The clouds had lifted from them, like gauze falling from a pair of jewels. They shone, like sunshine but murkier, darker somehow, a night time energy watching me evenly. She didn't flinch anymore. She was smiling. She said nothing. I didn't mention the nice man I'd met the night before while she'd taken her own partner into her bedroom, the man with gentle eyes and nervous way towards me that I liked so much. I didn't want her to feel resentful or threatened, and so I didn't tell her about the way he'd made me feel unexpectedly good, and comfortable, safe almost, like I hadn't felt with somebody for a very long time. But I told her, "With eyes as blue as yours, you could get anyone."

She only kept smiling, without words, like a mystery never to be unravelled. Her posture stayed bold. The starlight burned on in her stare. I watched her. I couldn't look away. She looked younger, brighter. It was like looking at the dead returned to the world of the living, a miracle in the middle of another trackless stretch of same-old. I said nothing, only basked in the fleeting moment of her.

Christina the Bloomed

It's another of many clandestine afternoons that he's returned to the water fields since the day the sun misfired and burned his heart black, but still his steps come heavily.

The wooden boards herald his passage despite his expertly stealthy progress, creakingly, like the bones of the elderly men he sees when he visits the park's general store with his mother; the ragged old men like scarecrows always seated on the wooden veranda before the general store as if in guardianship of its goods, who seem to groan and shudder with their every minute movement. The nodding willows and rushes on either side give back an opposing state, though, making their gentle, papery whispers in the languid breeze where they caress each other in a million places. He stares off across their slowly undulating landscape, crackling and bleached the colour of wheat by the tenacious sun. A v of Fish Crows takes flight from the marsh and wheels against the cerulean sky. An invisible Cave Swallow offers its warbling song to the new day. In the embrace of these old sounds and scenes, the boy feels comfort settle into his skin, displacing the unease with which he'd set out on his routine but difficult exploration of the marsh.

He walks slowly, slowly, seeking to savour the cicadas' electric songs playing on every side, the bite of the sun into his bare skin. Her words come to him then, as they've been haunting his thoughts incessantly throughout the past several days: *The sun turns us into chocolate, darker and darker every day.*

He makes a gesture of salute, shielding his eyes from the sun. In the eastern distance, the observation tower rears from the marsh like a looming Wickerman, the crooked horizon of the deciduous tree-line beyond. Its wooden skeleton shimmers waveringly in the heat haze as if it, too, is stirring subtly in preparation of its imminent march across the swampy land. He spies the lone figure in its crow's nest summit, bent over the toothpick-sized telescope. He knows even at this great distance of tricky air that it is his mother's telescopic eye which pursues him in his A.M. explorations. He'd felt her with him the moment he'd entered the central maze of the boardwalk, like an intensification of the sun burning into his skin, a close cloying warmth tickling his moist spine beneath his cotton shirt.

He turns southwards. The open stretches of the fenland shimmer in the light. Beyond, the brilliant light-speckles of Lake Erie stir, and stir something inside of him.

A soft splashing rouses him. Turning about, he's in time to witness the gargantuan carp recede beneath the pond surface following its brief emergence into the bright morning. He follows its progress as it submerges deeper and deeper beneath the murky water in an effect as of de-materializing. When it's gone and only bubbles and a widening arc of ripples remain in its wake, a pang touches him, and he wishes earnestly for the swimmer to return so that he can admire its silvery scales. But nothing disturbs the water now, and he only continues on his way, forlorn and discomfited beneath his mother's far-seeing eye. He tries to push thoughts of confronting her upon returning home from his mind and succeeds only when, a minute later, he stops to observe a pair of Tufted Ducks bobbing in the water. They drift but seemingly at the water's behest, languidly, as if he were in fact not watching birds with ornate, iridescent plumage at all, but striking models of Viking galleys with the sculpted likenesses of some obscure avian deity marking the vanguard of the warships.

In a desperate and paltry gesture to assuage his mother's certain displeasure with him, he reaches into one of the many capacious side pockets of his shorts and retrieves the persimmon that's been bulging the material all morning (as well as given him the pleasure of pretending that he, as a result of his courageous explorations into swamp country, has been stricken with the deadliest of illnesses, the first manifestation of which is the gross, elephantiasis-like swelling of one's body in various parts). Turning about so that he's facing the distant tower directly, he raises the fruit with deliberate slowness and great theatricality to his mouth, bares his teeth, and bites in. He stands poised with his teeth piercing the fruit's hide, relishing the cool juices jetting into his mouth in combat against the feral sun seeking to cook his skin darker while bleaching him of his energy.

He lingers in place a moment, eating with evident relish, and then continues onwards once more. He passes a couple seated on one of the intermittent benches which dot the boardwalk – a pretty girl with red hair and red corduroys and a thin, bespectacled young man sporting a beard and wearing a beret – speaking in low voices. He drifts past them unnoticed while they whisper to one another, a spectre stirring the cattails in his wake. Raising a hand to shield his eyes from the glare of the day he follows the winding path of the boardwalk, which has always reminded him of an immense serpent floating through the marshes. The path is empty everywhere he looks, but for drifting dragonflies catching the light in small brief bursts of silver and green like some Morse code of the natural world.

He arrives at the familiar juncture with a queer sinking sensation in his belly, the western path of which leads to the observation porch overlooking the great expanse of the marshland stretching out towards Lake Erie like some dark and ominous suggestion brewing in the horizon. He pauses, dusting the planks with the scuffed toes of his runners. A vivid blur flits past his nose: he turns to follow the shuddering flight of the large Monarch butterfly, an early arrival to the park and harbinger of the great orange hordes scheduled to arrive at summer's end. He watches the bright insect recede over the reeds like a fading ember. He deliberates on what feels to be a thousand pieces of information all congealed into a chaotic stew in his brain. Finally, he simply turns and scampers back the way he'd come. He feels mouse-like and cowardly as he goes, and when he passes the bench couple once more he makes certain to watch the boards racing past beneath his feet because the look of them – like a single organism entwined in rapturous observation of the spectacle of the awakening morning marsh – makes him somehow sad.

* * *

The wisteria blanching outside the kitchen window; the bouquet of delphiniums brightening the interior sill but just barely; the hanging fern like a head of dreadlocked hair spilling from the plain copper planter in the adjacent living room; all of this flora whisper to him, beckoning him to return into the world outside the walls of the house in escape of his mother's likewise worried and livid eyes.

"Where have you been?" She's speaking in her new-voice, lifeless but for the wrath imbuing it with the rancor that causes him to wince and cringe into himself. It parts the lush wall of his thoughts with its violent tinge, conjuring thoughts of her hacking away the encroaching tall-grass bordering their property with the rusty hatchet she keeps hanging in the shed for this purpose. He looks to her but only briefly, yet can't help but witness the pitiable if frightening sight of her; haggard and unkempt, her grey-black hair let down the way she never used to wear it, looking for all the world like a clump of iron wool; the pouches bulging from under her eyes like bloated tea bags; the deep lines like parentheses around her mouth and eyes, much more pronounced than he remembered them being only months before. Her shirt is the same she'd worn the day before, and he thinks the day before this as well. He grimaces at the stains down its front, the faded bloody residue of pasta sauce from last night's dinner, as if even the act of eating is one she's ceased attempts at being tidy with. Her work lies scattered across the kitchen table, lap-top open and humming laboriously, sheaves of papers covered in her hieroglyphic cursive, and the usual clutter of pens and hi-liters and opaque purple ashtray overflowing with the evidence of her sleeplessness the evening prior.

He turns his attention to the wisteria crawling along the outside window ledge, wishing in that moment he was an insect nestled within its verdant reaches, an ant or fly fortunate enough to be free of fear and condemnation and an atmosphere of decay. Then he considers the lifeless look of the flora, bled dry by the sun, and feels unease claim him again. He shivers, despite the humidity that's beaten the feeble efforts of the overtaxed air conditioner and invaded the cottage.

Her voice hardens, though her features when he turns to look at her remain drawn, bloodless. "I asked you a question: where have you been today? You've been gone all morning and nearly the entire afternoon. I don't like you keeping secrets from me. You know this."

She'd been a different creature in the before-days, one of myth, it now seemed to him. Her voice is rarely as soft as it once was. Her old tenderness towards him is a solace he yearns for constantly, but may be a fiction he's invented to comfort himself when her distant eyes and far-removed demeanour grow too difficult to suffer. He hears the accusation in the words she's given him. She's condemning him already so he sees no reason to evade her unspoken and true question like a weight between them.

"I was on the boardwalk, mama, but only a little ways in," he says pleadingly. He makes certain to widen his eyes in the rewarding way he'd mastered long before, although it wins him nothing from the face of gravity scrutinizing him.

"I told you," her voice is flat and hard, as if she's uttering curse words. "I told you so many times – *Never*. Never ever again. Do you hear me? Did you not hear me before? Just because spring's back and the people all go down there, it doesn't mean that you have to, too. It's dangerous there, like you well know. There are plenty of other interesting – and safer – places to visit around here. The forest, the trails. We have our own beach in the backyard, for Christ's sakes, where I can see you anytime from the window. Are you hearing this?"

He nods requisitely, mechanically, a survival gesture to earn him escape from this fearsome encounter. He waits tensely beneath his mother's baleful gaze, and only dares to patter off in his bare feet when the squealing of hinges intrudes into the silent kitchen what feels like hours later, signaling that she's turned her attention to the cupboards and the fixing of their dinner.

Rejoining the outdoors, he creeps to the wisteria gathered about the windows, making certain to remain hunched low to the ground so as to remain unobserved by his mother within. He searches for some sign of life among them but finds none in the bleached, crackling foliage. Disheartened, he drifts onto the abutting beach to kick at the sand in search of crabs or shells, and to scan the horizon for pirate galleys and other things that he won't find.

    He returns in time for spring rolls and salad and a cherry cheese cake dessert. They eat in silence, punctuated only by the whirring of the ceiling fan over the table, and the droning of the lone fly drifting languorously throughout the room in futile search for the outdoors. The boy watches the insect's wavering flight surreptitiously, but she sees his interest.

    "I'll open the screen door in a moment. It'll find its way out."

    He feels unworthy of her efforts to assuage his concern. He feels nauseous, as if he's eaten too much too quickly, though he's been known to help himself to double servings of cheesecake when she's been so generous. He nods wordlessly, pushes his plate away a moment later and shuffles from the room. It's only when he's on the threshold of his bedroom on the second floor of the house that he remembers his lack of manners – Spinning on his heel he patters downstairs so that he might thank his mother for the dinner she'd allowed him despite her anger at his disobedience and trespass into forbidden and dangerous places.

    He stops short in the kitchen doorway when he sees her broken posture. She hasn't yet vacated her seat, despite their dirty dishes and her perennial compulsion to wash their plates immediately upon finishing dinner. He examines her profile, sees the cigarette trembling between her thin lips as she weeps silently to herself. Smoke from the burning tip curls into the air and is swept away violently by the rotating fan blades. His hands fidget at his side. He always does this when overly pensive or anxious, this playing with his hands when words aren't allowed or are altogether too difficult to put into the world. He mulls on his mother's tears, as he always considers the things she does and says very closely. The daylight, he notices, has crept stealthily from the room during the brief interval of his exit from and return to the kitchen, colouring the walls in a wan sodium glow that, even as he watches, abandons the room, too.

He remains a moment longer in his secret vigil, trembling and wishing he knew what should be done to cure his mother. He gives up eventually and slinks back the way he came. His way is illuminated by frosty starlight spilling in from the hall windows and guiding his steps on the parquet floor. He whispers upstairs once more, leaving his grieving mother in the night-coloured room.

Of course he bends to the compelling voice of the marsh and – the following morning, no less – finds himself following the circuitous wooden paths of the boardwalk not long after being coaxed from his bed by the delicious drone of insect life outside his wee A.M. window. It is a voice he's followed from the beginning when it had first spoken to him – He recalls with a twinge of nostalgia the young days of wandering here, nestled between his mother and sister not long after they'd settled in their new home, their hands enveloping his as they explored the green places together in the early-June sunlight; mother teaching them the whole while in her wise scholarly voice, stopping to point out rare birds hopping gingerly along the brambles, to show them corresponding illustrations or photographs of turtles or wasps from her field books, or to name flower colonies blazing in the brilliant daylight.

In accordance with the passage of the days into weeks and as the months grew more humid, the marsh country and its incalculable denizens grew, as well, from the boy's hobbyhorse to his near obsession. Mother had even allowed the two of them to camp on the beach abutting their home on several occasions, in this way nurturing her children's connection to and love of the landscape around them. Pitching the bright orange canvas tent early in the day became common, a gleeful preparation for the forthcoming nighttime merriment – furnishing the interior with his transistor radio for late hour listening, as well as the usual assortment of books and nature magazines and the pair of flashlights by which to read them; a plastic treat bag rustling with chocolate bars and chip bags and other assorted sugary and salty junk; and magnifying glasses with which to examine any beach denizens who might chance to infiltrate their tent and become unwitting contributors to their mutual scientific scrutiny.

He stops intermittently as he walks to search the Wickerman's skeleton in the north, and to look overtop the crooked landscape of rushes and cattails to the boardwalk paths meandering away maze-like all around. It's a lonely day, with only a limping elderly couple creeping along the boards far behind him, and a man and his dog striding along the distant beach shore. The animal's barking reaches him after a moment's delay of distance, once it's already chased down the Frisbee its owner has sailed through the air and clenched it in its jaws. A muted sound of pipes drifts to his ears: following its song he scans the beach and, much further south along the shoreline, spies a queer, hunched figure loping against the tree-line, satyr-like and ungainly, but then he blinks and the vision has merged with the deep emerald thicket.

He walks and walks, and the boardwalk bobs buoyantly in the wake of his steps. The sloshing of water follows him, calming his nerves even when he's reached the familiar intersection. He dares this morning to hold vigil at the deadly place. It's the marsh-voice, difficult to define but always present, that draws him there, to the site itself. It's entered his dreams of late, as it had haunted them all of the previous Fall and early portion of the succeeding Winter, too, in the months following the tragedy. Always the dream is the same, the simple scene of witnessing himself, out of body and from a bird's eye perspective, padding along the cracked boards, lowering himself onto his haunches, and watching the still green water before him. Then a wind, insistent and frightening in the tenacious way with which it sweeps the landscape of surrounding reeds downwards into a cowed, submissive bending; his dream-eyes desperately scanning the blank face of the water but finding nothing except a patchwork landscape of lily pads and occasional water striders like precarious dancers daring to cheat science as they drift fleetly across the placid surface. Then he's awake and the dream is through with him, its final forlorn image indelibly imprinted across his eyes until the following night's fitful slumber when he would ghost the dream-boardwalks helplessly again.

He walks lightly but with a sprightly step along the

bobbing forbidden corridor. He comes into the observation deck with the familiar sinking feeling making a shambles of his stomach. He's alone. The willows' language of whispers strikes him as more eerie than soothing then. But still he edges forward to the narrow place among the surrounding railing where there is just enough room for a person to sidle onto the interconnecting plank-way and un-tether their rental canoe from the stout wooden post spiking from the green water like the bare mast of a sunken ship. Here he places his running shoe tips, just past the wooden safety of the boardwalk. Beyond its rim he stares into the deep green, swaying in the unmoving air like an acrobat mid-trick, on the cusp of his spectacle or calamity.

Suddenly, her voice is with him, on the baking air. He doesn't understand quite what she says, but certainly deciphers the familiar song of her from the gentle sloshing of spume against wooden timbers, the distant cry of water fowl taking to the sky. He searches near to him, among the rushes and willow branches swaying in the air, and then in the distance where haze makes the beach people uncertain as they go about their beach activities of wading into the surf or lounging on blankets with paperbacks across their laps.

After a time, he finds her in the unexpected middle distance, a tiny but beckoningly iridescent flash. He leans forward as far as he dares, and when he still can't reach her finds that he has more courage in him still, and on his very tip-toes leans forward; and stretching his arm outward, plucks her from the lone rogue milkweed stalk which he notices leans towards him as if in supplication. He comes away with her in his gentle grasp, his breath hissing through his teeth. He leaves the precarious planking and places his feet onto the considerably more firm boards of the observation deck. Gently, with nimble fingers, holding her like a precious jewel from which the sun reflects and abets his close scrutiny, he greets her, breathless:

"You came back," he says, making his voice a whisper, sensing the startling and clandestine nature of their reunion.

A moment after, wonder filling up his voice, he adds, "You're tricky – I almost didn't see you there." He examines her carapace in the thin light. A vibrant, seemingly palpable sheen radiates from its sleek emerald curvature, reminding him of pictures he's seen in books of the sun peering out from behind the inky shadow of an eclipse. He admires her prehensile digits gingerly investigating the clammy warmth of his palm, the antennae stirring in the humid breeze as if seeking to orient herself or map out the marshy terrain via some unfathomable intrinsic system of radar. Her new body mesmerizes him. She'd been beautiful before but now the whole world surely bowed before her splendour. He's never found a specimen such as this, he realizes breathlessly, and he'd been a diligent outdoorsman since he and mother had arrived here in the awakening days of summer over one year ago. It is his sister he holds in his palm, with her eyes like emeralds, once the envy of thieves and envious adults everywhere.

    He recalls his mother's words of long past, spoken on an afternoon of bountiful summer harvest, much like this day in temperature and A.M. light but less magical, of course. They'd been resting from an afternoon of bike-riding along the circuitous dirt paths of the Botham and Woodland Trails, leaning their bicycles against trees and swigging from their canteens. His sister had snuck off to relieve herself in the bushes and emerged from the thicket abutting the dirt trail several minutes later with a bouquet in each of her little fists; these she held out to the boy and mother respectively, the claret bushel for their mother (because her hair had once been red, the girl explained, and often overhead her speaking of her old colour longingly while combing through her graying roots before bed each night) and the green lot for her brother for the simple reason that this was his favourite colour.

    "I don't know their names," she'd confessed with a bashful expression. "But they're pretty, so..." She'd looked peaceful in the dappling sunlight filtering through the leafy roof over their heads, her round cheeks glowing from their afternoon activity, her long hair concealed beneath her bright yellow bicycle helmet. Taking the red bunch from her hand with a demure bow, their mother had said, "Why, thank you, my dearest. They're positively lovely and – although, as you well know – we should only *admire* and never *pick* the flowers here, still I'm very honoured. Thank you very much." And then, upon inhaling the fragrance from the vivid cluster, exclaimed, "Oh, my, you are the brightest specimen in bloom today – and I'm referring to you, my dear, not these pretty flowers. Let's head home, and I'll teach you both about these bouquets, after you've guessed their names on the ride home. We can look through my Pelee fields books after dinner, too, and pick out what we saw today."

The boy blinks. Salty beads mark paths down his cheeks. He examines his sister wondrously. His heart becomes filled with both the former and the new splendour of her. Tears fill his vision in profusion. He is, he understands suddenly, witnessing – *holding!* – the perfect pulsing heart of the summer unbound.

He smiles as an idea strikes him. Gingerly he places her to the left breast pocket of his shirt. A moment later she clings their easily, partly concealed within the aperture but with most of her legs and tiny swiveling head visible overtop the pocket. He wears her like a brooch or jewel the entire stifling afternoon.

The sun seems to flicker and through this subtle but incontrovertible sign he knows: she's discovered him in the forbidden place. He turns at the creaking of a footfall and she's there. She tells him with the storm of her eyes that he's trespassed too far on this occasion for clemency from her.

Her face holds unmitigated fury everywhere he looks – In the deep-set creases framing her mouth, the downwards sweep of her lips, the hardness of her gaze. She's brought along the dog, which whines anxiously at her feet, sensing the unrest in the air. He understands the immensity of her anger with him when she delivers the fidgeting animal a vicious kick to its ribs (she adores the animal as much or more than he does and never treats it like anything but royalty), eliciting a brief and pathetic yowl from its black-lipped mouth. The dog cowers at her feet like a reprimanded slave rooted to its place from terror, and watches her with servile eyes.

"You'd best be very careful in what you say right now," she spits at him. Sweeping the marsh with a violent motion of her hand, she proclaims, "This is wild country. That's the world out there. Look at it, damn it." Her eyes remain fixed on his and he knows he must obey. He looks. The water fields of rushes and willows, stirring subtly in the milky light, suddenly fill him with fear.

Narrating the landscape he surveys, her voice grown contemplative with distance, she murmurs, "This is wild, wild country. We have to watch our steps or be eaten up. You know this. If I didn't have my work, I'd leave here today. Don't you know this?"

He looks on until he feels enough time has passed that she'll allow his attention to waver. He looks to her, blinkingly. Still she's glaring down on him, her head and shoulders limned in the morose daylight.

She's unrelenting, and continues to demand the correct answer from him. "Do you understand? Tell me you do. Don't look at me all quiet. Speak. Tell me you understand this."

Yes, he nods. When this gesture proves insufficient and her deathly silence demands more from him, he murmurs, "Yes," willing the practiced statue-like rigidity into his face that might abet his lie when all he really sees at that moment is the ghost of his sister – his sister of old, before her rebirth – bobbing among the reeds like an immense dead fish, her long sodden hair like a tangle of golden seaweed partially shrouding her gentle face.

She watches him a moment longer. He shakes beneath her scrutiny, but he knows not exactly what her eyes tell, smeared out by the daylight as she is. A burning sensation stirs him from his fearful immobility. It throbs in his chest, and he realizes that it's emanating from his breast pocket. He feels the tiny touch of digits striving to clamber into the day. He places a hand to his chest, willing the movement to subside. When it doesn't, only grows more insistent, and then her golden voice rises from the pocket and to his ears imploring to be let loose into the day; and when he can bear no more his mother's stony observation of him cowering like an anxious rodent on the wooden floor at her feet, the words fall from him as if of their own volition.

"Chris is still here."

The boy's mother leans forward. He sees that her eyes have grown moon-sized and haunted in the wake of his confession. Fury seethes there. This same fury has made a gash of her mouth and seems to have paled her already waxen features considerably. The boy imagines an icy encroachment in her already grey hair, a creeping silvery glimmer to match that which blows from those eyes.

The gash parts and words fall from the crevice. "What did you say?"

He puts his eyes onto the slat-boards. He understands the fact of his wayward tongue if not the specific nature of its audacity. He's allowed to remain thus silent and cowed only a moment before fingers of iron dig into his bony shoulders. He rocks backwards and forwards in their slow but maniacal grip. Words fly about his thrashing head, and he picks up their thread and opens his mouth for his own words but none are able to come in the gale buffeting him.

"What. Did. You. Say. Tell. Me. What. Did. You. Say."

The mad turbulence abates and in the tense calm of its passage he trembles in his every part. He turns fearful eyes on his mother. She looms over him. Her fury with him seems to travel through every inch of her seething, twitching features like crimson thread through a loom.

"Tell me again. What were those words you said one moment ago," her glacial voice commands him. He recalls what she'd said concerning his vivid imaginings, and her belief that it was always wiser to know the difference between the real and the make-believe. He shudders, recalling the way he'd spent the previous day: how in the milky afternoon light, amid the rustle of insects in the reeds and the simmer of the sun baking the greenery and wood and water all around, he'd revealed his greatest fears and hopes in a way that he hadn't been able for over a year, what with his mother emerging from the past summer a new and distant person; in a hushed and comfortable manner, he'd whispered these secrets into his hand where he'd held her tenderly while the world ticked onwards indifferently as always.

He's much braver this morning for his recent experience, of course. He's been hardened by the tangible appearance of the impossible in the world. Maybe the firefly colonies he's watched burning in the forest while hunched inside of his bedroom window perch with the binoculars glued to his eyes are indeed the pixie tribes as he'd fabricated in his younger years after all. Perhaps pirate treasures long-ago buried do in fact lay interred beneath beach sands, while dragons glide from time to time through the marsh waters.

Thus bolstered by exhilarated romance and trusting in the truth as he knew it, he closes his eyes in anticipation of his dark fate at his mother's hands and says in his gentlest voice, "She's with me, mama. In my shirt pocket. I've got her here. She..."

But he trails off, his courage faltering at the sound of his words and the way he knows his mother might hear them.

The time springs to mind when he'd divulged a similar – if much less celebratory – fantastical encounter to her; in the younger portion of June only a few months prior, when he'd braved the observation tower's dizzying heights alone for the first time, manning briefly its telescopic gaze and through it witnessing a most peculiar vision occurring towards the eastern-most edge of the marshland serviced by the boardwalk: an immense disturbance of its water, long undulating waves the like of which only ever formed on the vastnesses of the lake, and foamed the surf along the beach-line running south. It had appeared as though a storm raged there, contained impossibly in this single, remote corner of the fenland. He'd left the battered telescope swinging in the wind and descended the precarious wooden staircases with fleet but ginger steps. Once his feet hit the dirt path at its base, life returned to animate his body and he flung himself courageously towards the mouth of the boardwalk beckoning him in the near distance. Several minutes later, his breath ragged and laboured, he'd arrived at the site of the disturbed marsh. Scanning the water earnestly, though, he found it only mildly agitated, as if whatever source of the happening had absconded the place. He'd been turning to leave himself, disheartened, peeling back the wrapper from the chocolate bar he'd snuck from the cupboard in the morning, when the boardwalk swayed beneath his feet. Jumping around he faced the fen and found it in unrest once more, though now its source lay revealed for him: he gaped at the gargantuan protuberance that had risen from the olive water, realizing belatedly and only after he witnessed the purposefulness in its movements, that it was the long neck of an immense marine creature rolling like a floundering galley beneath the water.

He'd pounded homewards, sending up flocks of Ivory Gulls in his wake like speckled confetti celebrating the miracle that had graced the marsh country and which he'd been fortunate enough to witness firsthand. Arriving out of breath and dashing past his mother's worried face and accusatory words – "What are you running so fast for? Is something wrong? You should slow down or you'll give yourself a heart attack in this temperature!" – he'd closed his bedroom door behind him and dove to a kneeling posture before the bookcase occupying the place adjacent to the window. He pulled forth one of his dinosaur books – the most colourfully illustrated volume he owned – and a moment later had the book cracked open on the carpet before him in rapt examination of the image there: *The Plesiosaur, he read, was a great swimmer, and one of the most fearsome hunters of the Oceans. It too died over 60,000,000 years ago.*

  Over dinner that evening he'd revealed the marsh's secret to her and suffered her indifference. Making him feel young and foolish, she'd muttered simply and with the new remoteness in her voice which she'd begun offering him more and more each passing day, "It's good to make-believe, but not too much. Not so much that we trick ourselves into believing the world has things in it that it doesn't. I'll read you my newest chapter when it's finished, all about the nesting birds of Point Pelee. That's just as interesting as your story, only this one's happening right now, all around us. Just this morning, I spent almost half an hour watching a pair of Bobolinks in the trees near Dune Beach. Amazing, just amazing. And when they flew off, and just when I thought my bird-watching was done for the day, I spotted a couple of Orchard Orioles right over my place – Like a pair of furry red tennis balls stuck up in the branches, just bobbing about and hopping around."

  "Show me," he hears from behind his clenched eyes, stifling his reverie. And when he makes no move to acquiesce, "I told you to show me. Show me what you've got in your pocket." He doesn't look to her, but knows that she too is seeing her in the moment: her daughter bobbing among a tangle of reeds, blue-faced and bloated, her once-lovely hair matted into a weed-like clump drifting indolently about her in the gentle but murderous current. The day when he'd led his mother to this very place, tears streaming from his eyes as he revealed his sister as he'd found her only minutes earlier; in that indelible moment when the fierce July sun had become obscured by cumulus as if of its own volition, as if in deference to the tragedy it too bore witness to.

"Show me," she says again.

Immediately upon the words being spoken, and at the precise moment he dares open his eyes, her hand arcs downwards from where she's been holding it trembling beside her ear. Her open palm strikes him across the mouth. He feels his teeth shake and his skeleton tremble and his heart shudder. A taste of iron spills into his mouth, exciting his tongue. He reels from the blow, taking a single heavy step backwards which results in an emphatic squealing of a loose plank in the boardwalk beneath his heel. Before he's able to regain his footing another falls across his cheek and sends him toppling to his knees. Somehow, through the salty smear of his peripheral vision he gleans the blurred motion of the runaway persimmon as it slips somehow from his shorts pocket and rolls erratically along the planking, bouncing up at intervals where the slats are uneven.

"Is. This. What. You. Want?"

His mother's shouted reprimands sound to his ears like the frenzied cacophony of hyenas, as he'd heard them on a nature documentary they'd watched together not long before. Maniacal and wild, less vicious than madly amused. Talons pull in his hair as she thrusts his whimpering face over the rim of the boardwalk. Water shocks him with its tepid contact, drenching his face and hair and staining the front of his shirt. He cries shrilly and scrambles in terror along the wooden planks. Slivers cut beneath his nails and his knees burn against the wood as he fights for purchase against the gale of his mother's madly swinging blows. She throws indecipherable words or curses into his ear and tears at his clothing and it's only when he's wrapped his arms fast around the stout anchoring pillar rising from the disturbed water adjacent to the boardwalk that she ceases her frenzied assault.

It's then, while standing over the boy, her fists brandished like hammers at her sides, that he sees a green glimmer rise from the wooden planks and lure her eye, too. Her hammerhands fall. She stoops in curious and fearful scrutiny. Her eyes widen and become wide moons. A cry tears loose from her mouth, inarticulate and primal. She recoils several steps, throwing a hand across her shuddering lips; she totters in her new place several feet from where the prostrate boy gathers himself onto the relative safety of the water-blackened boardwalk, takes one and then another tentative, trembling steps forward again. She peers closely at the green jewel pulsing from the boardwalk. It entrances her. She weeps. Words fall from her mouth, for the boy, for herself. "Oh. My. Sweet. God."

The boy sees this and begins to weep in joyful realization that his secret lives in the harsh and desolate world of adults, too.

She comes to her knees beside him and cries, her hands cupping her mouth and muting her crying while her mooneyes look on incredulously. Then she's standing on trembling legs, and a moment later careening a crooked path between the wooden guidelines of the boardwalk in the direction of home.

In the bottomless hours of morning the boy is shaken gently into wakefulness. Squinting through unseeing eyes and the lingering confusion of dreams, his mother's face materializes. For a moment, a very fleeting second or two, he mistakes the moonface features and immense eyes for another's. Her hair is a new season, golden and bright in the darkness, and wholly devoid of Winter. He says nothing, but responds to the smile she wears with a serene gaze. It has been long since he's seen her this way, and wonders if perhaps she's merely a sliver of dream that's followed him into the morning.

She pulls him tenderly from the bed. He sees that she's carried his shoes into the bedroom. Kneeling wordlessly before him with a soft popping sound inside her knees, she helps him slip his feet inside the runners, sock-less, the way she never allows him even on the hottest afternoons for fear of his dirtying his naked soles. She ties his fraying laces efficiently and, once finished, squeezes his toes firmly. Still her smile remains, bewildering him, lightening something inside of him, intriguing him like the best mysteries he's encountered. He feels a small stirring sensation in his pyjama shirt pocket. With it stirs a warmth in him, too.

She stands and drifts into the hallway. He follows her smile like a beacon in the dark. He follows it through the hall and adjacent kitchenette and onto the hushed backyard patio. From there they walk together, side-by-side, she taking his hand and leading them.

She guides them along the rustling beach and southwards to the mouth of the boardwalk. The marsh is drowsy. From the pond to their left, a group of turtles stretch their little beaked faces towards the moon. The pallid light strikes from their oily shells, making them look particularly rare and special. A tangled network of lily pads bob nearby and – thinking how perfect it would be if he were to find a frog reclining on one as he's always searched for them there before but to no avail – does, noticing nearly a dozen tiny obsidian heads dart towards him and then back again to their rapt worship of the moon, in which direction the tiny bullet-heads seem steadfastly pointed.

The boy gestures silently to their right, where a crew of almond butterflies have risen from the reeds like spirits and flutter across their path. Their unwavering bearing takes them over the still pond. She gestures wordlessly across the water on her side of the boardwalk, and he sees the Great Egret daintily wending its way among the reeds and driftwood on its long narrow legs like a graceful ballerina; discerning their passage it briefly turns its obsidian gaze upon them, observes them with one slender foot halted mid-air, then turns and continues on its way.

They walk on, too, the boardwalk bobbing in their wake, their steps soft but sending a gentle knocking rhythm outwards into the dark air, into the black water beneath them. He pictures fish stirring from their slumbers and wondering at their trespass, looking upwards with their glassy, inscrutable eyes and spotting their silhouettes moving against the moon-coloured sky.

They've rounded the first bend in the boardwalk. The immense darkness of the marshes surrounds them everywhere. A frog croaks nearby. Further off, a creature warbles a strange song and then returns to sleep. Daring the immense quiet of the morning marsh, the small warmth inside his pyjama pocket tickling his chest, the boy tugs on her hand and whispers, a little fearfully, "Mama. She wants to leave. She told me last night. She says so now, too. She wants to leave and go…"

He looks into the night fields of lilies and willows and still water like glass reflecting the sleeping sky. Like a mist hanging in the air he sees her image coalesce in the air. He admires her as he always has. Her jeweled eyes. Her moonface. Her golden hair like their mother's. Her mouth, pale and wondrous with the sweet and wise things it always told him. Turning to his mother, he sees that she's followed his gaze, too. She's nodding without words, and tear-trails shine silver on her cheeks in the lunar light as she, too, finally sees.

He takes the living jewel from his pyjama shirt pocket. It stirs between his limp fingers, many minute and tender caresses from her many digits. In the starlight, her shell shines brilliantly. He places his hand near to a willow stalk stirring in the agitated nocturnal air close to the boardwalk. He waits. The miniscule movements of her in his palm come slowly, uncertainly almost, as if she might be uncertain of what she wishes to do. Eventually, though, she passes from him to the beckoning foliage. In the fleeting moment of transfer the moon reflects brilliantly from her carapace, creating a mysterious glimmer in the darkness which both he and his mother will take with them into the new day.

They watch her stretch her legs atop her new perch. They watch entranced as she mounts the furry willow's very summit, upon which, with a tiny blur of emerald, she unfurls wings, as if in preparation for flight. A nearly inaudible humming sounds in the stillness, as of a hummingbird's invisible presence near at hand. They follow her passage as she lifts from the willow and drifts onto the air, disappearing a moment later, a fading emerald pulse over the marshland.

The boy turns from the watery field. His mother squeezes his hand and leads them on. Their footsteps creak on the wooden boards, though they tread as softly as they're able. In this way, he considers, they've let her go at last, and bid a final good night to the misery of unreliable sunlight.

The boy cocks an ear, listening. A moment later he discerns it clearly: the soft piping whistle of a flute's song drifting over the shadow-shrouded fen. It sounds perfect haunting the still air, he decides. He smiles within its melody, while images are conjured in his mind of similar ghostly sensations with which he's very familiar: wading through the invisible, gossamer puzzle of a spider's web in the forest; allowing the evening air to dry lake water from his body following a lengthy night-swim; the touch of his sister's hand in his during days of old.

A twin glow flares into being a ways ahead of them, from the hulking shadowed mass of the rushes, and then just as quickly fades. The boy points again. His mother squeezes his hand to show that she's seen it, too. They watch the spot while inching forward, slow as a pair of snails sliding on their way. Then, again, the pair of green lights appear and hover in the air, now directly over the boardwalk itself.

"It's firefly season," she reveals in an urgent whisper, the old enthused scholar merging with the jubilant child reemerged from her skin. She must have been as taken by the sight of them, too, he muses. Taking him by the hand again, she urges them forward in ambling pursuit, guided by the twin lantern lights of the fireflies, or pixies, only another of untold hushed, clandestine beauties or miracles holding sway in the midnight marshland.

I am the Stink Candle

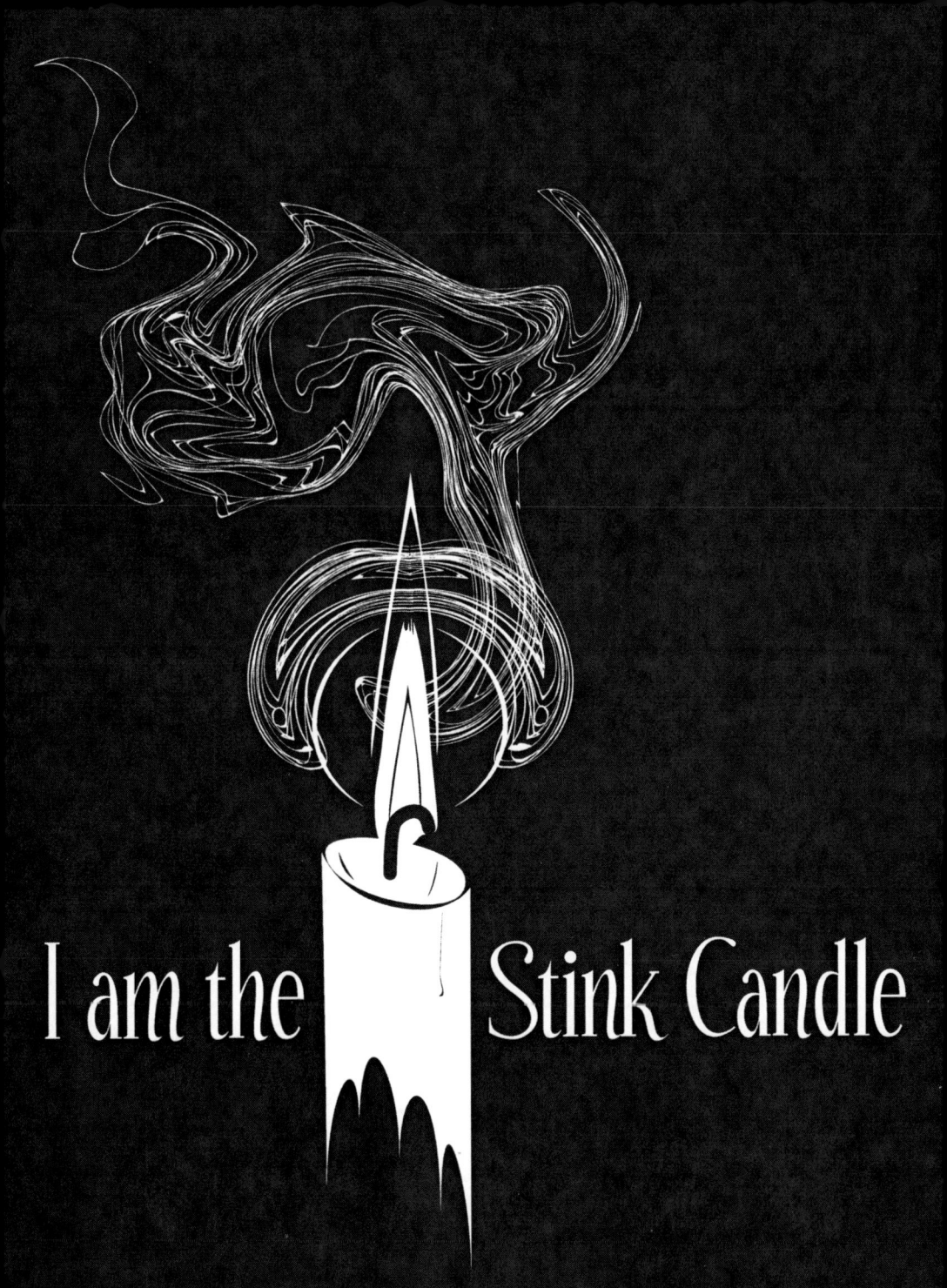

There's different invisible people here now.

Lynn and Barbara sat hunched in silence over their untouched coffee cups, hearing little Janice's words play over in their heads.

Different. Invisible. People. Here now.

And they remembered how choked her words had been, as she cried and shook with what looked like something worse than asthmatic tremors brought on by her terror; shook and trembled violently and they'd called an ambulance and now they were still waiting for its arrival out here in the deep woods, afraid to move the girl, wishing she was anywhere else but here, even in her father's careless arms in the city miles away.

Lynn placed her hand over her sister's, and Barbara could see the guilt eating at her, paining her pallid, fatigued features. It had been suffusing all of Lynn's thoughts that day, she knew, and knew also that she was reprimanding herself harshly as she recalled again and again her immense foolishness: *Hey, Barbara, I'm back with my smudge stick and this time around I think I know what I'm supposed to do.* As if one could actually gain any depth of understanding from a manual or guidebook when it came to dark subjects like these. But she'd come, yes she had, smudge stick in fist and amateur bravado filling her up as she surveyed the country house she would taint irreparably. Not knowing the ruin she carried with her, in the same way she'd always seemed oblivious to all of her regrettable and hurtful qualities. A moment passed, and into the great quiet Lynn began a renewed weeping. "How could I have been so stupid," she wailed, and she cried until Barbara's fingers squeezed hers tightly in vain reassurance: everything would be fine again. It had to be. Nightmares always drew to a close come morning. Right?

They gagged again, despite the open window to the rear of the spacious kitchen. A wendigo breeze of ice chilled them in their winter coats and scarves, and they pulled their toques down lower over their eyes in an ineffectual attempt to stave off its bite. And with the wind: the reek of death. Indoors and outside as well, this air of decay. Whenever they thought that they'd grown accustomed to the smell, they found themselves doubled over, spitting up phlegm onto the linoleum, their hands covering their mouths in case of sudden violent vomit. They'd taken to retreating to one wall of the room when they needed to throw up, mostly only brownish water now, since they hadn't eaten very much throughout the interminable day.

There's different invisible people here now.

Lynn whispered it as quietly as she could, for what felt to her sister like the thousandth time that night: "I'm so sorry, Barbara."

Then they were coughing vigorously again, gripping one another's gloved hands tightly on the kitchen table as they rocked to and fro with the ferocity of their seizures. The stench had suddenly grown more potent, it permeated the room and probably every other square inch of the house. It filled their nostrils and put tears in their eyes and it filled their heads and thoughts and stomachs and then they were leaning over their chairs, no time to retreat to the designated spot to the side of the room, to the plastic pails sticky with drying gastric fluids. And they were vomiting streams of yellow-brown onto the tiles about them, watching the liquid pool around their chair legs through reeling eyes. It was the most violent it had ever been, Barbara thought distantly, this latest bout of nausea and sickness.

She considered how big the stink was. It pervaded her world and Lynn's. It was everything because it stood in place of every other thought they might possibly have entertained then. It consumed them with its potency and they were driven to contemplate only it.

They left their chairs and sat huddled on the linoleum, sobbing and coughing and spitting in a futile attempt to rid their mouths of the acidic aftertaste of vomit. An hour passed, though it could have been two hours or perhaps several days because they could no longer distinguish very clearly the passing of time. They were becoming delirious, Barbara thought, unsuccessfully trying to repress the resentment from filling her as she saw Lynn's moist, red-rimmed eyes. The fear in them was a mirror, she knew, and she hated looking at her sister in that moment possibly more than ever before. "It's okay," she said in false consolation, realizing her mistake in speaking at all the moment the words left her. And her resentment at her sister grew with the strength of the stench in the kitchen until they were both heaving onto the tiles again, bone-weary and wishing they'd die finally rather than suffer more of this endless, maddening torment.

More time passed, another hour or year, and they remained in their places on the floor, staring at one another through eyes blurred with tears and exhaustion, stunned with the inexplicable helplessness of their predicament. Barbara could only consider how much she loathed her for this. For all of this. For always thinking she could help her when in the end, as always, Lynn was most incapable of helping anyone. I hate you, I hate you so *much*, Barbara thought, watching Lynn scratch feebly at her cheek, where red splotches had formed hours ago, always a manifest indication of stress and agitation rampant in her life. Good, Barbara thought. *Good*. If I could only tell you how ugly you look right now. Every time you're unhappy about your life and crying about how miserable you know you are, oh, you become so *ugly*.

But she only held her tightly when her sister crawled to her a moment later, because what else could she do. And they held one another for as long as they could, before the stench grew too strong and they were reeling drunkenly from it all across the floor, mad from it, their lungs pained from its relentless, vicious intrusion. They coughed. They screamed curses into the putrid air, and then they screamed only inarticulately. Then they lay on the cold tiles until sweet unconsciousness swept over them, slipping out from beneath the smell of their terror.

* * *

Years passed, maybe, possibly, or perhaps only minutes had crawled by.

Barbara peered through half-opened eyelids at Lynn wheezing near her. *How could you, Lynn,* and her thoughts drifted to the morning a lifetime ago when her sister's amazing pompousness choked out the world.

Hello, she'd called cheerily out into the large country house from where she stood owning its doorway: *Auntie's here, Janice. Come on down and see Auntie Lynn.* Always campy-ness with her daughter, and Barbara resented her all the more for her success with Janice. Janice, of course, as always, beaming and bright-eyed at the sound of her Aunt's effusive, booming voice, drawn to its confidence, sounding so much like a father's and wasn't it ironic the kind of substitute Ron had unwittingly found for himself in the midst of their family. Auntie Lynn, possibly the only more grossly inept parental role model than him, and there was Janice, always bounding with such excited and tragic haste into those open arms.

Just the scene this morning, if it had been this morning and not some long-past final morning before their descent into this strange hell. *Hello, sweetie, and look what Auntie brought with her today, Janice.* And Barbara closed her eyes to Lynn dozing fitfully on the cold kitchen floor across from her because she couldn't bear the sight of her as the events re-played themselves yet again in her mind.

She saw Lynn with the polished wooden stick in her hand, holding it theatrically aloft on the then un-ruined air as if it was a baton or magician's wand, smiling her confidently dumb smile. Her smiles had always been that way, all self-involved like a celebration of her winning charm despite the perpetual transparency of her motives. Barbara winced as she heard her little Janice's curious and excited exclamation: *What's that, Aunt Lynnie?* She'd probably thought it was just one of her Aunt's crazy old witchy toys, so fun and strange. Auntie was always bringing fun things in her colourful handbags for her to look at and hold in her hands: cloudy stones from the moon set in silver bands for her fingers, cards with archaic symbols in their corners which told you your tomorrows.

And her countless inventory of stories, Lynn always brought them along: *A man once watched his dog run beneath a rose bush in his front yard, chasing something that might never have been there, and the animal never came out into the sunlight again, and when the man himself followed he disappeared too, and his wife never forgave him.* And there was the time when Lynn had arrived in a mild state of panic talking her usual brand of nonsense to Janice, telling about the little green man she had inadvertently loosed in her apartment by lighting the wrong number of candles and uttering the right prayer but with one too many syllables. It had taken weeks, she still claimed, but at last she'd captured him, lured him into a durable Tupperware box by placing an entire head of lettuce in its bottom, and then slammed its thick lid home and prayed for days – the *right* prayer, this time – until the frantic poundings and hissings from inside the box finally ceased. Lynn was always painting herself as all-wise, but a poor disguise it was to those who knew her as well as Barbara always had.

Now Barbara saw the foolish smile on Lynn's face from that distant morning: *This is a smudge stick, Janice, and we're going to clean this old house of yours. And then, no more ghosties.*

Ghosts.

Janice had only been able to sleep soundly while sharing her mother's bed because of the invisible people. Her words, those, and they'd sounded so poetic to Barbara those first few weeks here in the woods, beautiful almost, in the way they allowed the dead some smidgen of their former status. *They're still people,* she heard Janice's explanation of weeks' past, *they're only harder to see. They're invisible most of the time, but you can feel them around the house. They're not really mean, but they're all so sad. They've been here for a long time, in the forest and in the house. They're so sad, but they don't tell me why. They only watch me all the time without saying anything.* And Lynn had arrived heroically with moon rings on her fingers and carven amulets hanging between her large sagging breasts, and with a powerful wooden stick in her hand and all of her huge ostentation and bigger stupidity and eagerness breathing out into the clean pine-scented air of her sister's new home. A haven in the woods, from which sanctuary Barbara would ostensibly be able to focus on her work and where Janice might enjoy some respite from thoughts of her parents' sad parting. A winter well-spent, or so had been their optimistic plans.

Christmas would never arrive now, it seemed. There could never be warmth again, or the holiday smells and sounds of hot chocolate and crinkly gift wrap and boiling pierogies and turkey all rolled into one.

Because then the mistake, and it had always been Lynn's way to master the worst possible moments and make them everyone's around her; dragging her sister down with her into all the sad regretful times. *It's okay,* Lynn had assured her, *just watch me,* and she'd pranced idiotically through the spacious rooms and down the long hardwood-floored hallways, covering in her jubilant thoroughness every landing and staircase and storage closet and even the deep basement with its single-bulb murkiness and spider web-clouded corners. Her large earrings were in the shape of stars, and they'd jiggled and glittered as she moved about, hypnotizing Janice to follow their movements as if the planet they orbited was incredible to watch.

Then she'd returned to the family room from which she began her fool's parade and claimed that she was finished, wasn't that easy – truly believing in her naïve and ignorant mind that it was an uncomplicated matter for her to master an old art like ridding spaces of spirits, or whatever the hell it was she'd thought she'd been doing. *I read it all in my guidebook,* and she was painting anew the air of the family room with the wooden tool for good measure, all helter-skelter in her mid-air weavings, making it all seem rather foolish like herself.

Then Janice screaming and pointing around the room, dashing from one room to another in terror, ceaselessly gesticulating and gasping and screaming until she was collapsed on the living room carpet, wetting herself and panting like a dog. Eventually wheezing hungrily as if she needed an inhaler to suck on even though she never had suffered from any respiratory sickness in her entire nine years.

And then: the lighting of the candle in the centre of the family room's coffee table, set flickering of its own accord.

No one's hand had been near to it, they'd both been huddled around Janice at the opposite side of the room and how could that be? They'd sat staring horrified at the trembling flame, a teardrop burning orange in the centre of the table in the centre of the room.

Then, the stink.

They'd gasped and coughed and covered their noses and mouths with their hands and shirt sleeves. But still, the colossal stink made them reel, their vision becoming washed with tears as they careened through the house, seeking clean air, of which there was none anywhere. The stench of rot, of corpses and sewage and burnt flora but carrying some indefinable putrescence more staggeringly grotesque than all of these combined, emanating from the room and from the outdoors beyond when they'd thrown doors and windows wide. Then, screaming at one another hoarsely, Barbara and Lynn, laying blame and hurling it back in anger, the old ways of two no longer young sisters much-accustomed to loathing each other.

Then the sudden clearing of the atmosphere and they were able to breathe again without gastric juices threatening to rise into their throats and mouths. The throwing open of the remaining windows of the cottage to the freezing night air and the sounds of the surrounding nocturnal forest; and then a dialling of the hospital one hour away and then the endless wait for the ambulance's arrival while Janice shook between them on the couch, covered in so many blankets and comforters. The hateful silence between two sisters who for too long had resented each other's presence in their lives, waiting, waiting for help for the little girl barely breathing beneath the shroud of blankets. And Janice's erratic semi-lucid murmurings while her eyelids twitched and worked as if she were dreaming awful pictures: *There's different invisible people here now. The new ones are different than the others. There's one especially. It's worse than my invisible friends. It's the worst thing.* And on and on, while something like fever scalded her cheeks and bathed her in sweat and made her shake and tremble and breathe raggedly.

There's different invisible people here now.

Tending to the girl in an atmosphere of tremulous peace,

the stench returned. The doors and windows opened only onto a forest of death. The putrid smell blew on the wind when they'd stepped onto the front porch, knocking them back indoors with its dank ferocity. They'd shut and bolted the door, leaving several windows open in case the outside air cleared up, though it seemed to follow the same erratic patterns as that of inside the house. What was it, they wondered aghast, and how could the wildlife not be running riot caught in the horror of it? And how could it have arrived so *quickly*? The breath of dying things, of rotten once-live things growing more rank and fetid by the second, enclosed in a small space with no circulation of outside atmosphere: this was their new and claustrophobic world. The two of them holed up in its midst, unable to breathe, unable to move for fear of disturbing the already weak girl or somehow triggering the stink to emanate yet more fiercely from its unfathomable secret source.

They'd waited and waited for rescue and were still waiting while Janice lay dying in the room with the malignant candle. There was nothing they could do. The fetid smell of dead things lingered in the air, or maybe it was only in their nostrils or their heads, they were no longer certain of anything. But it remained an ever-present, nearly tangible presence there with them. Barbara smelled it with all of her senses, and felt as though she could bear it no longer. It hung like a dense vapour inside her mouth, tickled the back reaches of her throat. It squeezed tears from her eyes and was a cloying touch on her skin. It conjured images of nausea: a rolling landscape of carcasses in varying states of decomposition, animals and humans heaped together, riddled with maggots like tiny convulsing beads, united in their rank, rotting decay.

Eventually, her weary head knocked softly on the linoleum and she slipped away again. I hate you, Lynn, she thought, and it was her final thought as blackness claimed her.

In her semi-consciousness she glimpsed things, a scrapbook series of snapshots and half-scenes, each featuring Lynn in one era or phase or another.

There she was: her sister the party girl at a time too late in her life, after a floundering marriage had driven her to whoring and drinking and a generally worthless trailer park existence. Then she was transformed in Barbara's hazy recollection, this portrait was of her several phases into her future, after undiluted envy at her sister's then-blossoming romance urged her back into academia and a brief tenure as a student of Philosophy, which led her right back into financial woe and trailer park bleakness. Quickly upon the heels of this image materialized the broken-hearted grocery clerk, a bottom-of-the-barrel life living meagre paycheque to meagre paycheque, wherein she gained solace only in her younger sister's own fragmenting marriage and difficult single parent lifestyle. Lynn's mouth was open in this picture, and questions, all the old ones, hung on her lips: *Another woman? How could Ron do that? When he has a daughter by you, even?* Her words tainted with a poorly veiled thrill, a glee not so much malicious as relieved: *Others can be unhappy, too. I'm not alone in the world.*

Then Barbara was time-traveling backwards in her reveries to long-distant youthful days, and there was Lynn as a teenager several years her senior, baring her breasts as if by accident when Barbara had a boy over: *Oh, I'm sorry, Barb, I was just getting in the shower, I didn't know anyone was...* Trailing off and exerting no effort in covering her large breasts with her hands while Tony or Jonathan or Charles or whatever his name had been followed her with his eyes; even later while his tongue was tasting Barbara's and he was groping her beneath her clothes, she knew his thoughts remained behind on her older sister and her flowering body. And afterwards, Barbara fuming and frantic and appalled as she stared at herself in their parents' full-length bedroom mirror, wondering if the boy from earlier in the evening had really found anything she was now witnessing attractive at all: the small breasts, the narrow hips with no curves except for where her bones protruded sharply, the wan pallor of her skin like cream cheese beneath lamplight. How could they, after a peek behind her sister's good-looking wardrobe, into her playful eyes like any boy's best fantasy.

Then the final picture superimposed over them all, the newest rendition of a woman without purpose: Lynn, mystic.

Mystic and seer, and she'll prophesize her way into brighter tomorrows with her decks of cards and with opals glimmering prettily on her fingers, never mind the battered old volumes on occultism and spell-castings gathering dust on her shelves. Except she never had led herself into that new kind of tomorrow. She'd never been a leader of anyone. She'd never be able to find a place to be happy except at her sister's side, a voyeur of her only competitor's miseries.

And in her half-sleep, this final image put tears in Barbara's eyes, and awakened the old anger and the old ache in her wheezing chest, and she hoped distantly to never wake into the stinking world again.

She awoke into dim consciousness, weak with hunger and fatigue. She went over the inexplicable events that had led to their imprisonment in the house. She dwelled on her sister, and the death-stench, and her daughter shaking and dying in the adjacent room while the candle burned and burned, bathing her in its awful glow. And her thoughts always returned to her sister and lingered there, against her will. She burned there, too – Lynn was like a candle in Barbara's head, too, and the thought of her made her feel sick.

And then she jerked up from off the kitchen tiles and was stumbling with stiff legs into the living room. Lynn stirred on the floor beside her, wiping sleep from her eyes quickly, fearful and blinking at this sudden animation in her sister. Barbara made straight for the candle in the centre of the table. It flickered resolutely, casting a wavering glow on the wood of the table upon which it sat. It was long, a pillar candle she'd purchased at a flea market long ago, deep purple in colour, a near-burgundy hue which made her think of milky-thick red wine. Barbara noted the absence of melted wax along its sides, which should by now have been moulding itself in pasty rivers over its simple ceramic dish, and mapping the table-top in strange geographic designs. She pinched her nose at the stench, more potent at this close proximity to the candle, covering her face with a hand. With her other, she reached forwards tentatively, bringing the tips of her gloved fingers towards the edge of the darting flame. She held her hand there waveringly, feeling no sensation, then removed her glove and – hesitating a moment with her heart hammering behind her chest – plunged her naked hand through entirely. The orange flame licked hungrily around her fingers and she shook reflexively, holding herself determinedly rigid.

The flame was cold, an icy prick across her fingers.

She darted her hand away as the sensation registered fully in her mind, backing slowly away from the candle. What are you, but she didn't dare speak the words aloud into the rank room, because of course there was no telling what might happen if she did. She feared an answer would be forthcoming, and wouldn't hearing it push her further than she'd been yet, even? Wouldn't it lure her into a rose bush from which she would never return?

And she recalled her daughter's words of a thousand mornings past, little wise Janice with fear haunting her large eyes: *There's different invisible people here now. The others are gone. They were too scared to stay. You smudged it wrong, Auntie Lynn. What did you do so wrong?*

She sensed Lynn stirring behind her, and shuddered when her fingers found Barbara's shoulders and held her tightly. "It's cold," she told her in a quavering voice, and they watched the candle fearfully as the stink of rotten things grew more fetid in their nostrils. They should have known by now that speaking was dangerous in its presence, at least most of the time. They coughed at the renewed stench, and were spitting profusely onto the carpet a moment later. Barbara glanced to Janice on the couch, wrapped up tightly as before, a wad of restless, quaking girl cocooned beneath a mound of blankets. She waited for the even rising and falling of her breathing, grew cold as she waited for what she felt were too many seconds, her breath held up in her throat. At last, she saw, and allowed herself to resume into a fit of vigorous coughing.

She felt a kind of intent there in the room with her, and knew that it came neither from Lynn nor Janice nor herself because they were each helpless with tears in their weary eyes, and vomit on their breath, with empty stomachs and weak, shaking limbs which made it impossible for them to contemplate anything very lucidly. This intent – this sense of an invasive sentience – hung over everything and yet emanated most potently from the candle itself, and from which they'd instinctually shrank with immense revulsion from the moment it first flared into baleful life. She saw Lynn's smudge stick lying discarded on the carpet, half-beneath the couch. A simple piece of wood, smoothly formed and with a comfortable handle. It had a sheen of polish which made it seem too new to Barbara, too generic in the realms of dealing with the kind of things an instrument such as this was originally made to deal. It fit her sister perfectly, she mused, imperfect in its brash boldness, incapable of achieving what it set out to do. A fraud, a Ouija board made and distributed by Parker Brothers and sold mass market at Toys 'R' Us department stores all over the country. And then their whole predicament struck her again, in all its hopelessness and inexplicability. And she thought, helplessly, angrily, *what did you do, Lynn? What did you let into my house with us?*

Then, she reeled, making straight for the candle. Lynn covered her face as she anticipated what her sister was preparing to do, uttering a choked cry of despair. The odour grew instantly in power, veritably slapping her back in her place, but still she plodded on. She reached the table and with an anguished cry lashed out as hard as she was able, an open-handed slap sending the candle and the plate it rested on clattering across the table and onto the carpet. She and Lynn watched in trepidation and then mounting horror as the orange glow continued its wavering movement, despite its violent trip down to the floor; and the plush carpet, to their astonishment, remained unmarred by the licking flame, its soft velvety contours seemingly untouched.

Barbara cried then. It was all she could do. There was nothing else. Everything was the stink of the candle, and the fear she felt for her daughter dying on the couch, and for herself, and even for her foolish sister awestruck behind her. Barbara wheezed, her breath constricting in her throat as never before. She could barely see for the tears, and her hands went instinctively to her throat, to no avail. She was going to die.

And then she heard Lynn begin her renewed weeping behind her. An infant's blubbering which penetrated Barbara's thick, congested atmosphere of throbbing temples and ruined oxygen. And it brought her up from her plummeting trip into unconsciousness, back upwards into realms of lucidity as she tuned in to the old sound of her sister's woeful voice. "I'm sorry," were the words she was wailing, a fruitless lament in that moment of despair and imminent loss. "I'm so sorry, Barbara."

You're always sorry, Barbara thought, always sorry for the things you do and then you want to just smudge them away.

Barbara heard her sister's next words very, very clearly: "I don't want to die."

And it gave Barbara strength, hearing those words. Because, she thought, *Lynn: you* should *die. You should die in place of Janice and myself, because you always were the one to heave your problems onto everyone else. Now we're both completely alone here, and so is my daughter. Now you live with this thing you've done and die with it, too.*

And Barbara turned about and lunged at her sister with all her remaining strength. They collapsed onto the carpet in a heap, rolling about lethargically, each trying to secure purchase atop the other. Then, Barbara's fingers scrambling madly along the carpet, suddenly clasping the cold oily candlestick in her fingers, raising it and slamming downwards with all her might, once, twice and three then four times, then over and over beating her sister over her face and head with the hard candle. It was resilient, withstanding totally the impact of Lynn's skull where its waxy base slammed into her temple and eye sockets, bruising and blinding. Barbara didn't stop, she only kept plowing downwards with the candle. She suddenly had unsullied air in her lungs, she could breathe and the taste was sweet. Her fingers ached fiercely and her wrist, too, from the impact of the waxy stick she gripped so relentlessly with the face of her sister lying motionless on the carpet beneath her.

One final stabbing downwards with the candle, and Barbara blinked down at the vision of Lynn before her. The candle had punctured her left eye, its base and a good several inches of its body were rooted deeply within the cavity, blood and other milky eye-gore lining the crevice and streaking downwards over the ridge of her smashed nose and between her parted lips. She stared at the wick of the candle, and watched its flickering flame.

She thought: *Some things don't die, Lynn.*

And she was only dimly aware that she'd spoken the words aloud, panted them hungrily, her fury ebbing only slightly in the wake of this act that had been so long a time in coming. And a moment passed, and the air remained sweet-tasting, and it caused her to wonder, how in the midst of her red rage the air had returned to its pre-rot normalcy. And hadn't it done the same hours past, when she and Lynn had been screaming at one another until their voices had grown hoarse and she'd felt as if she might throttle her like she'd wanted for so many years? And again and again, each time during her and her sister's intermittent hateful exchanges, their awful words and the biting truths they carried: the sudden arrival of sweet, delicious and untainted air.

She thought again: *What did you do, Lynn? What did you do in my house? What did you invite in?*

And then she was crying, weeping with an overwhelming regret and sorrow as she gingerly caressed the inert form of her sister whom she was still straddling in the centre of the room; reaching blindly outwards to the side for her daughter barely breathing beneath her blankets.

And then the suddenly changed atmosphere as the stink returned, making her choke and cough and gasp for air again; only this time more pungent than in any of its previous manifestations – violent, hateful in the way it attacked her senses with its foul and indefinable ingredients, the fetid fumes of eviscerated and putrefying, plague-ridden corpses; the stench of the world razed by fire; all of these horrors but carrying somehow something so much more awful, too. And then the charged quality to the air, the actually changing wind currents as the bustling bodies of the medics dashed madly around her, first gently pulling her from atop her sister, and then administering to Janice on the couch nearby.

Through the narrow tunnel of her fading hearing as vertigo reeled her senses and she neared unconsciousness once again, Barbara strained her ears, listening hard, and she heard:

"What the hell happened here?"

And, "My God, she must have lit it after she killed her."

And, "Put it out, for God's sake."

And finally, the last words that she heard amid a chorus

of coughing like thunder in her ears, "I can't breathe. What *is* that? God, I can't breathe in here."

And then the distant thud of bodies collapsing all around her and the pervasive stink of everything bad filling the world up, permeating its every secret nook and crevice. And then everything was black except for the teardrop flickering orange which was the last thing Barbara saw.

Grandmother and the Mars Relentless Call to Arms

There's a rent in the air, she told me in a conspiratorial whisper as if she was letting me in on her greatest secret.

That was grandmother: mastermind reader of the universe's myriad plots against her and hers. I thanked her for the useful information and promised her that I'd get right on top of it, returning my attention to the newspaper in my hands and thinking little of my words to her like I usually did. Grandmother was, after all, completely and unequivocally insane.

She grabbed me under the arm and squeezed the upper area of flesh near my armpit, the most painful spot – I'd learned long ago – on the human body. I hated her when she did it, her old punishment for inattentiveness and other criminal behaviour. I'm not six years old, you crazy witch bitch, I wanted to shout in her weak ear and then throttle her until an iota of sense returned to her straying, forgetful mind. But I only folded the paper and placed it neatly across my lap and asked her what was the matter.

The gods of war, Kelsey, she whispered, her yellow eyes intense through their veil of mucus cloud cover. Can you see my annoyance through your ten million cataracts, I wondered as I watched her placidly. No, said those eyes, fervent and demented and to my eternal dismay somewhat endearing in their genuine concern for me. The gods of war, she repeated it, and then went on to tell me that they'd contacted her only last night, while the nurse had been scrubbing her beneath her arms in the shower, they always use those really rough bathroom scratchers, the ones with bristles like knives on your skin and why would they use those on elderly people with our weak skins and feeble bones.

Because I didn't know how to answer her meandering words, or even to follow them very accurately, I shrugged my shoulders and watched her as she shook her head in irritation. Sons of bitches, them nurses, that's what they are, she spat and swept the air with her bony hand in a gesture meant to encompass all nurses the world over. I nodded along helplessly, of course not daring to refute her claim. She then fell abruptly into silence, looking around the room and seemingly having forgotten entirely about her warlike visions. I returned to the newspaper, glad of the silence in the room, punctuated only by the intermittent mechanical coughing of the central air conditioning system pumping cold air throughout the facility. The front page was talking about something interesting, a great fire out in the county, only a few miles west of where we were. I looked through the bedroom window: the afternoon was milky, a dead kind of sky shone through the glass and illuminated the drab walls with their faded beige and olive green floral wallpaper pattern. It fit my mood as I sat by her side, turning my attention again to the newspaper and trying my best to read, and forget her insanity and wild eyes.

But she recalled her gods a moment later and pinched my arm once again. I turned to her, irritated, smiling falsely, wondering as I've often wondered how Dana could put up with this craziness as well as she always had, but then remembering that she'd always been the best and most tolerant child of our secretive family. The gods of war, Kelsey, she whispered with renewed vivacity in her cloudy eyes, yes, it was them, and do you want to know what they said to me?

I nodded my head perfunctorily, yes, I wanted to know. She leaned in closer and I smelled her old malodorous breath: she'd been eating fish cakes recently and had evidently neglected to brush her dentures. It had to have been from last night's dinner and her breath was a wind of slaughter contained lingeringly in a fisherman's netting. I winced but nodded along, looking as interested as I could manage.

The gods of war were named Max and Chorus and Olivia. They were named thus simply because they were, they'd told her this themselves, each introducing themselves personally, and don't question them because questioning them will only make them angry with you. They lived directly above the clouds, walked and slept on their cushiony topsides, from which vantage they apparently conducted their sundry games of warfare, using mankind as their game pieces. They travelled to and from the Earth via a rend in the cloud lining, a rip in the air through which they visited and communed with select ladies and gentlemen. Grandmother knew all of this because she'd been told only last night, by one of their number personally - Olivia, the girl god, who also went by the name of Mars. A *goddess*, grandmother whispered and smiled, proud to have been selected for this illustrious group of contacts by a fellow woman. She has long flame-red hair, straight and like a carpet all the way past her knees, like a cape, and boy wouldn't you like to sleep in that carpet, and she clucked deep in her throat which meant that she was laughing, the vaguely disgusting sound she made whenever she found something funny.

    I looked at my watch: only another ten minutes or so remaining before I could leave her, having paid my monthly dues. She slapped my forearm in annoyance, and then another slap found the backside of my head. She was greatly bothered by my inattentive behaviour, I was like a particularly distracted pupil of hers from her teaching-days, she fumed, his name was Kelsey Bermer, and he couldn't pay attention if his life depended on it. I didn't remind her that I was, in fact, Kelsey Bermer. I smiled and made as if I was giving her the entirety of my attention. I sat a while longer, mostly only thinking about Cassandra Wallings from my work, with her prodigious breasts and ample behind good for pounding hardily, or so I imagined. I imagined her often, mostly once I'd returned from a long day's worth of fantasizing about her while actually interacting with her at work. Once I imagined having her while I stood stroking myself in a washroom cubicle during my lunch break, and then felt embarrassed a few minutes afterwards when I ran into her en route to my desk.

    Slap, upside my wandering head. What's wrong with you, my goodness, Kelsey Bermer, Kelsey Bermer. Either she'd remembered my name or else she was mocking me in her sing song way which annoyed me so greatly. That even got to Dana, grandmother's lilting voice singing its insults into your incredulous ears. You're not the world's most perfect granddaughter after all, Dana, I thought weakly, no longer really caring about our old gripes.

I tuned in to grandmother's voice: she told me she likes you.

I stared at her and a moment later I was seeing Cassandra Wallings in the same pair of baby blue panties I envisioned her in every night. Then I realized what she was blathering about. I nodded, remembering. Olivia, grandmother's goddess of war.

Really, I asked, feigning interest. What did she say about me?

Don't think like that, I was rebuked by the diminutive madwoman in the bed before me. She cares for you but not in *that* sort of way. I felt embarrassed, having been thinking lustfully about Cassandra in grandmother's presence, and I examined my hands bashfully. That's right, you *should* be ashamed, Mister Dirty Mind, she chortled towards my downcast eyes. This particularly bizarre portion of our interaction caused me to wonder what the hell was going on exactly, and whether she might be succeeding in driving me crazy right along with her own crumbling mind.

I stood suddenly, reaching for my coat, determined to leave the room for a moment in order to clear my thoughts. Wait, she called, the old sound of plea infusing her cracking voice. I tried hard to ignore her but couldn't stop myself: I looked to her, to make certain she wasn't faking me. She was, the look in her eyes was mocking, but innocent in its own mad way. I relented. What do you want, grandma? I asked her, replacing my coat at the edge of her bed.

A glass of water, she told me plaintively and, as I turned gratefully towards the door, her words stopped me in my steps: she says that she lives inside me.

I turned to her, but she was staring vacuously around the room once again, her eyes lost and drifting. Thankful for any respite from the torment of watching her deteriorate before my eyes, I left in search of the cafeteria and more minutes ticked off from my allotted stay with the craziest lady in the world. But I wondered at her last words: had she meant the war-like girl, the Mars goddess, what was her name - Olivia? Olivia. A good name for a war goddess, I thought as I walked along the sterile white halls with their depressing lighting illuminating everything much too clearly: the nurses pacing to and fro in their bright white runners, stoic-faced, hard-eyed, as if they'd seen it all and were hardened to the mournful atmosphere permeating the building; pushing residents along in wheelchairs en route to the dining room or television room or the showers, those wizened creatures of bone and gaunt, sunken cheeks and milky, somnolent eyes staring into the ether and seemingly seeing nothing except perhaps the ghosts of who they were before time had ravaged them so mercilessly. Olivia: a strong name, the name of a woman I'd maybe like to meet some day, if she really did like me at all.

I remembered him as I was receiving my change across the counter.

Mr. Orange had been my favourite toy of all for two reasons: he was given to me on my birthday, a fact which makes any toy a boy owns a little more special than the others. And secondly, he was alive, a rambunctious little ball of orange fur and tiny fangs, my tawny ferocious kitten who pounced on and nibbled at socked and bare feet alike, or any other moving or inanimate thing which happened to lie before him.

I spent most of my waking hours with him engaged in housebound and outdoors adventures both. We hid from one another and found each other behind couches, under beds and behind stacks of Tupperware crates in hallway closets. We climbed trees together and explored the dark musty corners of the shed with flashlights and whiskers feeling the path ahead of us. We braved the wrath of hanging crawlspace spiders and my furious mother, who always became more livid when she'd catch us roaming about on all fours in the living room amid her vases and pristine furniture. He's a cat, he has claws, he can't help it, I'd plead with her as her raised hand hung in the air, ready to find Mr. Orange's soft-furred behind. I don't care, his scratching post is beside the litter box, not every piece of my furniture that he fancies – he has to learn. And the open hand would fall down, time and again, and Mr. Orange's eyes became wide and frantic orbs as he pleaded with me: make her stop.

I suppose she got it from her mother, that quick rage, the onset of which was so sudden it became frightening the more we were exposed to its malevolence. Her open handed punishments found me, too, many times, clapping my head and boxing my ears and then it was ringing ears for the better part of the next unhappy hour I sat fuming and resenting her in my bedroom.

I had Mr. Orange for five years or so, and he'd grown into a wiry cat brimming with energy and a lust for life fuelled by the copious amounts of dry food he was wont to devour every day, as well as the morsels of leftovers I'd sneak him whenever the opportunity arose; whether when mother was immersed in her cookbooks for new recipes to rival her old dishes in tastiness or loading the dishwasher with her back turned away from me where I lingered at the dinner table, feeding the cat surreptitiously as he hovered around my ankles. It was towards the middle of the fifth year that grandmother became sick and her doctor suggested she stay with her family for an indefinite period of time. It was the first time I'd seen her exhibit a hint of the insanity which would later rule her life.

It had been many little things and a few bigger things as well: her strange habit of passing scribbled notes to us while at the dinner table, hastily scrawled messages pertaining to nothing at all, all very nonsensical – one which I've always remembered and which Dana and I still chuckle about to this day having to do with the secret ingredient purportedly found within the roast beef stew we'd been eating that particular evening: worms live in this meat, my children, juicy specimens that make your livers strong – eat up! Then there was her ritual of stacking all the non-perishable cans outside of the cupboards, along the countertops with the largest on top and decreasing in size so that the most narrow cans, which were always Campbell's chicken noodle soup cans, formed the bottom-most component of these often gargantuan, precariously-constructed structures. This landscape became a dangerous fixture of our bizarre household, and on one or two occasions resulted in a bruised hand or foot when one of the strange pieces of architecture collapsed upon one of us obliviously passing through in search of a snack or drink. Then there was the night we came home after a movie to find every piece of uncooked meat removed from our freezer and placed before an open window or doorway, her method of keeping ill-tempered spirits from entering and running rampant in our home.

Grandmother was strange, but often entertaining in her eccentricity. It was when we grew older and mother – in her compassion or emotional weakness - hadn't yet committed her to the old care facility in which she so evidently belonged that Dana and I began to dislike her presence. We grew resentful of the attention she'd always stolen from us, and we became fed up with never being able to invite our friends over for fear of embarrassment at her hands. She became the monstrous secret we had locked up in our basement, so to speak, and I suppose it was the single most important factor that caused Dana and I to grow close over the years.

But the worst moment came towards the end of the summer before I would begin eighth grade. Dana was just starting high school and was very absorbed in herself and the clothes she was buying so frequently those days in a determined effort to remake herself from the bookworm of primary school days to some infinitely more trendy creature in the secondary school world. We'd stopped hanging around the way we'd used to and I found myself a little more lonesome when I wasn't at my friends' houses or talking to someone on the telephone. Everything was awful enough, but then the worst of it had to occur, at the beginning of what I assumed to be a cursed school year, my last before I discovered the difference between grade school and secondary school bullies and their malicious methodologies of torturing the green juniors of which I'd surely be the smallest and most readily picked on.

I came home and mother, waiting for me in the doorway, took me aside immediately. I knew by the stern look she wore that it would be bad. She only ever had that face when there was news and it was of the overwhelmingly terrible variety. It had been the face she'd worn when father died years before, and the same one that informed Dana and I that we would be moving across the city and so she and I would have to switch schools and suffer through the impossible task of making new friends.

So I stood looking bravely into that face, her kneeling before me so that we could see each other's eyes easily. She was going to be open and just flat out tell me - that's what that face said.

And she did. Mr. Orange is dead, Kelsey. I'm so sorry. He got – he was hit by a car in the street this afternoon.

I remember crying. I cried more then than when father died, I think because he at least understood what was happening to him. He was logical, sentient, a human being and human beings are always better to die than animals, which don't understand their dire circumstances. Cancer was an awful killer, but father could define its malignant presence in his bones and gather what energies and fortitude he had to combat it as he could. Mr. Orange never knew what hit him, and I kept seeing him lying broken at the side of the road, or worse yet, smashed and bloody in the road's centre, situated along the yellow road lines while cars continued to flatten his broken legs and crushed ribs while he died an agonizingly protracted death, seeking to understand in his heartbreaking animal logic why he was in so much terrible pain.

Dana was especially kind to me for the next few weeks following the tragedy. She even took me to the movies a few times with some of her friends, who were also nice to me, a grand gesture since everyone knows that little tag-along brothers are the worst pesky nuisances the world has to offer to their elder siblings. It would only be years later, during a heated argument between the two of us, that Dana would let slip something which I'd always chalked up to her being particularly livid and malicious and spiteful at that time, but which nevertheless remained with me from then onwards.

She didn't have to be so cruel, in either case, but she was. We'd been arguing passionately, more so than usual because mother was at work and so we had free rein to hate each other as vociferously as we felt. Brian, her football-tossing boyfriend and several years her senior, would be staying for dinner. Fuck you, that asshole's not staying for dinner. Yes, he is, you little shit-stain. No, he's not. Why do you even like that douchebag? He only hangs around you so he can fuck you, you slut.

My mistake, I suppose, to point out so succinctly the truth of Dana's cheap and shallow life at that time. I remember the look of indignant triumph in her eyes as she towered over me, looking down at me hatefully. I win, her eyes said, and I haven't even said it yet. She relished the moment before the kill, and then she went ahead and unleashed her secret artillery.

Hey, just so you know, your precious Mr. Orange didn't get hit by a car, asshole. He died different than that.

A dramatic pause while I stood waiting, riveted against my will to my evil sister's tantalizing words. Then: Grandma killed him. She *ate* him. She fucking *ate* him. Stuffed that piece of orange shit in her mouth after biting him and tearing him into a hundred pieces.

She stood staring at me, looking triumphant for a few seconds, until a hint of remorse replaced the victory in her wide eyes. Then a renewed fury in her face and she told me to fuck myself and stormed off into the upper reaches of the house, probably to tidy her room in expectation of her boyfriend's arrival, who I suddenly was too weak to hate as ardently as I always seemed to have the energy for.

I shook my head, wondering how my sister could be so cruelly creative. How twisted - how *insane* - to come up with a story like that, and in its wake I considered how grandma's brain condition must certainly run inside the blood stream, holy. I went to my friend's house where we played video games for the better part of the night, and came home only when I knew mother would be returned from work and Dana's shitty football hero had finished with her. But her words never left me, and their illogical formula always nipped at my late night thoughts while I lay in bed waiting for sleep: where *had* grandma been that day when Mr. Orange died in the street a hit-and-run victim? Mother had explained before and I'd never thought to question her: Grandma's sick. She's really weak. We just had to take her to the hospital for a day or two so she can get her strength back.

Could it be that doctors had been keeping her for an entirely different sort of examination? Could they have been cleaning her up - rinsing her mouth of slivers of splintered bone and matted orange fur - even as my mother's grave face like a mask of stone had given me the news that ruined my day?

I shook my head and forced a laugh in an effort to free myself from my unsettled mood, pocketing the coins which had grown warm in my cupped hand while I stood staring off into the cafeteria drabness. Then I walked slowly back to grandmother's room, the water bottle I'd bought for her sloshing softly in my hand in time with my rippling, troubled thoughts.

When I returned, I saw her under the milky outdoors light filtering in through the gauzy curtains and I couldn't help it: I liked her again.

I didn't love her, I never had, really. But I was fond of her, and admired the way she could tune out the world and maintain her own weird sense of equilibrium within herself and with the rest of the universe spinning on its course around her.

There she was, surprised to see me, apples in her cheeks as she beamed up at me from her upright position propped against her stack of pillows. I wanted to say hey grandma, there's Mars bright and red in your cheeks, but I didn't want to startle her, or get her going in a war-oriented direction again. What a nice present to find on a Sunday morning, she beamed, and her arms were open for me to walk into. I did, and as always marvelled at the weight of feathers I was suddenly holding. How could a human being weigh so little and qualify as a living, breathing woman with a long history and a cache of memories, as faded and skewed as they might be.

I held her closely, smelling her old person smell of stale perfume and fish cake breath and old urine, and I thought of my history in relation to hers. I thought of Mr. Orange, my favourite toy I'd ever owned, the best one because he purred like a motor when you stroked him under his chin and behind his big flopping ears, the best toy because he arrived with a little green bow around his neck marking the anniversary when I'd turned eight years old so long ago. I was tempted in my moment of nostalgic reverie to ask foolish questions of her, about past events and the different truths that might make them up, but the promise of receiving claps to my ears as reprimand silenced me, or perhaps it was something altogether else that stayed my words.

She noticed my jacket on the edge of the bed and exclaimed merrily that it looked as if I was planning on staying a while. So I did, and I asked no questions besides the old standards of how the staff had been treating her, and how her suppers and lunches had been lately, and what had she been eating, oh really, fish cakes, that sounded delicious.

A quarter of an endless hour later, my jacket was in my hands again, and I was turning towards the door. And again, a warning in her crackling-cackling voice halted me in my steps: Remember, my boy - Olivia lives inside these bones and runs through these varicose vein rivers.

I turned and stared at her, suddenly very frightened. The timbre of her voice, deep and husky and foreign to my ears, as of a different woman made of anything but feathers and brittle bones. The uncharacteristically lyrical quality to the words, as if she were reciting from a book of dark verse. Then apples were returned and glowing in her cheeks and her open arms were beckoning me for a parting embrace, and we held each other in goodbye and I promised that I'd be seeing her in less than a month's time, take care and yes, I'll take care, too. I left it at that and hurriedly pulled my jacket on as I raced down the halls and past the nurses in their starched whites and greens, wielding clipboards and pens with stethoscopes encircling their necks like mechanical snakes.

I got in my car and pulled the newspaper from the jacket pocket into which I'd stuffed it and tossed it onto the passenger-side seat. I sat there a moment, feeling the usual post-visit drain of my physical and emotional energy, while remembering her yellow eyes and the acute sensibility burning there when she looked at me from her bed at the end of our time together that afternoon. She looked so lucid sometimes, despite the unanimous diagnosis of the many doctors over the years. She sounded so reasonable sometimes, so utterly cogent.

I glanced by chance to the paper beside me, sat staring at it a moment, not seeing the words printed there. Eventually they registered on my dazed senses, and I found my place and finished reading the article concerning the fire in the county. It had taken place in an abandoned factory in nearby Comber, and was what the authorities were calling an accidental blaze, caused by the combination of extreme seasonal temperatures and persistent sunlight and a years-old roof that had caught fire and collapsed inwards into an interior filled with the residue of a hundred flammable substances.

A fire in an empty shell of a derelict building. It was her to a tee, and I remembered her lucid eyes watching me from her bed as I stood staring at her in sad and unsettled goodbye only minutes past. And I forgave her, for all her crimes of amusing craziness against all of us.

And then I was pulling the car from the lot and out onto the street, shaking my head and laughing it all off, a little nervously but still laughing it off: Dana could be the bitchiest, meanest sister in the world sometimes, just as crazy as the rest of us.

The guilt was relatively big in me as I entered the building a month later than I'd promised and made my way down the familiar depressing corridors. The too-white light that coincidentally matched the light outside once again coloured my mood as I walked, placing a weight on my steps as I went. It was humid still, the tenacious mugginess would probably be following us into September this time around, according to the predictions of weather forecasters. I passed the common area where a commotion had three nurses doing their best to restrain a very large woman wearing a voluminous nightgown like a toga, I'd seen her here before in passing, who'd always appeared very sedate but was now wildly frantic as she shrieked and flailed and clawed at the uniforms and faces of the nurses trying to subdue her. The scene had a comical gladiatorial quality to it which might have caused me to chuckle on another occasion when my mood wasn't as subdued as it was then.

I passed quickly, averting my eyes, wishing instinctively for grandmother to never have to witness lunacy such as this while she still lived here in this awful place that had always seemed to me less the old care facility advertised in its brochures than a disheartening asylum from decades past. I pit-stopped at the cafeteria and bought her the requisite bottle of water for her constantly parched throat, as well as a small bag of M&Ms and a larger bag of Skittles, for when she woke up after one or more of her frequent unplanned afternoon siestas with her sweet tooth yearning and dinner too many hours away.

Her sweet denture tooth, I'd once remarked good-naturedly while in her presence, and received a particularly vicious pinch from her, and for which she'd offered no explanation other than commenting, as though she were teaching me some very important lesson: Teeth like these serve a lady well, Mister Bermer!

The moment I entered her room I felt it. I looked at her and my old practiced smile froze. She was wearing the old face, mother's face when she was prepared to tell me some hard truth or another. I said nothing, only braced myself and bit my lip when I heard her begin to cry softly in the stuffy room, her wizened features wrinkling even more in the grip of her emotions.

I closed the door softly behind me and seated myself quietly at her side. I allowed her time to collect herself, knowing she'd talk to me when she could or when she wanted to. Whenever she entered a crying-mood, patience always proved the best way, and eventually she'd resurface in a brighter mood and with peace in her eyes, as if she hadn't descended into hysterics at all. I waited, surreptitiously perusing that day's newspaper which I'd brought with me and placed on the mattress. No stories of fires or other catastrophes marked its front page, and I was about to turn to and scan the sports section when she made a sound.

It was a muffled noise only, but I knew she was trying to speak, to articulate something to me. I pushed the paper near her feet and gave her my undivided attention. I died when I saw the look on her face. Her eyes welled. Her thin chapped lips trembled. Her scrawny frame shook everywhere. She was made of anguish and it took her nearly a full minute of incoherent stammering but in the end she regained her composure enough to tell me in a clear but cracking voice: You're not safe with me anymore. I love you still, Kelsey, but you have to go and never come back to visit me. She's here in me now and she'll never leave. Not ever.

I discerned something peculiar in her speech, some subtle aspect which sounded amiss yet eluded definition. I examined her closely, and when she saw my eyes fix on her mouth she nodded, as if coaxing me along towards an understanding of some unspoken lesson, waiting for understanding to dawn on me. Yes, she nodded up and down, as she apologized. I'm sorry, my boy. I'm sorry. And she reached two bony fingers into her mouth and popped out her dentures into her cupped palm. I stared at the row of upper teeth, their discoloured areas looking particularly unsightly under the honesty of the room's lighting, dark splotches, brown-ish and ugly. I stared aghast: between two of the incisors on one side of the appliance, a bright feather jutted, its fine tip matted down with saliva into a sharp point. It was brilliant green in colour, the emerald plume of a parrot but belonging more likely, considering its relatively small size, to the common budgie. My mind reeled as I sought to glean meaning from the scene before me, until the hard truth of the answer came to me. It stared out at me from the lucid eyes of the frail woman before me. And I took in the sight of the small mound of mangled meat clutched in her hands, broken and bloody, its insides streaking her fingers. She nodded when she saw the recognition seep into my face. Kelsey does good when he pays attention in class, doesn't he, words she might have said but didn't. She only remained rigidly in place, studying me closely and with something like curiosity in my moment of startled epiphany.

    I didn't move, only looked at her helplessly, thinking of my childhood and my sister's scathing words to me, spoken in the heat of a brash and unfortunate instant of sibling quarrelling that I've never forgotten. My grandmother spoke to me then, and they were the last words she ever spoke to me. She said in a hard but wavering whisper – as of two voices vying for mastery of the same speaker - as brittle as a Fall leaf crisping away to nothing in a child's eager and violent hand: you're not safe with her now.

    There was regret in her face, in its every nook and crease and wrinkle like an intricate map etched into her leathery skin. Then she shrieked a shriek like I've never heard before or since in all my days and she flung the dead bird at me. Then she was flailing in her bed and reaching for me with her frantic curling fingers like claws for my eyes. At least if she'd caught a hold, I no longer would have seen the horrid image of her writhing like a person possessed in her creaking bed.

    Nurses barged in and rescued me but really didn't help me. The picture continued floating before my eyes, of the old woman lunging for me with war in her eyes. It's a ghost that still haunts me. I cried while they subdued her with leather bonds pulled taut, bringing full circle my impression of the facility as one of antiquated barbarism, while muttering their own exclamations as the pieces of their twisted hospital puzzle fell into place - a weeping patient lamenting the absence of her pet budgie, and then the mad woman with demons in her veins fighting her grandson in her room with the blood-spattered remnants of the bird staining the tiles at the foot of the bed. One of the nurses swore, an oath murmured under her breath after grandmother had been wheeled away, bed and all, to another room, but loud enough for me to hear: sweet Jesus, she's got the demons in her. Did you see those eyes?

    I corrected her, speaking through the words of the nurse trying to console me, as if she could, as if she or any of them knew anything of the truth in that moment of conflict and possession. I said to that nurse, and I said it really to all of them and to myself, too: Not demons. *Olivia.* She was the goddess of war in my grandmother's eyes.

    Then I wept more violently even than before. I shook with my crying until a nurse's hand sought to comfort me by touching my shoulder. But I swatted her away and swore at her, something unintelligible, and I'm certain I looked and sounded as much like a lunatic as any they'd ever seen. Then I rushed out to my car and never returned to those rooms of too-white light and ruined memories, where peace was always endangered by war breathing at its gates.

    When she asks, I tell her it had been a peaceful way to go.

    It's been long since the funeral, a year or more since the conquest and ultimate occupation of the gods grandmother spoke so passionately of. Dana asked me once on that day, and she asks me every once in a while still during our weekly telephone conversations, as if she doesn't quite believe my words to her: How did she go?

    Peacefully, I say. In her sleep, dreaming good dreams, probably. And I never change my explanation or alter the gentle tone of my voice as I say the words. It's a good truth, the one Dana knows uncertainly to exist. A small gift of peace from a brother to his older sister. And now when the sunsets burn spitefully bloody and savage after a season of milky skies and oppressive air, I can even enjoy them, the fiery grand look of them.

Where the War Bird Leads

Burma. 1942. August.

The air steamed. The vegetation baked in the heat. The sun hung relentlessly overhead.

The men cowered through the thick brush, low-slinking, noses brushing the wild grass through which they'd been wading for a thousand days. Demoralized, the ragtag survivors of a platoon fallen victim to relentless dawn ambush. They'd never seen the snipers, glimpsing only fleet green shadows among the fronds. The firefight, if it could be deemed thus, had been over in a matter of minutes. A slaughter in the fetid verdant gulfs. Death in those trackless miles where the group had been wandering for days following an earlier defeat and retreat. Hungry and without provisions, thirsty and with empty canteens and no healthy water in sight.

Pursuing the faintest trickling murmur had led them to no stream. The lieutenant stared dejectedly into the shallow black pool, its rim encrusted with a threatening-looking film of green scum. The heat-shriveled, sun-bleached remains of some small unidentifiable animal lay embedded in the mud along its perimeter. "Shit," he swore softly under his breath, but his men heard his voice of fraying resolve. He was turning away when he noticed the small movement like a flare in the air. He looked, saw the tiny crimson bird stretching its wings aflutter in a whirr of red. From its beak a mellifluous song issued, gentle on his ears, calming after the racket of invisible simians in the trees, the screech of more raucous avian life, the endlessness of a tour of duty haunted by firefights and the screams of the dying.

He watched the bird until it fluttered off, merged into the green morass. He gazed after it, remembering its soft voice.

Its memory stirred something in him, causing him to consider his situation, its hopelessness and the greater futility of his place in this country of conflict at all.

"Sir?" one of his men murmured, puberty or fear cracking his hushed voice.

"We go on," the lieutenant said, with as much assurance as he could muster.

They trudged onwards, the men trusting to their lieutenant to lead them to salvation. This his duty, and their right. Through jabbing crab grass as tall as a man which made them feel like insects traveling through a land of giants, beneath shadowy, rustling roofs where snakes draped like vines near to the ground, hissing death into the faces of those not wary enough. The men's steps trailing their leader's closely, even when they noticed with a start the rectangle of cloth discarded in the grass in his wake. An eagle grounded forever, a bird of regiment torn from the lieutenant's shirt by his own hand, disowned as any symbol or insignia of his suffering and his men's in the futility and madness of the conflict they'd been steeped in for what felt like centuries. They followed suit, the soldiers, wordlessly tearing themselves free of the shackles of names and duty to greater causes they remembered little of. A small tribe of new men wandering the wilderness.

For hours more they ghosted the green depths, lost. Days and nights and weeks and years. Always the monotony of thick air and mosquito clouds and rustling bush and the sun like a circle of death beating down from above and baking them mercilessly in their hellish trek. Peeling leeches from their legs like hideous black tongues and dropping them back into the dank pools through which they waded. Anxious of flitting shadows which might spit bullets and snipe them one by one into oblivion.

Then, the green world wholly changed.

The screaming of monkeys fallen into silence. Birds ceased their wild and savage song. Insects hushed from their buzzings and whirrings and twitterings. No leathery slipping of serpent through bamboo rushes, and no splashing of alligator like rolling logs in nearby pools.

All was primordial stillness. The gargantuan quiet before

life began. A scene before prehistory's dawn had awakened.

It strode from the jungle like a shining silver god, amazing the soldiers into fearful immobility, guns dangling harmlessly in loose fingers.

Taller by a full two heads than the tallest of the remaining platoon's members. Silver-skinned and deadly. Nearly blinding to look upon directly. Sleek-limbed, with razor-sharpened extremities. Fingers like knives spiking the air. Blades sprouting like ostrich plumes from its head. A colossal gun grasped easily in one hand, a howitzer in the grip of a giant. The most violent of deaths blazing in the light, parting the noxious jungle mists with its hulking insidious arms.

A moment of bended time, seconds elapsing queerly, prolonged and strange as the men and the divine or unholy being beheld each other.

The thing swung its sharp taloned hands upwards, and tore off its head.

A man lay revealed beneath, grey-haired, hard-eyed, and he held his sun-glittering helmet in his immense hands.

His voice was deep, his eyes stern as he examined the men.

"We've come for recruitment purposes. Our latest foray to your world. You've provided a rich supply of killers over the years. Your people. Your species."

The lieutenant only gawked, stunned into silence. His tongue remained cleft to the roof of his mouth. A moment, and he stammered, "I'm...We're no killers." He sounded uncertain, his words wavering. Distantly, he thought of his many days skulking and fighting through the jungle, of those things he'd seen and those things he'd done in the green depths.

The towering man furrowed his brows, as if grown irascible at the lieutenant's inadequate reply, frustrated with the incomprehension meeting his own words. He said simply, "Of course you are, man. What is it that you hold in your hands? What is it that lives in your eyes?"

The soldiers looked to their rifles, forgotten in their limp grasps.

The silver man turned to look the way he'd come. He parted the fronds with a hand. A saucer stood revealed in the glade beyond, flashing iridescently in the sunlight. A dozen or more silver men like porcupined deities milled there, sparkling in grandeur, bristling with arms. In the huge silence, only the small efficient electric clamor of their communications sounded. Among them sat huddled a group of soldiers, of differing uniform and physiognomies but sharing the same dead stare; sprouting from the grass like a strange crop of dusty fruits, bound and tethered to each other with thick steel cords.

The silver man spoke, his voice impassive, professorly.

"There is a war. It rages, on and on and without respite. Greater and greater than your puny conflict, but made still of the same ingredients. You'll come with us, of course." His eyes were hard, uncompromising.

He held aloft the large steel ring. A collar, as for a dog, but this stout chain made for the necks of men.

The company of soldiers stared silently.

Suddenly a small flash of movement, a crimson sizzle in the air. A bird the colour of fire lighting upon the towering figure's shoulder. Familiar in design to the dazed soldiers' eyes, yet alien its beauty, too. The flame bird riding the giant fearlessly, cocking its diminutive head from side to side in rapt examination of the scene. It sang. A wailing din from its sharp little beak. Filled with spite, brimming with fury. A song of fire erupting from its little rotund body, rife with savagery as potent as the scalding sun. And in its wild wake, the jungle around the group erupting once more into its old savage clamor. The wilderness song renewed.

The silver man continued to proffer the steel ring, wordlessly, like a dark offering or bloody promise, unheeding of the small red rider perched atop his magnificent shoulder, hopping from foot to foot among the long sharp spikes like an alien thicket.

The lieutenant, after some rumination, dropped his flimsy rifle in the grass. He stepped forward, bowing his head, eyes moist, lost, his shoulders sagged and defeated. His weary men followed.

Another Light Called 1-47

The summer of 1-47 proved to be one of peace and gallantry, and particularly so in the small but historically significant town of Spring's Grove, Ontario. Boys held doors open for the girls they crushed on and for those whom they'd never dreamed of at all, too. Police officers saved careless children from the turbulent river and helped stranded cats from trees, and apprehended the very occasional villains who held up confectionaries before midnight struck and shop doors were closed for the night. Bullies were rare that summer, too, either hiding indoors and out of sight or else electing instead to revel in the chivalry of those days, too, and simply joined the ranks of their former victims.

Over the years that summer grew to be remembered as one of fairy tale splendour and good will among people everywhere; though of course nowhere in the world was this more true than in the small town which lay at the heart of the summer's most wondrous ingredient. *Oh, the Summer of 1-47* – An incomplete phrase yet containing all of the indescribable emotion born that momentous July night, to be spoken with wistful and nostalgic fondness for years and years to come.

1-47 was a handsome model, and would remain so, even in the eyes of future generations accustomed to norms of increasingly streamlined design as well as technologically- and structurally- advanced capabilities. 1-47 represented a utilitarian and efficient – and handsome, in its simplicity – beacon of hope for anyone who dreamed, and in the summer of 1-47 who didn't dream? It was these qualities, in fact, which remained wholly inherent to 1-47 alone, to the exclusion of all of its brethren. Some would reason that this was due to its being the first successfully completed model of its kind, and the first to be sent away on the quest for which it – and its many failed predecessors and future brothers and sisters – were created.

Some – perhaps the more romantic of heart – claimed 1-47's nostalgic favour stemmed from its golden voice, like the very pulse and heartbeat of summer. Like a million cicadas singing their electric song; the sound of moonlight paling hillsides and rooftops; and of stars trembling in their constellation-bodies while children scampered excitedly through cascading sprinkler waters.

1-47 was – at its most fundamental element – a promise made to the men and women and all of their children, ensuring all that the future awaited them, and that its sunrises and sunsets would rival those of even that most idyllic of summers.

Ten-year-old Angela Samson was present that day on the sward on the town's outskirts, several miles from the government facility where 1-47 was born; there among the majority of the townsfolk and many visiting people who'd traveled from afar to witness the milestone event, and the indelible spectacle that it was, and the bright light of hope that it represented. She'd stood with her mother and father and younger sister Abby, who was too young to fully understand the portent of the event they'd gathered to witness but was more interested in the ice cream cone she was licking and which was dripping fat chocolate drops across the front of her orange-and-white polka-dot summer dress. Angela also had an ice cream cone that afternoon, but she rolled her tongue across hers with less gusto than her younger sister, because her eyes were riveted the whole while on the colossal needle spiking from the field and stabbing towards the dusking sky.

A simple parting from 1-47, delivered in its golden sunlight's voice. "Goodbye, friends. We will see each other again." And the politest of waves to the gathered – returned by all, with tears running freely across the cheeks of everyone with their hearts thumping a din inside their full chests – and 1-47 entered its gargantuan needle, disappearing from sight.

The silver needle spitting fire and smoke, and roaring a roar felt for years to come in the souls of all the watchers. And the needle shooting into the star field overhead, merging with its countless distant shimmering points. And the long wait was begun, while life sought to return to a semblance of normalcy, as if the world hadn't been witness to all of its collective hope shot into the ominous eternity of the heavens.

    Little Angela Samson cried that night, too. Her tears washed the celestial scene above into an oblique silvery smear, and she would forever associate this colour – the saddened portrait of evening skies – with feelings of fearful hope.

    A blackened carcass arrived from the sky some thirty years later. A husk, charred and broken and though its beauty was ruined and its once healthy heart lay cold and inert in its chest, the name emblazoned thereon remained, if only barely visible beneath the scabbed, scarred steel skin:

    1-47.

    It fell to Earth with neither grace nor dignity, a careening wreck spouting fire and smoke-plumes like a red and filthy beard in its wake. A dark comet, like an ill augury for all those witnessing the furious descent across the skies. The site from which the remnants of 1-47 were recovered was near to but not precisely upon the site of its original departure – the wounded needle having nearly plummeted it into close-by Lake Molnar – a clear indication that its trajectory had been severely tampered with by unknown means. Little else could be learned from the remains, despite the arduous study devoted them in the years to come.

    People fretted everywhere. Some called for doom soon to fall from the Heavens, while others prayed for salvation. But neither doom nor salvation arrived, only the same day-to-day joys and sadness as always.

    Angela Samson was then a forty-year-old widow, childless and though not quite destitute what with her husband's life insurance preserving her, yet she wasn't altogether financially secure. She had her pets (two terriers named Luke and Bernard), and a tabby she called either Hunter or Sleepy depending on its mood. She'd never left Spring's Grove and, until her husband's passing, believed that she didn't want to; in the days afterwards she felt a distant tugging inside her but by that point felt too tired and old to follow its voice anywhere but through the same day-to-day ennui and menial work drudgery to which she'd been a slave for the past twenty years.

    The day she'd heard the news she was sitting before the television in the kitchen, alone, a cigarette in her fingers and a half-eaten T.V. dinner grown cold in its foil tray before her. She watched the television and cried. When she could bear no more watching of this same news on every channel she came to, she shut the television off and went to her room.

    There, sitting on the edge of the bed she'd shared with her husband for twenty good years before he'd died suddenly of a bad heart, she held the naked razor blade she'd popped from the plastic shaver in quivering fingers. She fingered its sleek edge, pressed it first to one wrist and then the other. She drew blood, a dribble from the line she scratched across her left wrist, and the itchy, stinging pain it aroused caused her to abandon her efforts, too afraid to continue. Even in this instinctual act of self-preservation she wasn't able to gain any sliver of confidence or optimism; thinking instead only of her younger sister, who three years before had taken herself from her own downtrodden futile life with a razor much like the one she so ineffectually wielded. Even her kid sister had shown more courage and determination than she could muster.

    Things had not turned out for her the way she'd dreamed the future days would unfold. The days carried far more dismal and discouraging a character than she'd foreseen, or even believed possible when she'd occasionally considered the worst possible scenarios that might lie waiting. Little money and an assortment of tedious jobs following a failed tenure in the local community college, and her eventual resignation to the fact that she'd never be the writer of children's stories that she'd aspired to become during her more sanguine academic years; and her husband, faithful and loving towards her but eternally unhappy in his own work, doomed to toil long bone-wearying shifts in the local foundry until his untimely passing.

    She went to bed, and slept only fitfully, and dreamt of her husband; but her husband as the boy she'd fallen in love with when she'd first grown to know him, in the distant summer of their shared youth, at an age before girls and boys fell in love with each other but maybe only felt the nascent strange tugging that would one day blossom into true love.

She saw, recurring throughout that hopeless night, his child's eyes, wide and blue and sparkling and filled with all the potential she'd needed in order to imbue her vibrant young world with contentment.

After many years, the ravaged husk of 1-47 was inducted into the Museum of World Wonders, and served as a dual reminder to those who traveled to look on it, of the lofty pursuits humankind is famous for, and the fragility of our dreams.

Severe and debilitating arthritis came to eat Angela Samson's joints in the ensuing years. She grew crooked and became imprisoned in the confines of a wheelchair, thereby joining the ranks – in her mind – of the near-useless citizenry of society, no longer able even to engage in the day-to-day activities that had made her who she was. No more pottery sculpting at the kiln, and gone were the days of her being able to stand for long hours before canvases and paint the blobs and swirls and eddies which gave her such joy, even in the face of the bewildered reviews given her work by her neighbours and few friends; and even her pastry recipes – famed throughout the old neighbourhood – seemed to have lost their indefinable magic, tasting less flavourful and much more flat and dull than she, or anyone, recalled them tasting. The future had brought with it technologies capable of placing men's dreams into the furthest corners of the sky, but still she was destined to wheel her way through her remaining days as an invalid. Her dogs and cat had passed on, too, like all of her family and those few of her friends whom she'd considered herself close to. She'd never felt so alone in all of her life, and she often fingered the old naked razor blades and toyed with ideas of the salvation they might provide her if only she could muster the courage for the simple but difficult cutting act the way her sister had mastered it years and years before.

It was then, nearly sixty years after the day the little girl she'd once been had watched in rapture as a giant silver needle spiked into the heavens, that an answer came from the sky.

A light descended. It hung in the sky for eleven days – as if ruminating on the fates of all those watching it raptly – before falling, on the twelfth day, to earth. It had hung over the small but important town of Spring's Grove, and that's where it fell, too, early in the evening. People came from near and far to live the event, of course, awakening Spring's Grove from its decades-long somnolence, like a ripple through a placid pond.

No needle landed upon the sward that night. A sliver of bright light descended slowly and, with a ginger grace uncanny to behold, settled itself softly upon the grass. The luminescence seemed to hum a hum felt by everyone gathered in their deepest parts. It stirred them to whisper among themselves, and ponder the course of their lives over the past sixty years.

It was – wondrously, almost *magically* – a renewed 1-47 which strode forth from the shard of light.

Its skin was pristine, new and lustrous, yet undoubtedly encased the 1-47 of old. It seemed to reflect each of the gathered people's faces of wonder and awe – many of whom were old and grey and had seen this sight before, on a night imprinted upon them forever – as well as the stars trembling in the sky. Its steps were sure and measured and fluid. Its gaze as it surveyed those people convened in the field held vitality. It radiated this vigour in a way unmatched by any of its successors throughout the years. Fleet, graceful, mighty and reassuring.

Of a sudden a pair of arched tents unfolded from its shoulders, and the masses stared in wonder at 1-47's silver wings which hadn't ridden there those many long years ago. They fanned the balmy air, stirred the hair on the watchers' heads and mosquitoes into more excited heights.

A pervasive hush fell over the throng.

"Hello," it said into this great and expectant quiet, and its voice was exactly as golden as that long-distant dusk nearly sixty years past. And it said, "I have a long and strange story to tell you all, about where I have been and of the things that I have seen and learned. I have a message for you. I have for you a story dark with death and bright with birth. Will you listen to my story, which is also your story?"

1-47, nearly sixty years on, was just as polite and respectful of people as in the far past.

A collective sigh escaped the thousands gathered. No one

stirred. The night birds had grown hushed in the surrounding trees. The crickets' evening serenades were paused. The world listened. Overhead, dusk had descended in its full celestial glory. The sky was clear and cloudless in all directions, and the earliest stars, it seemed, had begun their frostings with a greater insistence than usual; pulsing, pulsing, as if eager to impart some of their stories into that being told on another very special night in history.

And Angela Samson, hunkered down inside of her rickety steel and rubber wheelchair, felt the old crone she'd become straighten its crooked skeleton; felt the blood flow more freely through her withering veins and stiffening arteries; and she remembered the little girl she'd lost through the long hard years, along with so many other friends; and she felt that girl's heart becoming a slow, sure, steady pulsing behind her frail chest, suddenly filled with something she'd believed long lost to her, too: Excitement. Strength. Hope.

She placed her feet from the steel chair's footrest and onto the lush lawn. The thousand tiny pricklings of grass blades reached her numb callused and bunioned soles and toes through her threadbare slippers. She gripped the sides of her chair with fingers suddenly stronger, and stood; so that she could gain better vantage of the drama unfolding; to hear better the words being told; to feel like she once had, long before when she'd stood with shoulders straight and head held high.

"Well, listen then, friends," sang the golden voice, having received its answer from the tears flowing all around. "And listen well."

And the tears that ran from her eyes as she listened to the story told by 1-47 watered the July grass below her new feet, a small rain of renewal while everyone remained huddled close together in the night, hushed, in rapture, and – for the first time in a very long time – wholly at peace with one another and the world held enthralled all around.

Poppy, the Girl of my Dreams, and the Alien Invasion I can Detect like Radar through my Braces

"We can't read this," protested Poppy, wanting to.

Jill looked from the sheaf of dog-eared papers her friend was clutching and rolled her brown eyes skywards.

"What??" exclaimed Poppy anxiously, her grip on the papers unrelenting.

"You want to – you *HAVE* to read it," persisted Jill.

"It's too mean! Evil, even! If Raymond found out –"

"He worships you! Read it!"

"But he–"

"READ IT!"

A pause of perhaps one second, then, "Okay."

The two friends hollered in combination mirth and excitement and their two heads came together to peruse the papers simultaneously.

The bunch of papers was a diary of sorts. It belonged to the boy next door, Raymond Hoop, who had no clue that his two friends were reading it, with wide eyes. And if he did know that they were reading the sheaf of papers, with his secret thoughts made out into words and set onto paper, he would have to make certain that he died right there on the spot, for sure.

The title he'd given the diary/mess of dog-eared papers summed up why, and concisely.

"Poppy, The Girl of My Dreams, And The Alien Invasion I Can Detect Like Radar Through My Braces," read Jill aloud. She swivelled her curly head to look at Poppy, who's eyes continued to burn holes into the cover page between them.

Folding this initial page back over the rest of the

manuscript, Jill took in the blotch of blue ink that covered the paper with awe. "That's a lot of writing."
Then, starting at the top, the two girls began to read.

One hour and a half later, they were finished.
"Holy cow," murmured Poppy.
"Yeah," nodded Jill in agreement. Then, "Um, Pop? Like, do you think Raymond's a psychotic?" A tiny smile accompanied her query.
Poppy shook her head no.
"No?", cautiously.
"No," affirmed Poppy. "Raymond is not insane. Well, he is, but you know. He's a fun insane, not like, you know, a psychopath insane."
"Yeah," said Jill very tentatively. "But you realize he does think he can hear aliens from another dimension talking across the, uh, airwaves of space or whatever, and that he says here that they're planning to invade Earth by tonight at three after midnight?"
Poppy was silent a moment. Then, thoughtfully, she looked up at the pure blue of the afternoon sky.
"Why not?" she then said. "He said he could catch a radio station through his braces last year. He'd hear baseball games and oldies music."
"Poppy. Poppy...A radio station, aliens from another dimension. Do you see a difference?"
Poppy looked strangely at the diary, which lay pinioned to the hot cement of the driveway by a white rock. "He said he loves me in there."
At this, Jill grew less anxious. "Yeah. He says it all the time, Poppy."
Poppy smiled. Picking up the papers and shuffling through them, she came to the page she sought. Picking it out, she handed it to her friend. "Read the third paragraph."
Jill looked at the designated string of words.
Her eyes are like stars tossed in a milkshake and all shook

up, and that's all I need to know.

"Wow," nodded Jill. "You're lucky."

"Yeah?"

"Yeah."

"Yeah."

Jill leaned back and stretched herself out on the driveway. The blue blanket above them stretched on for, most likely, forever and forever. "It's beautiful," she sighed. "Why would anyone want to ruin that?"

Poppy followed her friend's gaze. "Maybe they don't plan on ruining it. Maybe they're just jealous."

"Jealousy hurts."

"For sure."

A minute passed as the friends stared into the blue.

"Raymond's more in love with you than anything. Wanna know how I know that?"

"How, Jilly?"

"Because somewhere on I think page three, he said that you're better than a sparkler lying on the grass in July."

Poppy wanted to smile, but felt pleasantly too tired and so she just lay there, warm.

"And somewhere else on that page, he described the aliens as looking like a big dark cloud coming out of space and making all the stars wink out of existence in their wake. Or something."

"Yeah."

"And then he said that although he's not sure why, he has a feeling that they're a few feet taller than the average Earth man and that they're blue-skinned with orange and brown spots and that they're going to exterminate the entire human race with laser rays."

The two friends dwelt on this a moment, then chuckled quietly. Peacefully.

"And he's right, you know?" murmured Jill, her eyes all over the sky.

"About which?"

"You're better than a sparkler lying on the grass in July."

Poppy felt warm there on the driveway, and she smiled.

Poppy had just finished apologizing to the boy she loved, Raymond, for reading his diary that they'd stumbled across in his garage earlier that afternoon.

"Do you hate me?" asked Raymond, as he stood there on Poppy's porch, all elbows and knees.

Poppy smiled. "You make me happy."

They stood there, in the fading afternoon light.

"Meet me on my roof tonight around eleven-thirty?"

Poppy nodded yes, and turned to retreat into the cool blue of her house.

Raymond was just unlocking the gate that led into his backyard when Poppy stopped him. "Raymond."

"Yeah, Pop?"

"Do your braces hurt, nowadays?"

"No," Raymond answered, a crooked smile upon his face.

The stars were everything.

They were a spiralling, cascading rain that gave promises you knew they could keep. If you chose a direction and were vigilant, you might see yourself any way you liked to. Better, stronger, or the way you once were, but always, always against the twinkling backdrop of the strange universe.

"Holy cow," whispered Poppy in Raymond's ear.

He craned his neck down and looked into her eyes, which reflected the sky about them. Silently agreeing with what she'd said, he squeezed her shoulder gently.

"You know, you're a pretty good writer, Raymond."

He shook his head. "I write non-fiction. It's not hard."

Poppy breathed in deeply. She reached to Raymond's side and drew his arm about her small shoulders. He loved the way

Poppy, the Girl of my Dreams, and the Alien Invasion I can Detect like Radar through my Braces

her ugly green sweater felt to his touch there on his roof in the cool fall night. Underneath the emerald weavings he felt the warmth of everything he ever loved to think about.

Casting his eyes upwards was difficult but he managed. Raising his left arm, he gestured that-away and said, "Hey, Pop. Watch that spot over there."

Poppy followed his peter-pointer with her smaller hand atop his. She saw.

A wonderful swirl of dots that were stars were the object of the friends' scrutiny.

"Name it," said Raymond, indicating the constellation.

"Name it?" laughed Poppy. "I can't. I...I don't have the right to name it."

"Actually, you do," nodded Raymond assuredly. "You really do."

Poppy thought for a quick moment, and then announced, "Q-Tip."

Raymond laughed, and Poppy joined in. "Q-Tip! That's great. I love it."

Poppy had her blue-painted lips apart to say something, but she stopped herself as her panning eyes discerned something in the blackness above.

"Look," she breathed, pointing to Q-Tip, although she didn't have to point at all.

Raymond knew what he'd be seeing before his eyes located the spot. There, in the middle of the gorgeous constellation Poppy had just named, lights were winking out. Where a billion Christmas trees had shone their joys and sorrows mere moments ago, blackness now reigned. Where there had been many somethings to gaze into and wonder about, was now a steadily growing nothing.

"Well, here we go," whispered Raymond, eyes fixed on the spot.

"Void," said Poppy, and she repeated it. "Void."

Raymond held her tightly in his frail arms.

Then, suddenly, that entire portion of sky was gone.

Gone and that was it, except in the two friends' memories, where it would linger.

"Goodbye, Q-Tip," whispered Poppy solemnly.

Raymond echoed her with the grief in his eyes. The oncoming blackness was resolute. Lights winked out of existence, here, there.

Poppy felt cold, even beneath the might of her ugly green sweater, so she turned to Raymond. "Raymond," she spoke softly. "Do your braces hurt right now?"

"No," he answered Poppy with a straight smile, and accompanied it with a kiss on her cheek.

The blackness came on, turning off the sky in its wake.